The new Zebra Regency Romance logo that you see on the cover is a photograph of an actual regency "tuzzy-muzzy." The fashionable regency lady often wore a tuzzy-muzzy tied with a satin or velvet riband around her wrist to carry a fragrant nosegay. Usually made of gold or silver, tuzzy-muzzies varied in design from the elegantly simple to the exquisitely ornate. The Zebra Regency Romance tuzzy-muzzy is made of alabaster with a silver filigree edging.

A DANGEROUS PASSION

As she neared, he lowered his gaze to rove over every inch of her.

"You're dangerous," he whispered.

"I hope so." With shaking fingers, she touched his smooth shaven cheek.

He removed her hand quickly. "You're making me forget you're a lady." The words sounded strained. "We have obviously been raised under differing rules."

She nodded, knowing all too well that they were worlds apart.

Her lids fluttered closed as she went into strong arms that opened only enough to enfold her.

She had been kissed before, but never like this, never so completely that it encompassed her very soul. She clung to him, meeting his desire with a desperate abandon that would have startled her had reasoning thought been possible.

FOREVER IN TIME

JANICE BENNETT

ZEBRA BOOKS
KENSINGTON PUBLISHING CORP.

ZEBRA BOOKS

are published by

Kensington Publishing Corp.
475 Park Avenue South
New York, NY 10016

First printing: September, 1990

Printed in the United States of America

For Helen, Betty, Jennifer, and Judith Marie

Also by Janice Bennett:

An Eligible Bride
Tangled Web
Midnight Masque
An Intriguing Desire
A Tempting Miss
A Timely Affair

One

Riki's fingers dug into the loose shale of the rocky ledge, slipped, then captured a grip. Rain bombarded her, plastering her dark auburn hair against her neck as the wind whipped wet strands into her eyes. She had enough trouble seeing in the darkness of the storm without that. She shook her head, but it didn't do much to clear her vision. Determined, she inched farther, found another fingerhold on the barren face, another toehold for her hiking boots.

Lightning flashed, jagged and long, directly above her, to the accompanying crash of thunder that would have done credit to the entire percussion section of the London Philharmonic. A shudder ran through her and she clung to the ledge, trembling. Panic and nausea vied within her, only to be fought down. Dear God, how she hated electrical storms!

She forced open eyes she'd closed tight and sought her goal. There, still a good six feet above her and a yard or so to the right, she could make out the dim shape of the peregrine falcon, huddled against the fierce weather, one wing hanging limp and broken at its side. Only an idiot would risk her life to climb a slippery rock in the middle of the worst downpour of the year to save one stupid bird. One stupid, rare, endangered species of a bird. All right, she was an idiot.

Riki slid her foot along the sheer rock face, dislodging pebbles and debris, but the questing toe of her boot encountered no solid haven. She tried again, higher, gripping her fingers tight to keep her balance. Lightning flashed, nearer now, accompanied once more with that resounding thunder like a timpani player gone mad. The shale broke loose, crumbled in her hand, and her foot slipped. Painfully, she slid down the three jagged, rocky feet to the last solid ledge.

"Are you all right?" A man's deep voice shouted from below.

She started, then turned carefully to look down. Twelve feet beneath her, the churning waves of the English Channel beat among the rocky outcroppings of Falconer's Folly, her tiny island. A stranger stood on one of these, his oddly old-fashioned clothes dripping wet. Dark hair hung damply over his eyes, which he shielded from the rain with a hand as he gazed up at her.

"I—I'm fine." But even as she spoke, a shattering flash illuminated the afternoon sky and the rumbling thunder reverberated through her. She clung to her ledge, trembling, hating herself for her weakness.

"Can you get down?"

She forced her eyes open and her anxious glance sought the bird, which seemed oblivious to both the storm and her aborted attempt to save it. "I can't. I have to—"

"You have to come down!" He shouted to be heard over the surf that crashed behind him, washing about his booted feet.

Torn, Riki bit her lip. Afraid of heights and terrified of lightning, she made a pretty rotten rescuer; but she couldn't—wouldn't!—ask anyone else to do this for her.

"Better hurry, this is only getting worse. If you don't—"

10

His words vanished in the resonant drumming that beat through her as the sky lighted up once more. Tears brimmed in Riki's eyes, mostly at the frustration of once more giving way to this disabling panic. As the thunder faded, the man's voice took its place, calm but authoritative, filling her mind. He ordered her movements, directing her to inch her way down the rock's face; and not quite certain why, she complied.

As she neared the bottom, strong hands grasped her slender waist and she felt herself lifted free of the giant rock. A moment later, the man set her gently on her feet. She turned to face him, and her shaky words of thanks died on her lips as she stared up into eyes as dark as coal.

"You're a female! Good God, what the devil did you think you were doing?" His gaze moved across her tightly clinging navy windbreaker which had afforded her scant protection against the elements, then came to rest on her drenched jeans.

She dragged her gaze from his hawk-like features. "A 'female?'" An unsteady laugh escaped her as her fears found relief in humor. "I suppose you call yourself a 'male.' Is this some new version of 'Me Tarzan, you Jane?'"

He stared blankly at her. "I beg your pardon?"

Riki stepped back a pace and wiped the rain from her eyes, regarding him askance. Maybe he didn't have a sense of humor—but those gleaming falcon-like eyes set in that tense face were meant to twinkle with merriment. And as for the rest of him! He might not be handsome, but his face held more character and strength than she previously had ever encountered.

"Are there any men on this island?" he demanded.

"No. I—"

He swore. "Have you a boat I could use?"

She shook her head. "Not in this weather. You'd never be able to control it."

11

He drew a deep breath, then nodded as if he unwillingly accepted an unpleasant but inescapable reality. For a long minute, his worried gaze scanned the churning waters of the Channel, then rose to the rock where she had been clinging not long before. "What were you doing up there?"

She cast a measuring glance over his broad shoulders and the peculiar garments he wore. She had seen their likes in the sketches her cousin David had plastered about his wargaming room—civilian clothes of the Napoleonic era. He must have been a gaming acquaintance of David's. That might make him strange, perhaps, but not dangerous.

"There's a falcon with a bad wing perched in the rocks. Just before the storm, I heard someone shooting—probably tourists." She spoke the word with loathing. "I've had boys with BB guns out here before. Anyway, I've got to get her safe. She's quite young—this will be her first nesting season."

His frown deepened. "A pet, I take it?"

"Not really. I try not to tame any of them. It can prove dangerous if they trust people too much—as you can see." She bit her lip. "I've got to get her down."

He nodded, and determination intensified the grim lines about his mouth. "Why don't I give it a try? I climbed a bit when I was a boy. I might as well save *something*." The last words, spoken to himself, were barely audible over the howling wind. Without waiting for her response, he strode forward and reached up, feeling along the steep incline for a fingerhold.

"Here!" She stripped off her windbreaker and handed it to him. "You'll have to wrap her in something to bring her down. I'd planned to tuck her inside."

He took it and started to shove a corner of the thin nylon into the top of his pants, then stopped and stared at it, running his hand over the slick fabric.

12

With a puzzled shake of his head, he stuffed the jacket securely in place, found his grip, and started up.

Thunder and lightning struck again and Riki huddled in her cream fisherman knit sweater. Another flash followed almost at once, and she didn't open her eyes until the last rumble rolled away. Craning her neck and shielding her face from the driving rain, she peered up and saw the man made excellent progress. *He* wasn't hampered by any irrational fear of electrical storms.

He moved carefully, though with an athletic ease that drew her envy. He was far better at this rescue business than was she. In only a few short minutes, he attained her previous position—which had taken her half an hour to reach—found the footing that had eluded her, and crept higher and closer to his quarry.

He eased himself up until he knelt on the ledge at the falcon's side. The bird struck at him with its sharp beak; the man shielded himself with his leather boot, then swooped down, grasped the bird by the legs and effectively bagged it within the confines of Riki's windbreaker. He secured his furious bundle by tying it up with one sleeve, then knotted the other about his arm and started down.

Very efficient, Riki nodded in approval. The injured wing should hold securely in that makeshift sack. She found her appreciation of the man growing. She was darned lucky he appeared when he did—even if it did go against her to accept aid from anyone.

With another resounding crash of thunder, lightning flashed through the darkened sky. She turned her face into the shoulder of her dripping wool sweater as a shudder ran through her. Dear God, she only wanted to get inside, close the shutters, insulate herself against this storm.

"What are you going to do with her?"

Riki looked up as the man jumped the last three

13

feet and landed on the rocky outcropping at her side. He held the bagged falcon with care, for her windbreaker jerked about with the bird's frenzied struggles.

"That's not going to do her any good, poor thing. Come on, let's hurry. I've got supplies in the aviary." She shivered as the lightning flashed once more, and closed her eyes tightly in an attempt to block out the dreaded rumbling that seemed to shake the very ground beneath her feet.

"It's only electricity in the sky," he said. "It won't harm you."

"I—I know. It's just—there have been so many of these storms of late. Let's get under shelter." She hurried across the slippery rocks until she reached the solid footing of the ground. There she broke into a run, as if she might dodge the pelting rain. Heavy footsteps followed, keeping pace easily.

She ducked through a gate set in an arbor entwined with the thorny, bare branches of climbing roses. A rambling two-story stone cottage faced them across the courtyard. Riki ran to a long building on the left side of this, threw the door wide, and stood back for the man to enter with his precious burden.

She led the way past the generator that hummed and chugged, and ran lightly up the stairs to the next floor. The man, after staring at the machine, followed more slowly. In here, the thunder sounded muted and the lightning remained unthreateningly outside.

The upper chamber formed a long, spacious rectangle. Numerous perches stuck out along the window-lined walls, and three large cages stood at the back. To the right of the door stood a long row of cabinets, a refrigerator, and a microwave. Riki stopped at a table, above which were a number of cupboards. She opened one, drew out wooden splints and bandages, then turned to the man.

"Is she all right?"

"The way she's fighting, she must be." He set the thrashing sack of nylon onto the table and carefully unfastened the sleeve that knotted it together. "Did you really plan to just stuff her into this thing while you were wearing it?"

A rueful smile touched her lips. "I'm not sure."

The furious falcon broke free of the confining fabric, spread her one good wing and hopped away. The other wing hung limp. The bird, no stranger to humans, cocked its head and shrieked, as if protesting the rough treatment.

"The poor dear. I raised her, you see, so she's not really afraid—which is lucky. Easy, now, Guinivere." Riki reached out toward the falcon. It struck at her with its beak.

"Watch out!" The man caught Riki's wrist and jerked her hand back.

Riki looked at him, surprised. "I know how to work with peregrines. But I want to get that wing strapped up before she does any more damage to it. Don't I, Guin? Yes, I know we treated you terribly, but I've got to look at your wing."

This time, Guinivere submitted to the gentle voice and touch. Carefully, Riki stroked the reddish-brown feathered neck, then eased around to the cream-colored throat, sliding her fingers ever nearer the injured wing. Dark, piercing eyes regarded her balefully. Forcing herself to ignore the ominous rumbling and flashes without, Riki kept up a soft, almost crooning, conversation.

"She's a beautiful falcon, isn't she?" Only in part did she address the man who stood at her side. "She's almost twenty inches long. I weighed her in the fall, and she was already just over two pounds. She's going to be a marvelous bird. It would be terrible if she didn't reproduce."

She found the injury without actually touching it.

15

Feathers were torn away, revealing a clean break of the wing's bone. If it were kept immobile, it would heal nicely. Deftly, with the man holding the protesting bird, she taped a splint into position.

"What now?" He stroked Guin's neck while the falcon watched him warily.

"Now she gets some rest. And hopefully eats something. There, would you open that one on the end?" Riki picked up the bird, carried it to the waiting cage, and placed it gently inside. The man closed the door as soon as she pulled her hands out.

"How are you going to feed her?"

"Oh, I'm prepared for emergencies." She went to the refrigerator, opened the freezer and drew out three white paper-wrapped packages of varying sizes. She stuck the smallest into the oven and set it for two minutes.

The man stared over her shoulder. "What in heaven's name is that?"

"A microwave. Oh, you mean the package. It's a mouse. And no, I couldn't kill it myself. There's a falconer on Jersey who catches and cleans them for me. Then I just freeze them so they're ready for whenever I have a sick bird. I look at it as little as possible. And no, I don't watch the falcons feed."

The oven dinged and the man jumped and stared. Riki opened the door, withdrew the package and unwrapped it gingerly. She wrinkled her nose.

"Do you think it's defrosted?"

He took it from her. "It's cold!"

"Put it back in for thirty seconds, then."

The man stared from her to the oven, then back again. "How?"

"Good heavens, haven't you ever used one of these? I thought everyone had them. Just set it like this." She did, and thirty seconds later it dinged once more, and the man jumped and stared again.

16

"How does it do that?"

Riki shrugged. "It's just set to let you know when something is ready. There, would you mind giving this to Guin? I'd rather not look at it if I don't have to."

He carried the loosely wrapped offering down the long room to where the falcon sat on a mock rock ledge only inches off the floor of the cage. Riki defrosted the other two packages, then followed with a bottle of water, which she poured into the waiting dish. The falcon prodded her dinner, accepted the offerings, and Riki turned hurriedly away.

"Well, if she's eating, she can't be in too bad shape. That's always a good sign. Thank you. For all your help."

A slight smile just touched his lips, and some of the strain seemed to ease from his face. It was a shame he appeared so solemn most of the time, she decided. Even as faint as it was, his was a smile to be shared.

"You said there were no men on the island. Are your servants away at present?"

"My *what?*" She raised humorous eyebrows.

His frown returned. "The people who look after you?"

"I look after myself."

He blinked, momentarily nonplussed. "You can't mean you live here *alone!*"

"Why not?"

"That's hardly proper. Have you not even some female to bear you company?"

"Of course not! Why on earth should I?" She laughed, more at his disapproving expression than at his antiquated notions of propriety. "I'm fine on my own."

He shook his head, as if unable to accept her words. "There must be *someone*. A scrubbing woman or a—a cook?"

17

She considered a moment. "Well, there *is* Mr. Fipps, of course. He's the falconer I mentioned. He comes over once a week with supplies and checks the generator." Her tone took on an edge. "Just because I'm short doesn't mean I'm helpless."

"I didn't intend to imply that you were. Only that you are a most unusual female to live in such a manner. Did your family not object?"

"My family objects to everything I do," came her dry response. "My mother feels I should 'adorn society' the way my older sister does." She broke off. And the way her younger sister was about to. That defection on the part of Susie still hurt.

The man inclined his head. "It is society's loss that you do not."

That brought her smile back. "It would be mine, if I did. I'm hopelessly addicted to worthy—and usually lost—causes. Quite a trial to my family, I'm afraid."

"I find you charmingly original."

She tilted her head, regarding him in a mixture of fascination and uncertainty. She liked his rather courtly manners—probably carefully cultivated to go along with the clothes and the Napoleonic era of his wargaming. "I've never encountered anyone like you before," she said before she could stop herself.

That brought an unexpected touch of amusement to his piercing, hawk-like eyes. "I can certainly say the same about you. Since there is no one to perform the introduction, I fear we must take it upon ourselves." He stepped back and bowed with an elegance in keeping with that by-gone age. "I'm Bedford, and completely at your service."

She had learned to curtsy in ballroom dancing class, but to do so while wearing wet jeans and a soaked fisherman knit seemed absurd. Instead, she held out her hand. "Erika van Hamel. I'm David's cousin."

He took her hand, but instead of shaking it, he raised her fingers to his lips. "Am I acquainted with 'David?' "

She drew back, suddenly perplexed. "But—aren't you? Your clothes—"

He looked down at himself. "They are certainly wet. Under normal circumstances, I would never present myself to a lady in such a state."

"You're dressed like the pictures in his room. Weren't you one of his wargamers?"

The tiny lines in his brow deepened. "I hardly consider war a game, Miss van Hamel. It's a very deadly business."

"Especially the way they fought in Napoleonic times. If you weren't one of David's group, then why are you dressed like that?"

He ignored her question. "What do you mean, 'in Napoleonic times?' "

"Don't I have that right? I thought that's what David called it. Or should I say the 'Peninsular Campaign?' That's his favorite period—or era, or whatever you call it."

"Good God, how could anyone *enjoy* that!"

She moved a step farther away, unsettled by the sudden anger that glinted in his dark eyes. "We seem to be talking at cross purposes. Look, you said your name as if you thought I should know you. If you aren't a friend of my cousin's, then who are you?"

"Gilbert Randall, Viscount Bedford."

"Oh, it's your title!" Her frown cleared. "I'm sorry, I should have realized. But I'm an American, you see. I've only lived over here for two years, and I seldom get off my island. I don't meet many people."

"Except your Mr. Fipps? Did he create that—that *thing* over there?" He gestured to the microwave.

"The oven? No, of course not. But he's a marvel with engines. I don't think that generator would still

19

be working if it weren't for him, and I rely on it for everything. Even my shortwave, though I have battery backup, of course."

"Of course." He stared at her once more as if she spoke a foreign language. "I don't suppose you could tell me where I am, precisely?"

"Only about a half mile from Jersey. This is Falconer's Folly—hardly large enough to be called an island, but we try. You're lucky you landed here. There's a fisherman's hut on one of the other piles of rock, but no one's there in January. Was your boat badly damaged, or do you think we can repair it?"

He shook his head, and the grimness returned to his expression. "It sank."

"It—how awful! But you're all right? I'm sorry, here I've been going on about poor Guinivere, and you've been through a boatwreck!" She led the way to the stairs as she talked. "No wonder you're so wet. Let's go over to the house and dry off."

They reached the entry hall below and he paused once more to stare at her generator. She couldn't blame him. It looked more like a pile of junk than her preserver. Mr. Fipps had built it primarily from salvaged engine parts left on the tiny island after the German occupation of Jersey during World War II.

A jagged flash of lightning eerily lit the charcoal sky as she opened the door. She cringed as the dreaded thunder boomed overhead with gusto, and she drew back into the aviary. A strong hand closed on her shoulder and she turned toward Bedford, instinctively seeking shelter from her unreasoned fear.

"It's only thunder." He spoke gently, as if to a child.

For one long moment she knew the temptation to bury her face in the smooth wet wool of his coat, to seek this secure haven. But safe-seeming harbors, in her experience, invariably hid dangerous shoals. She pulled free and, still trembling, strode out into the

20

storm. The deafening rumble faded, leaving the late afternoon silent except for the steady pelting of the rain.

"Were—were you driven into rocks, or did you just take on water?" She focused her attention on her companion's plight rather than on his broad shoulders.

He shook his head as she closed the aviary door behind them, and they started for the cottage. "We were pitching about quite a bit, but we could have survived that. If it hadn't been for the whirlpool—" He broke off. "We didn't stand a chance, even if the lightning hadn't struck our mast."

"My God!" she whispered. "You said 'we.' Were there others?"

He nodded, and the strained lines that marked his face deepened. "There were five of us. I thought they jumped free of the boat before we were fully into the whirlpool."

"You're not sure?"

His mouth tightened. "I was knocked out. I didn't come around until I was lying on a rock, with no trace of either the boat or my companions anywhere."

Riki drew an unsteady breath. "You searched?"

"Of course! Then I saw the outline of your cottage, and swam for it—and hoped they'd made it here. I'd just finished circling the island when I spotted you on that cliff."

"Why didn't you tell me at once? Come on, let's call a rescue team."

"You said there weren't any men!"

"Not here, maybe, but we can get some people from Jersey."

Hope eased the tension from his features, replacing it with determination. "How do we do it?" He quickened his pace.

"Radio, of course." They reached the cottage, she threw open the front door, and hurried inside the spa-

21

cious, tiled entry hall. Bedford followed, but stopped just over the threshold, looking about. Riki tossed her dripping windbreaker over the brass arm of an antique coat tree.

"Go in the kitchen and dry off. I'll see if I can raise anyone." She hurried down the hall to her small office, the old study that looked out over a sharp drop to the churning Channel below. There'd be interference, but with this storm, the ham operators would be standing by for emergencies.

To her dismay, all she got was static. *Damn* electrical storms! There'd been so much thunder and lightning in the past two years, but this storm created even worse problems than usual.

She returned to the hall and found her unconventional guest standing where she had left him. He had removed his coat and waistcoat, both of which now hung on her hall tree. He stood before her in what she supposed must be breeches, a drenched, clinging shirt of equally old-fashioned design, and salt-encrusted boots.

"Forgive me for removing my coat, but—"

She cut off his rather stiff apology. "It's better than freezing in those things. I couldn't get anything but static."

"The searchers—?"

"I told you. Just static—interference. I'll try again in a bit, and if I still can't get through, we'll take brandy and blankets and go ourselves as soon as it's safer."

"Is there any way I can go now?"

She shook her head. "The motor's down on the outboard, so I've only got the ketch—and there's too much wind for a sail. We'd be driven straight into the rocks. I'm sorry, we'll have to wait."

She led the way into the kitchen and flipped on the overhead light with the switch near the door. "Let me get some coffee started, then I'll show you to a bath-room. If we can find you something to wear, we can throw your clothes in the dryer."

"The what?"

The light went off, then back on and off again, and she turned to see him flipping the switch as if he'd never seen one before. "A dryer. Believe it or not, I've got all the modern conveniences. And thanks to Mr. Fipps, they even work most of the time."

"Your Mr. Fipps must be a miracle worker!" He returned the light to the "on" position. "I've never seen anything like it!"

Riki stiffened. Was he teasing? Or had that blow he said he'd received to his head affected him? Resolutely, she shoved a filter paper into the coffee maker and began measuring out coffee grounds. He'd feel better after he'd gotten a cup, stiffly laced with brandy, inside him.

The humming of her kitchen microwave reached her, followed by a ding. Firmly, she banished the niggling suspicion she might be alone on the island with a lunatic. There had been calm sanity in those dark eyes. Perhaps if he had been part of some play acting or war gaming group a severe blow might leave him temporarily confused. A good night's sleep should restore him to health. If he showed any signs of concussion, she could handle it.

Running water sounded just behind her and she glanced over her shoulder to see him playing with the tap in the sink. This continual fiddling with gadgets as if he'd never seen them before left her uneasy. He moved on to open the door of the oven, then turned a dial on the stove.

"It's hot!" He turned to stare at her. "Is this more of your Mr. Fipps's inventions?"

"You might say that." She poured the water into the coffee maker's reservoir and turned it on. He appeared

23

confused, but sane. Perhaps it was a form of shell shock, after what he'd been through. Or was he playing a game with her? David's miniature enthusiast crowd had warped senses of humor, she knew from bitter experience. The one who gave the eulogy at David's memorial service—

She turned abruptly away. It had been just over two years ago, in a storm just like this, that David disappeared. Only his sailboat had been found, dashed to pieces on the rocks.

The water began to perk and bubble, and coffee dripped into the carafe. On the other side of the kitchen, her guest poked a finger into her freezer and watched the wave of cold air that floated out.

"The coffee will take a few minutes. Let's get dried off. There are two bathrooms upstairs. Are your clothes wash and wear? We should get the salt out of them."

He looked down at his sodden shirt sleeve. "My man usually takes care of everything."

"Well, here we're on our own." She returned to the hall and started up the mahogany staircase. She had forgotten she was dealing with a member of the British upper class. He probably never entered his own kitchen. Useless and pampered, that's what he was. No wonder he was in shock. His companions had probably been servants, crewing for him.

But he had been very capable climbing that rock rescuing the injured Guinivere. She decided to reserve judgment.

At the top of the stairs, she flipped on the hall switch. White stucco walls, decorated with bright prints, were interspaced with arching mullioned windows that reflected the fluorescent lights. Outside, all was darkness. She would try radioing Mr. Fipps again the minute she got her guest settled. The sooner they got a helicopter out looking for his companions, the better; it would be night all too soon.

The sky lit with another crackling flash and she turned away as the rumbling thunder followed hard on its heels.

"In here." She preceded Bedford into the blue tiled bath and opened a cupboard. "Heater's down there, towels in here. If you want a shower, we have plenty of hot water. In there," she added, pointing to the tiled tub as he looked about in curiosity.

She eyed him, measuring. From the low vantage point of her own five foot and a hair, he seemed tall. Probably under six feet, though; but his shoulders were very broad. He seemed solid—like a brick wall. "David was taller and lighter than you, but I may be able to find you something to wear."

"Thank you." Already, he had flipped the heater off and on twice and now stood warming his hands, an expression of fascination on his rugged face.

Riki backed out, closed the door, and hurried downstairs.

This time, she raised Mr. Fipps on her third try. His cheerful voice sounded shaky, more crackly than usual, but it was better than she'd hoped for after her earlier failure.

"Riki, my love? Trouble with old Mortimer? Over,"

"No, the generator's fine. There's been a boatwreck. One man—a Viscount Bedford, he said—is safe with me. Four others are missing. Over."

Static filled the air, then cleared enough for her to make out the words. "—call the emergency people." More static followed, then "—find them before dark. Over."

"Thank you. Over."

More crackling disturbed the air. "—eight o'clock tomorrow morning. Got that, Riki, my girl? Eight o'clock. Over."

"I'll be waiting. Just get the helicopters out. Bye for

25

now. Over."

She switched off the set and stood, smiling. Mr. Fipps was the sweetest old man.

"Who the devil were you talking to?" Bedford's deep, bewildered voice sounded just behind her.

"Mr. Fipps." She turned, and saw he had not yet availed himself of the shower. He remained fully dressed, though he held a towel.

"How? I thought you said he was on Jersey."

"Radio. There's interference from the storm, but I got the message to him about your friends."

He came forward, staring at the box of dials, switches, and lights that rested on the table. "You actually mean to tell me you are talking to someone who's more than a half mile away?" Disbelief shown rife on his dramatic features.

"I told you, the interference isn't as bad as it was. I don't think I could reach London, though, if that's what you had in mind. But if there's someone you want to let know you're all right, I'll get Mr. Fipps again for you. He can telephone."

"Tele—This is impossible! A communication system over great distances!" He shook his head, marveling, and an arrested gleam lit his eyes. "Can you see its potential? Its use for the war? Why doesn't your Mr. Fipps tell the government? Don't you realize what this could mean to us? We could get information—accurate information!—and in minutes rather than days!"

She'd had enough. Riki hugged herself, but close contact with her sodden sweater only made her colder. "Look, I'm not in the mood for your games. I've sent out word to look for your friends. If there's anyone you want to call, fine. Otherwise, I just want to get out of these clothes and get warmed up."

"Are these things common in America?" he demanded, refusing to be diverted from her radio.

"They're common everywhere. If you're going to

26

keep playing like this, I'll throw you back out in the storm. And I mean it. It's not funny."

"I'm not trying to be funny." He slammed the towel down to the tiled floor, strode up to her and grabbed her by the shoulders. His fingers dug into her skin, and the pungent odor of wet wool surrounded them. "What is going on, here? I've never seen so many queer things as you have on this island!"

She tried to pull free, but couldn't. She hadn't expected violence, and fear at this abrupt turn flooded through her.

"Are you in the middle of a game?" She tried to keep her voice calm, to humor him. "Is this one of the rules, pretending to live in the period?" She managed a false but bright smile. "You're welcome to use my cousin's equipment if you've lost yours."

If she could get him out of the room, she could lock the door and radio for help. She could try it now, for he seemed interested, but she didn't want to excite him any further.

As if sensing her panic, he released her and backed off a step. He still remained between her and the door, though. She couldn't escape.

"How long ago did he invent these things?" Bedford demanded, a queer, tight note in his voice.

"He didn't invent them." She picked her words with care. "David set up the radio when he took over the island and the rookery five years ago. Mr. Fipps *did* build the generator, but I bought everything else in London."

He stared at her in silence. Slowly, his head swiveled, the muscles in his neck taut, and he found the light switch on the wall. With his eyes on the ceiling fixture, he flipped the switch, and the room darkened. When the bulb came back on the next moment, he was still watching.

A steady, rhythmic hum began, growing louder and

closer. Riki's spirits soared. Rescue! If she could just get outside, she could signal the helicopter. There was nowhere they could land, but maybe, if she waved wildly enough, they'd let down the rescue sling. She might be able to escape this lunatic.

"What's that?" Bedford's voice sharpened and his head jerked toward the window.

"The helicopter. I told you I'd get someone out to look for your friends."

"A what?" He strode over and peered out the window, looking up into the sky. The small two-seater rescue chopper came into view, hovering, dipping close, then moving on.

"My God, what in heaven's name—" He reached out, clasping her arm.

This time, she felt no menace from him. Only confusion, complete and utter bewilderment. Sympathy replaced her panic.

Still wary, she spoke gently, soothingly. "Everything will be all right, now. You're safe. I'll go outside and signal them, and they'll let someone down in that sling you see hanging below it. They'll take you to hospital. Everything's all right, now," she repeated.

The helicopter swooped out of sight from the window. The man turned back to Riki, saw he clutched her arm, and released her. "Have I gone mad?" he breathed.

"You said something hit you on the head. You'll be all right."

"Just tell me this is the Eighteenth of January, 1812, and I'll be fine." He looked back to where the helicopter could now be seen, dipping around a nearby pile of rocks.

"Well, it's the Eighteenth of January, but you've been wargaming too long. You're about a hundred and eighty years too early."

"A—" He broke off, and every trace of color drained

28

from his face. "That's impossible. It's—"

"Look, let me signal the 'copter before they get out of range."

But it was too late. The chopper lifted and moved away, heading to the next group of rocks some distance off. Riki fought her returning fear. She wasn't alone. She still had the radio—and the man hadn't shown any real sign of hurting her.

"Why don't you take a nice hot bath?" she suggested.

Those dark, mesmerizing eyes came to rest on her. "You think I'm an escaped Bedlamite, don't you?" A humorless laugh escaped him. "I'm beginning to think it myself." He turned on his heel, scooped up the towel, and left the room.

Two

Riki knelt beside the heavy trunk on the floor of the large storage closet and dragged up the lid. Inside, where she'd laid them a scarce two years before, were a number of David's clothes. Most, she'd given to charity, but these she remembered too well to part with—the robe she'd given him one Christmas, the jeans with the patch she'd sewn on the knee, the sweater he'd loved that she'd knitted for his birthday. . . .

Tears filled her eyes, but she fought them back. She missed David, as irresponsible as he might have been. But nothing could bring him back. She might as well let her peculiar guest wear his things. This Viscount Bedford, if that were really his name, would look ridiculous in her robe, and her flannel shirts and knitted sweaters would never stretch across his broad shoulders.

She selected an armful of likely prospects and carried them down the hall. Opening the door to the spare bedroom next to the bath, she heard the shower running full force. He'd be done in a minute, then she could take her turn with the hot water. She tossed the garments on the bed, then rapped loudly on the connecting door. The water shut off.

"I've put some things on the bed in here," she called. "I hope they fit. I'm going for my shower, now."

"Thank you," he called after a moment of silence.

She made her way to her large chamber with its connecting bath and gratefully dragged off her cold, clinging clothes. The efficient little heater had the tiled room warm in minutes, and beckoning steam rose from the shower she turned on. With a sigh of relief, she climbed in.

Twenty minutes later, her dark auburn hair still damp from her brisk toweling, she descended the stairs. She wore jeans again, but these were soft, faded and, most importantly, dry. A bulky green cowl-neck sweater hung low over her rounded hips. Sloppy, perhaps, but she liked her comfort.

She found her guest in the kitchen, pouring coffee into mugs he had unearthed from the cupboard. He looked up at her entry and grinned, and she stopped dead.

Lord, what eyes the man had! Dark, piercing—like a falcon's—yet warm with enjoyment. Rugged character marked his face, someone to be depended on and trusted—despite the warped sense of humor he had shown her earlier. Her uneasiness faded. At the moment, his features were marked by an unexpected boyish charm.

Her gaze drifted to the warm rust turtleneck sweater that stretched across his muscular torso. It had looked good on David, but on this man it caused an unexpected reaction in her. She'd always had something about broad shoulders, and this man had them, with spades. The jeans, she noted with appreciation, could not possibly have been tighter and still allowed him to drag them on. His feet remained bare, and somehow that added the final panache to the homey effect.

"Is this how you like your coffee?" he asked.

She looked up to find his eyes resting on her with much the same appreciative light that hers must hold. She managed a smile. "Do you prefer yours black, or would you like cream and sugar? Or something stronger? I've got brandy and a few other things."

She brushed past him, and found she liked the contact. She must have been alone too much these last two years. She could almost get used to sharing her kitchen — and the rest of her house — with someone like him.

She brought out her bowl of raw sugar and a carton of milk, then turned to her liquor cabinet. This she allowed Bedford to sort through. He came out with a bottle of V.S.O.P., which he opened and sniffed with approval.

She held out her mug for a dollop, then made her way into the living room. Wood and newspapers lay stacked by the fireplace, in which she'd installed an efficient air-tight stove with a see-through door. The van Hamel money came in useful if one wanted to remodel a nearly 200-year-old cottage.

By the time her guest joined her, she had started the fire. He watched as she struck a match and closed the door.

"Very practical." He came up and studied it.

"It'll be warm in just a few minutes." She remained where she was, curled up on the floor. She reached over and pulled a large pillow into position behind her.

He glanced at the comfortable chairs placed near by, then followed her example, sinking down to the area rug with an unconscious athletic grace. He, too, used one of the large cushions she kept in an inviting pile by the wall.

"This is a very pleasant way to be shipwrecked."

"All the comforts of home." She sipped her steaming coffee and regarded him over the rim of her mug. Apparently, he had abandoned his earlier game. She was glad; she felt so comfortable with him at the moment, she'd hate to discover he was nothing but an irresponsible gamer who thought everyone should play along. His infectious smile flashed, and she discovered it was dangerous.

She glanced out the long glass window toward the sheltered cove beyond. "I wonder if they've found your friends. I haven't heard the helicopter for a while."

"If they're there, they must have." Abruptly, he changed the subject. "Have you lived here long?"

He must be worried—and there was nothing he could do as night closed about them. The occasional lightning provided an irregular and erratic illumination. She shuddered as thunder rumbled once more.

"I came here two years ago, after my cousin drowned. It was in a storm much like this. They—they found pieces of his boat, shattered on the rocks just a little way out into the Channel."

"I'm sorry."

She didn't look up, though she sensed the gentle honesty of his response. "The island was mine—I'd inherited it from a distant cousin on my mother's side. The rookery was already here, and I guess I told you I'm a sucker for endangered species and worthy causes. David offered to run it for me, if I'd provide the funds, and it seemed like a good place for him. He hadn't liked the family businesses, you see." She glanced at the man, found those dark eyes resting on her thoughtfully, and she concentrated on her coffee.

"Were you here when he died?"

She shook her head. "I hadn't seen him in nearly six months. Mr. Fipps telephoned me when David's boat was found. He's the dearest little old man. He stayed here, keeping an eye on the falcons in the aviary, until I arrived. One look at the place and I decided to stay."

Her companion nodded. "I can see why. I don't think I've ever been anywhere so restful."

She managed a slight laugh. "And you've only seen it during a storm. It's beautiful here. It might almost have been designed with me in mind. It was built by—" She broke off and stared at him.

"By?" he prompted.

33

"Viscount Bedford. It just clicked. You're using his name. Why?"

"I'm using no one's name but my own. We have a long family history, though." Here, his lips quirked in an odd smile. "Longer than many would imagine. It could very well have been built by a Viscount Bedford. When was it, by the way?"

"1815, I think. Right after the Napoleonic wars ended."

"The—" He broke off and seemed to struggle with himself. "The wars ended," he repeated. "Undoubtedly, I—my ancestor—built it in celebration. We have long been falconers, you must know."

"Have you been? I thought you handled Guin as if you knew birds. How fitting this place should give you shelter, now."

A wry smile just touched his lips. "Fitting, indeed." He yawned. "Lord, it's been a—" He broke off and a somewhat shaky chuckle set his shoulders quaking. "—a *very* long day for me."

Riki glanced at her watch. "It's only just after five. Are you hungry? We could have an early dinner. You'll probably be better for a good night's sleep."

A slight frown creased his high brow. "If you will show me where you keep your spare blankets, I'll make up a bed for myself in the aviary."

"In the aviary? What on earth for?"

To her utter amazement, a dull flush crept under the light tan on his cheeks.

"It is your reputation I am thinking of." He sounded embarrassed. "You may live in a highly unconventional manner, but you are undoubtedly a lady. I have no desire to compromise you in recompense for your kindness in giving me shelter from this storm."

"*Compromise* me? Good heavens!" Amusement vied with consternation and won. "I had no idea anyone worried about things like that anymore."

He inclined his head, though he did not appear

34

convinced. "Under the circumstances, I must be guided by your judgment."

"Then you might as well use the guest room and be comfortable." She swallowed the last of her coffee and rose. "Let's fix something to eat."

He trailed after her into the kitchen and leaned against the doorjamb, watching as she rummaged through the freezer. She emerged with a couple of steaks, which she put in the microwave to thaw. A second search of the freezer produced a loaf of sourdough French bread she had baked two weeks before. She set it on the counter, waiting its turn for instant warming.

"How are you at making salads?" She looked over at the man, who had once more stuck his hand into the freezer.

He came out with a tray of ice cubes, which seemed to fascinate him. "Making what?"

She rolled her eyes. "You know, lettuce, tomatoes, carrots, whatever other veggies you find in the 'fridge?"

He flexed the plastic tray he held, and jumped as one of the cubes popped free. He examined it, then restored the whole works to the freezer. "I can always learn."

"Haven't you ever cooked *anything* for yourself?" He must be about thirty, she decided. Had he always been pampered and catered to? Somehow, that didn't mesh with the image of capability and command he projected.

"I served on the—" He broke off. "I was in the army, before I sold out."

"Sold out?" That had a dishonest ring to it.

"Returned to civilian life," he amended.

"Oh, a British term." She shook her head. "Sometimes I think we speak different languages. I still haven't gotten used to calling sweaters 'jumpers.'" She found a head of lettuce, tore off a few leaves and washed them. "Here, use that bowl down there and

35

tear these up." She turned her attention to finding more vegetables.

The microwave dinged, she handed her findings and a knife over to her guest, and she concentrated on tenderizing the steak. The broiler fascinated the man, and he stood at her side, watching as the meat cooked. Having money and servants when she grew up hadn't kept her from learning how to take care of herself. But perhaps, since he had been heir to a title, his parents hadn't thought it proper for him to hang about the kitchen. She knew an impulse to introduce him to basic survival skills.

They ate dinner on trays before the fireplace, which Bedford filled with more wood. Riki leaned back against the base of an overstuffed chair, watching the man as he swirled the wine in his glass. His shadowed expression betrayed his concern. He looked up, caught her gazing at him, and smiled.

"Why do you choose to live in so isolated a place?"

"The falcons. I feel I'm doing some good here."

"In what way?" He stretched his legs out before him, toward the briskly burning flames, and poured more wine for them both.

"Protecting the fledglings, caring for the injured. Making sure they have a safe place. When David first came here five years ago, he recorded only six eggs, and only five of those produced hatchlings. Last season I had fourteen, and all of them hatched safely. Plus two in the aviary, which I brought in and incubated when the mother was killed."

"That's a lot of birds, considering you're alone. Do you hunt them?"

She nearly spilled her wine. "They're *endangered!* We're preserving them, not using them for games. There are too few left in the world. It's a lucky thing your ancestor built this rookery."

He started to speak, then changed his mind. He gazed out over the Channel, where the lightning

36

flashed in the distance. Only the slightest rumble of thunder sounded.

"It would be a tragedy if peregrines disappeared," he said at last. "They're such beautiful birds."

"They are. And each one has such a unique personality. Have you noticed?"

He smiled suddenly. "I have one—a tiercel—that takes the longest baths. I'll swear he spends over an hour in his stream. Then he perches on a rock and dozes while he dries."

She nodded. "Guin does that, too, though not for as long." His love for the birds seemed to match her own. In subtle ways—in his keen eye, his majestic stance—he reminded her of them. She hurried into speech. "We've put in a fresh water stream with an electric pump. That's one of the things that keeps the birds coming here, I think. A guaranteed safe and reliable bath."

He didn't answer, and she stole a look at him. He still gazed out over the Channel, his expression unreadable. He must be worrying about his companions. They couldn't search at night. It must be terrible for him, not knowing, not being able to do anything. But they could check.

She stood. "Let's try to reach Mr. Fipps, and see if there's been any word on the rescue." She led the way to her office.

The radio produced only static. Bedford leaned over her shoulder, fascinated, watching as she adjusted the dials, trying to find just the right frequency. The crackling became unbearable, and at last she switched the unit off.

"I'm sorry. There's too much interference from the storm."

"Thank you for trying. And don't worry so. I think my companions are safe—back there."

"On Jersey? I hope so."

"Possibly not on Jersey."

He murmured the words, so she might have heard wrong. His solid assurance made her feel secure, and she allowed herself to stop worrying. It was pleasant to have a guest for a change, someone to talk to, someone just to be with. She felt oddly at ease with this strange man. The thought disturbed her.

"Are you tired, or would you like to look around the rookery?" Anything was better than sitting before him, staring up into the darkest, most compelling eyes she had ever seen.

A slow smile lit their depths. "I should be honored to see your home."

She stood, suddenly nervous. "This is my office. I keep the records on the birds over there." She gestured to an oak filing cabinet. "I've computerized almost everything, which makes the record keeping easier. The birds are all banded, of course."

She moved past him, into the hall. Suddenly, her little office seemed too small, his large, solid body too close to hers. The not-so-irrelevant thought came to her that she hadn't shared her bed since that summer five years ago when she'd camped out with the Save the Whales protesters. They'd used a sleeping bag, of course, and an air mattress that wouldn't stay filled. . . .

She strode down the hall, trying to shake off the sudden yearnings raised by those memories. She'd dropped Greg when she realized he was more interested in the van Hamel money than in her van Hamel body. But she knew what desire was, and the solid male keeping pace with her at the moment wasn't doing a thing to help her forget.

She threw open the only other door on the ground floor. "This was David's gaming room. I kept it the way he left it."

"You must have been very fond of him."

The deep, understanding voice did little to calm her heightened awareness.

"He was like a brother—only a year older than me. We were raised together from the time we were about four or five, when his mother died."

She flipped on the light, illuminating the large chamber. Twelve rectangular wooden tables were arranged down the center of the chamber. The tables contained large Plexiglas domes encasing battle scenes with hundreds of detailed period reenactments. Colorful prints of Napoleonic military uniforms, weapons, and engagements lined the wall.

Bedford took two steps inside and stopped, slowly turning around to take it all in. The table before him bore the legend "Talavera, July 28, 1809." The label on one dome read "As-it-occurred." The other said "As-it-should-have-been."

Bedford leaned close, studying first one scene, then the other. The first showed the actual course of the battle, with the British cavalry being routed in the city square, but with the French army of Joseph Bonaparte and Marshal Victor retreating in defeat anyway. The second dome depicted an altered strategy on the part of the French, by which the defeat of the British cavalry brought about a French victory.

Bedford rose slowly and turned to regard Riki through narrowed eyes. " 'As it should have been?' " he demanded, his voice like ice.

She shrugged. "That's the way the wargamers play it. Since Napoleon lost the war, they like to replay the battles and see if they can get him to win. If the French won, everyone would want to play Wellington, I suppose."

"Napoleon lost," Bedford repeated. He walked between the lines of tables, glancing at the labels, then stopped before "Salamanca, July 22, 1812."

Riki heard his sharp intake of breath. "Is something wrong?" She joined him.

He shook his head. "He let the British win this, I see."

39

She examined the two domes. "I think the "Should-have-beens" are actual games he played, where he altered the French and British strategy. Apparently at this one," she gestured to Salamanca, "the French didn't stand a chance."

Bedford continued, stopping at last at Waterloo. He stared at it for a very long while. "This is the last battle?"

That almost buried uneasiness resurfaced again. "Even *I* know that."

A lop-sided, but decidedly charming, smile just touched his lips. "I am far more familiar with the earlier battles and campaigns." He came toward her, pausing before the table labeled "Torres Vedras, winter 1808-1809."

She joined him, and together they examined the painted plaster-of-paris terrain of Portugal. With loving detail, David had recreated the line of mountains that stretched across the peninsula. Walls were carefully constructed between the peaks, with openings left for the heavy artillery that aimed down into the valley below, discouraging a French siege. Miniature figures, carefully colored to represent the uniforms of the diverse armies, held strategic positions.

"It's exactly like I—like I imagined it." Bedford bent down. "There are even Portuguese *cacadores*. Lord, they were the surliest—" He broke off. Turning abruptly, he looked about, then crossed to the table bearing the label "Fuentes de Onoro, May 3-5, 1811." He stood in silence for a very long time.

Riki remained where she was, frowning. His odd manner bothered her, yet she wasn't the least bit afraid of him. Whatever he might be, he wasn't dangerous. Well, not in any violent way, at least. His danger for her lay in a very different vein—despite his peculiarities. She'd been alone too much, that was the problem.

"I've kept everything exactly the way David left it,"

40

she said, feeling the need to distract her attention from the muscular back in that tightly stretched rust sweater. And as for the jeans—! "He sealed up each 'should-have-been' dome when he managed to get the greatest French advantage."

"Have you noticed how similar these two are?" Bedford still stood before Fuentes de Onoro. "Look, here. The only difference is on the Fifth of May, where Craufurd's Light Division was forced to withdraw. Your cousin has Massena pressing the advantage and following through, taking the British. In actuality, Massena let them retreat and attacked Fuentes instead, and was defeated himself."

"Oh?" She regarded him askance. He claimed not to be a wargamer, but he sure knew what happened at that battle! There weren't any labels on anything giving the generals' names.

He wandered on, examining the other domes, paying particular attention to the final battles of the war. Riki trailed after him, more interested in his reactions than in the battle scenes, which she had seen any number of times. She had spent a great deal of time in here after David's death. It had brought him closer to her, somehow.

At last, he turned his attention to the prints on the walls. A British dragoon atop a showy bay caught his attention. He glanced down at his jeans and sweater, shook his head, then moved on. He stopped suddenly before a photograph.

"My God! That's a clever likeness. That *can't* be a painting!"

She looked over his shoulder. "Of course not. It's a photo. You know, camera? Those are some of his gaming friends. David's in the next one."

Bedford turned to it and Riki felt him tense. He remained silent for a very long minute.

"David Warwick," he breathed.

"Yes, I thought you must know him. Is your memory coming back, now?" A wave of relief washed over her. "That must have been a nasty blow you got on your head. I'm so glad you're better."

He spun about to face her, and she took an involuntary step back, bumping into a table. "Your cousin. But he's my assistant."

Apparently, he still needed humoring. She managed a nonchalant shrug. "Probably. Which general were you?"

"I wasn't a general, damn it, but I *was* a captain before I sold out. I wintered with Wellesley at Torres Vedras." He pointed at the dome. "And my brother fought at Fuentes de Onoro." He gestured to the scene, then swung back to face the framed photograph. "And David Warwick is my junior assistant in Whitehall—in the War Office, to be exact. And the date isn't Nineteen-whatever it is, it's 1812!"

"I don't think that's funny."

The dark eyes he turned on her burned with his raging thoughts, but showed no sign of insanity. He paced along the wall, looking at the other photos and prints. At the far end of the room, he stopped.

"Your cousin isn't dead. He was very much alive when I left him two days ago—in 1812."

"I said that isn't funny."

He strode up to her and Riki backed away until she collided with the wall. The door stood open, but several feet to her left. His broad shoulders rose and fell, his chest expanding to the limits of the sweater as he drew one deep breath after another. She watched, mesmerized. Like a rabbit with a snake, the thought drifted through her mind.

"You said he drowned in a lightning storm two years ago, didn't you?"

She nodded.

"And David Warwick—he's American, like you, isn't he?"

Again, she nodded, not risking speech.

42

"Yes, an American. He came to my office in Whitehall and offered his services in late November of 1809. I'd just started there, myself, after selling out." He stared at the prints on the wall behind her, unseeing. "He said he had inside information on French strategy, and Bathurst listened to him, then took him on."

"Bathurst?" Her voice almost squeaked, but she controlled it.

"Our Secretary of War. I don't suppose your cousin disappeared in October or November, by any chance?"

"He—yes. It was the first week of November." She gazed up at him, caught up in his growing excitement.

"My God!" He whispered the words in all due reverence. "You see what happened, don't you? He must have been transported back in time, the same way I've just been brought forward!"

Three

Riki broke away from Bedford, but stopped in the doorway. "Quit playing your games!"

"Games, is it?" Bedford reached into the incredibly tight jeans pocket and drew out a sealed oil-skin packet. He hesitated, then broke it open, yanked out the single sheet it contained and thrust it at her. "Look at the signatures. Don't bother with the orders, they're in code. But they're meant for Wellington, in Torres Vedras."

Hesitantly, she accepted the paper. It felt odd, like a parchment. The writing was distinctly old fashioned, spidery thin yet perfectly formed. The words made no sense. She looked down at the signatures. Three looked similar, in that same, old fashioned spidery style. The fourth stood out like a sore thumb. She'd recognize David's sloppy hand anywhere.

"You—you gamers really go in for realism, don't you?" She handed the sheet back. "Can you buy these things at your supply stores?"

He almost snatched it from her. "You don't believe me, do you?"

"That you and David switched places in time? Of course, I don't! It's ridiculous! You're carrying this joke too far, and I don't like it!"

He stuffed the sheet into its pouch and restored it to

44

the pocket. "That's why everything's so strange, why *you're* so strange." He spoke more to himself than to her, and ignored her indignant gasp. "It's the only explanation."

"Will you quit this pointless pretending?" She spoke through clenched teeth.

"Madam." He regarded her with serious eyes. "I would if I could. But this is no game of your cousin's devising. Somehow, I must discover how to return to my own time—and return your cousin to his."

Riki turned on her heel and left him. Why did he have to sound so sincere? And why did he have to raise the hope within her that David was still alive? That was even more unforgivable than the rest of his teasing. She had been closer to her cousin than to her own two sisters when they were all children.

She returned to the living room, threw several more logs onto the fire, then curled up in her favorite chair with her knitting. If she concentrated very hard on the intricate cable and popcorn stitch pattern, she might be able to force her unwanted guest from her thoughts.

Gilbert Randall, Viscount Bedford, watched the petite figure, rigid with anger, stalk away. He couldn't blame her. The whole idea was preposterous.

He leaned against the door jamb and closed his eyes. The side of his head still ached. He'd dismiss this whole experience as the dream of an obviously disordered intellect, except that not even in his wildest imaginings could he have created the wonders he had seen in this cottage.

He looked back at the rows of tables with their domes that looked so much like glass, yet felt different to the touch. *Badajoz*, he repeated to himself. *Salamanca. Waterloo.* He'd take notes—copious ones—before he began his search for a way home.

45

On impulse, he returned to the kitchen and once more opened the freezer door. How did she get it to stay so cold in there? That was actually ice in those trays! And those white wrapped packages contained meats, already cut into small portions. Just like the mice and gophers in the similar contraption in the aviary.

A soft whir startled him. It came from this thing she called the "refrigerator." He frowned, closed the top door, but the noise continued. He waited, watching, until it stopped. He opened the door again, and the odd humming began almost at once.

He turned his attention to the box his reluctant hostess called a "microwave." He liked the light that came on without candles and the musical bell that sounded when it went out. The fact it made frozen food warm was merely an added bonus. His brother Hillary would go mad over it.

He flipped the overhead light on and off several times, then dragged a chair over and climbed up on it to examine the odd bit of glass that shone. It was hot to the touch. Not a trace of wax or oil or even the slight odor of the coal gas that had begun to fill the streets of London at night. He shook his head, marveling. In future—if he succeeded in getting home—he would attend the lectures at the Royal Academy of Sciences with extreme interest.

He jumped to the tiled floor and discovered a number of his muscles still protested from his forced swim. *Had* the others made it to safety? He'd give a great deal to know. When the whirlpool opened up before the yawl, the officer who'd accompanied him and two of the sailors had dived overboard. The other sailor followed only moments before the lightning struck the mast. Bedford closed his eyes, and a vision of the glowing luminescence that had danced along his body returned to haunt him. It hadn't touched the others, of that he was certain. They had swum clear—to

46

safety, he was almost sure—before the boat had been drawn down into that whirling vortex of water.

What he needed right now was a good night's sleep. He'd probably wake up in his own bed in his house on Half Moon Street. Either that, or he'd find himself on the yawl, and discover this was naught but a disordered nightmare of *mal de mer*, caused by the pitching of the boat in the storm that blew up out of nowhere.

At any rate, he would not be remiss in his manners. He would say good night to that lovely illusion who was his hostess before seeking his couch. And that, he hoped, would be the end of this whole impossible affair.

In the doorway to her drawing room—living room, had she called it?—he paused. If this were indeed a dream, he had certainly created the ideal female to populate it. She sat curled in her overstuffed chair, her bare feet tucked beneath her, her delicate frame enveloped in the massive folds of her huge sweater. Her smooth, thick hair glowed with red highlights amidst the dark satiny brown, reflecting the light from the odd lantern at her side.

She looked down, studying the knitting that hung from needles held in delicate hands. Her eyes dominated her face, he decided. Lovely eyes, of an appealing gray, he remembered, though he could not see them now. He did notice the slight bump on the bridge of her nose, as if it had been broken at one time, and the sprinkling of freckles across her cheek.

Freckles. Now, why did the simpering misses of society strive so hard to remove those delightful marks and call them blights? He liked the effect. In fact, he would like very much to kiss one of them. The one on the side of her nose, perhaps. And if he were to think of kisses, he could not ignore those lovely, full lips.

Abruptly, he turned away, abandoning his intention of bidding her a correct and formal goodnight. The way his thoughts were taking him, he'd behave with shocking impropriety. He could not so take advantage of a defenseless female, alone in her own home, when she had taken him in to shelter him from a storm.

Resolutely, he made his way upstairs and to the room she had told him to use. His clothes still hung in what she called the "bathroom." He'd rinsed them out and laid them over the metal bar at the top of the large bathing tub.

Now, that still fascinated him. When he'd stood under that strange metal thing on the wall she called a shower and started twisting those knobs, he'd been hit by an icy blast that quickly gave way to scalding heat. Judicious—and quick—experimentation had produced a comfortably relaxing temperature in the water that beat down on him. On the whole, an enjoyable invention.

He turned to the washbasin and watched in amazement as the water gushed out with only the turn of a knob. Wishing he had a toothbrush, he made himself ready for bed as best he could. And while he was at it, he'd give a great deal for Pervis, his valet. Or even his old batman.

He peeled off the sweater and jeans, again marveling at the odd fastening device. Those two metal strips that joined together were far more efficient than buttons—once he discovered how they worked.

He sifted once more through the garments Miss van Hamel had provided for him. Apparently, Cousin David did not leave any nightgear behind. Feeling self-conscious at wearing nothing, he climbed quickly between warm fuzzy sheets and pulled up the thick down comforter.

He had nothing to complain about in his accommodations, he decided. He'd suffered far worse at posting houses. The storm raged on outside his window, but he remained warm and dry inside, enveloped by the pleasant aromas of roses and violets that wafted from a bowl of dried petals and leaves on the lace-covered dresser. No damp sheets, no fireplaces that gushed smoke, no inferior tallow candles to add their unpleasant odor to the room. And hot water—and other luxuries—readily at hand. Considering he'd been shipwrecked, he had come through amazingly well.

He closed his eyes, but this time it wasn't visions of the whirlpool or lightning that haunted him. Instead he saw Miss Erika van Hamel, knitting quietly in her chair, the picture of peace and serene beauty. So very fragile, yet brave to climb those slippery, sheer rocks for her falcon. Her huge gray eyes kindled and burned, reflecting her every emotion. . . .

He groaned at the stirrings in his groin, and rolled over. For his peace of mind—for his sense of honor!— he couldn't allow this. He forced himself to concentrate on the message he carried to Wellington. At the moment, he was almost two hundred years too late to deliver it. That thought drifted off in a dreamy hazziness as exhaustion overcame him.

Slowly, he became aware of the steady beating of rain on the paned window. The grayness of an overcast morning hung about the room, and it took him a few minutes to come fully awake. It must be later than dawn, but the storm prevented any brightness from seeping in through the drawn curtains.

He rose, pulled these back from the window, and stared out over the rock-filled Channel toward Jersey. A streak of lightning sliced through the charcoal clouds, followed by the muffled rumble of thunder. He couldn't remember an electrical storm lasting this long.

He turned slowly and examined the unfamiliar chamber. Those odd clothes remained on the chair where he had tossed them the night before. Not a dream, then, as part of him had hoped. His head no longer ached, exhaustion no longer dulled his perspective. This was real. Somehow, he had been thrown into the future.

In the bathroom he found his own clothes, still damp and considerably wrinkled. Definitely, he needed Pervis—though a brief examination of his things showed them to be beyond the talents of even his inestimable man. At a rough guess, they must have shrunk beyond the point of his ever being able to get into them again.

Leaving his ruined garments where they were, he donned the tight jeans and the warm rust sweater he'd worn the night before. Barring his man, he could use a stiff brush or two—Pervis would never forgive him for the shocking state of his boots. But at least they were wearable, and he didn't have to go downstairs with his feet bare this morning.

As he neared the kitchen, the sound of off-key whistling reached him. A rather nice tune, if somewhat botched in performance. He entered to find his hostess measuring coffee into that marvelous machine they had used the night before.

She looked up and a wary expression entered her eyes. "Good morning. Did I wake you?"

"No. Did I sleep long?"

"It's almost nine." She shuddered as a flash of lightning outside momentarily brightened the room. Thunder rumbled only a moment later.

He watched, fascinated, as the contraption hissed and water bubbled down, coming out as coffee in the carafe.

"Do you like eggs? Not falcon, by the way. I keep chickens."

"Yes, thank you." He watched as she removed several from the refrigerator and carried them to a counter, where she set about scrambling. It amazed him that she could cook without fire in the stove, but somehow she managed it by merely turning a few knobs.

Feeling useless, he opened cupboards until he unearthed plates and mugs. He found silverware in a drawer. Not for the first time, he wondered why she didn't have servants. It was rather satisfying, though, doing everything for themselves. Much like being back on the Peninsula—though there he'd at least had his batman.

"There's orange juice in the 'fridge. Go ahead and pour some." She didn't even look up from the fresh herbs she chopped.

That meant finding more glasses. This he did, then poured juice for both of them. He retired to the comfortable nook with his.

He liked this place, he decided. It made him feel at home. And he liked Miss van Hamel, despite her antagonism.

Riki dropped thin slices of bread into a metal box, then scooped the cooked eggs onto a plate and carried it to the table. Next she brought a small yellow block from the refrigerator, and with a sense of surprise he realized it was butter. When the metal box made an odd clicking sound, she pulled out the bread, which had become brown and toasted. He accepted the slices and watched, fascinated, as she put in two more.

"Mr. Fipps radioed this morning. The searchers didn't find your friends." She brought mugs of coffee over and sat down.

He nodded. "I didn't think they would. I'm sure they're safe—back there."

She put down her fork and glared at him. "Look, did you let me call out a rescue helicopter for nothing? *Were* there others? Or is this all part of your warped game?"

He shook his head. "There's nothing I can say to convince you of what's happened, is there? I could give you my word as a gentleman, but I know how insane this whole idea must seem to you. It seems insane to *me*, and I have the evidence of my senses—I see things all around me that I *know* are impossible. I would assume I am now residing in Bedlam, except

51

that in every other way, my mind appears to be functioning in perfect order."

"Damn it, you make it all sound so — so *possible!*" She pushed her plate away and stood. "I'm going to check on Guin."

He watched her stalk out of the kitchen into the hall, where she paused to pull on her windbreaker. Without looking back at him, she left the cottage, ducking her head against the rain and wind that greeted her.

With a sigh, Bedford turned back to his breakfast. He had some thinking to do. If he actually had gone forward through time, if those battle scenes in David Warwick's gaming room were real, then the details he could learn, the information he could provide the army, would be tremendous. But Warwick already did that. David obviously knew French strategy perfectly; he had studied it minutely, it seemed. That meant the advice he gave the War Department was sound, and could only help them.

Or could it? A chill ran through him. In his wargaming, David Warwick played for the French to win. What if he did the same, now — or rather, in the past? He could well make it very difficult for the British, or even arrange for Napoleon to conquer Europe!

Bedford pushed back his chair, and strode to the gaming room. With new insight, he studied the battle scenes, paying particular attention to those that had taken place since he had accepted the assistance of David Warwick. Was it his imagination, or were the "As-it-should-have-been" renditions disturbingly similar in many critical aspects to the "As-it-occurred?" The British came off the victors, but not by much. The British strategy was faulty. He closed his eyes, wracking his memory. Had any of that been at the recommendation of Warwick?

He returned to Fuentes de Onoro. His brother Aubrey had had a near brush with death, there. If

Warwick—his own assistant!—had anything to do with that. . . .

Struck by the prickly sensation of being watched he broke off the thought. Looking up, he saw Miss van Hamel standing in the doorway. He straightened.

"Did your falcon enjoy her breakfast?"

She wrinkled that delightful nose, causing the freckles to bunch up. "Not yet. I left Guin bathing as best she could, and occasionally poking at the wood pigeon I gave her. I do *not* enjoy cleaning up her leavings."

That brought a smile to his lips. "You need a rookery attendant. Someone to cater to the birds for you."

"I manage very well, thank you." She drew a deep breath and let it out audibly. "The storm's still too bad for you to try to leave. You're welcome to stay—if you quit playing games."

"I'll not disturb you, that I promise. Do you mind if I remain in here?"

"Be my guest." She sounded stiff.

"Thank you. May I borrow paper and pen?"

She gestured to a small table at the back of the room, where several books on wargaming stood on a shelf. Beneath, in a small drawer, he found a tablet and several white sticks of an unidentifiable material. With a little experimentation, he discovered they contained ink, and he could write with ease. He returned to the domes and began making notes.

The storm continued throughout the morning, but he paid it little heed. Details of French battle strategy filled his mind to the exclusion of all else. Finally, the rumblings of his stomach succeeded where that of thunder failed, and he laid aside the pen. A tantalizing aroma reached his nostrils, and he followed it as if it were a will-o'-the-wisp.

He found his hostess once more in her kitchen, stirring the contents of a large kettle. The smells were more pungent, even harder to resist, in here. He peered over her shoulder into the simmering concoc-

53

tion that contained a multitude of different ingredients that Riki identified as chowder. Lord, what he would have given for this young lady in the Peninsula, where their meals were frequently of such a hodge-podge nature, yet rarely appetizing. When she placed a bowl before him, he ate with undisguised pleasure.

Across from him, she sat without speaking. It bothered him that he distressed her, yet what could he do? He could think of no topic of conversation that would be safe, for his mind teemed with questions that would only serve to anger her, make her think he feigned ignorance deliberately.

He took another sip of the thick creamy soup and savored the flavor. She knew how to cook, all right. He could just envision his youngest sister Felicity if confronted by a stalk of celery or an onion. Or better, his other sister Clarissa. A chuckle escaped him at the thought of the horror with which Clarissa would regard a kitchen.

Riki looked up, eyeing him uncertainly. "Is everything all right?"

"I was just thinking of either of my sisters trying to live without a household staff."

"Mine also. Though I had hopes—" She broke off and stood abruptly. "Excuse me. I have work to do." She set her bowl on the counter top beside the sink and left.

He finished his chowder, then returned to the gaming room. Those books he had glimpsed might prove useful. If nothing else, he would like to discover what "gaming" was, and why Miss van Hamel obviously regarded it askance.

He opened the first, entitled merely *Miniature Campaigns*, and soon was bewildered by talk of scale, handicapping, and morale factors. He leafed farther into the heavy volume, only to stop as he found himself staring at a map labeled "Salamanca." The positions of the generals and field marshals were clearly pointed out, along with their lines of charge and retreat. He continued until he reached a section labeled "biographies" and found himself staring at details of Napoleon's death.

The blurring of the page and the strain on his eyes warned him of the hours he had spent perusing the volume. Outside, the sky grew dark with the coming of night. His first thought was to summon reading candles, but an easier solution lay readily to hand. He strode to the wall, found the switch, and watched the ceiling fixture as it sprang to life with blazing light. Feeling immensely smug over his mastery of this device, he returned to his studies.

The next chapter "Communications and Supplies" caught his interest, and he began reading, in rapt fascination, how many loaves of bread, and at what cost, must be purchased to maintain an army. The problem of spoiled foodstuffs, and the percentage of men he could expect to desert if he provided them with bad food, appalled him.

He flipped the page, but before he could discover why the author labeled the next section "Medical Atrocities," the light above him flickered, then went out. He sat in complete darkness, for the heavy clouds and barrage of rain effectively blocked the rising moon. A jagged streak of lightning momentarily illuminated the scene, then faded away to the accompaniment of a thunder that rivaled his unnerved memories of cannonading.

A spot of light appeared in the hall, growing brighter as it approached. Candles, he thought in relief, and began feeling his way among the tables. A brilliant circle of yellow appeared in the doorway, showing his path.

"Miss van Hamel?" Taking advantage of the illumination, he hurried forward. He could barely make out her petite shape, for whatever she held cast only the dimmest reflection upon her. It must be a shuttered lantern, he surmised, with its opening directed at him.

"Bedford?" She sounded tentative. "The generator has gone out. Are you any good with engines?"

"Is that not your Mr. Fipps's specialty?" He reached her side and took the peculiarly narrow, cylindrical lantern from her to examine it.

A shaky sigh escaped her. "He can't get out here after dark. Do you think you could at least look at it?"

She sounded nervous, which surprised him. But as the lightning flashed again at that moment, she took an instinctive step nearer, as if seeking his protection. The amazingly capable Miss van Hamel possessed a very distressing bugbear.

He resisted the urge to slip a comforting arm about her. For all her nonchalance of the night before, she might also be frightened of permitting a strange man into her home. It was amazing what light—or the lack of it—did to normally rational people.

"It's in the aviary, isn't it? Come on, then. Do you have an umbrella?"

She produced a very serviceable one from a stand in the hall, and he opened it and held it for her as they raced across the courtyard. Inside the long building, silence greeted them. Miss van Hamel directed her lantern toward the large, peculiar contraption. Bedford suppressed the eerie sensation that it smiled at them in defiance.

"Lord Bedford, meet Mortimer." Riki knelt down and dragged open the curved door. "Maybe it's just out of fuel. Damn, I can't read the dial." She peered closer, then shook her head. "About three quarters of a tank, still. I was afraid of that." She shook her head again, setting the smooth, silky mass of her hair glinting.

Bedford resisted the urge to touch it. "What does your Mr. Fipps do?"

"A wire's probably come loose. The thing shakes so

much that a connection is always breaking." She regarded it uncertainly. "Sometimes he just kicks it and it starts up again."

"That much I can probably manage, if you think it will help."

She turned to look up at him, much as if she expected him to work some miracle. It irritated him that she so obviously thought he should know all about the damnable thing—and even more so that he could not rise to the occasion and fulfill her expectations.

He cast the umbrella aside, took the light from her, and examined the contraption. Never, in his entire life, had he beheld anything quite like it. But he was prime for any adventure. If only he could understand how it worked, he might be able to do the trick.

"What is the principle behind it?" He asked the question while he studied the mystifying switches.

Silence answered him. He looked over his shoulder and encountered her sheepish expression.

"I—"

Her complexion had undoubtedly taken on a delicate flush, could he but see it. He regretted the lack of sufficient light.

"Yes?" he prompted, beginning to enjoy himself.

"I've never been very good at machinery," she admitted.

He shook his head, and in spite of his nobler instincts, his voice took on a lofty tone. "If I could understand it, I could probably fix it."

"Of course, I was forgetting." She recovered admirably. "They hadn't invented gasoline engines yet in Eighteen-whatever, had they?"

He inclined his head. "Unlike you, I never had the opportunity to learn."

"That's right, rub it in. That's going to do us one hell of a lot of good, isn't it?" She turned her back on him, found her umbrella, and stalked out the door.

He followed, still smiling at her outrageous language. He found it distinctly refreshing. It allowed him, if he so chose, to express himself with similar freedom. He couldn't help but wonder if all females of this time were as outspoken — and enjoyable — as this one.

They dined before the fireplace on salad, leftover bread, and wine. Somewhat to his disappointment, all the conveniences he enjoyed so much appeared not to be working. This thing called a generator — or a Mortimer — must be a very powerful contraption, indeed.

On the whole, he decided, he didn't really mind that much that Mortimer stopped working. Those sconces or whatever they were in the ceiling were too bright. Firelight definitely suited Miss van Hamel. She sat across from him, silent, sipping her wine and gazing into the shielded hearth. She was beautiful. And the gleaming play of reflected flames along her auburn hair did interesting things to his senses.

Riki glanced up and caught his eyes resting on her. Heat flooded her cheeks and she looked quickly away. *Damn* the man for being so attractive. The very least he could do would be to appear outwardly as peculiar as he behaved. But no, his features had to be strong and piercing.

She gazed down at the burgundy in her glass. It didn't hold a candle to the sparkling luminescence of his eyes. Irritated with her fancies, she stood up and needlessly brushed off the seat of her jeans.

"Did you enjoy yourself today?" she asked abruptly.

"Very much. I found your cousin's gaming room fascinating."

"I'll bet." She breathed the words. "I suppose you particularly liked the battles in which you claim to have taken part."

"No, actually I spent my time studying the ones that have not yet taken place."

"What would you gain, even if you really were from the past? Napoleon lost, anyway. It's not as if you'd change history."

He set his glass down. "I wasn't thinking of anything that drastic. But consider the lives that could be saved if our generals knew the enemy's plans in advance. This would be better than any intelligence information we've been able to obtain. Come, let me show you." He sprang to his feet, grabbed up her flashlight, flipped it on, and led the way to the gaming room.

Why hadn't she kept the curiosity out of her voice? She had made the mistake of encouraging his pretending. Now he probably wouldn't give her any peace until he showed her whatever he had in mind.

She followed as he led the way among the tables until he came to one labeled "Ciudad Rodrigo."

"There," he said. "This would be the next battle. Look carefully at the 'As-it-ocurred' rendition. Do you see where the French have concentrated their defences? If the British troops moved from over here —" He broke off, staring.

Riki stared, too. It was crazy, but she'd swear the British assault wasn't the way she remembered it. It must be the meager light from the flashlight that seemed to alter the positions of the tiny figures. She'd gazed at these silly domes countless times, but everything looked different in these shadows.

"Look at the other dome." Bedford's voice sounded strange.

The "As-it-should-have-been" scene appeared just as she remembered it, in spite of the eerie illumination. She looked back at the other dome, and a sudden, unpleasant idea struck her.

"You changed it! They're almost alike, now, with the French having a powerful advantage." She glared at him, furious. "How *could* you?"

"How, indeed." His words sounded clipped. "If you

59

will try to move the dome top, you will find it is impossible."

She tried, and it didn't budge. "All right, you glued it back down. How *dare* you move his figures!"

"I didn't." He gestured at the card bearing the battle's name and date. "Read that."

"January Nineteenth, 1812. January—" She broke off. "No, I know what you're getting at, and this isn't funny! So what if its anniversary was today! There was an eleven day siege! It says so right there!"

"And the battle scene altered, of its own accord, because now that your cousin is in the past, he changed the course of the battle to favor the French!"

"No!" Riki screamed the word at him. She spun away, but he grabbed her wrists, preventing her from escaping.

"Listen! You're damned right, this isn't funny. Check the way the dome's been sealed. It hasn't been touched."

She stopped struggling. She honestly couldn't think of any way he might have lifted that Plexiglas top, but somehow, he must have.

"Can't you see what is happening?" Bedford turned the full force of those dark, blazing eyes on her. "Your cousin has gone back through time and is changing history in Napoleon's favor!"

Four

Bedford's eyes blazed with intensity. "Warwick is sabotaging the British effort. Give me the benefit of the doubt for one minute. If what I suggest is true, could your cousin tilt the scales so Napoleon could come off the victor in the Peninsular campaign?"

Riki stared at him, then looked down at the domes. "Yes. But the British win!"

Bedford's jaw tightened. "But was that without your cousin's influence?"

"That's ridiculous. It happened almost two hundred years ago!"

"I arrived here, in your time, on the same day of the year that I was swept out of my own time. What if there's some correlation between our two times? What if something that happened because of his interference on today's date in 1812 only has an effect starting from today, in this year?"

Riki leaned back against the table behind her for support. "You're mad!"

"Do you want to see the notes I took earlier? *That scene has changed!*"

She shook her head, feeling bombarded, almost frantic.

"Damn it, how can I prove it to you?" He turned away, running an agitated hand through his tousled hair. Suddenly, he demanded: "What do you know about the Viscount Bedford who built this place?"

"I—I have the diary he kept. It's locked in the safe."

"So I keep a diary, do I? Then I'll undoubtedly put in some clue to prove my story to you."

"What?"

He shook his head, smiling suddenly. "How do I know? I haven't done it yet. Of course, it's possible I'm not able to get back to my own time. In that case, viscount Bedford will be either Aubrey or Hillary." He looked around the room, shaking his head. "This place isn't like either of them, though. But it is like me. Where's the diary?"

There was something powerful, sincere—and desperate—about the man that made her almost believe him. Now, alert to danger, his resemblance to her birds became more than merely physical. He had the heart of a falcon, she realized, the keen instinct of the hunter. The comparisons both fascinated and frightened her.

Mutely, she led the way to her office. Built into the wall beside her desk was a fireproof safe, which she opened. She pulled out a handful of papers, then drew an ancient book wrapped in plastic from the bottom shelf. Carefully, she opened it.

"When the time is right, the need for the following chronicle will be understood." The neatly inscribed words on the opening page jumped out at her. She had often wondered about them.

Bedford laughed shortly as he read over her shoulder. "That's my hand, all right. I suppose I wanted to make it mysterious to intervening generations."

"There's nothing in here. I'd have discovered any message addressed to me at once."

"Then obviously I wasn't so coarse as to leave one. No, I'd be more like to leave something subtle. There isn't by any chance a portrait or a sketch, is there?"

She choked. Carefully, she turned the aging manuscript pages to the back of the book. There, attached firmly to the padded back cover, was a miniature.

Riki gazed down at the now-familiar hawk-like features, that pepper-and-salt hair waving with a life of its own back from the high forehead. The mouth held a secret, sardonic smile.

"Gilbert Randall, Viscount Bedford," she whispered, reading the painted inscription. She looked to the man who stood beside her, then back to the painted features.

There couldn't be any doubt. It was the same man, both in the almost 200-year-old portrait and standing now at her side.

She shook her head, fighting against the evidence of her eyes. "You planted this here!" she exclaimed, turning her wild, frightened gaze on him. "You and David—"

But even as she spoke the words, she knew they could not be true. David had never seen the diary. She had locked it away in the safe before ever turning the rookery over to her cousin. She hadn't wanted the diary, which recorded the construction of Falconer's Folly as a sanctuary for peregrines, to become a mere wargaming prop. The lines, written in almost poetic prose, amounted to a love sonnet to Bedford's "dearest lady" and their birds.

Bedford took the book from her and directed the flashlight at the pages as he leafed through them. "I don't suppose I really ought to read this. But it's interesting to know what I'll be doing in three years' time."

"If—if history hasn't been changed by then." Even to Riki, her voice sounded thin and nervous.

He looked down at her, his expression unreadable in the near dark. "Do you believe me, now?" he asked gently.

"It can't be true." But she was no longer so certain. That dome, which she would swear had been altered, the almost 200-year-old picture of the man who stood at her side. . . . Perhaps it was she who was insane, from living alone too long. But if his story were true, then at least Bedford wasn't peculiar, or playing a cruel joke on her! The relief that thought brought startled her.

Riki raised her gaze to his and found him watching her with so much understanding for her confusion that her last doubts fled. Only someone who had been faced with the impossible, who had been forced to accept it as true, could understand how she felt at this moment. Tentatively, she raised one hand to him, and he took it in a firm hold.

"It's preposterous," she said, her tone purely conversational.

"I know." His smile faded and a grim note crept into his voice. "And now I have to discover how to return to my own time and prevent your cousin's traitorous actions."

"He's not a traitor, though. He's not British. He's Ameri—" She broke off, as horror dawned on her. "The War of 1812!"

"The what?"

"The British and Americans go to war. It must be after Napoleon is defeated in the Peninsula and heads into Russia. Our countries go to war." But David and his current activities couldn't be responsible for that! There were sound reasons, economic ones, for that conflict with England—weren't there?

"With your cousin meddling, there's a good chance Napoleon may win in the Peninsula after all."

The potential consequences appalled Riki. If the utterly impossible had indeed happened, and David now lived out his wargaming fantasies to the detriment of history, he had to be stopped! And, with a gripping fear, she knew someone must convince him of the dangers of altering what had already occurred—someone from his time, someone he knew, liked, and trusted. In short, herself.

"No!" Bedford shook his head, his features adamant.

She realized she had spoken her thoughts aloud. "I *must* go," she repeated. "There's no one else he'd listen to." She saw the cold, unyielding determination in the depths of Bedford's dark eyes, and shivered. "You aren't even planning on talking to him, are you? You're just going to storm in there Rambo-style and get rid of him—kill him!"

"I cannot permit such treachery, and in my own assistant!"

"I won't let you murder David! He has no idea what he's doing, it's just a game to him!"

"Were you in love with your cousin?" he demanded.

"What? Of course, not! We grew up together as brother and sister. You've got to let me talk to him."

Bedford's expression softened, but he shook his head. "It's too dangerous for you to try to go back through time. I must try, for that is where I belong." He turned over the diary that he still held, and gazed for a moment at the neatly inscribed cover. "This is no guarantee I will make it. This might be history the way it *was*, not the way it will now be." He looked up and met her gaze. "There is every chance I will merely drown."

An unexpected rush of fear swept through her—for him. She fought it down. "David is my cousin. It was my money that provided him with financial freedom to pursue his wargaming hobby till he became a fanatic. So it's my duty to stop him."

"That's utter fustion." He tossed the journal onto the table and turned on his heel.

"Where are you going?"

"To make preparations. My staying here to study the battles didn't seem to matter, before. I thought your cousin was using his knowledge to help our people. Instead, he's using it against us. I've got to get back and stop him."

"*We've* got to stop him."

65

She shoved the book into the safe, locked it, and ran after him. He stood in the hall, his head bowed, lost in thought. Slowly, she came up behind him.

"It's going to be a hazardous endeavor," he said.

"I know. But you're not leaving me behind. Damn it, it's *my* fault!"

He faced her and placed his strong hands on her shoulders. "So very brave. You even climb rocks in this storm to save a falcon. What would become of your Guin if you left?"

"I'll radio Mr. Fipps. He prefers staying here to living on Jersey, anyway."

"I can't let you risk your life."

She ignored his comment. "How do you plan to do it?"

Absently, his fingers stroked her shoulders. As if suddenly aware of what he did, he drew back and strode quickly into the living room. Riki followed.

"What are you going to do?" she repeated.

"The key to shift through time must be a lightning storm." He stared into the fire. "Your cousin disappeared in one and I came forward during another."

Riki shuddered. "It *would* have to be, wouldn't it?" She fought down the surge of terror she felt at the mere prospect of being outside during thunder and lightning. She had done it the day before, to save Guin. She could do it again. "Do we just set sail?"

"*We* will do nothing." He studied the flickering flames behind the fireplace door.

She expected him to elaborate, but he didn't. "David will listen to me. He must! I can convince him to stop whatever game he's playing and come back with me."

"I'll need a boat." He didn't seem to have heard her last argument.

"I told you, the motorboat isn't working—until Mr. Fipps looks at the engine. I have a ketch—" She broke off, and a slow smile of satisfaction just touched her lips. "She takes two people to handle her."

He turned at that and fixed her with a piercing re-gard. "No other vessels? And you, alone on the is-land?"

She shrugged. "David had the smaller sailboat. I've only taken the ketch out with Mr. Fipps. Normally I use the motorboat if I have to run over to Jersey."

He glared at her. "I'll try it alone."

"You'd be guaranteed to drown, then. With two of us, you'd at least stand a chance of controlling her. What's more important to you, playing hero or getting back to your own time and saving your country?"

She didn't give him the opportunity to answer. Tak-ing the light from him, she turned back toward the of-fice. "I'll radio Mr. Fipps right now."

"How soon can he get here? The storm isn't showing any signs of letting up."

"That won't bother Mr. Fipps if he thinks the fal-cons need him. He has a forty-foot fishing boat that can get him through this," she called over her shoulder. She sat down at the radio, switched its power source to the battery, and turned it on. A low humming filled the air.

Mr. Fipps, standing by for emergencies as he always did in such weather, answered at once. The prospect of spending a week or two on the island delighted him. With promises to come over first thing in the morn-ing, he cut off. He must be anxious to pack, Riki thought, amused.

She started to rise, then returned to her position at the desk. There was one more thing she really ought to settle. What if they didn't make it back through time? Bedford had been right, they might very well drown. The whole idea was so crazy as to be unbeliev-able. No sane woman would undertake such an adven-ture.

A slight smile playing about her lips, she drew a plain piece of paper before her and carefully penned the words: "I, Erika Teresa van Hamel, being of sound mind. . . ."

The document took her only five minutes to compose, being merely an update to her existing will. But just in case something happened, she wanted to leave Falconer's Folly to Mr. Fipps. The lack of witnesses couldn't be helped, but no one in her family was likely to go against her expressed wishes—at least, not where this island was concerned. They simply wouldn't care.

She found Bedford in the living room, staring into the fire with a deep frown creasing his brow. His intensity radiated from him, enveloping her as well until her skin prickled with his tension. This was no joke; he believed in his story—and in the danger of his intended undertaking.

She swallowed hard, summoning her inner strength. "Well? How do we begin?"

"There isn't much we can do until morning. The clouds aren't letting any light through from the moon or stars, and I don't care to try navigating through those rocks solely by lightning." He raised his gaze to stare out the window. "I don't like your coming."

"Neither do I, but I'm the only one who can get through to David. Do we take provisions?" She didn't quite control the quiver in her voice.

He turned to look at her, and his expression softened. "By all means, if it will make you feel better."

"Nothing about this makes me feel 'better.' " She moved up beside him, seeking the warmth of the fire. "This is all preposterous. What makes you think we *can* travel through time?"

"Because it has been done before—by your cousin going back and by me, coming forward. On both occasions, we were sailing during an electrical storm."

"Other people have been crazy enough to do that, and *they* haven't gone hopping about in time. Why you and David? And why should we?" She shivered as a

68

jagged streak flickered in the distance.

"The lightning struck one of our masts," Bedford mused.

"That's happened to boats before. What made it different for you?"

"The mast, I should think. It struck the shorter of the two. One of the sailors had rigged up a makeshift attachment for the sail on that one, using a metal link from a chain."

"That would attract lightning, but I don't see why that would cause a jump through time. Damn it, you're talking as if this were *reasonable,* as if it happens every day!"

"I hope it will happen tomorrow."

She could get no more out of him, so she unearthed another flashlight from the hall cupboard and made her way up to her room. Would this be the last night she spent in her bed for a very long while? she wondered as she crawled in between flannel sheets. She shied away from considering the entire matter. Determinedly, she concentrated on a sleep that eluded her.

She emerged from her room at first light, once again dressed in her jeans, bulky sweater, and nylon windbreaker. She reached Bedford's door and saw it stood open; the quilts had been drawn hastily over the pillow and his own rumpled antique clothing lay in a heap over a chair, alongside a neat pile of David's things that hadn't fit.

As she reached the foot of the stairs, Bedford strode in the front door, shivering, his scraped-up boots leaving muddy prints. Riki stopped in her tracks.

How could anyone look so overpoweringly attractive at six in the morning? His shoulders stretched the knit wool of the sweater and those jeans should have prevented his moving without ripping seams. His rumpled, pepper and salt hair curled back from his high forehead, above thick brows that almost met over his aquiline nose. But instead of giving him a frowning

69

expression, today they emphasized that hawk-like, piercing gaze. He reminded her of a tiercel, circling his prey, preparing to strike.

As if aware of the steady gaze on him, he looked up and saw her. No smile lightened the intensity of his features. "I've had a look at the ketch. It'll take both of us."

Riki nodded, unable to find words. She had only managed to drift off to sleep last night by convincing herself this would be a normal day, that nothing untoward was about to happen. The alternative was too ludicrous—and too terrifying.

"I—I can make coffee," she managed at last. "I have a little camp stove that isn't electric. Would you like some?"

Bedford nodded. "I borrowed a link from a chain in the boat shed and attached it to one of the masts."

She cringed as a distant rumble of thunder reached them. "What will we need?" How did one plan an impossible journey—especially a journey in which one really couldn't quite believe?

"Warm clothes and food. I'm as hungry as a bear. You said you had brandy, didn't you? Did your cousin keep a hip flask?"

"Yes, and I have one, too."

He regarded her quizzically, but refrained from comment. "I think we should get underway as quickly as possible."

"Then help me make sandwiches."

He followed her into the kitchen, and in a very short time they had assembled a selection of food that should last them well into the following day. While Riki spread cream cheese and strawberry preserves on sliced bagels for breakfast, Bedford filled the flasks. He thrust one into his already tight back pocket and handed her the other.

Riki didn't lock the rookery—there was no need. Mr. Fipps would come within the next two hours. She paused in the trellised gateway, hunching her shoulders to the rain, and looked back at the cottage. Suddenly, she hated to leave the safety of her home.

"I can't even feed Guin this morning without the microwave to defrost her something."

"Your friend will take care of that." Bedford took her arm and pulled her along with him.

The tiny drops stung her face as the wind whipped them along. Lightning, for the third day without cease, flashed across the sky and the accompanying rumble thundered as if it tore the charcoal clouds.

"At least the storm's still with us." An edge of repressed excitement touched his voice and his eyes gleamed.

Riki cast an uneasy glance at him. Her tiercel, having spotted his prey, was about to swoop for his kill. The comparison caused an icicle of fear to jab through her chest, and the chill seeped all the way into her stomach.

The steep path led to a dock constructed of wood and rock. The ketch tossed and pitched at its mooring, ramming safely into the tires that lined the pier. Bedford threw their sack of provisions on board, then turned to hand Riki onto the heaving deck.

As soon as she found her footing, Riki grabbed the boathook and steadied the vessel against the tires while Bedford cast off the lines. In moments he clambered aboard and together they eased the thirty-foot ketch away from the rocks and headed her out into the Channel.

Icy wind whipped wet hair across Riki's eyes. She shoved it aside and crawled to the bow to secure the jib. The main sail luffed wildly in the wind, but Bedford drew in the sheet, bringing it under control. Only the mizzen remained loose. Ducking under the boom, Riki returned to the stern and secured it.

Another fiery streak tore across the sky and she gritted her teeth, waiting for the rumble to fade in the distance. She was crazy to go out in this! They were both insane!

"Where did your boat go down?" She called.

He shook his head, but whether he indicated he didn't know, or that he hadn't heard her, she couldn't be certain. For several long minutes, he peered across the Channel, as if searching for some familiar object to give him his bearings as he steered the treacherous course. Only low, rocky outcroppings surrounded by foaming white met their searching gazes.

Drawing the mainsheet with him, he returned to Riki's side and took the tiller. A streaky flash shimmered, barely feet away from the mizzenmast, and Riki cringed as the thunder crashed on top of them. She gripped the varnished rim, then ducked under the boom and inched forward to catch the flapping jib. The boat hove to, throwing her against the gleaming brass handrail.

"Careful!" Bedford's cry of warning reached her, thin and distant in the wind.

She didn't even attempt to reply. She clung where she was as angry waves buffeted against the sides of the light craft. The deck rose up beneath her feet, then plunged downward, throwing her to her knees. Her fingers whitened on the rail as lightning flashed directly overhead.

The ketch reared back again, then dropped with sickening force as a wave crashed over the bow. Riki dragged herself up from the outer cabin wall where she had been thrown, only to be flung hard against the rail. She hung on as the vessel rose once more, knocked about by the heaving waves as if it were a toy. Her nose and hands felt like ice.

Behind her, Riki heard Bedford shout, but couldn't make out his words. She stumbled back toward the stern, only to be thrown hard against the man's strong chest as the ship pitched violently to port, at the mercy of the raging Channel.

Bedford gripped her, holding her tight, shielding her face from the freezing sting of the rain and salt spray. The pungently smelling sopping wool of his sweater tasted of salt, but she clung to him, welcoming the solidity of his body.

A violent lurch of the ship threw them against the cabin. Bedford caught himself, but as the wave receded, the ketch plunged downward, tearing Riki from him. She staggered backward, only to be knocked to the deck by a freezing wave breaking across the stern. The water dragged backward, pulling at her drenched legs, but she struggled to her knees and reached for the hand Bedford held out to her. The ketch pitched to starboard, throwing her to her side as another wave swamped the boat.

Thunder exploded above their heads as the sky lit with a vivid streak of lightning. Riki clung to the open cabin door as a wave rushed over her and down the companionway.

"We're taking on too much water!" Bedford shouted.

Rocks loomed up dead ahead, glittering in the streaky illumination of the storm. Bedford threw the tiller and the boat lurched to port, skimming the outer rim of the jagged outcroppings. Riki's sigh of relief vanished into a gasp of pure terror as a wave slammed them hard and the ketch was thrown leeward. The rasping screech of splintering wooden planks sounded loud above the wind.

Another wave swamped them, spilling over the side, as Riki clambered to her feet. She clung to the door frame, trying to keep her balance. She could see Bedford clutching the rail with one hand and the tiller with the other in a vain attempt to steer clear.

They were sinking! Riki stared in horror at the chill water that slapped her ankles. This was madness! Had she honestly expected some magical intervention to sweep them up and carry them across time to safety?

Frantic, she scanned the sky. Never would she have

dreamed she'd pray her boat would be struck by lightning, but she did so now. In only minutes they would be floundering. They were sinking, they would fail in this desperate, impossible mission — they would drown.

The churning of the waves took on an eerie echoing sound and Riki turned in horror to see the swirling arms of a whirlpool form about the bow. Faster and faster the water spun, drawing them into the vortex, pulling them down in a frenzied spiral. A scream tore from her throat as the craft began to gyrate. The sails flapped, useless, as the funnel deepened, opening like a mouth to swallow the spinning boat.

"Hang on!" Bedford shouted over the tumult of the storm.

Dizzy, Riki clung to the side. As the ketch plunged beneath the black sea, a shimmering iridescence illuminated the water and danced along the brass hand rail. Blinding light flashed directly above them, filling the sky for one brief moment before the dark waters closed over them and Riki lost consciousness.

Five

A smell strong enough to curdle her stomach penetrated Riki's befuddled mind. She wished she could sink once more into oblivion. Sink. . . .

Their ketch sank, she was as certain of that as her groggy state allowed. Yet the revolting odor that filled her lungs, blocking out the fresh salt spray, was pitch. And from the wild tossing of the uneven board surface on which she lay, she *must* be still on a boat.

And she was drenched. She lay in a pool of icy water and rain pelted down, matting her hair but not diluting the pungent odor of the sealer on the rough hewn timbers. She gagged.

Her other senses began to check in, and the rumble of noise separated into wind, distant thunder, and churning waves. The murmur of harsh voices reached her, coarse, heavy with unfamiliar accents. Something about landing kegs.

"Two extra pairs of hands will make for lighter work." Bedford's voice sounded somewhere close at hand.

Bedford. He was there, with her. She was safe. Too exhausted to analyze or remember, she drifted off again.

She roused to the sensation of someone stabbing her leg over and over with thousands of needles. Either that, or the circulation had been cut off and now chose

75

to return with a prickly vengeance. The odor of wet wool, not pitch, surrounded her. The rocking motion of the boat had slowed, become gentle, as if she were instead cradled securely in strong arms.

A stubbly chin brushed her forehead. Bedford. Riki rubbed her head against his broad shoulder and contentment filled her. Whatever had happened, they were together. For the moment, that was enough.

Wavelets slapped against his legs as he waded through shallow water onto a sandy beach. Riki opened her eyes to a blackness that would have been complete except for the strange lanterns carried by several of the most oddly dressed men she had ever glimpsed. Explanations were beyond her. She closed her eyes again and shifted into a more comfortable position with an arm about Bedford's neck.

He strode up a slight rise and stopped at last. Gently, he disengaged her hold on him and lowered her to the cold, wet ground. Scrubby bushes reached out, whipped by the wind, tangling in her dripping hair and catching at her sweater.

"Lie still," Bedford murmured, and slipped away into the darkness.

She did as he suggested. The rain had let up to a steady drizzle, but she shivered in the cold night air. Night? She blinked, coming more fully awake. The last thing she really remembered, it still had been morning. She decided to think about it later, when she was warm and comfortable.

Thick, dark clouds obscured any moon or stars. Where, she wondered, had Bedford gone? Dimly, she could make out the shapes of about a dozen men, some near the ocean's edge, some heading toward them leading small horses. Everyone seemed busy.

One of the dark figures moved away from the group by the shore and headed up the beach toward her. She caught her breath, then released it as she recognized Bedford. She sat up.

"Well, we made it." He sounded unusually cheerful for someone who had just been through two boatwrecks in three days.

"We're alive," she agreed as she struggled to a sitting position. She kept her voice low. "Who are those men? And what on earth are they doing out on a night like this? Fishing?"

A deep chuckle set Bedford's shoulders shaking. "In a manner of speaking. They've brought in quite a catch tonight."

"You mean us?" She must be more dazed than she had thought. She felt as if she were missing something.

Bedford took the hand she unconsciously held out to him. "They're freetraders. Smugglers," he explained at her blank look.

She felt the blood drain from her face. "Smug—oh, my God! You mean *dope?*" Her horrified gaze flew to the figures who moved about less than twenty yards away.

"I don't know what 'dope' is, exactly. It's brandy they're landing."

"Brandy!" A shaky laugh of relief escaped her as she looked back up at Bedford, who knelt on one knee at her side. "Why on earth smuggle brandy?"

"I said we made it." His sustaining hold tightened on her hand. "I don't know what the situation is in your time, but you've got a lot to learn about mine."

"Your—"

He nodded, and a glimmering twinkle showed in the depths of his dark eyes. "Welcome to 1812."

"To—" She shook her head as memory flooded back. David's wargaming room, the altered displays, Bedford's crazy story, the picture of him in that diary, her own reluctant half-belief, their insane journey in the middle of a thunder storm. . . . "Please, tell me this was all a joke."

He smoothed the straggly, dripping hair back from

her face with his free hand. "You'll believe soon enough. Right now, if we want to get out of this little escapade alive, you're going to have to act a little. I've told them you're my young brother."

She rose to her knees. "Shouldn't we try to slip away?"

He shook his head. "They'd shoot. Our best bet is to join them."

"Join. . . ." Her voice trailed off.

"That's right. Can you pretend to be a boy? About twelve or so, I should think. If anyone asks, you're at school at Eton, but you got sent down for some prank. Can you remember?"

She nodded, too numb still to do anything but play along to his direction, and allowed him to help her to her feet. "Why will they believe I'm a boy?"

"Ladies of my time don't wear breeches—or 'jeans.' And they certainly won't expect a lady to have gone sailing in a storm."

"Now, there they have a point." She steadied herself, then brushed the clinging wet sand from her jeans and sweater as best she could.

"Look excited." He moved a step away from her. "Remember, helping a band of cut-throat smugglers to land their kegs is the secret dream of every school boy."

She threw him a comical look of horror, then forced her expression into wide-eyed delight. As they neared the men, she didn't say a word, merely allowing her jaw to drop. She moved slightly behind Bedford and peered out as if hardly able to believe her luck.

Five oddly assorted men met her uneasy gaze. All wore hats, enveloping coats, and boots, but she could see little else in the darkness. One, solidly built and with a straggly beard, stepped forward and peered right back at her. His cap hung low over a face dominated by a bulbous nose.

"Scrawny little whelp, ain't 'e?" He grabbed Riki roughly by the arm, looking her over with disfavor.

"Are ye strong, lad?"

"Yes!" The word escaped her in a squeak, and the others laughed. They probably thought her a gangly youth with her voice cracking.

"Get the cargo up to the ponies," he ordered and let her go.

Riki hurried to where four men waded back and forth between their boat and the beach. A small pile of brandy kegs lay on the sand, and Bedford picked up one. Riki grabbed another.

It was surprisingly heavy. But that man, apparently the leader, watched her with narrowed eyes. Without betraying the strain, she fell into line with the other carriers and lugged her keg to the waiting ponies. There another man took it from her and strapped it to a harness.

They worked for over an hour. One pony train disappeared into the darkness to be replaced by another. They would go in different directions, Bedford murmured to her, to help throw off pursuit by any excisemen who might have gotten wind of their run. Riki nodded, too exhausted to summon her voice for an answer, and staggered back up the beach with another keg. Somehow, it didn't seem like a good idea to suggest they open one and share the contents.

But she had her own! She had forgotten it completely, for she didn't normally carry a hip flask. Now she could see the reason for them. She released her keg into waiting hands and started back toward the water's edge. A subtle feel of her back pockets, though, told her she had lost the flask.

The men no longer floated casks to shore, she noted with relief. They must be almost done. She bent down to lift one of the remaining ones in the stack, only to have a booted foot placed on it. She looked up, startled.

"Well, lad, are ye goin' t' tell all yer friends about yer adventure?" The leader of the smugglers leaned over her, breathing a mixture of brandy and onions into her face.

With difficulty, she didn't recoil. She allowed her face to fall in dismay. "I can't!" she wailed.

"And why not, lad? Ye'd be the envy of yer school." He watched her through narrowed eyes.

"Because I gave my word we wouldn't speak of this, and my brother knows, as do I, that the word of a gentleman is his honor." Bedford placed a firm hand on her shoulder. "You need not think we'll go to the nearest exciseman."

The man let out a guffaw that sent Riki backward a pace from the impact. She'd missed the garlic, before.

"It will make fine telling for him in a year or two, when it can do you no harm." Bedford met the smuggler's gaze squarely.

"Best shoot 'em both and be done with it."

Riki spun about as the leader of the second pony train strode up to them. Her stomach tied a bowline that would have made a boy scout jealous. This man looked capable of committing any number of murders—and of enjoying himself while he did them. She lowered her gaze.

"After the work we did?" Bedford straightened up and regarded the man with hauteur. "I should have thought we earned our rescue."

The leader guffawed again. "Spoken like a gen'leman. Leave off, 'Arry. 'E's not one to open 'is gaff. Nor the lad, neither."

"Yer not jus' turnin' 'em loose, are ye?" The one addressed as Harry glowered at his leader. "Damme, if I works wi' the likes o' ye again."

"Ye'll work for me. You, take yer brother and get back in the boat." He jerked his head without moving his gaze from Harry's.

Bedford grasped Riki's elbow and hauled her down the sand into the slapping waves. "Do as he says," he muttered in her ear.

She shivered as the water rose to her waist. Bedford dragged her along until they reached the boat's side. One of the smugglers had already returned to it, and Bedford scooped Riki up in his arms and handed her over the side to him. With an athletic grace that drew her admiration, Bedford followed.

Riki glanced back at the shore. A single lantern bobbed in the distance, then disappeared among the trees as the land smugglers led their ponies away. Darkness engulfed the beach once more. Only dim shapes could be glimpsed as the freetraders made their way back toward the water.

Riki huddled in the stern of the yawl beside Bedford. Under cover of darkness, her hand stole into his. He gave it a reassuring squeeze, but that didn't help much. If the smugglers wanted to dispose of their unwanted guests, it would be much easier to take them back into the Channel and dump them overboard. Between the icy cold and the choppiness of the waves, they didn't stand much of a chance of getting back to shore alive. Then there wouldn't be any messy corpses with bullet holes in them to explain away.

The leader returned to the boat last. Silently, they raised anchor and manned the oars. The clouds separated and one star peeped out as they eased out of the cove.

"Where are you putting us ashore?" Bedford kept his tone conversational, as if he had only the most passing interest in the answer.

"There's a safe landin' a few miles along. No need t' fret, now, m' bully. They don't go a-callin' us 'gen'lemen o' the trade' for nuthin'. I said ye'll go free, and so ye will."

He returned his attention to his crew, and Riki huddled against Bedford's arm, welcoming the warmth of his body that reached her through the drenched wool of his sweater. Apparently, they weren't to help with the rowing. She was relieved; she'd gone through quite

81

enough for one day. Her arms ached with the carrying.

The single star disappeared again and the drizzle resumed. Riki gazed across the dark waters of the Channel, seeing nothing. Where were they? Somewhere along the southern coast of England, most likely. If she knew for certain, maybe she wouldn't feel so vulnerable.

In spite of her tension, exhaustion overcame her and she dozed off, only to be awakened by Bedford's movement. He came to his feet, standing easily in the pitching boat. She joined him.

"This is where we part company?" He offered his hand to the smuggler.

The man hesitated, then grinned suddenly, wiped his own on his bedraggled breeches, and shook. "We'll leave ye tied, but not so's ye can't get free." He turned away. "Bring 'em."

The man nearest Riki secured his oar, then turned to her. She cringed, but he merely grabbed her and heaved her over his shoulder like a sack of potatoes. Another latched onto Bedford's elbow and followed their leader. The small band made their way ashore in the sheltered cove.

Riki's carrier dumped her unceremoniously face down onto the sand, and she closed her eyes and mouth tight. He dragged first one of her wrists, then the other, behind her back. The rough rope with which he tied her cut into her tender skin, and she gritted her teeth to keep from crying out. Next her ankles were secured, then her captor rolled her over and she gasped for air.

Dimly, she could make out the shape of Bedford lying a few feet away from her. The bulky figure of the smugglers' leader bent over him.

"On yer 'onor as a gen'leman, not a word o' tonight's 'appenin's. Now, ye should be able t' work yerselves free in a 'our or two. Our thanks fer lendin' a 'and."

He signaled his companions and the three freetraders strode away, back to where their yawl rocked in the shallow water, awaiting them.

"They left us above the high tide line," Bedford remarked after a moment.

"How thoughtful."

His deep chuckle sounded, low but unmistakable. His enjoyment of this horrendous situation eased her own nerves, which felt about as stretched as they could go. She tried to move her hands, but found them too securely bound. At least the circulation wasn't cut off.

Bedford pulled himself into a kneeling position and tried to bend so his hands, which were behind him, could reach the ropes about his booted ankles. He muttered something under his breath that Riki couldn't catch.

She tried to copy his pose with more luck. She found the ropes, but the knot was on the bottom, buried beneath her feet in the sand. She gave up with a sigh. "What other delights does your time have in store for us?"

"You believe it, then?" He sounded curious.

She considered. "No, but it's easier than arguing with a madman. Or a figment of my imagination. What we just went through *can't* have been real."

He chuckled again. "Can you roll over here? If we turn our backs to each other, we may be able to do something about our hands."

"You're enjoying this!" she accused.

"I am." His tone held more than a little surprise. "Lord, I must be getting as bad as my brothers. Are you coming?"

She complied, and for the next several minutes they were silent as they tried to position themselves where they could reach each other's bonds. Under different circumstances, Riki decided, this activity could prove quite provocative. Rather like playing twister, in fact. They knelt in the wet sand, backs barely inches apart, her lower legs between his. He, at least, remained in possession of the flask in his back hip pocket. She felt it as they maneuvered into position.

"I believe, Miss van Hamel," he said at last, "it will be best if one of us remains still to give the other a chance to work unhindered."

"Yes, I was noticing it wasn't easy with us both moving our hands. I don't suppose you have a knife on you?"

"I had, but our erstwhile friend relieved me of it."

"A pity the flask isn't glass. We could break it and use it as a knife."

"Speaking of flasks, I don't suppose you could reach it, could you, Miss van Hamel?"

"Call me Riki. Everybody does." She felt behind her for his back pocket and the brandy within. Those jeans couldn't possibly have been any tighter. She concentrated very hard on removing the flask and not on his powerful muscles. Now was hardly the time for an intimate encounter. The thin metal bottle came free in her hand at last, and she breathed a sigh of relief.

"Thank you." His voice sounded tight. Apparently, her search for the brandy had affected him, too.

She placed the flask in his hands. "If you'll hold it, I'll try to get the lid off." His grip tightened, and in moments she loosened the top. The tiny cup dropped to the side, secured by a delicate silver chain.

"Now, what?" he asked, his tone purely conversational.

"Oh." After a moment's thought, she shimmied away from him, turned around, bent down, and got her mouth over the top. She started giggling, but whether from her ridiculous position or from reaction to all that happened, she wasn't certain.

"By all means, take your time."

Thus admonished, she got herself under control. By leaning far to one side, she managed to tilt a little liquid into her mouth, and she swallowed. It burned like

84

fire shooting down her throat, then a welcome warmth and lassitude crept through her aching muscles. She turned around and took the bottle from him.

He copied her form, then with his back once more to her he recapped the bottle. "I believe you will do best to set it on the ground, Miss—Riki."

She quite agreed; the prospect of searching for that tight pocket intrigued her too much. She let the flask drop.

The sip of brandy helped steady her. She remained still while Bedford worked on the knot binding her hands, but to no avail. At last, too stiff to remain where she was, she pulled away, only to collapse unceremoniously on the sand.

"Are you all right?" He looked over his shoulder, then dropped into a roll. In a moment, he pressed tightly against her, his warm breath fanning her cheek.

"I'd be a lot better if we could get these knots undone. Sorry, my legs cramped up. Shall we try again?"

His gaze did not meet hers. Instead, he appeared to be studying her mouth. A slight smile just touched his lips. "By all means."

This time, he succeeded in loosening the knot. Riki remained frozen, afraid to move and undo his work, as numbness crept through her fingers. Then suddenly the ropes eased and she could move her hands. The bonds fell away and she pulled her arms in front of her in relief to massage her bloodied, hurting wrists.

Feeling returned, and she set to work on the knots that cut cruelly into Bedford. The smugglers had been less kind to him. His skin was raw from the ropes, which were soaked with salt water, rain, and his blood. It must sting like mad, but he made no comment as she tugged and eased at the ends. His rigid stance never slackened by so much as a fraction.

"There, it moved!" Elated, she pulled a little too

85

hard and saw him flinch. Biting her lip, she moved more cautiously. Another ten minutes or so passed before she could free him.

His breath escaped in a ragged gasp as he dragged his arms in front of him. Her fingers were covered in blood, his and hers. She picked up the flask and handed it to him.

He took a long swallow, then passed it back. She sipped carefully and let the fiery liquid slip down her throat.

"Aren't you going to indulge in a fit of the vapors?" He regarded her with an odd smile playing about the corners of his firm mouth.

"In a what?"

"Hysteria. After what you've been through, you've earned it."

"Maybe when the shock wears off. Right now, all I want is to get my feet free." She moved to a sitting position, curled her legs up, and started working on the last of her bonds. If her fingers weren't so stiff and sore already, it would be a lot easier.

"Here." Bedford stood, albeit unsteadily, and joined her, his own ankles now untied. Kneeling before her, he helped.

The light colored ribbing at the cuffs of his sleeves showed dark stains, and his wrists looked raw and ugly. She could see him quite clearly, she realized.

"It's morning!" Riki looked about, startled. She had been so absorbed in freeing herself, she hadn't noticed the pinkish tinge of dawn that crept into the heavy clouds hanging low in the lightening sky.

"So it is." He pulled the ropes away and helped her to her feet. Slowly, his eyes roved over her slender body in the wet, clinging jeans and the bulky sweater. "How the devil am I going to explain you?" he muttered.

Riki bristled. "What do you mean, 'explain me?' "

"It would be best if I could keep you from meeting

anybody except your da—your cousin." Bedford rubbed a blood-stained hand over his stubbly chin. "There'll be the devil to pay if you talk to anyone."

"And just what do you mean by that?"

"If anyone just *sees* you dressed like that, it will be bad enough. I knew I shouldn't have brought you." He muttered the last words to himself.

"Let's just get one thing straight. I'm not some baggage you hauled along. You didn't 'bring' me. In case you've forgotten already, you *needed* my help."

"And now look where it's got us."

She looked around, deliberately misunderstanding. "A rather nice beach, I'd say. Coarse sand, a bit of driftwood. A terrific sunrise with all those clouds. Not bad at all, considering the boatwreck and smugglers."

He ground his teeth. "We are in exactly the position we most ardently need to avoid, madam. Our purpose, in case *you've* forgotten already," he mimicked, "is to remove your cousin from my time before he can do or say anything more that might alter the future. And now *you* are here, able to do as much damage as he."

"I wouldn't!"

"Not intentionally, of course. But what about—" He started to gesture to the zipper on his jeans, and dull color flooded his face as the blatant impropriety of mentioning such a subject in feminine company obviously struck him.

"We get new clothes, as quickly as possible." She kept her voice purely matter of fact.

"You will have to keep a guard on your tongue at every moment. It would be best if you could be prevented from meeting anyone."

"I am not such a fool as you obviously think me. I daresay if you will instruct me in how a well-behaved young lady acts, we shall 'manage to scrape by tolerably well.' Have I that expression right?"

A reluctant smile played about the corners of his firm mouth, easing the exhaustion from his face. "For one thing, a lady doesn't go off on hare-brained adventures in the company of a gentleman."

Riki's hauteur collapsed. "There's no hope for it, then. Perhaps you can pass me off as your half-wit brother. You did say you had one, didn't you?"

"Two, in fact. And both more hare-brained than half-witted. They would enjoy this situation far too much." He drew a deep breath, apparently coming to a decision. "There's no hope for it, you will have to meet a few people at least. As soon as we get our bearings, we'd best find you something suitable to wear."

"As long as it's dry, I'll take anything." She looked away from the shore, but saw nothing but shrubs blending into forest beyond the sand. "Where do I buy—"

She broke off. She had no money. For the first time in her twenty-seven years, she honestly had not one single cent.

"What's wrong?"

She shook her head, shattered by the knowledge but unable to explain. For all her life, the van Hamel money had been behind her. It colored the way people saw her, made instant enemies of some, instant cloying hangers-on of others. But now she was on her own without that glittering aura of family gold.

"Riki?"

"I—I don't have any money."

A deep chuckle escaped him. "You looked as pale as death for a moment. Is that all?"

"How would you like to find yourself totally bereft of funds?"

A crease formed in his brow. "Does it matter so much? You'll be in my time for as short a while as possible. I'll provide what you'll need for a few days."

"I've *never* been . . . on my own."

"What? Afraid?"

If he intended to rally her, it worked. She brought her chin up. "Of course not," she lied.

"Then I think we had best decide how to get ourselves out of this mess. Stay here while I look around."

She shivered. "I'd rather come with you, if you don't mind. I could use a walk."

"I will thank you to stay out of sight until I know where we are. Neither of us is exactly dressed with propriety." He sketched a brief bow and started up the beach, leaving her to stare after him.

Damn the family money. She'd never before realized how complete her dependence on it had been. Finding herself alone, stripped of her golden security blanket, she felt naked, vulnerable. This adventure suddenly took on nightmarish overtones.

Except for Bedford. He fell under the category of a pretty fantastic daydream.

Six

Riki would be safe on the beach, Bedford told himself as he strode briskly through the shrubs toward the forest. He spotted an overturned dory and his spirits rose. There would be a house or even a town nearby, and probably a path that would lead him there. Once he knew where they had been left, he could set about obtaining help. He wished he had money — even one of his cards — on him. In these unconventional garments he had borrowed, no one would take him for a gentleman. He had only his voice — and his habit of command.

A few minutes' walk beneath the wind-swept pines brought him to a narrow cart-track. Fresh hoof prints mingling with the narrow ruts of wooden wheels, neither completely washed away by the overnight rain, encouraged him further. There must be frequent traffic. Five minutes of following this brought him to a lane — and to the conviction that his boots had suffered irreparable damage.

A signpost pointed the way to Rottingdean. Satisfaction washed through him. They were in East Sussex — and not that far from Brighton. Still, he'd be damned if he'd walked the whole way in these boots. And now he had to return to the beach to get his companion. He turned to start limping his way back, only to draw up short.

90

A sigh of exasperation, not unmingled with relief, escaped him. "Don't you ever obey simple requests?"

Riki moved out from beneath the trees and joined him. "Only when they're sensible. I couldn't see any point in your coming back for me, and the way you're walking, you ought to be glad. Does the sign post help any?"

"It tells me where we are, but it fails to suggest how we are to reach help."

"Walk?"

"It's all of nine or ten miles."

"To—" She looked past him. "Rottingdean? Do you know anyone there who would help us?"

"To Brighton. I have a friend—Sir Julian Taggart—who keeps a house there. Even if he's not presently in residence, his servants will give us shelter."

"Are you in the habit of calling on your friend in unusual circumstances?" She started along the lane at his side.

"One of my brothers has, upon several occasions." Was he becoming as madcap as Aubrey? The thought startled him. The responsible and always proper Viscount Bedford, engaged upon some lark? If Julian were indeed at home, his friend would never let him live down what would seem to him an unparalleled freakish start.

He could always tell his friend the truth, of course. Then Julian would merely have him conveyed to Bedlam without further ado. A muscle twitched at the corner of Bedford's normally sober mouth. He'd been raised to respect his position and his dignity, while Aubrey and Hillary kicked up larks and got up to every sort of entertaining bobbery. Just this once, it wouldn't hurt him to enjoy himself a little.

"What will you tell your friend about me?" Riki spoke quietly. "Or do you intend to leave me hiding in the bushes outside so I won't inadvertently blurt out I'm from the future?"

91

"Vixen," he murmured. He looked down at her. She hugged herself against the cold and water trickled down her neck from her auburn hair. There were freckles there, too, he noted with interest.

Such a delicate little creature, yet she faced storms and smugglers without one word of complaint. Only the absence of her fortune made her tremble. Well, he could understand that, he supposed. Any other female of his acquaintance would have succumbed to a fit of hysteria by now, and without nearly as much provocation. Except, perhaps, for his sister Felicity.

Unfortunately, his thoughts concerning Miss Riki van Hamel were far from fraternal at the moment. Those tight fitting "jeans," which clung in a most unseemly and enticing manner to her slender legs, wreaked havoc with his gentlemanly intentions. The wispy Grecian drapery worn by the *ton* ladies over the past few years had never affected him as strongly as did the bulky sweater that had lost its shape and now clung to the slender curve of her breast and her fully rounded hips. He moved a step farther away from her.

"Your friend will know I'm not your brother," Riki continued. "What was his name? Sir Julian—?"

"Taggart. And anyone who sees you in the daylight will not be fooled into thinking you a youth, despite your shocking attire." He spoke more sharply than he intended. She was temporarily under his guardianship, he reminded himself firmly, and it irritated him when that thought chafed.

"My presence *is* going to make things awkward for you, isn't it?" She peeped up at him from beneath her long, thick lashes, sudden mischief lightening her somber expression, mixing with unspoken apology.

"As you say." What a damnable little minx, to create havoc in him with just a look! It would serve her right if he succumbed to impulse and kissed her. But a Randall of Falconer's Court—and the Viscount

Bedford, at that—did not behave in an improper manner. For the first time, he found that dictum frustrating.

"I suppose we'd best stick as closely to the truth as possible." Her brow wrinkled in concentration. "He'll know I'm an American from my accent—if you let me speak—and the boatwreck will explain a great deal. Where should we have met?"

The next few minutes passed in a discussion of the most plausible story. Bedford encouraged this, for it kept his thoughts in a more proper vein. They were still arguing over details when he became aware of the steady clomping of a horse's hooves and the rattling of an ill-sprung cart approaching.

He broke off in midsentence and turned to see a farming wagon nearing them. A weathered, slightly built man of indeterminate years perched on the seat as his placid old cob plodded along. Bedford waited, and the man at last drew abreast.

"Could you give us a ride? We were fishing and our boat sank."

The man's eyes narrowed as Bedford spoke. "Quality," he muttered, shaking his head. "Aye, climb in back. I'm goin' t' Brighthelmstone, if that'll be of any help t'ye."

"Thank you, it would," Bedford grabbed Riki's hand and strode around to the rear of the wagon. She had a remarkably tiny waist, he noted, as he picked her up and set her on the floorboards. The wooden planks smelled suspiciously of fertilizer. He didn't even have a coat he could spread on which she might sit.

"Where is he taking us?" Riki whispered as he jumped up beside her and the cart started forward once more.

"Brighton. He used the old name—though I don't suppose it's old, to him."

They fell silent as the wagon lurched along. Despite the crawling pace, they were jarred considerably, but Bedford resisted the temptation to cushion Riki by drawing her against himself. An inner voice warned him he might not stop at that, and a gentleman did not take advantage of a lady. *Damn* being a gentleman, he thought, for the first time in his very proper life.

"How soon can we reach London?" She didn't look at him, but stared back along the lane the way they had come.

"By tomorrow afternoon, I should think. My friend or his household will help us obtain suitable clothing and there will be no trouble hiring a carriage. We should be able to confront your cousin by the day after, at the latest. I don't like it, though."

"I know. Don't worry, I'll be good. And maybe when I see David, I'll really start to believe in all this." She fell silent. A few minutes later, she asked, in a very small voice: "What will happen then?"

He stiffened. "Provided I don't call him out, you mean?" In her disturbing presence, he had almost forgotten the traitorous activities of her cousin, the reason for her presence in his world.

"You mean challenge him to a duel? You can't! I won't let you murder him. Promise me you won't!" She caught his arm, gripping it tightly in her vehemence. "Promise!"

He drew a deep breath, then let it out between clenched teeth. "Very well, I promise. Only get him out of my vicinity—out of my world!—before I forget and treat him as he deserves."

She didn't ask him how she was to remove Warwick, for which he was glad. How the devil were she and her cousin to get back to the future, where they belonged?

He studied the tiny patches of blue sky that peeped through the heavy gray clouds. By tomorrow, the last traces would be gone. The prospect of Miss Riki van

Hamel being stranded in his time should not please him so much. It was too dangerous. They were a world apart, and had to remain that way.

Farms replaced the pine forest, with small fields separated by hedgerows or low stone walls. The road led through the center of Rottingdean, and Bedford sat in stony silence as village children stopped and stared at the plodding wagon's unconventional passengers. His companion, he noted with stoic philosophy, gazed about with wide, avid eyes. They would probably prove a seven days' wonder, providing the local people with a topic over which to bless themselves and marvel. At least no one would know who they were.

The village passed at last, Bedford relaxed, only to come to another unwelcome realization. He had no idea how long it had been since they had eaten, and a gnawing hunger made it a matter of considerable importance. Yet they had no money, nothing with which to purchase food. They would have to wait.

He glanced at his companion, who sat as erect as possible in the lurching cart. At least he had the hope of rectifying his penniless state in the near future. Undoubtedly, she would be anxious to return to her own time, to the security of her own life.

"Not much longer," he assured her, but whether he meant till the end of their journey or the end of their adventure, he wasn't certain.

She managed a wan smile. "Just as long as your friend doesn't take one look at us and throw us out."

It must be almost two o'clock, Bedford judged by the sun that peeked out from between parting clouds, when the cart jolted onto the cobbled street of Brighton. He wished they could have arrived under cover of darkness. This might not be the fashionable quarter of town, but he loathed being stared at by every vulgar mushroom or farmer who happened to catch sight of them.

They turned into the yard of a rickety old inn, and the farmer drew the cob to a halt. He knotted his reins over the brake and the horse dropped its head.

"Far as I'm goin'," he called back to his passengers. They were the first words he'd spoken since picking them up hours before.

"Thank you." Bedford climbed stiffly to the ground, vividly aware of far too many sore muscles. He offered a hand to Riki, but she took it only for balance as she jumped down. He turned back to the farmer in time to see that worthy disappear through the darkened doorway into the tap room.

"You'd think no one had ever seen a couple of people wearing jeans and sweaters before," Riki murmured as she moved a step closer to him, as if for protection.

Bedford resisted the urge to put a comforting arm about her. "Come on. The best course would be to hide somewhere until dark, but I'm too hungry for that. Let's just brazen it out." He walked out of the yard.

Riki followed. "Pity we can't juggle. People might take us for clowns. Or do you call them Merry-Andrews?"

"Merry-Andrews," he confirmed. "We should have my brother Hillary with us. That's one of his questionable talents."

"Being a clown or juggling?"

Bedford actually smiled. "Both." Somehow, walking through Brighton dressed in these remarkable garments, looking as if they had just dragged themselves from the ocean, didn't seem so bad. Was it because few Fashionables populated the summer resort in the freezing cold of January, or because he found a measure of enjoyment in the companionship provided by the young lady at his side?

He led the way through a maze of narrow back streets, always heading toward the beach. By walking

96

along the sand, they should be able to avoid curious eyes. The overcast sky would not lure many people out to enjoy the icy sea breezes.

Sir Julian Taggart's tall brick house stood on the Marine Parade, a bare block from the Steine. Casting a quick glance about to assure himself no one was watching, Bedford grasped Riki's elbow and drew her across the paved street and up the four steps to the porch. Resolutely, he applied the knocker.

Several interminable minutes passed, in which Bedford imagined the occupants of the neighboring houses to be staring out at them from behind the curtains. At last the door opened and a very proper butler faced them, his expression of outrage fading beneath justified shock.

"Good afternoon, Ferndale. Is Sir Julian at home?" Bedford managed a nonchalant smile.

"My—lord?" Shaken, Ferndale retreated a step. With obvious difficulty, he mastered his expression. "If you will wait in here, Lord Bedford, I will ascertain." His eyes rested a moment on Riki, who hovered behind Bedford.

The butler escorted the visitors to the front salon and tottered off to find his master.

"It is to be hoped Ferndale is not one to gossip with his fellow butlers." Bedford glanced at the comfortable upholstered chair, considered the state of his jeans thanks to the ocean and the farming wagon, and remained on his feet.

"At least he let us in. For one moment, I thought he would slam the door in our faces."

The door into the salon flew open and a dark-haired youth half-swung inside, "I say, Julian, I—" He broke off, and an expression so horrified as to be comical replaced his engaging smile. "Gil?" His voice squeaked.

"Hillary?" The name exploded from Bedford as he stared at his young scapegrace brother. "What the

97

devil are you doing here?"

"I—I thought you were still at Whitehall." The boy took a cautious step into the room and managed a grin. "What a surprise!"

Bedford drew himself up, imposing in spite of his bedraggled garb. "And you, you young jackanapes, should be at Oxford."

"Oh, I just thought I'd pop down for a visit. You know how it is." Hillary Randall folded his arms across his brilliantly flowered waistcoat and tried to brazen it through.

"I rather think I do. What was it *this* time?" Bedford regarded his enterprising young brother with resignation.

"Oh, it wasn't anything bad, just the greatest lark. We wanted to see how many chairs would fit in one of the dons' rooms. You'd be amazed how they can stack!" The youth's eyes twinkled as he assumed an air of breezy innocence. "Aubrey would have done the same."

"There is no need to tell me that. There was never much to choose between the pair of you. Why didn't you go to the Court?"

"What? And upset Mamma? I'm not such a shab-rag as that! Lord, when I think how glad she was to pack me back off to school after the Christmas—" He broke off, his grin broadening. "I say, Gil, you're not going to lecture *me* on propriety at the moment, are you?"

A dull flush crept into his cheeks. Hillary crowed in delight, obviously feeling that for once he'd gotten the better of his eldest brother. And Bedford couldn't disagree.

He turned to Riki. "This, Miss van Hamel, as you may have gathered, is my youngest brother, Hillary. Hil, you are forgetting your manners. Come make a leg to Miss van Hamel."

"Miss—" Hillary's dark eyes widened in delight.

"And you accuse *me* of getting up to bobbery!" he murmured. He swept her a magnificent leg, accompanied by a winsome smile. "How do you do?"

Uncertain, Riki held out her hand. "I'm pleased to meet you."

"You won't be, when you know him better," Bedford informed her.

Hillary threw his brother a quizzical look, but refrained from comment. A sound at the open door caused them all to turn.

"Bedford?" A dandy, beautiful to behold in a lavender swan-tail coat and white small clothes, stepped daintily into the room and stopped dead at the sight that met his shocked eyes. He groped for the quizzing glass that hung about his neck from a purple velvet riband, and raised it to inspect his friend. It dropped from his fingers as an exquisite shudder ran through him. "Bedford!" he repeated in failing accents.

"Hallo, Julian. It seems the entire Randall clan is descending on you for help."

Sir Julian's gaze lighted on their bloodied wrists, then moved on to search for other signs of injuries. "Help, is it? What the devil happened to you?" His carefully cultivated affectations fell away, and he strode forward, for once forgetting to mince.

"Our boat sank. And if you are about to offer aid, some food wouldn't come amiss."

"Certainly." Sir Julian, whose glance had come to rest on Riki, seemed incapable of movement.

Hillary, enjoying himself hugely, obliged by pulling the bellrope. "You haven't introduced *Miss* van Hamel," he pointed out.

"Haven't you somewhere to go?" Bedford cast his brother a fulminating look, which promised a rare rake-down at the first convenient moment.

Hillary grinned in response, obviously thinking the ensuing scene would make it worth being hauled onto the carpet. "No, nowhere at all. What an unnatural brother I'd be if I didn't want to hear all about your adventures."

Riki touched his arm. "I believe it will be safe to let these gentlemen into my secret," she whispered in a voice calculated to let everyone hear.

Bedford made a show of hesitation. "Perhaps it will be the best way to assure their silence," he agreed at last, in that same hushed tone. *That* ought to send Hillary into alt.

The youth's eyes widened. "Lord, Gil, is this some secret mission?"

"Not a word out of you!" Bedford fixed him with a compelling eye. "Miss van Hamel is an American agent. If you have been reading your newspaper of late, you will know that relations between our two countries are strained. She has come to try to prevent war by exposing another American who may have infiltrated our government with the purpose of sabotaging our effort against Napoleon."

"Has she, by Jupiter!" Hillary stared at her in round-eyed awe.

Sir Julian swung his quizzing glass by its riband, his thoughtful gaze narrowing on Riki's face. "An American agent," he murmured. The next moment, he recovered, and drawled: "My dear Miss van Hamel, you are to be congratulated. I do not believe our friend Bedford has ever before engaged on so dramatic an undertaking."

That nettled. "I did spend a couple of years on the Peninsula," he pointed out.

Sir Julian's reply was cut off by the arrival of Ferndale bearing a tray with decanters, glasses, and a plate of cakes and biscuits. Sir Julian sent him back to the kitchens to obtain more sustaining viands, then returned his attention to his guests.

"And what, pray, brings you to my humble doorstep?" He poured wine for Bedford, then hesitated.

Neither of the two decanters contained a beverage suitable for a lady.

"Our feet. And a farming cart." Bedford solved the problem by handing Riki his own glass, then poured himself another.

Sir Julian raised an eyebrow but made no comment. Instead, he caught Bedford's eye and held his gaze. "Unless I am very much mistaken, you were headed in quite another direction."

"Now, where did you hear that?" Bedford took a swallow of wine, but his unwavering regard remained fixed on his friend.

Sir Julian shrugged. "Something someone in your office said just before I left town."

"And what might that have been?"

"That you were headed for Dover, dear boy, and not, as you had been at pains to imply to me, to Kent."

"And who, may I ask, passed on this interesting bit of information?"

Sir Julian raised his quizzing glass and studied Bedford's sweater. An exquisite shudder ran through him, and he allowed the glass to drop. "Now, to whom was I speaking about you? Was it young Warwick? No, I have it. I believe it must have been Lady Linton."

"Clarissa? How the devil—" Bedford broke off.

Sir Julian inclined his head. "It is so difficult to keep things secret, is it not, my dear Bedford? But I am quite certain Lord Linton would have spoken of your movements to no one but his wife. She is, after all, your sister."

"I don't see where that makes any difference when our entire department was sworn to silence over my mission." He took a deep breath and forced his jaw to unclench.

"Especially if he told Clary! She's the worst gabster," Hillary stuck in, obviously relishing his inclu-

101

sion, in however minor a capacity, in Great Events. "It's Lombard Street to a China orange she'll spread your doings all over town."

"I'll thank *you* to keep your tongue between your teeth, you cork-brained young rattle-pate." Bedford checked his rising temper. The events of the last few days had taken their toll on him. Clarissa possessed more decorum than to speak of his activities to any but such an old friend as Sir Julian—though in this case, even he should have remained in ignorance. He didn't like his brother-in-law passing on information gleaned in Whitehall. He would take him severely to task for it, even if Lord Linton were a senior official and his elder by fifteen years.

"I assume your journey was aborted?"

He looked up to find Sir Julian watching him. The hairs prickled along the back of his neck, as if he were a dog sensing danger. He forced back the ee-rie—and ridiculous—sensation. "Actually, our boat sank. We were rescued from drowning by a band of smugglers."

A gasp escaped Hillary. "Smugglers? No, really, Gil? You're not shamming it?"

Ruefully, Bedford noted his young brother's undis-guised wonder and dawning respect. The boy must always have taken him for a slow-top. Nettled, he continued the story. "We helped them land their kegs, then they ferried us to a cove near Rottingdean, and left us bound on the shore. When we freed ourselves, we were able to flag down a farmer, who brought us to Brighton."

Sir Julian shuddered once more. "And all this, Miss van Hamel, you have been forced to endure? What a very odd notion this must give you of a Brit-ish gentleman."

She shook her head. "Oh, no. Lord Bedford has tried to—to invest our adventure with what propriety he could. He told the—the freetraders I was his young brother."

Hillary shook his head, for once awed into silence. When Bedford asked for the plate of biscuits, the youth passed them over without a word.

"You will have lost your baggage." Sir Julian addressed Riki.

With her mouth full of almond cake, she nodded. After she swallowed, she asked: "How do I go about getting suitable clothes? I obviously can't go around dressed like this."

Sir Julian closed his eyes. "I should say not. A maid will be dispatched at once to see what can be obtained. In the meantime, I shall have my housekeeper conduct you to a bedchamber. At the very least, she may supply you with *something*, so you need not dine in *that*."

Bedford intercepted a mischievous glance from Riki and directed a reproving look at her. She was more than capable of announcing that she wore such garments every day. Here, in his own time—in his own world—he suddenly felt improperly clad himself. That was odd, for he had grown quite accustomed to "jeans" and "sweaters" in only a couple of very short days. It appalled him now to think that he had dined with a young lady without so much as stockings on his bare feet.

When the butler returned, Sir Julian sent him for Mrs. Ferndale to take charge of Riki. His housekeeper, already informed by her astounded husband of the shocking presence of a young female in outlandish gentleman's garb, entered stiffly. But the hint of secret government business, combined with Riki's unconscious air of well-bred gentility, went a long way toward soothing her righteous indignation. In a very few minutes, the motherly woman was clucking over her new charge, sending maids scurrying for hot water, towels and any clothing that might fit the unfortunate dear's petite frame.

Riki numbly followed her guide up a wide stair-case to the third floor, then down a blue plush car-peted hall to the open doorway of an unused bedchamber. Inside, a maid knelt at the hearth, ar-ranging twigs in the grate to start a fire. A branch of beeswax candles provided the sole illumination. Riki entered slowly, staring about a room that was as ele-gant as it was antiquated.

Before her stood a large canopied bed with rose-colored velvet curtains. A highboy, a dressing table, an amoire, and a small writing desk were positioned comfortably about the large chamber. A round pedes-tal table, flanked by two Hepplewhite chairs, stood near the hearth. She turned back toward the door and spotted a china basin placed in a wooden wash-stand.

If Bedford felt lost upon abruptly finding himself faced with modern conveniences, Riki thought, how much more lost was she without them? She shivered.

Another maid entered, bobbed a curtsy, and handed the housekeeper three long gray dresses. The girl's wide-eyed gaze rested on Riki, but Mrs. Fern-dale sent her quickly about her business.

Riki did no more than glance at the garments. She wished the woman would leave her alone so she could pull off the scratchy sweater and indulge in a good wash. What she wanted, of course, was a shower, to wash the salt and who knew what all else from her hair. Her face and skin felt as if she were encrusted. A tentative mention of this brought another flurry of activity, and ten minutes later, two stout footmen car-ried in a huge tub and placed it before the sputtering fire.

Only by persistent requests did Riki at last clear the room. The moment the door closed behind the housekeeper, Riki turned the key, then dragged off her ruined clothes. She washed out her underthings, then left the flimsy wisps of nylon hanging over the firescreen to dry.

Next, she turned her attention to the steaming water scented with violets and indulged in a thorough scrub and hair wash, followed by a leisurely soak. With the easing of her muscles—and tension—the unreality of the last few days hit with a vengeance. It wasn't possible—none of it could be! Yet here she was, taking a bath of all things, in 1812, approximately one hundred and fifty years before she was even born.

And Bedford . . . Thoughts of him steadied her reeling world. He must have gone through this same sense of disorientation, of unreality, when he had been thrown into the future. He had survived it—and returned to his own time. She would do the same. For as improbable as it seemed, it *had* happened.

She climbed out of the tub, caught herself looking for the plug, remembered there was no such thing as plumbing yet, and instead dried herself off. The chamber pot, discovered in the cabinet of the washstand, proved another lesson in the rigors of premodern life. She was living in the past, all right.

And that meant no blow dryer. She looked at the tangled mass of her hair and groaned. It was so thick, it would take forever to dry without help. Well, she'd faced it before, when her generator had gone out. At least then, though, she'd had her makeup to make herself feel a little more human.

She checked her underthings, found them almost dry, and pulled them on. Next, she donned the white, coarse chemise-affair that lay beside the three plain gowns. It brushed the carpeted floor, making her feel as if she were a child again, dressing up in her mother's clothes. She winced at the memory. Candace, dear elder sister that she was, had suggested the game, then assured their furious mother that she had tried to talk Riki out of such dreadful behavior.

Riki turned abruptly to the dresses. The shortest touched the ground by more than an inch. If she tried walking in this, she would either tear the hem or more likely fall flat on her face. There were definite disadvantages to being five foot and a hair. Candace, from the vast reaches of her five foot six, had pointed them out regularly when they were in high school.

A knock on the door announced the return of Mrs. Ferndale, who set about at once bandaging Riki's wrists with a sweet-smelling salve and strips of cotton cloth. With that completed to the motherly woman's satisfaction, she turned her attention to the hem of the gown.

In a very short time, Riki found her skirt and chemise pinned up so that she could walk with safety. A pair of fabric slippers, which tied about her ankles, fit well enough so she didn't have to go barefoot. Feeling foolish, as if she had donned a costume for some play, she ran a comb through her damp but clean hair and allowed the housekeeper to lead her downstairs to where dinner—and Bedford—awaited.

But so, too, did his brother and friend. Who knew how many unintentional traps lurked for her tired, unwary tongue?

Seven

Sir Julian, Hillary, and Bedford awaited Riki in a long drawing room on the first floor. All three gentlemen stood at her entrance, but she had eyes for only Bedford. He, too, had changed, though his appearance when compared to that of his two companions seemed every bit as peculiar as her own. The somber black garments, she guessed shrewdly, had been borrowed from the butler, whose portly stature did not quite mimic Bedford's muscular breadth. The smile in his dark eyes dominated Riki's thoughts as he came forward to take her hand.

"You make a lovely maid," he murmured, for her ears alone.

"Thank you. Am I now dressed properly enough for you!"

He shook his head. "We will have to do better for you."

She frowned. "I don't have any money."

"You won't be here long enough for that to become a problem, and I have thought of a much safer plan than our original one." He seated her on the sofa, then took up a position beside the blazing fire. "Hillary, it is possible your presence here may be turned to good account. I would like you to perform a commission for me."

The youth nodded vigorously. "Gladly! Am I to

107

follow some dangerous spy?"

A slight smile just touched Bedford's lips as he shook his head. "Nothing so dramatic. I need you to carry a message for me to Whitehall."

Hillary's face fell, only to brighten the next moment. "You mean I'll be a secret courier!"

"As you say. I will write a letter. And so you won't be tempted to break it open, it is merely to my assistant, asking him to join me at the Court for an urgent meeting."

"With Miss van Hamel?"

"No, I do not believe we will mention Miss van Hamel. Bear that in mind, please. The information she has to impart will best come as a complete surprise to Mr. Warwick."

"Do you want me to go at once? Tonight?"

"Tomorrow will be soon enough. How did you travel down here?"

"By stage." A sheepish grin replaced the boy's earlier eagerness.

"Without a feather to fly with, I suppose. For once, bantling, I cannot come to your assistance."

"I shall be delighted to oblige." From his pocket, Sir Julian drew a beautifully enameled box, which he offered to Bedford.

As Riki watched, fascinated, the viscount took an infinitesimal pinch of the contents, held it to his nostril, and breathed in. Snuff, Riki realized. Sir Julian copied the procedure, then dusted his fingers with what Riki would swear was a rabbit's foot that hung from the box by a golden chain. Meeting Bedford's amused eye, she tried to look bored, as if she had seen such peculiar activity every day of her life.

"I will not loan you my grays—nor my curricle, Hillary, so do not look so excited." Sir Julian returned the box to his pocket. "You may take my roan and ride."

Hillary nodded, obviously disappointed.

"When you have delivered my message—" Bedford broke off, considering. "For how long have you been rusticated?"

"Only a fortnight. I'd planned to return at the beginning of the week."

"You've had him here for more than a se'nnight?" Bedford turned to Sir Julian. "You have my condolences."

"He serves to alleviate boredom." Sir Julian's normally lazy gaze rested intently on his friend. "And what may I do to assist *you* in your—er—endeavors?"

"Arrange the hire of a post chaise and four, to leave in the morning. I fear my pockets are in the same shabby state as my brother's—though for a far better reason, I make no doubt. Other than that, you may oblige me by forgetting you ever encountered Miss van Hamel and myself in those unusual garments."

"The mere thought of them is repugnant to me, dear boy. I shall be only too happy to comply."

The entry of Ferndale, announcing dinner, ended the conversation. Bedford offered Riki his arm and led her across the hall to another comfortable apartment decorated in deep reds and gold. The long table, on which two ewers rested, had been arranged so that all four settings were grouped at one end. Bedford led her to a seat, then took the one next to her.

For the next twenty minutes, Riki thought of little besides the delectable dishes from which she was served by a footman. She didn't care what they were, as long as they were hot and filling. But her eyes proved proverbially bigger than her stomach, and she shortly sat back to sip her wine and toy with a floating island. Long before the gentlemen finished, she found herself drifting off toward sleep.

The deep, masculine voices reached her without really penetrating. They made plans, she supposed,

109

but they need not worry her at the moment. Tomorrow would be soon enough to deal with the myriad problems that undoubtedly awaited. When Mrs. Ferndale appeared at her shoulder to take her back to the guest room she had used earlier, she made no objection, merely wishing the men a hazy goodnight and trying not to stumble as she climbed the steps.

She awakened slowly in the morning to a sensation of warmth and comfort. Rolling over, she snuggled her face into the soft feather pillow. But something was wrong—the mattress didn't support her properly. She opened a reluctant eye to find herself enclosed in a cocoon of rich rose velvet.

Rich rose velvet! She sat up abruptly, memory flooding back. It hadn't been the dream of a too-tired mind. This wasn't her room. She was in Brighton, in the house of Sir Julian Taggart, in 1812.

A thrill of excitement raced through her and she drew back the enveloping curtains. Faint sunlight streamed in through the thick drapes at the window. She climbed out of bed onto the chill floor and hurried over to fling them wide.

An empty expanse of beach and the gray ocean beyond met her eager eyes. It must be early, still, probably no later than six or seven. She looked about the quaintly furnished room and spotted an elaborate bronze clock on the mantel above the fire, which a maid must already have kindled because it blazed invitingly. Six-fifteen.

A ceramic pitcher stood on the hearth. Curious, she crossed over and glanced inside. It seemed she would have warm water with which to wash her face. Smiling, she held out her hands to the rising heat from the dancing flames.

A sing-song cry reached her and she returned to the window to see a woman, selling milk from cans suspended by a wooden shoulder yoke, approaching along the cobbled street.

A whole new world awaited. The prospect elated her—and left her just a little afraid. Everything would be alien, strange to her. She was truly alone for the first time—except for Bedford.

Would he be awake and wanting to get underway? Or did he dread the coming day? They would go to his home instead of to London. In some ways, that made everything easier for him. He could keep her under his constant eye and make sure she spoke to no one.

But what of his family? Perhaps taking her to some impersonal hotel would be safer, after all. Though she'd never admit it, she agreed with Bedford on one point: the fewer people she encountered, the less chance she'd have of affecting history.

Well, the sooner they set forth, the sooner their goal would be accomplished and the sooner she could return to the safety of her own time. And she wanted to see David. Joy at the prospect of her cousin being alive temporarily overshadowed her anger with him for the game he tried to make of history—and people's lives. The sooner she took him home, where they both belonged, the better it would be.

She carried the jug over to the washbasin, poured in some warm water, and splashed it over her face. Her skin stung, hurting as if her cheeks, and not her wrists, had been rubbed raw. Peering into the elegant mirror at her reflection, she was aghast at the ravages wrought on her complexion by the wind and salt spray. She'd give a great deal for her moisturizer. Even hand lotion would do.

The dressing table offered nothing, however, that might make her look or even feel a bit better. Perhaps she could ask for some of that cream the housekeeper had used on her wrists.

She donned the same dress she had worn the night before and combed out her hair. That, at least, hadn't suffered too much damage. It swept back smoothly, framing her reddened face. With a last wistful thought for her absent makeup, she set forth in search of food. Breakfast suddenly seemed like an excellent idea.

She found it more easily than she had expected. At the landing on the next floor down, the welcome aroma of coffee reached her. Following her nose, she made her way to the front of the house where an open door revealed a sun-filled, cozy apartment with a lace-covered table set into a bow window. A sideboard stood against one wall, its gleaming mahogany surface covered with chafing dishes, plates, silverware, cups, and saucers.

Bedford, clad in those same somber garments, rose from the table and came toward her, his hand extended. "I didn't expect you to be up so early." His strong fingers closed about hers.

"I'm always an early riser." She drew her hand back. When he looked at her like that, with a smile lurking in the depths of his dark eyes, it unsettled her. She stepped up to the sideboard and lifted a lid at random. "What's for breakfast?"

"Hillary demanded a beefsteak, in hopes it would take a while to cook and he could stay abed a few extra minutes." He handed her a plate. "I believe you like eggs?"

She made her selections, then poured coffee while Bedford carried her dish to the table. "Has your brother already left?" she asked, over her shoulder.

A deep, vibrant chuckle answered her. "A half hour ago. And protesting all the way, I assure you. He will arrive at Whitehall by noon."

She took the seat opposite him at the small table, and fought back the cozy image of the two of them sharing breakfast in her cottage. It had been only two days ago—and so very far away in the future.

"Are you certain it would not be safer to take me to London? If I stayed at your home, you couldn't

112

hide me from your family. But if you took me to a hotel, you—"

"No. No respectable hostelry would permit us through the front door. You have no luggage, no female to bear you company. There would be too many questions we would not be able to answer."

"Oh. Not even if we signed as Mr. and Mrs. John Smith?"

He returned only a blank look, so Riki abandoned her teasing. "Won't your family ask equally awkward questions?"

"There you need only say you are sworn to secrecy and no one will pursue the matter."

She took a bite of her toast. "How long will it take David to reach your estate?"

"He probably won't set out until tomorrow. He should be with us by late afternoon." He sipped his coffee, appearing in no hurry himself.

"Where do you live?" Suddenly, she wanted very much to see him against the backdrop of his own home.

"Near Canterbury. It's a bit more than sixty miles from here. But have no fear, I will be able to place you in my mother's charge before nightfall, I promise you."

She hesitated, her delicate china cup hovering less than an inch from her mouth. "You make it sound as if that were important."

"It is." He set down his own cup and stood, as if seeking to put some distance between them. "It will be best, in fact, if I hire one of Julian's maids to accompany us."

"Whatever for?"

He regarded her through half-lidded eyes. "Propriety, my dear Miss van Hamel. In your time, it is very obvious that a young lady enjoys a number of freedoms not acceptable in my time. Since we must travel in a closed carriage, you ought to have an abigail — a lady's maid."

"Is she expected to serve as a chaperone? How ridiculous! Are you supposed to try and seduce me in a bouncing vehicle?" A soft laugh escaped her. "That might be rather interesting."

To her amazement, a dull flush of embarrassment tinged his face.

"It is also not considered proper to joke of such things." He spoke shortly.

She forced her face into a sober expression to match his. "Will your poor mother be scandalized if I arrive without a maid — to protect me from her evil-intentioned son?"

In spite of himself, Bedford smiled. "No. My mother, shameful wretch that she is, would be delighted."

"Then we will dispense with the maid. Besides, I'm dressed as one, aren't I? And you make an admirable butler. Who will care what we do?"

"You're incorrigible. Very well, then. I don't suppose we can damage your reputation, since you don't really exist in my time." A sharp edge crept into his voice. "I have requested that a bonnet and pelisse be found for you. If you can be ready, we will leave as soon as the post-chaise arrives."

She drained her coffee and rose. "Should we not thank Sir Julian?"

"He never leaves his room before noon, except in the direst of emergencies. I have written him a note expressing our thanks. You need not worry about standing upon ceremony with him."

Less than half an hour later, Riki came down the stairs again, ready for their journey. Her face, thanks to Mrs. Ferndale's excellent strawberry and green pineapple cream, no longer stung. Nor did her wrists, which the housekeeper had bound in fresh bandages. In her hand she carried a small valise that contained her jeans, sweater, and tennis shoes. Bedford, who awaited her in the entry hall, looked up and a sudden frown creased his brow.

"Very dashing," he said in a flat tone that robbed his words of any compliment. He took her bag and led the way outside to the waiting post-chaise.

"I feel old-fashioned and silly." The chip straw bonnet felt odd on her head, as did the ribbon tied in a bow beneath her left ear. The high-waisted long coat he called a "pelisse" hung about her feet, completely covering her gray maid's uniform.

"You will do very well." He handed her into the carriage, then climbed up after her.

The post-boy, who sat mounted on the near leader rather than on the box, spurred the animal and the vehicle set forth over the uneven paving stones.

Riki peered out the window. No trace of anything modern met her searching gaze. No Palace Pier, no amusement centers. Not even any colored beach umbrellas lined the expanse of beach. The whole concept of traveling back through time still seemed impossible, yet she couldn't discount the evidence of her eyes—or of her other senses.

She peeked up at her companion to find his gaze resting thoughtfully on her face. She looked down quickly. "How should I behave? What will be expected of me?" She rushed into speech, unaccountably—and uncharacteristically—embarrassed.

"You will do very well, have no fear. But be somewhat reserved. If you think you have made a mistake, do not appear uneasy. No one could possibly guess the truth about you, and you may be very sure that any peculiarity of manner will be ascribed to your being an American."

"What a delightful reflection on my country. Tell me, are all Britishers so insular?" She smiled sweetly at him, hiding her touch of irritation at his unintended slight.

His frown faded before a sudden smile. "Worse," he

115

admitted. "With luck, though, you will only meet my mother and sister."

"What are they like?"

"My mother likes to be thought of as a gorgon, but don't let her frighten you—it is all an act, for her amusement. And Felicity is much like Hillary."

With that, Riki had to be satisfied. A few questions provided her with the facts that Prince George currently reigned as Regent, that appearances were everything, and that a lady was expected to think of nothing but her gowns, the upcoming season and other frivolities. Riki felt revolted and lapsed into moody silence.

The countryside, though, soon enthralled her. Fields, hedgerows, farmhouses, and forests slipped past. In the distance, she glimpsed an occasional church steeple or rustic village. After two hours, they pulled through a bustling town and into the yard of a busy inn. Riki watched, fascinated, as three uniformed boys ran forward and began unhitching their horses.

Bedford consulted a pocket watch, apparently borrowed from Sir Julian. "We're making excellent time."

"Are we?" For one accustomed to cars, this seemed a rather slow way to travel.

"Provided the new team doesn't boast any bo-kickers, we should reach the next stage in just over an hour."

The ostlers harnessed four fresh horses into position. The lads ran clear, the post-boy mounted and collected his team, and they rolled forward out of the enclosed yard. Riki looked back to see another carriage taking their place, and the ostlers once more engaged in their swift work.

A steady, fine sleet began to fall after they passed Hastings. The horses, perforce, slowed, and Riki hugged herself against the chill wind that penetrated the carriage. Her wrists had begun to throb again.

116

Bedford muttered something beneath his breath, and promised at the next stage to order a hot brick, a carriage blanket, and coffee.

Delicate flakes of snow began to touch the carriage window, melting at first, then clinging, creating intricate patterns. A thin, filmy blanket of white covered the ground and the hoofbeats became muffled as the horses' iron shoes struck the cushioning substance. Bare tree limbs donned their icy wintry foliage as the world filled with swirling flakes. The post-boy reined the team to a walk.

Bedford peered ahead, but the air was thick with flurrying snow, vision almost nonexistent. "It appears we will be somewhat delayed."

To Riki, that sounded like an understatement. It looked suspiciously like a blizzard in the making out there. Still, and despite the post-boy's suggestions that they find a likely inn, they kept doggedly on. Suddenly, the carriage lurched to a stop.

"What happened?" She leaned forward but couldn't see anything blocking their path. The post-boy, in fact, stared hard back over his shoulder.

Bedford let down the window. "Is something wrong?"

"N—no, m'lord."

The horses started up once more at a walk, and the vehicle swayed on. About a half hour later they stopped once more, and the post-boy again seemed more concerned with the road behind them than with whatever lay ahead.

Bedford threw open the door and hopped down to the snow-covered ground. "What the devil is going on?"

"There's someone followin' us, m'lord."

Bedford's brow creased and he cast a swift glance behind them, but the air was thick with swirling white. "What do you mean? I don't see anyone."

"I can 'ear a carriage, m'lord. It slows and speeds

up right along with us. So I tries stopping, and so does it. Every once in awhile I gets a glimpse o' the 'orses, then they drops back, like."

Bedford drew a deep breath. "Can you lose them?"

The post-boy chewed his lower lip. "I don't knows as I dare try, m'lord. The footin' is slippery, like."

Bedford looked ahead. "Do you know this stretch of road?"

"Yes, m'lord."

"Would you know if we were to approach a side lane? In time to spring the horses and get far enough down to get out of sight? I'd like to follow our friends for a bit and see if this is just coincidence."

The lad nodded, pleased with the idea, and Bedford returned to the carriage. They plodded on for another quarter hour, then abruptly the carriage jolted forward. Riki grasped a hand strap and Bedford's strong arm swept out, holding her safe against the squabs.

"Can you see anyone behind us?" Bedford peered out the window, his narrowed gaze searching.

Riki shook her head. "If they really are following us, they'd have to be keeping us in sight, wouldn't they?"

"Not necessarily. If they know who we are, they'll have a good idea where we're going. We're not likely to delay on the road. Whoever they are, they were probably biding their time until we came to a long deserted stretch of road to overtake us."

Riki shivered: "What delightful thoughts you have. Any idea *why?*"

"My journey to Portugal seems the likeliest, doesn't it? Word leaked out about that, thanks to the ineptness of my brother-in-law — and possibly others. There is always the chance I was spotted in Rottingdean or Brighton."

Riki turned from the window to fix him with a fascinated eye. "You sound quite accustomed to being followed."

Bedford shook his head, never looking away from the road behind. The carriage swung sharply, the wheels skidding through the snow, and they headed down a lane so narrow it would have been possible to miss it altogether. Here, tall evergreens screened the road so that little snow impeded their path. The horses broke into a gallop and Riki clutched her hand strap even tighter. Behind them, on the main road, a carriage swirled past in a spray of muddy slush, heedless of the treacherous footing.

Abruptly their own horses slowed to a walk, and Riki nearly flew from the seat. Bedford steadied her as the vehicle turned laboriously in the narrow confines of a country cross-road. They started back at a brisk canter the way they had come.

"It's madness to spring horses under these conditions," Bedford remarked, his tone purely conversational. He drew his flask from his pocket and offered it to Riki.

She took a sip and handed it back. "You think they *were* following us, then?"

Bedford nodded. "Why else keep pace like that? A normal carriage would have passed us when our postboy stopped."

"And now we follow them."

"If we can."

They emerged once more onto the main road and the horses leapt forward. This time, Riki was prepared and held on tight. But no carriage came into sight before them. At last, for the sake of the blown team, they were forced to slow. At the next posting house, they stopped for a change.

Their lad came to the door of the post-chaise while the ostlers backed a fresh team into harness. "No one's stopped 'ere for the past hour or more, m'lord. They weren't prepared for us, with the snow fallin' so 'ard."

Bedford nodded. "Either our friends have gone ahead searching for us, or they pulled our trick and are once again behind."

"Do you want me to keep tryin' to race 'em?"

Bedford shook his head. "The snow's too heavy. You were only hired until this stage. Do you want to go the rest of the way with us?"

The lad nodded, an impish grin crossing his unprepossessing features. "Adds a bit of excitement, it does, m'lord."

Bedford nodded. "Then have the landlord supply us each with a pistol. It doesn't pay to take chances."

Locating the pistols caused some delay, but the guns duly arrived, along with blankets and hot bricks. The latter helped alleviate Riki's discomfort of body, if not of mind. Mostly, she appreciated the dollop of brandy Bedford added to their coffee.

They started forth once more, and would have been much more comfortable except for the shadow of uneasiness that now hung over them. Riki cast frequent, darting glances out the window, but no other carriages could be seen venturing forth in the heavily falling snow. Her alert vigil gave way to tedium as they plodded along.

One glance at Bedford's face discouraged her from asking questions. Deep lines creased his brow and the firm set of his square jaw bespoke his preoccupation as clearly as if he voiced his concerns aloud. She couldn't blame him. Even if their mysterious follower never caught up with them, journey's end wouldn't be any picnic for him, either. He still had to present her to his family.

At the next stage, Bedford obtained a pack of playing cards, and the atmosphere inside the post-chaise lightened immeasurably. He poured them both a brandy from his flask, shuffled, and his pensive mood faded as he introduced her to the intricacies of piquet. Only occasionally did he cast a searching glance behind them.

Increasing darkness put an end to both the watching and the cards. Riki returned her attention to the countryside, and noticed the snow had let up to a light fall.

"We've reached Canterbury," Bedford announced as the outline of a large town came into view. "Not much farther, now."

When at last they turned off the road onto a narrow lane, a couple of stars peeped out from between the clouds. A few miles later, they slowed for a turn and the crunching of gravel beneath a thin layer of snow announced they now traversed a private drive. Riki peered ahead, but could not see their destination.

"Around the next bend. There, you can just make out the outline of the chimneys."

Falconer's Court looked to be a massive house of low, rambling design. Riki found herself more interested in the lights that illuminated the multi-paned windows on the ground floor, and their promise of warmth and comfort. She shivered, and wondered what Bedford's mother and sister would think of her.

They drew to a stop before the front door, which opened as Bedford jumped to the ground. A man in somber black waited, stiffly correct, apparently not impressed by visitors who arrived under cover of darkness without warning. Bedford strode forward, and the previously impassive face of the butler crumpled in amazement.

"My lord?" He hurried forward.

Bedford handed him their borrowed valises. "As you see, Newly. Have Mrs. Wicking prepare a room for my mother's guest." He offered Riki his arm and led her toward the house.

The butler bowed them into the hall, then took Riki's pelisse and Bedford's topcoat. Appalled, the man stared at his master's unusual attire.

121

"Shall I send Mr. Pervis to you, my lord?"

Bedford fought back a smile. "Later. I will see my mother first. Is she in the Blue Drawing Room?"

"She is dressing for dinner, my lord. If the young person will—"

"Young *lady*, Newly. Have Mrs. Wicking assign a maid to assist Miss van Hamel."

"Very good, my lord."

Riki remained poised under the butler's curious stare, returning it with only the slightest smile touching her lips. Newly bowed to her with dawning respect, and Riki turned to take Bedford's offered arm. They started for the stairs.

"Mr. Sylvester is with us, my lord." The butler added the ominous words in the accents of one long inured to disasters.

Bedford stopped dead. "The devil he is."

Newly bowed slightly. "As you say, my lord."

"When did he arrive?"

"A little more than an hour ago, my lord."

"Traveling, in this weather?" But he murmured the words to himself.

"Mr. Sylvester?" Riki whispered as the butler made his stately way toward the back of the house. Not even in the presence of the smugglers had she seen Bedford so taken aback.

"*O my prophetic soul! My uncle.*" His mouth twitched into a wry smile.

"*O villain, villain, smiling, damned villain?*" Riki murmured back.

"So a number of young ladies not of our order might say. He has been a source of entertainment for my mother and chagrin for my father for as long as I can remember. It was, in fact, upon the occasion of one of Sylvester's visits that my father was taken off in a fit of apoplexy."

The last was said without any trace of tragedy or grief, so Riki accepted it as a statement of fact and offered no condolences. "What brought him out in such a storm?"

"*O villain.*" Bedford's eyes narrowed.

Riki gasped. "You don't think . . . ?"

"It's ludicrous." Yet still, obviously, he had thought of it. "He has no reason to follow me."

"No, he could quite easily just meet you here," Riki agreed. She met his frowning gaze, but could find no answer to the unspoken question she read in his eyes.

"Let us—"

Bedford broke off, for a slightly built gentleman with silvered hair and an elegant manner appeared on the landing above them. His green velvet cutaway coat fit him to perfection, showing an elaborate brocade waistcoat shot through with gold thread beneath. The gentleman waved a delicate white hand on which an overly large emerald sparkled, matching the one nestled in his cravat.

"I say, Newly, where—" He saw the arrivals in the hall below. "Bedford?" He raised his quizzing glass and regarded them through it, then allowed it to drop. His face wreathed in a welcoming smile, he hurried lightly down the curving oak staircase. "My dear Nevvy! I thought you out of the country."

Riki blinked. Despite the elaborate show, she detected no real surprise in that greeting. *Could* he have followed them in so odd a manner? It just didn't seem likely.

Bedford accepted his uncle's hand, but a sudden frown creased his brow. "Did you, Uncle? Now, why would you have thought I had left England?"

"Stopped in to visit you at Whitehall." He twisted the giant emerald on his finger. "The day before yesterday, I believe. Yes, definitely, for I had been playing at White's all night and thought I'd pay my respects to you on my way home."

"By which I may assume that you dipped rather deeply."

123

"Only a slight flutter." A frown replaced Sylvester Randall's expansive smile. "I may have been a trifle muddled, dear boy, but I distinctly recall someone saying you were headed to Portugal. I am delighted to see it was not true, after all."

"As a matter of fact, I was on my way. But an unexpected problem came up, and I have returned, as you see. What brings you to the Court, and in such inclement weather—or need I ask? Under the hatches again?"

"Oh, tol-lol, dear boy." Sylvester waved the question aside with a grand gesture, and beamed once more. "London can be so very dreary in January. I was prompted by an ardent desire to see my lovely sister-in-law once more."

"That, and the somewhat pressing demands of your creditors?"

The elegant gentleman directed a look of pained reproach at him and straightened his slight shoulders. "Do I look like a shabster?"

"Yes."

A twinkle entered Mr. Sylvester Randall's not-so-innocent blue eyes. "How well you know me, my boy. How well you know me. And what of this delightful creature? A maid?" He raised his quizzing glass and directed the scrutiny of the connoisseur on Riki.

"Not a maid, Uncle—and not fair game for you, either. Miss Erika van Hamel is an emissary from the American government who had the misfortune to be involved in a shipwreck with me. Miss van Hamel, I am sorry to introduce to you the black sheep of our family, my father's brother, the Honorable Mr. Sylvester Randall."

Sylvester took her hand, bowed deeply over it, and managed at the same time to raise her fingers to his lips with an artistry that demanded admiration. "Pay him no heed, my dear. Every family must have a profligate or two hidden away."

"And he has been forced to carry the role alone for too long," Bedford stuck in, unconsciously playing straightman to his uncle.

"Very true." Sylvester shook his head in exaggerated sadness. "Until my brother had the good sense to marry Lady Prudence, whose humor, I am pleased to say, she passed on to *most* of her children," here he cast a roguish glance at Bedford, "the duty fell solely to me."

"And now you have assistance?" Riki couldn't resist the question.

"You have already met Hillary," Bedford reminded her.

"Has she?" Sylvester raised an eyebrow. "I distinctly remember him saying he was off to Oxford. Devilish flat, I thought at the time. Has he had the good sense to go elsewhere?"

"You see what we have to endure." Bedford turned to Riki, his eyes holding a rueful smile as his tension eased.

Riki inclined her head toward the elegant gentleman. "I understand you have only just arrived. How was your journey from London?"

"Cold, my dear. Devilish cold."

Bedford took her arm. "And so was ours. If you will excuse us, Uncle? I am certain Miss van Hamel would be glad of a chance to freshen up before dinner."

Sylvester bowed low once more to Riki. "Forgive me for delaying you. You will have need to make haste. Lady Prudence sets an admirable table, but insists on dining at the ungodly hour of six when in the country."

He nodded affably to them both and glided toward the back of the house, apparently set upon discovering the butler, who had long since vanished from the hall. Bedford watched his departing figure with a slight frown still creasing his brow.

"Will his presence complicate our business with my cousin?" Riki whispered.

"What?" He glanced at her as if he had momentarily forgotten her presence. "Complicate? No, I shouldn't think so. We will merely take care to keep Warwick out of his vicinity."

"It couldn't have been your uncle following us, you know. The idea, as you said, is absurd."

"It does seem unreasonable. Yet he arrived a bare hour before we did, and in weather that normally would have kept him safe at home. And I especially do not like the number of people who appear to have been cognizant of my journey to Portugal."

"Only your brother-in-law, your friend, and your uncle. Secrets have a way of being talked about, you know, especially within a family."

He looked down at her, his dark eyes barely discernible beneath half-lidded eyes. "Some coincidences I believe in. Others I do not. Julian 'just happened' to encounter my sister, who 'just happened' to mention my whereabouts after her husband had been sworn to secrecy. My dear Uncle Sylvester 'just happened' to drop by Whitehall, which I might add he has done only once before in the two years I have worked there. Next, I suppose you will tell me we 'just happened' to be followed on the road by a carriage that 'just happened' to behave strangely?"

Eight

Riki shook her head. "I don't know about the other 'coincidences,' but I believe your uncle's visit to Whitehall—and subsequent journey here in a storm when he found you gone—can be explained quite easily. He was in somewhat urgent need of a loan, wasn't he?"

Bedford's lip twitched wryly. "He is always at Fiddlestick's end. That would make an excellent excuse, though, would it not, to call at the War Office?"

Riki regarded Bedford uncertainly. "Are you accusing your uncle of having some surreptitious purpose?"

Bedford ran a hand through his already disordered hair. "No." He sounded tired. "I don't seem to have been thinking clearly since I was shipwrecked on your island. Whoever is talking freely will get the finest trimming of his life, though, of that you may be certain."

"Perhaps—" Riki broke off.

A motherly woman of comfortable proportions approached from a side corridor, and Bedford introduced his housekeeper, Mrs. Wicking. He handed Riki into her charge, hesitated a moment, then followed the route so recently taken by his uncle toward the nether regions of the house.

Mrs. Wicking and her maids had been busy, Riki noted as soon as she stepped into the large, airy apartment on the second floor at the back of the vast, rambling mansion. Four triple branches of candles stood on polished tables about the room and a large fire crackled merrily in the hearth. A pitcher stood before it and steam spiraled from the hot water within.

"There, miss, you'll be wanting to change, I make no doubt." She went to the valise, which rested on a mahogany Sheraton chair.

"There's nothing in there." With a quick movement, Riki stopped her. She didn't feel up to explaining about jeans and zippers at the moment.

The woman drew herself up, the suspicion of a frown forming between her brows. Apparently, Riki reflected ruefully, luggage was another necessity for a lady of this time period. No wonder Bedford had been loathe to take her to London. On the whole, she was surprised he had dared to bring her to his home under the circumstances.

She went to the fire, extending her hands to it as she threw a disarming smile over her shoulder at the affronted Mrs. Wicking. "Did Lord Bedford not explain? Our boat sank in the Channel, and we were lucky to be rescued at all in that dreadful storm."

"Shipwrecked?" The woman clucked her tongue, and her comfortable warmth returned. "There, now, miss, what a dreadful time you must have been having, to be sure. It was very right of Master Gil—his lordship, I should say—to carry you straight to his mamma's charge. If you'll let me help you out of that gown, I'll see it's brushed and pressed at once."

Already, she worked on the two small buttons that fastened the neckline in back. In a trice, she dragged the gray maid's gown over Riki's head. Stopping only to pour hot water into the china basin, she hurried from the room, muttering under her breath about the "poor miss" and the "unsuitable dress."

Riki availed herself of the washing facilities, then strolled about the room while she waited for her gown to be returned. It felt good to move again, after so many hours of jostling in the carriage. Her muscles still hadn't recovered from the swimming—or the carrying of the brandy kegs.

A light tap sounded on the door, and she opened it at once. It was not a maid carrying her newly cleaned dress who entered, though, but a petite brunette with large, laughing eyes as dark as Bedford's. She tripped into the room, cast one last peek down the hall, closed the door, and turned to Riki with all the air of one engaged on a delightful and slightly reprehensible lark. Riki had no doubts as to her identity.

"I'm Bedford's sister, Felicity." She held out her hand, suddenly shy. "Oh, don't disapprove of me, please. I know I shouldn't have come to your room like this, but it would be just like Bedford, in that *odious* elder brother way of his, not to let me meet you."

Riki blinked. "Why ever not?"

"Because you're an *agent*," she breathed in awed accents. "I heard him telling Mamma. Please, don't send me away. The moment I heard you were here, I knew I had to meet you. Bedford is so dreadfully stuffy, he never introduces me to any *interesting* people."

"I'm not so very interesting," Riki said, but knew her words fell on deaf ears as the tiny hand clung to hers. "If Bedford would rather we didn't meet—"

"Oh, that's just his nonsensical notions of propriety! He is forever trying to hold me in leading strings. I don't know why he never wants me to have any fun. He doesn't kick up a dust when Hillary goes off on some spree. And Hil's two years

129

younger than I am, and I'm already *out!*"

"Are you?" Riki wondered if she sounded as bemused as she felt. It was no wonder Bedford had sobered before his years if he'd been left in charge of this lively young lady. Hillary must prove a constant worry, as well. And hadn't there been mention of a second brother? Her respect for Bedford's patience soared.

"Yes! This will be my second season," Felicity rattled merrily on. "And Bedford really is a dear, though so *fusty* at times. He's not pressing me to marry at all, which I must say is very kind of him."

"You don't want to?" Riki felt her way with care. She had always thought young ladies in earlier times wanted to be married before they were twenty.

"No, why should I? I may not be an heiress, but I am quite comfortably situated. And I am having far too much *fun* to become leg-shackled. Have you been an agent for long?" She rushed on to the new topic without pausing for breath.

"No, not very," Riki answered truthfully.

Felicity sighed. "Oh, how brave you must be. I wish Bedford would let me help. Was it dreadfully difficult to persuade him?"

"Yes, it was rather. But he had no choice."

Felicity giggled. "Bedford *always* has a choice. No one ever forces his hand."

"Don't they?" Somehow, she could believe that. Yet here she was, when he hadn't wanted her with him in his time. Or had he? That proved an intriguing thought.

"Did you lose everything when your boat sank?" Felicity regarded her with wonder in her wide, clear dark eyes. "Have you not even a change of gown?"

Riki cast an uncertain glance at the flimsy folds of the chemise she wore. "My—my own things were utterly ruined. What I am wearing now once belonged to one of Sir Julian Taggart's maids."

130

"Sir Julian? *He* knows about your adventure?" Felicity's marvelous eyes grew even wider. "I must say, that is the outside of enough if Bedford is going to let a simpering fop like Sir Julian help, but not his own sister! Well, I can do as well as he can." She cast a considering glance over Riki's petite figure. "You're only slightly smaller than I am. Stay right here, I'll be back in a trice."

Before Riki could protest, Felicity darted out the door and ran down the carpeted hall at a most unladylike gait. Sighing, Riki returned to her contemplation of the crackling fire. She had the distinct feeling Bedford was not going to be pleased with whatever his lively young sister had in mind.

Apparently, Felicity intercepted Mrs. Wicking and the maid's uniform, for they returned to Riki's room together, accompanied by a stern-featured woman of middle age garbed in sober black. In the arms of all three were an assortment of gowns in a variety of colors and fabrics. These the women laid down on the bed, except for a simple creation of dull gold silk that Felicity clutched.

"I had this made up at the beginning of the little season, but Mamma won't let me wear it. She says its not *proper*." The girl made a face, conveying the message that she, for one, did not agree, but after all, what could one do in the face of silly parental vetoes? "It would look beautiful on you," she added with a touch of envy.

Silently, Riki agreed. She couldn't imagine anything farther from her beloved jeans and bulky sweaters, but it might be fun to dress up again. She hadn't had occasion to put on an evening gown in almost four years, not since that night her mother entertained the Swedish ambassador and the maid had spilled an entire trayful of caviar and salmon pate crackers over his white-starched shirt front and cummerbund..

The dour-faced maid proved to be Miss Bexhill, Felicity's autocratic and highly-paid dresser. Riki, accustomed to the occasional supercilious servant who lorded it over her mother's household, merely inclined her head and permitted the faintest smile to touch her lips in acknowledgment of Felicity's sketchy introduction. Bexy, as Felicity called her, knew Quality when she saw it, and however outlandish Miss's appearance and arrival might be, she knew her clear Duty in caring for the needs of a Lady. Miss Bexhill sniffed and ordered Miss to stand still while she expertly tossed the golden folds of silk over her head and twitched them into place.

It fit better than Riki would have expected. The tiny puff sleeves that perched on the points of her shoulder might be more fitting to a young deb, or whatever they called them in this time, but the skimpy bodice fit well enough, thanks to Riki's lack of generous endowment in that department. While Bexhill fastened up the tiny buttons at the back of the low-scooped neckline, Riki examined her reflection in the mirror. The excellent cut of the high-waisted skirt and the dramatic fall of the heavy silk fabric lent her an elegance she had sadly missed of late.

"It *is* beautiful." Felicity heaved a sigh. "I must say, it looks better on you than ever it did on me."

Miss Bexhill sniffed again. "Miss stands with her shoulders straight."

Felicity made a face at her naggy dresser from behind that worthy's back. "It doesn't even need to be altered. Look, the flounce just brushes the top of your feet. A little long, perhaps, but no one will notice for tonight. Can you do something with her hair, Bexy?"

Bexy could. After only a few minutes with a curling iron, which Riki regarded with a certain amount of consternation, tiny ringlets surrounded

132

her face. A gold riband threaded through these, drawing back the rest of her thick auburn hair. One gold silk rose added a final touch that pleased even Riki.

After ordering Riki not to stir until she came back, Felicity dragged Miss Bexhill away to assist her in completing her own dressing and to collect shawls for them both. She rejoined Riki barely twenty minutes later, dressed now in a white muslin gown Riki suspected had been chosen to show her beleaguered parent how plain she forced her own daughter to appear. The mischievous sparkle in the girl's eyes confirmed this, and Riki's sympathy for the still unknown Lady Prudence grew.

It faded ten minutes later as Felicity ushered her into the drawing room where the family gathered before dinner. On a brocade sofa near the fireplace sat a stately silver haired dowager who put Riki forcibly in mind of a purple silk stone wall. Riki approached slowly, feeling very much as if she were about to be presented to a Grand Duchess.

"Mamma, this is Miss van Hamel. Gil has told you all about her. My mother, Lady Prudence Randall, the Dowager Viscountess Bedford. She won't bite," Felicity added in a voice just loud enough to make certain her mother heard.

Lady Prudence didn't so much as bat an eye. She extended a beringed hand, permitting Riki to just touch two fingers. No stranger to haughty society dames, Riki curtsied ever so slightly, implying a respect due to years rather than superior breeding. Lady Prudence noted and her dark eyes twinkled in a manner that reminded Riki disturbingly of Bedford.

"We are pleased to have you with us," Lady Prudence intoned.

Whether she employed the royal "we" or referred to her entire family, Riki wasn't certain. The former, she suspected, and found herself enjoying the formidable matron.

"It is very kind of you to permit me to visit in such a—a ramshackle fashion." She hoped that was the correct adjective.

"It is quite the norm in this family, though I had not expected Bedford to become involved in the sort of escapades normally indulged in by my younger sons." Lady Prudence regarded her visitor with a mock condescending smile that only served to emphasize her rampant curiosity—and patent approval of anyone who could shake her first born out of his respectable and dull rut.

With difficulty, Riki kept a straight face. Not a doubt of it, Felicity and Hillary took after their mother. Riki could almost pity the late viscount, who had passed his more sober disposition on to his heir—and apparently to none of the others. Lady Prudence, who had obviously regarded her eldest son as a changeling amidst her lively brood, now seemed to see hope for the first time.

The door opened to admit the Honorable Sylvester Randall, who stopped dead just over the threshold to stare at Riki in blatant admiration. Unconsciously, he straightened his cut-away velvet coat and squared his shoulders, every inch the aging roué. He strode forward, a predatory gleam lighting his blue eyes.

"Miss van Hamel." He clasped her hand and raised her fingers to his lips for a lingering kiss. His gaze traveled slowly over her borrowed finery and came to rest on the rounded curve of her hips, which filled the skirt more fully than Felicity's more youthful figure would have. "Delightful, my dear. Delightful." He patted her hand, which he showed no signs of releasing.

"It is indeed." Bedford's deep voice sounded from the doorway.

Riki looked up quickly and encountered his quizzical gaze. Slowly, the amusement faded from his eyes to be replaced by a smoldering glow that left her breathless.

She had found him attractive in a rugged, self-confident way before, even in his bedraggled or ill-fitting clothes. Now, in his own element, dressed with a precision and neatness that had little to do with the fastidiousness of his Uncle Sylvester, she found him overpowering. The long-tailed coat of claret-colored velvet fit to admiration, emphasizing the breadth of shoulder and narrowness of hip. A white waistcoat could be seen beneath. No fobs or chains cluttered his person, his only ornamentation the large signet ring he wore on the middle finger of his left hand. His pantaloons of buff stockinette outlined his muscular thighs. With difficulty, Riki redirected her gaze to the intricate folds of his starched neckcloth.

He came forward, his regard never wavering from Riki's slight form. "How did you manage this transformation?"

Warmth crept into her cheeks at his patent approval. "Your sister—"

"My sister." He turned his suddenly amused gaze onto Felicity, who regarded him with a certain amount of trepidation. "Felicity, my dear, you are to be congratulated."

"It *is* a beautiful gown," the girl pointed out.

"It is. And far more suitable to Miss van Hamel than to yourself. Remind me to have you order something more appropriate to replace it."

Felicity beamed, obviously having achieved at least part of her intent.

Newly entered to announce dinner, which had merely been held until the two late arrivals had an opportunity to change. Sylvester made a beeline for Riki, but Bedford forestalled him, offering her his

135

arm and throwing his rakish uncle a challenging glance. Sylvester backed off and instead escorted both his sister-in-law and niece.

She must be more tired from the journey than she realized, Riki reflected. As curious as she was to see his home, it all seemed too much to assimilate. Bedford led her into a spacious, elegant apartment, but she gained merely impressions of a high painted ceiling, huge gilt-framed paintings, rich tapestries and hangings, and silver gleaming in the light of a multitude of candles. The heavenly aroma of food surrounded her.

Bedford seated her at his right, with Felicity on her other side, before taking his place at the head of the long table. As at Sir Julian's, only one end of this had been set, gathering them all together to make conversation possible in this lofty apartment. Lady Prudence sat opposite Riki, but confined her conversation to her son and to her brother-in-law, who sat on either side of her.

During the second course and her third glass of wine, Riki started yawning. As soon as Lady Prudence rose, announcing the end of the meal, Riki gratefully accepted her suggestion that she might like to retire at once. Mrs. Wicking appeared in the hall, almost as if she had expected a summons, and led Riki back to the chamber that awaited her.

Miss Bexhill had been busy. Across the great bed lay a nightgown and nightcap, undoubtedly purloined from Felicity's abundant collection. Riki made a mental note to thank the girl as she doffed one borrowed gown to don another, then promptly forgot everything as she tumbled into bed. Her last, hazy thoughts were of comfort and sleep.

She awoke slowly to the sound of someone moving about her room. Already, the green velvet curtains had been drawn back from about her bed and a tray bearing freshly baked rolls and a cup of steaming chocolate rested on the bedside table. A young maid poked at the fire, added another log, then drew the drapes back from the window to expose a snow-covered vista and gray threatening skies.

Riki yawned, sat up, and tried to focus her tired eyes on the ormolu clock on the mantel. It remained a disobliging blur.

"What time is it?" She yawned again.

The maid turned, bobbed a quick curtsy, then hurried over to arrange pillows at Riki's back. "It's gone on nine o'clock, miss."

"Nine? Am I late for breakfast?"

The maid giggled. "No, miss. His lordship and Miss Felicity were down over an hour ago, but her ladyship never rises before ten."

"And Mr. Sylvester?" Riki hoped this didn't constitute gossiping with the servants. She really had to learn how a household of this era—and this one in particular—operated so she would make no glaring gaffs.

"He never stirs from his chamber before noon, miss. Nor will Master Hillary nor Lord Linton, arriving as late as they did."

"Master Hillary?" That brought Riki fully awake and sitting straight up. "When—did anyone else come with him?" She couldn't keep the eagerness from her voice.

"Only Lord Linton, miss, who is his lordship's brother-in-law, being married to Miss Clarissa."

Riki suppressed her disappointment and climbed out of the raised bed. At this moment, she would give a great deal for a pair of sheepskin slippers. The floor, in spite of the thick carpet, was cold. The maid helped her into a rather pretty muslin wrapper, then pointed out the bedside tray. Dutifully, Riki sipped the rapidly cooling beverage and took a bite of the flaky, buttery roll.

Today, she decided, she would remove the bandages from her wrists. The cream supplied by Sir Julian's housekeeper should relieve the itching caused by the healing. Her face still felt too raw to wash, so she simply made generous use of the soothing contents of the jar.

The maid produced a pale green Circassian cloth morning gown from the wardrobe, along with a corset and a fresh chemise. Riki donned these quickly, along with a pair of Felicity's slippers. She was anxious to see Bedford. After all, Hillary might have told him when David could be expected to arrive. Almost convinced that was her sole reason for rushing, she accepted the soft woolen shawl the abigail held out, and made her way downstairs.

To her disappointment, the breakfast parlor to which the butler directed her stood empty. She hesitated in the doorway, then retraced her steps. After the roll and chocolate, she wasn't particularly hungry at the moment, and a far more urgent desire filled her. She went in search of her host.

After one false start down a long corridor, she found her way to the Great Hall, where she came to an abrupt halt. Last night, she'd just been so glad to get out of the freezing carriage and inside a house, she hadn't taken in any details beyond the pleasant warmth that surrounded her. This morning, she saw the luxury. The vaulted ceiling, which rose two stories, appeared to have been carved from mahogany. Silk banners and Renaissance tapestries from Italy lined the paneled walls. She walked slowly across the dramatic geometric patterned tiles of green, pink, and white marble, then stopped uncertainly near the massive oaken front door.

"May I help you, miss?"

She spun about, startled, so silently had Newly approached. "Is his lordship in the library? I'm afraid I don't know where that is."

138

"Down the left corridor, miss. But his lordship is in the rookery." With due ceremony, he escorted her through a maze of short hallways, through a magnificent ballroom and to a set of French windows that looked out onto a tiled terrace now covered in a light dusting of snow.

"Down those steps, miss, and through the rose garden. The rookery backs up against the stables. If you would wish, one of the footmen will accompany you."

"I think I can manage. Left past the shrubbery?"

He nodded, and she set forth. It was colder out here than she'd expected and she shivered in her shawl as the icy wind cut through her woolen gown. What she really needed was her nylon windbreaker. And the snow wasn't doing her silly thin slippers the least bit of good, either. She missed her pile-lined waterproof boots. But the thought of talking to Bedford—about David's arrival, of course—sped her onward.

She easily located the large cobbled stableyard, surrounded by low stone boxed stalls. The carriage house stood on the far side. Smoke rose from numerous chimneys, heating both the barns and the grooms' quarters. Apparently, Bedford's horses lived as well as did the rest of his household.

She circled to the far side and found a low structure backed up against the carriage house sharing the warmth of the fires, she supposed. She opened the door and entered the comfortable interior, which was illuminated by a row of lanterns hung from the beamed ceiling. Hawks were everywhere, some in individual cages, others free to fly at their will.

Bedford stood at the far end of the aviary, one gauntleted hand raised high. As the door closed behind her, he turned to look, but didn't move. The next moment, Riki saw why.

A large tiercel swooped and landed on Bedford's

139

protected wrist, digging in with its sharp talons. With a fluttering of wings, it settled onto the living perch, then cocked its head and regarded the man. Bedford murmured something Riki couldn't hear and the peregrine rustled its feathers and relaxed.

Riki took a step closer, not wanting to interrupt their rapport, yet drawn by a yearning she couldn't resist. It was as if they had stepped out of her half-remembered dreams, this strong, noble man and his hawk. A lump welled in her throat at the sheer beauty of their harmony.

"Now you see *my* rookery." His soft tone, almost a caress, invited her to come closer.

Slowly she trod the length of the room, and the birds nearest cocked their feathered heads and sidled or hopped away. For once, she had eyes for only the man. His regard, every bit as piercing as that of his birds, never wavered from her face.

As she neared, he lowered his gaze to rove over every inch of her in a manner that brought prickling heat to her cheeks. Those dark, brooding eyes glowed as they once more rose to her face, his regard lingering over every feature until he looked into her eyes, which she felt certain must reveal the chaos he created in her.

He lowered his arm and the indignant peregrine flapped the short distance to a more reliable perch. "I see Felicity has provided very well for you. But it is too cold out here for a mere shawl."

Reaching out, he lowered the thick woolen folds from about her head so that they fell across her shoulders. He drew off his gauntlet, cast it aside, and gently rearranged the soft warmth about her neck. His controlled tenderness proved too much for Riki. She caught his hand and pressed it against her throat.

His thumb traced the line of her jaw, then down her slender neck until his fingers brushed her exposed skin at her collar bone. Warm breath fanned her cheek, and she gazed into eyes that smoldered with a passion too intense to be denied. Her lids fluttered closed as she went into strong arms that opened only enough to enfold her.

She had been kissed before, but never like this, never so completely that it encompassed her very soul. She clung to him, meeting his desire with a desperate abandon that would have startled her had reasoning thought been possible. Now, she only experienced, and savored the delicious sensations that shot through her, that awakened long-buried yearnings.

It wasn't reasonable to want a man this badly, not when she had known him only a few short days. It had to be the unreality of the whole situation, the time gap that would always separate them, that made him irresistibly forbidden fruit. And she couldn't resist.

His mouth moved over hers, evoking visions of him joining her in that huge bed in her chamber. She moved even closer, until she pressed tightly against him, molding her softer curves against his hard, muscular body. She needed him, more than she could say—more, even, than she could understand. It was as if here, in his arms, she found something for which she had searched in vain all her life.

A low groan escaped him and he grasped her shoulders, setting her firmly several inches away. His eyes burned into hers and his breath came more quickly.

"You're dangerous," he whispered.

"I hope so." With shaking fingers, she touched his smooth shaven cheek.

He removed her hand quickly. "You're making me forget you're a lady." The words sounded strained.

"From a different time. If we were in the future,

141

in my time—"

He turned away. "We're not." He spoke savagely, through clenched teeth. "We're in my time, and you—you'll be returning to yours." He looked back at her over his shoulder, his expression closed except for the blazing light that illuminated his dark, mysterious eyes. "We have obviously been raised under differing rules."

She nodded, understanding all too well. She could act on passions, he could not. They were, as she knew well, worlds apart.

Tears of frustration threatened to fill her eyes. Gathering the shawl more closely about herself, she turned away. Maybe they weren't that far apart, after all. She wasn't one to indulge in a brief but passionate affair, no matter how overwhelming her desire. For her, only a lasting relationship would do. And that she could not have with a man who would shortly be separated from her by nearly two hundred years.

A shout, of Bedford's name, sounded from outside, and Riki thought she recognized the voice; Hillary must have awakened. That put her in mind of the ostensible reason she had sought out Bedford in the first place, and she forced her thoughts back to David.

"Bedford!" Hillary came closer, bellowing loudly enough to send the falcons into a rustling flutter that made Riki think of broody hens.

"As you may have been told, my brother arrived late last night." Bedford had his voice, if not the lingering embers in his eyes, under control.

"I came out to ask you why, and if he had a message from David."

Together, they started for the door, the awkwardness of the preceding minutes heavy between them.

"He did. Warwick—" He broke off as Hillary gave tongue once more.

"Bed—" The cry broke off abruptly, followed immediately by the muffled sound of something heavy falling on the cobbled stones.

Bedford pushed past Riki and threw open the heavy door of the rookery. In the yard beyond, next to the white-frosted shrubbery, a great-coated shape lay crumpled in the snow, blood oozing sluggishly from a swelling gash on the side of his head.

Nine

Bedford reached his brother in six running steps and fell to one knee on the snow-covered ground at his side. The boy groaned, and Bedford heaved a heartfelt sigh of relief. His worst fear removed, he set about discovering how badly Hillary was hurt.

"Is he—" Riki, breathless, ran up behind him.

"All right." He checked his brother's pulse, just to reassure himself. "But how—" He looked about, searching for something that might have struck him hard enough to knock him unconscious, and sharp enough to cause that cut. If Aubrey were here, he'd have suspected snowballs. But Aubrey's humor, as erratic as it was, did not run to including rocks in his frozen weapons. Sylvester, though—

"Why would your uncle throw a loaded snowball?" Riki demanded.

He had been speaking aloud, Bedford realized. "He wouldn't," he said with more conviction than he felt. "Besides, Sylvester has the aim of a drunken artilleryman. He can't hit anything he chooses as target." Yet Hillary had been struck with something, and with evident intent to do harm. *Why?*

"Maybe it was an accident," Riki suggested, "and he was in fact aiming for something else."

"He'd have come to help. And you don't throw a

144

snowball with a rock inside unless you're planning to do some damage."

A second groan sounded from the victim, and Bedford turned his attention to his brother, who showed definite signs of reviving. Riki placed a small handful of snow against the swelling on the side of the boy's head, and a moment later Hillary raised a shaky hand to bat it aside.

"What—" He dragged open his eyes.

Bedford wasn't about to plant unfounded suspicions in his brother's mind. "What did you run into, you young idiot?" he asked with true brotherly spirit.

Riki glanced at him in surprise and he gave his head a slight shake.

Hillary struggled to a sitting position and touched his throbbing skull. He stared at the blood on his fingers in disbelief. "Someone hit me!"

"What makes you think so?" Bedford rested his hand on Hillary's shoulder, preventing the boy from staggering to his feet.

His brother ran a hand over his face, dislodging the flakes of snow that clung to his cheek. "I heard something. Someone just behind me in the bushes. I started to turn—" He shook his head slowly. "That's all I remember."

"You didn't see anyone?"

Hillary shook his head with less caution this time and winced.

Bedford's fingers tightened on Hil's shoulder a moment, then he strode over and poked among the straggly line of hawthorn shrubs. Holding back several branches, he bent to peer through. The thin layer of snow on the far side, barely discernible between the thick twigs and leaves, showed signs of being kicked about. Someone must have stood there for some minutes. He continued his survey, and a moment later dragged a two-inch-thick branch about three feet long from under cover. At one end, several dark hairs clung to a sticky purplish red stain.

"It seems there was a weapon," he said slowly.

Someone must have been lying in wait—but there was no reason for that. More likely, Hillary had been struck down to prevent him seeing something—or someone. The questions loomed large in his mind, momentarily unanswerable.

Hillary came unsteadily to his feet, and Bedford thrust those questions aside in the face of a more pressing concern. He wanted to get the young scapegrace tended.

Riki already slipped an arm about his waist, trying to take part of his greater weight on her slight shoulders. She staggered, and Bedford stepped in to relieve her.

They started around the corner of the barn, with Riki still determinedly helping. As they crossed the yard, a wiry middle-aged groom came into view, putting the final polishing touches on a newly oiled whip stock as he walked. He cast this aside and hurried toward them.

"Have you seen anyone about, Jem?" Bedford asked.

Jem shook his head, his wide eyes resting on Hillary's blood-streaked face. "No, m'lord. Mr. Sylvester came out to check on his horses, which he does every morning he's with us." His tone indicated that the grooms did not take kindly to this implied distrust of their abilities. "And Sir Julian Taggart, o'course."

"Sir Julian? What the devil is he doing here?" Bedford muttered the last words to himself, but Jem seemed to think an answer had been required of him.

"He arrived about twenty minutes ago, m'lord." He gestured across the stable yard they had entered, to where they could now see the undergroom assisting Sir Julian's man to push a white-winged, low-slung curricle into the shelter of the carriage barn. The legendary grays were nowhere in sight, probably already rubbed down and snugly housed in warm stalls.

Bedford glanced at Riki, and met her look of startled inquiry. What a ridiculous moment to realize how very appealing and expressive were her huge gray eyes. He thrust the disturbing thought from his mind. Thanking Jem, he nodded dismissal and watched as the groom retrieved the whip and resumed his polishing.

Shifting his hold on Hillary's arm, Bedford started once more toward the nearest entrance to the house. Friends one had known practically from one's cradle—well, dating back to Eton, at least—did not go about tipping one's brother a rise. Not without good and sufficient cause, at least. His frown lightened briefly. That fastidious dandy might have considered Hillary's waistcoat to be just that.

They turned through the shrubbery toward the tiled terrace behind the ballroom, and Hillary began to show signs of reviving more fully. It took more than a crack from a thick stick to down his intrepid brother, Bedford reflected in relief.

The boy straightened up, pulled his arm free from Riki's hold, and thanked her. "Pray forgive my lack of manners in not making you an elegant bow." The words sounded thick, and were uttered with exaggerated politeness, but a flash of his usual humor showed through. "Bedford may rake me over the coals for it later, but it would be far more improper to fall on my face, I assure you."

"I shall consider the bow made." A slight smile touched Riki's full lips.

Lips definitely worth kissing more than once, Bedford decided. He was sorry he couldn't try

147

again. He still hadn't tried for those freckles, either.

The French window opened and a frail man of medium height came out. He stopped, and his pale blue eyes widened in his kindly, if somewhat drawn, countenance. He ran an unsteady hand through thinning sandy brown hair and regarded the trio uncertainly.

"Has something happened? What have you done to yourself, Hillary? An accident?"

"He fell in the snow." Bedford brushed his questions aside. "I don't believe you've met my mother's guest, Miss van Hamel. This is Linton, my sister Clarissa's husband."

Lord Linton recovered, took Riki's hand and made an elegant leg. "Delighted," he murmured. "Fell, did you say, Bedford?" He shook his head. "Careless of you, my boy, but it's always the same, isn't it? You're forever getting into some scrape or another. But we shouldn't keep you out here talking. You're like to catch your death of cold standing in this wind." He shivered himself as he opened the door he had just closed, and he ushered them inside.

"What caused you to brave the elements?" Bedford stood back for Riki to enter, but kept a concerned eye on his brother-in-law.

George Linton waved this aside, though the gesture lacked strength. "I was coming to look for you. I couldn't imagine what you were doing out of doors on a raw day like this." He managed a smile.

"Not that raw. You came all the way down from London in worse yesterday." And apparently paid the price for it, today. From the looks of him, Linton must have passed an indifferent night.

"Don't remind me." The faint amusement faded from Linton's eyes, leaving his pale face more drawn than ever. "Only a sense of duty dragged me out, you may be sure. That, and young Hillary's refusing to tell me what you were about, and why you wanted to see Warwick so urgently."

"A matter of personal business. Not, as you seem to fear, connected with the War Office at all."

Linton's lined brow cleared. "Ah, then that's why you didn't just go to Whitehall. The young jackanapes here made it all sound like some great mystery." He shook his head, his lips curving upward as if with an effort. "There was no need for me to come at all, and risk the drafts in a carriage."

"That's what I told you," Hillary informed him, sounding aggrieved.

Linton nodded, but didn't appear to have paid much heed to Hil's comment. "What we need is a good hot toddy," he murmured.

"Why don't you ring for one?" Bedford suggested.

They crossed the huge, empty ballroom and emerged into the spacious corridor that led, by way of connecting drawing rooms, to the Great Hall. Before they reached it, Sir Julian Taggart rounded a corner and strode toward them, only to stop short at sight of the procession.

With a visible effort, Linton pulled himself together, resembling once more a senior member of His Majesty's government rather than the frail, infirm figure he had become. He raised politely surprised eyebrows. "I didn't realize a house party was gathering." He looked at Bedford as if it were his fault he had not been informed of Sir Julian's presence in advance.

"I didn't know, either." Sir Julian raised his quizzing glass to survey the others, then allowed it to drop.

An undercurrent of animosity ran between the two men. Bedford glanced from one to the other, noting it, then reluctantly stored it for later consideration. He returned to the more pressing matter at hand. "Has Newly taken care of you, Julian? Then if you will excuse us? I will join you as soon as I can." He pushed past, one arm still firmly supporting Hillary, and turned in at the door to the library.

Riki ran after him and cast a rapid glance about the spacious chamber filled with a multitude of volumes, large, comfortable furniture and the musty odors of leather and beeswax. As Bedford lowered Hillary onto a sofa, she snatched up a beautifully embroidered pillow and shoved it under his head to cushion it. The boy flashed his sweet, deceptively innocent smile at her.

Bedford rang for Newly, then set about examining Hillary's temple. Twice, his brother winced as his fingers probed the cut, but Hillary showed no signs of permanent damage.

"Well, doctor?" the boy asked as Bedford at last sat back. The swelling lay buried beneath his thick, unruly curls. Only the pallor of his face and the crusted blood that turned his dark brown hair to mahogany betrayed the injury.

"Your skull is hard enough to take any number of whacks." Bedford kept every trace of the sympathy he felt from his tone. "Now, lie still until we wash it off. Linton, will you pour him a brandy? There's a decanter on the table over there."

"You're making the greatest fuss over the merest trifle," Hillary protested, but took the drink gladly enough when his brother-in-law handed it to him.

Linton also poured one for himself, which he sipped slowly, savoring it as if it were the source of what little strength he possessed.

Newly entered, and Bedford sent the butler for a basin of water and bandages, which the man brought a few minutes later. With him came the always capable Mrs. Wicking.

Hillary eyed her askance. "No, really, I don't

want a pack of women hovering about me."

No one paid any heed to his outburst. Between them, Newly and Mrs. Wicking tended to his bruised and bleeding temple. Linton positioned himself at his side, offering at frequent intervals the brandy glass, which Hillary kept waving away.

While they worked, Bedford strode toward the hearth in which a fire blazed. Turning back, he eyed the group gathered about the sofa, and he fought back a smile. Poor Hil, to have that lot plaguing the life out of him.

His glance brushed over Linton, whose color slowly was returning, thanks to the brandy. He even seemed to stand more erect. Then Bedford's gaze came to an arrested stop at the toes of his normally glossy top boots. They were scuffed and showed traces of mud. Now, how could that have happened? His man would never permit him to leave his chamber in such a state, and he had only just started out the door when they encountered him.

As if aware of Bedford's scrutiny, Linton looked up, met that piercing regard, and looked down.

"What happened to your boots?"

Linton smiled weakly. "My man will probably give his notice," he said, shaking his head. "Dreadful, isn't it? And I took no more than a dozen steps from the terrace in search of you when I gave up and turned back for a warmer coat."

"I shall have to see to paving the path between the ballroom and the stable." Only with difficulty did Bedford keep the dry note from his voice. "Bye the bye, you never did tell me where Warwick is and why he didn't come."

"Didn't I? I'm sorry, it must have been the exhaustion of the journey. Really, I feel quite foolish, thinking I came on a matter of great urgency. Young Warwick was caught up in the midst of meetings, occasioned by your aborted trip and the conflicting reports of your disappearance."

"Your—" Riki looked up quickly.

"My crew made it back safely, you'll be glad to know," Bedford said smoothly, catching her eye. "Apparently they arrived in Whitehall only hours before Hillary."

He turned back to Linton. "It was good of you to come to tell me about them, but you shouldn't have put yourself to the trouble. Hillary is an able messenger." He poured his brother-in-law another brandy, and had the satisfaction of seeing his pallid complexion take on a more normal tone. The man should abandon London and spend more time in the healthy country air, Bedford reflected.

Sir Julian strolled in and paused just over the threshold. "What, are you all still here?" He watched Mrs. Wicking stand up, having put the finishing touches onto Hillary. He shuddered. "My dear boy, surely you are not going about looking such a figure of fun?"

Hillary bristled. "I won't leave that bandage on for long," he said darkly.

"Yes, you will." Bedford turned back to Sir Julian. "What brings you down to the Court?"

"To discover the end of your adventure, dear boy, what else?" he answered promptly. "You didn't think I could stay out of it, did you?"

Nor refrain from following them, perhaps? No, that was ridiculous. Why should Julian have gone to such pains just to keep them in sight? Had that been his desire, he could simply have traveled down with them and saved himself a great deal of bother. No, he must merely have decided shortly after their departure that whatever was about to take place at the Court might well provide him with some amusement. Bedford shook his head. Their mysterious carriage and its occupant remained a puzzle.

At the moment, though, it lay beyond his abilities to solve. The duties of a host, however, loomed large before him. Leaving the others in the library, he took Sir Julian to pay his respects to Lady Prudence.

Newly and Mrs. Wicking, carrying their soiled lint and bowls of water, took their leave to return to their own duties. Hillary headed for his chamber, with Linton still solicitously hovering at his side. Riki remained where she was, alone in the large, comfortable apartment, lost in thought.

Lord Linton, she gathered, worked in some capacity at the War Office with Bedford and David. Doing what? she wondered. He looked too ill to be of much use. She shrugged the question aside. The only thing that mattered right now was seeing David, talking to him — and taking him back to their own time. She tried hard not to think of the difficult explanations to be made when he suddenly turned up after having been believed dead for over two years. They'd work it out, somehow. Still, her spirits sagged.

Bedford's kiss — and worse, her reaction to it — proved depressing. What future could there be with a man who would be dead long before she was even born? They each belonged in their own era; that they had even met, that they had crossed the barriers, was an anomaly. It would have to be set right — and then they could never see each other again.

Suddenly, she longed to go home, where everything was safe and familiar. At the moment, though, that was impossible. She'd have to settle for some solitude, which was not likely to be guaranteed indoors.

On inspiration, she returned to her room, donned her borrowed pelisse and a pair of Felicity's leather half-boots that fitted reasonably well, and set forth to explore the grounds. Instead of going by way of the ballroom, she slipped through the front door, strolled down the drive, then turned to look back at the house.

It was beautiful, parts of it three stories, parts of it four, irregular in shape from constant building throughout the generations. Chimneys stuck up from everywhere and an old round stone tower rose near the front door. Mullioned windows and ivy thick on the walls added the final panache.

The snow had stopped, and the clean, crisp air beckoned. She set off briskly down the neatly raked drive toward the stable, which she passed without turning in to the cobbled yard. She had no desire to be stared at by the grooms. The rookery beckoned her, but now it held memories of Bedford's kiss. She hadn't recovered fully from the effects of that.

She strolled a little farther, then found a paving stone path and followed it. This brought her toward the back of the house, where she walked across what must be a beautiful expanse of lawn in the summer. Now, the patches that peeked through the light covering of snow were brownish and barren. Straggly, leafless trees rose at irregular intervals across the landscape, and a sheet of gray that glittered in the distance with unexpected sparkles must be an ornamental pond. A small gazebo, an imitation of a classical temple, had been built on its far side. To her right she glimpsed a barren rose garden.

She strode on, trying in vain to banish her lingering depression. A high hawthorn hedge bordered the lawn, and she headed toward its arched opening. Ducking under the leafy lintel, she found she had come upon a maze.

Intrigued, and momentarily diverted, she set

forth to explore its mysteries. It couldn't be too difficult; the shrub walls reached to well above her head, but the outer circumference didn't seem that great.

Following the age-old rule, she placed her left hand against the neatly pruned wall and started walking, never losing the contact. This led her down several short dead end passages, but steadily she worked her way farther from the entrance. She should reach the center any moment, she decided, when the deep rumblings of voices reached her.

Bedford. Her heart lifted at the thought of seeing him. She couldn't identify the low murmurings of his companion, but that didn't matter. She hurried forward.

"What are you implying, Nevvy?" the other speaker demanded, thus identifying himself as Sylvester.

"Nothing," came Bedford's calm response. "I merely asked if you saw anyone behaving in an unusual manner this morning behind the stable."

A momentary pause followed, then Sylvester's reflective response reached her. "Well, I saw you go into the rookery. Then a few minutes later, Miss van Hamel disappeared inside, as well." Amusement crept into his voice. "I would have joined you, dear boy, but thought I might be somewhat *de trop*."

Silence greeted this comment, and Riki could just imagine Bedford's offended sensibilities. Actually, Sylvester was quite right. They hadn't needed him in the least.

"Anyone else?" Bedford pursued in a tight voice.

"It is not my habit to spy on my fellow creatures," Sylvester responded with a virtuousness Riki found hard to believe.

The two men moved off together and Riki hurried after, convinced she would encounter them as

155

they left the center of the maze. But five steps later, she turned a corner and found herself standing opposite the entrance. A cleverly constructed maze, indeed. Bedford and his Uncle Sylvester must have been outside, and she must have been near the outer edge all along. She hoped the other puzzles that had crept into her life wouldn't be as difficult to solve.

She shivered, less from the chill air than from her troubled thoughts. She no longer felt like tackling the maze. Instead, she went back to the house and made her way to her room to take off her pelisse and dampened boots. She barely closed her chamber door behind her when a light tap sounded on the panel and Felicity peeped inside.

"I thought I saw you return." She bounced down on the bed, her bright eyes brimming with mischievous laughter. "Whatever has brought Linton here? Did Bedford tell you? Oh, do, pray, don't frown at me so. Is it all secret?"

"No, his arrival has nothing to do with my—my mission." Riki hated to disappoint her, but it wouldn't be wise to have the girl tip-toeing about the halls, listening at keyholes so she wouldn't miss anything "fun." Hillary already had a cracked skull from being in the wrong place at an apparently strategic moment.

Felicity's face fell. "Well, he's such a—a slow-top, I suppose I'd be surprised if he *were* involved. So *useless!* I cannot think what Clarissa sees in him, though to be sure, she's more interested in her important position than in adventures. Can you imagine, Miss van Hamel, having a sister who positively *worships* society?"

"I have one very much like that. And my other—" She broke off abruptly.

"Is she also bent on making a splendid marriage, or has she, already?"

156

Riki nodded. "I had such great hopes for Susie, too. I thought she showed more sense than Candace, but then her last letter was all filled with parties and the important people she was meeting."

Felicity nodded. "A season is quite enjoyable, of course, but one shouldn't take it so seriously. Or one might get stuffy, like Linton, or a slave of fashion like that odious Sir Julian."

"You don't like him?" This seemed an excellent time for investigation.

Felicity wrinkled her nose. "No. Can you honestly imagine a man whose most cherished ambition is to be the chief Pink of the Ton?"

"No, I don't think I can," Riki admitted with all honesty.

"All he ever thinks of is the set of his coat!" Felicity gave a delicious shiver. "He would make the most marvelous villain, would he not? So precise as he always is? I vow, I cannot like him. Nor can I imagine why Gil does. Yet Hillary and Aubrey both run to Sir Julian when they're in scrapes and don't want Gil to find out."

If anything, Riki reflected, that sounded like an excellent character reference. "What does your Uncle Sylvester do?" she asked abruptly.

Felicity giggled. "Wastes the ready," was her prompt response. "He is dreadfully expensive and forever hanging on Gil's sleeve since he became Bedford. I don't know what he wouldn't do for money," she added naively. "Oh!" A sudden smile of devilish delight lit her bright eyes and she stood abruptly. "I must dash. I have thought of the most delightful trick to play on Sir Julian. I've a pine cone I've been saving this age, and it's just aching to be put in someone's bed." She hurried from the room, apparently bent on putting her reprehensible scheme into immediate action.

Riki watched her jaunty departure with a slight

smile. She'd remember to check her own bed before crawling between sheets each night. She crossed to the window and stared out, her amusement fading as the puzzle returned to the forefront of her thoughts.

They had three likely—or rather, unlikely—suspects for that attack on Hillary—Linton, Sir Julian, and Sylvester. It simply didn't make any sense for any of them to have done it. Unless they didn't want to be caught spying on Bedford?

Obtaining material for blackmail might be a possibility. That might let out Sir Julian. He must have enough reminiscences from school days to hold over his friend's head. But he well might have wanted to learn more about her. Somehow, he had that appearance, as if he needed to know everything that occurred, especially if it were none of his business.

No, that didn't make any sense, either. Idle curiosity was not a sufficient motive for knocking out Hillary.

What of Lord Linton? Again, she faced the unanswerable question of *why?* Unless, perhaps, his obvious ill-health made him fear for his position. He might very well dread being pushed to the outside, especially if, as Felicity hinted, his wife married him only for his important rank in political circles. Would it have driven him to the point of distraction to think Bedford might be organizing a conference at Falconer's Court to which he had not been invited? Still, that was no reason to knock out Hillary.

Then there was always Sylvester. Could he have been trying to catch Bedford in a compromising situation to cadge money from his nephew? Next time she saw Felicity, she would have to ask how open-handed Bedford was.

She frowned. Of course, whoever had struck Hillary might not have been interested in the rookery at all. It might well have been nothing more than a stable lad up to some nefarious business and afraid of getting caught. And Bedford, she decided ruefully, had probably come to that conclusion over an hour ago.

Still, a discussion of that possible solution provided an excellent reason to go in search of him. She did, and found him in his library staring off into space, a deep frown lining his brow. He looked up as she entered and his expression lightened as he rose to his feet.

"Where is your uncle?" she asked by way of greeting.

His gaze remained disconcertingly on her lips. "In the cellars, selecting tonight's wine."

"Not sampling?" She seated herself across the desk from him. She liked the way his eyes followed her every movement, as if he found pleasure in the mere sight of her. She broke off that thought. She liked it *too* much. She couldn't let this wild, exciting feeling he roused in her get the upper hand. She would miss him terribly enough when she went home, as it was. And she *had* to return to her own world. She didn't belong here.

How soon do you think David will come?" she asked abruptly.

"He won't. I believe I will have to go up to London myself and drag him down here."

"Can you order him to come?" She managed to insert a note of skepticism into her voice.

He hesitated, then shook his head. "He can refuse if he wishes."

"He probably will, or he would have come in answer to your message."

"What do you suggest?" Amusement softened his dark eyes.

"Take me to London with you?"

Obviously, the suggestion didn't surprise him. The next moment, she realized the thought had already occurred to him. When he nodded, her heart lifted.

"The problem remains of where to take you."

Her face fell. "Hotels are out, aren't they. What should we do?"

A twinkle lit his eyes. "There seems to be only one course open to us. We must throw ourselves upon my mother's mercy."

Ten

A decidedly charming grin transformed Bedford's face, giving him a marked resemblance to Felicity as she set off in pursuit of her pine cone. "We will open Bedford House."

"You mean drag your poor mother up to London in this weather?"

"She'll be delighted—as long as we make it mysterious enough for her. She can't resist meddling in things."

Remembering the monolithic Lady Prudence, the severity of her purple silk belied by a distinct twinkle in her dark eyes, Riki reflected that the woman would dearly enjoy pulling the wool over society's eyes. It was almost a shame they couldn't tell her the whole truth. The story of a spy they concocted for Sir Julian had delighted her, though, and with that they had best all be content.

"What will you tell the others about leaving so soon after your arrival? Lord Linton and your uncle—"

"As neither was invited, I don't believe we need concern ourselves overly much." He stood. "I shall speak to my mother at once." He escorted her out of the room, but parted from her at the foot of the Great Stair.

Riki mounted the first step, then paused. If she went to London, she would be seen by any number of people. The thought frightened her. She was nobody here, she had no fortune to make her eccentric ways acceptable. This was only for a little while, she reminded herself. She could go home soon, where the van Hamel money awaited her and she knew who she was—as did everyone else she met. She had never realized until now just how much she relied on her family name.

At the moment, though, it was time to be brave—and under the circumstances, that meant blending in to this alien society. Thoughtfully, she bit the tip of one finger. Felicity was disposed to regard her as a heroine. If she appealed to her sense of intrigue—or, based on her brief acquaintance with the girl, on her sense of adventure and humor—she was sure to get hints on how to behave and dress.

She made her way slowly upstairs to her bedchamber. She would have to borrow more clothes, she supposed, though she couldn't like the idea. Yet she had no money. With luck, this whole business shouldn't take long—provided David didn't dig in his heels and refuse to cooperate. She could always resort to threats, if necessary.

Then she only had to face the lightning and thunder and the savage sea. What a situation to which to look forward!

Her room, she saw as soon as she entered, had been invaded in her absence. Two more dresses lay across the bed. She picked up one, a high-necked gown of a light woolen fabric with a single flounce at the hem. The other was an evening gown of pale green gauze with a low-cut bodice and full short sleeves confined in three bands.

More of Felicity's kindness, Riki reflected with a twinge of guilt. That solved one of her problems.

Now, if only dealing with David would be as easy!

A tap sounded on the door and Riki hurried to open it. A footman bowed slightly.

"If you please, miss, his lordship's compliments, and will you join him in her ladyship's sitting room?"

Riki thanked him and followed as he led the way through a maze of corridors to an ancient wing of the house she hadn't yet visited. The family's wing, she decided, for here, even more than in the hall where her chamber stood, there was an aura of hominess. A rather pretty yellow straw paper lined the walls above the wainscoting and landscapes and still lifes were interspersed with silhouettes and miniatures of what must be various family members.

The footman opened the door to an elegant salon decorated in regal tones of purple and gold. Lady Prudence Randall had certainly created a setting for herself. Riki felt as if she were being ushered into a royal presence. Lady Prudence sat enthroned on a huge purple velvet winged chair placed squarely before a high, arched window.

A fire burned merrily in the grate. Bedford stood before the hearth, leaning on the gilded mantle. He looked up as Riki approached, laughing glints dancing in his eyes.

Lady Prudence inclined her head, setting the ostrich plumes nodding vigorously from their precarious perch in the purple silk turban wound about her head. Perfect silver ringlets clustered about her high forehead. Matching purple silk swathed a figure that Riki had, the night before, likened to a brick wall. The impression didn't change. Not even the queen, she reflected, could appear more regal. And obviously, Lady Prudence was highly pleased with herself.

"My son informs me that I am to have the pleasure of your company in London," she said with an

163

indefinable air of disapproval.

"I fear it is too great an inconvenience, to ask you to travel at this time of year," Riki protested. "It looks ready to snow quite dreadfully."

The dark, hawk-like eyes sparkled. "If it is necessary to Bedford's work, I would be an unnatural parent indeed not to put my own comfort aside and lend him whatever assistance I may. If he needs a chaperone for you," she inclined her head once more, "then I shall of course not consider the weather."

More like, the weather wouldn't dare interfere with her plans. Riki met Bedford's amused glance and looked hastily away. "It would be a very great help to my—my mission, ma'am. If it is not too great an imposition, I would welcome your support."

"Of course it is an imposition," Lady Prudence declared, the twinkle in her eyes becoming more pronounced.

"Thank you." Bedford intervened. "If it will not incommode you too greatly, I would wish to set forth early tomorrow morning. As you have already gathered, Miss van Hamel's mission is of extreme urgency to our government."

"You may dispatch Sylvester and Linton for me, then, Bedford. And send up Newly and Mrs. Wicking."

With that, Riki gathered the interview was over. She stifled the impulse to curtsy and instead thanked her hostess and left the room. Bedford followed her out.

"I'm glad to see she didn't put you into a quake," he murmured as the door closed behind them.

"No, but will she mind? She can't like being forced to travel in such weather."

"She will enjoy it. She finds life dreadfully flat unless there's something to be done. And don't believe a word of her complaints. She has the constitution of an ox, and you will note she will never make use of the vinaigrette she will call for at regular intervals tomorrow."

Riki hesitated, then looked up into his rugged face. "We are causing you and your family a great deal of trouble, David and I."

The muscles of his jaw tightened. "Just get your meddling cousin out of my time, before I forget my promise to you not to call him out."

Preparations for the journey began at once. Bedford dispatched a groom to ride to London and alert the elderly retainer living there to make all ready for the arrival of the family. The remainder of the morning passed in a blur of activity for the staff— and Bedford—and Riki, doing her best to remain out of the way, retired to her chamber where she settled in a window seat to stare out over the peaceful, snow-covered gardens.

The serenity of the scene filled her with an unexpected contentment. She could be very happy in this world, it dawned on her. Everything was strange but wonderful. The air was clean, no industrial waste killed the lakes and rivers, no acid rains tormented birds and trees. No pollution of any kind marred the land. The innocence of pre-industrial-era life suited her exactly. Yes, she could be very happy in this time.

For the next few days, only. No longer. This wasn't where—or rather when—she belonged. It did her no good to think wistful thoughts of a life that could never exist for her.

She stood abruptly and went downstairs, in hopes of being given something constructive to do.

Hillary, who had passed the morning lying down in his room, put in an appearance in time to request an extravagant nuncheon. This suggestion was seconded by Sylvester, who then suggested a game of billiards. The two took themselves off after the meal, with Hillary firmly insisting their stakes be wholly imaginary, as he hadn't a feather to fly with and was willing to bet his uncle was in the same disreputable state. Sir Julian strolled along with them, listening to their easy banter with a slight smile touching his lips.

Bedford excused himself and left the table to join his bailiff. Lady Prudence, after consuming the last mouthful of a gargantuan meal, announced that she must busy herself with her correspondence. Felicity eyed Riki, but before she could speak, Lord Linton rose.

"Miss van Hamel, may I have the privilege of showing you about the shrubbery maze?"

She hesitated, for she had no desire to be private with anyone to whom she might betray herself, but it would be rude to refuse. She rose and allowed him to send a footman for her pelisse.

"Don't forget half-boots," Felicity declared, sorry to have her quarry thus removed.

In a very short time, Linton ushered Riki outside into the chill afternoon. Threatening clouds gathered above, but the snow held back. Probably it planned a bombardment for tomorrow, when they would be traveling.

She walked quickly, hoping against hope that the frail gentleman at her heels merely intended to be polite. She had known, of course, that wasn't the case. The door barely closed behind them when he spoke.

"It was a terrible thing, the boatwreck. One can only be thankful you and Bedford escaped with your lives."

"Yes, we were most fortunate." She moved ahead, hoping to discourage conversation. Had his department begun to phase him out? She couldn't blame them—but neither could she help sympathizing with one who found himself, because of his health, no longer in the midst of the excitement.

"And where do you come from, my dear?" He offered her his arm as they entered the shrubbery maze.

"America—Massachusetts." At least she had been to college there, and if called upon to recount landscape, she probably could manage something.

"Boston?" he asked, prodding gently.

"No." She left it at that, hoping he would take the hint.

He didn't. "And what brings you to England? It seems odd you would have been on the same ship as Bedford. No one at the War Office mentioned your presence on that journey."

"It was a carefully guarded secret, known only to a very few."

"I should have been told," he murmured, sounding more lost than aggrieved.

"I'm sure you would have been, had it been possible. It was kept secret from—from everyone, until I actually boarded that boat."

He brightened. "You mean Bedford didn't know, either?"

She shook her head, at last on secure ground. "I came as a complete surprise to Bedford."

They traversed the shrubbery paths without so much as a hesitation while they talked, arriving at last at a small central clearing in which four benches had been placed in a square, back to back, each facing an identical appearing entrance/exit. The maze had been cunningly created to confuse.

Linton handed her to a seat. "Are you cold, Miss van Hamel?"

For a moment she considered lying, to grab that excuse to escape his company and return to the house. But though the air was chill, they were protected from the wind by the high bushes. She made a show of fastening the top button on her pelisse,

167

then shook her head and smiled brightly.

"Do you work in the same department as Bedford?" After all, the best defense was a rousing good offense.

He inclined his head. "In a very minor capacity, only, these days. My failing health, you see. I was far more active in previous years."

Her heart went out to him. It must be dreadful to view only from the sidelines what one had previously led. No wonder he seized the opportunity to accompany Hillary to Falconer's Court. It would have made him feel important and busy once more.

"I understand you wanted to speak to Warwick," Linton pursued.

Riki bit her lip. Bedford had told him that it was a personal matter. The truth, whenever possible, was safest. "He is my cousin. My visit will be a complete surprise to him."

Linton nodded, apparently satisfied — at least for the moment. "A very pleasant one, I make no doubt. It's damned cold out here," he added.

He did seem to be feeling the weather. Wind and cold had reddened his pale complexion and his slight figure trembled as he folded his greatcoat more closely about himself.

"Perhaps we should return to the house." Riki stood, but hesitated over her selection of the path.

Apparently pleased to be needed in even so minor a capacity, Linton took her arm and guided her through the shrubs. They re-entered the house through the door into the library. Before they had gone many steps down the hall, the door into the billiard room opened and Sir Julian came out. He halted, raised his quizzing glass to better examine them, then allowed it to drop.

"Have you really been outside?" He gave an exquisite shudder.

Linton straightened his wilting shoulders. "A good

brisk walk never does one harm."

"Never?" Sir Julian considered, then dismissed the matter as beneath his consideration. "A leisurely stroll down Bond Street, perhaps, or a gentle airing in the Park. But you're begging, simply begging, for an inflammation of the lungs to go out on such a raw day as this. Really, Linton, I'd advise you to seek your room and send for a mustard plaster. At once."

"I shall change, certainly. Miss van Hamel?" He bowed over her hand, took his leave of her, and strode off with great dignity.

Sir Julian swung his glass by its velvet riband. "Poor Linton. That was his intention, of course. The mustard bath, I mean. Now he may pretend it was forced on him." He shook his head.

"That wasn't kind to make sport of the poor man. He is obviously in uncertain health."

"Was I unkind? I thought I merely rid us of an intolerable bore."

Riki awarded him a scant half smile and turned away. She didn't like Sir Julian, she decided—despite Bedford's obvious trust of the man. Probably that friendship went back to a time before Sir Julian's funning humor turned acidic.

She made her way quickly to her room to take off her pelisse, but found the chamber to be full of people and chaos. This settled into the abigail assigned to her, Felicity, and Miss Bexhill. A large trunk lay open on the floor and into this, under Felicity's direction, the two maids placed neatly folded gowns that had been wrapped in sheet upon sheet of tissue paper.

"What is all this?" Riki demanded, staring at a forest green riding habit that lay across the bed, waiting its turn to go into the trunk.

"Just a few things you'll need." Felicity smiled brightly at her. "You are not to think there is nothing to do in town at this time of year, just because the season hasn't started yet. All the public men and their families will be there, and as soon as it is discovered we have arrived, we will be invited to various parties."

"We will?" Riki regarded her uncertainly. She had hoped to be seen by as few people as possible. With Felicity in charge, that seemed to be impossible.

"We'll have the gayest time." Felicity's enthusiasm neared the bubbling point. "My sister Clarissa is in town, and so are my dear friends, Miss Athercombe and Mrs. Marley. You'll love Marie Marley, I know you will. She's a widow already, and she's barely four years older than I am."

"How terrible for her."

"No, it isn't in the least, for her husband was the most dreadful brute, and it was a—a Judgment from Heaven when he was struck down in the Peninsula eighteen months ago."

Miss Bexhill clucked her tongue in disapproval, and Felicity turned her large, teasing eyes on her.

"Pray, don't pull down your mouth and frown, so, Bexy. I know my tongue rattles on, but it is only to my dear Miss van Hamel, and she would never betray me. *Would* you?" She appealed to Riki.

"Of course not. We probably won't be in town for long, though, for once I have spoken with someone there, I must continue with my mission."

"With David Warwick." Felicity nodded wisely.

"How do you know that?" Riki regarded her in wonder. But of course she'd know. Hillary did not appear to be one to keep secrets from a persistent sister.

Felicity dimpled roguishly. "It will be dreadfully cold in town, but I have any number of gowns you should be able to wear." The girl sighed. "I do wish I had your lovely figure."

Riki blinked. There was nothing wrong with the

girl's slender hips. She'd give a great deal to carve off a few inches in that department, herself.

"It is the most fortunate circumstance that you are able to wear my gowns, is it not?" Felicity went on.

"It is," Riki said with real feeling. "For me, at least. I don't know how I shall ever be able to repay you."

"Oh, I shall merely have Bedford buy me some new ones," she said airily.

"Then it seems it is Bedford I must repay." Adding more to the debt she already owed him. She did not look forward to the day of reckoning . . . when they would part forever.

"Linton plans to travel with us, but since Uncle Sylvester also intends to accompany us, you may be sure we shall be a merry party after all."

"Your uncle is going to London?" Riki watched the abigail fold away the riding habit. "Excuse me."

She hurried out of the room. The fact that Sylvester and Linton were both going to London with them was disturbing.

She found Bedford in his library again. He looked up as she entered in response to his call, and the frown vanished from his features. It returned the next moment.

"Is something the matter?"

"I don't know. Probably not." She perched on the edge of a large armchair across from him.

He rose and came around to her side, then leaned back so he half sat against the mahogany surface of his desk. "What is it?" he pursued, gently.

"Why is your uncle going to London with us?"

A soft chuckle escaped him, deep and reassuring. "Because, my dear—Miss van Hamel, he has, once more, outrun the constable. At frequent intervals, he finds it necessary to bury himself in the depths of the country—at someone else's expense, of course— until quarter day brings him about again. If we

171

leave, then so must he."

She nodded, relieved at so simple an explanation. "When Felicity told me that both he and Lord Linton intended to accompany us—" She broke off and shook her head. "I am being foolish."

"It has been rather unsettling of late for both of us, hasn't it?" he agreed. "But neither that carriage nor what happened to Hillary can in any way be involved with you. It's not as if we don't *know* who is betraying the British cause. We are just in high fidgets because we have a secret we want no one to guess."

She nodded, glad of his common sense. "I know. Yet if you told me Sir Julian, also, had decided to go to London instead of to his home in Brighton, I'd begin to think we were in the middle of some dreadful conspiracy."

The expression faded from Bedford's face, leaving his features shuttered. He said calmly: "He has."

Eleven

Riki stared intently at the imposing facade of the War Office building in Whitchall, waiting, shivering from the cold as she huddled in the carriage. More than thirty minutes had already crept by, yet still Bedford had not come out of his office—with David. Each time a stately gentleman exited the building, she jumped, and her heart beat erratically until she realized it was only a stranger.

She couldn't sit still, she kept craning her neck, anxious for her first glimpse of her cousin after two years of thinking him dead. She still wasn't certain whether she would throw her arms about his waist or her hands around his neck. He deserved strangling, but she could hardly wait to see him.

At last, after what felt like hours, Bedford emerged—alone. As he neared the crested town-drag in which she sat, she could see the grim tenseness of his expression. Her heart sank into her stomach.

"Warwick is not there."

"What do you mean?" She caught his arm as he opened the door, and her fingers clutched his sleeve. "Has something happened?"

"Only of his own doing. It seems he has taken a short leave of absence." He climbed in beside her and slammed the door closed. "How dare he, when he'd received my message to meet me at the Court!

He must know how da—that it's important for him to see me."

"Maybe he's gone to the Court," Riki suggested.

Bedford stared at her. "I'll send a messenger at once."

Probably David and the messenger would cross paths, Riki thought, but prudently held her tongue. If anything, Bedford was even more upset than she.

"We'd better plan our reception of him," she decided, trying to tease him out of his mood. "Should we throw a party? Or should we solve the whole problem by inviting him on a sailing trip, the date to be determined by prevailing weather conditions?"

To her relief, that brought a slight smile to his lips.

By the time they returned to Bedford House, he had unbent considerably, though she still sensed his anger beneath. He jumped to the paved street and reached back to assist her out. She hesitated, holding his hand tightly as she joined him on the flagway.

"Remember your promise," she begged softly.

"*If* you can keep yours and get your bloody cousin out of here."

They entered the house to find Hillary and Felicity engaged in lively game of jackstraws with a young gentleman of approximately three years. Bedford's ill temper evaporated upon the instant and he swooped down on his young nephew and swung him up in his arms.

"Is Clarissa here?" he asked as he settled the boy on his hip. A reserved expression settled over his features where a moment before he showed only untrammeled pleasure in the boy's company.

"She's gone shopping," Felicity explained. "She was quite put out to find Miss van Hamel from home. She left Nurse here and is giving Mamma a chance to see Lawrence—or so she says. *I* think she wants an excuse to come back."

Bedford nodded, and Riki sensed he was relieved to find Clarissa gone. Apparently, these three were not overly fond of their sister.

Bedford carried the boy over to Riki and little Lawrence instantly buried his pale blond curly head in his uncle's shoulder.

"Hey!" Gently, Bedford coaxed the boy to look up, then performed the introduction. Young Master Lawrence Linton bestowed a beatific smile upon Riki.

"How do you do?" she responded solemnly and offered her hand.

The boy giggled and quickly reburied his face, nuzzling into Bedford's cravat. Riki was charmed but whether by Lawrence or this new aspect of Bedford's character, she wasn't certain.

A middle-aged woman of determined aspect bustled in, carrying a baby. Felicity jumped to her feet to take the infant girl from Nurse.

"This is little Emily," she announced to Riki.

"Whose sole distinction in life so far," Hillary put in, "is that she ruined the little season for her mamma by forcing her to be confined in October."

Nurse made a disapproving clucking noise and Felicity laughed. Bedford kept a straight face with a visible effort, and drew Nurse aside to discuss her charges' progress.

Riki slipped away from the delightful domestic scene to run upstairs to the Yellow Room, the large chamber allotted to her, to take off her bonnet. Seeing Bedford with his family proved an enlightenment, and she was loathe to break the homey spell for him. She didn't belong in it, she reminded herself. She was an outsider, permitted no more than tantalizing glimpses of his world before returning to her own. The thought brought a pang, which she quickly stifled. There was no point in longing for something she could never have.

She dawdled over straightening her hair, then at last, knowing she could delay it no longer, returned to the morning room.

Bedford, oblivious of his title and dignities, sat on the floor while little Lawrence bounced on his lap, giggling with delight as his uncle tried with exaggerated ineffectiveness to reclaim a jackstraw from him. The viscount looked up as Riki entered and a dull flush crept into his complexion. He tried to stand at once, over the loud protests of the indignant child.

It proved too much for her. Without hesitation or thought for her non-wrinkle-proof clothes, Riki forestalled him and joined them on the Aubusson carpet. Before they could once again spread out the sticks, however, a young woman of about Riki's own age swept into the morning room, drawing off her gloves as she came. Riki blinked, for before her stood a younger version of Lady Prudence, minus that formidable dowager's air of enjoyment.

Clarissa, Lady Linton, removed her hat, dislodging the dark brown tresses that had been carefully cropped short about her face and teased into ringlets. Her eyes were as dark as those of the rest of her family, though lacking the humor Riki had come to welcome. Her plumpness was of the solid sort that would shortly become stoutness on her meager inches. Another Randall brick wall.

"And this must be Miss van Hamel. How delighted I am to meet you." Instantly, Clarissa went to Riki's side, taking her hand as she gushed her greeting.

Riki answered politely as she rose from the floor. She experienced the disturbing sensation that her social importance was being assessed.

"How delightful," Clarissa repeated. "Why, it is almost time for a light nuncheon, is it not? I shall stay, Bedford.

"Nurse, do take the children upstairs to the old schoolroom. They are the greatest dears," she explained to Riki, "and of course I simply dote on them, but they make such a racket during a meal, it is simply impossible to think." She waved an airy hand, dismissing the subject of her offspring.

Lady Prudence marched into the room in time to hear this last, and regarded her daughter through glacial eyes. "It is my wish they remain."

For a moment there was a facing off, then Clarissa gave way with ill grace. They adjourned to the breakfast parlor, where a cold collation awaited them on the sideboard. Clarissa left the tending of the two children to Nurse and Felicity, and concentrated once more on Riki as they settled at the table.

Her knowledgeable eye ran over Riki's gown and her smile became a shade warmer. "Will you be staying long in London? Linton wasn't able to tell me."

"Lord Linton mentioned my visit?" Riki asked, surprised.

Clarissa shook her head, setting her dusky ringlets bouncing about her face. "No, odious man that he is. He didn't breathe a word of you until I particularly asked him. It is to my Uncle Sylvester I'm indebted for the information. Men can be so tiresome, they never give a thought to *important* things. I'm holding a *salon* next Thursday, and you simply must come. As Bedford can tell you, the political world flocks to my door. You will be the rage, I feel quite certain."

Hence the invitation, Riki reflected dryly. Why, though, had Sylvester spoken of her—and why had

Lord Linton not? She cast a perplexed glance at Bedford, but his frowning gaze rested on his sister.

He rose abruptly. "If you have finished, Miss van Hamel? Perhaps we can settle that matter now. If you will excuse us?" He addressed the last to his family.

Riki stood with alacrity. "So many pressing duties, when one represents one's government," she murmured, shaking her head.

She hurried out of the room. "Business?" she whispered to Bedford as she preceded him into the hall. "Is there something you haven't told me?"

He closed the door behind them. "There is. My sister is one of the most avid gossip-mongers in the *ton*. I strictly forbade Linton to mention you. I should have known Sylvester couldn't resist. It was undoubtedly her intention to steal a march on the rest of society by being the first to present such an unusual American visitor, just dropping a hint, of course, that you have business in government circles. In another minute, you would have been subjected to a detailed interrogation of your ancestry, connections, and anything else that might make you a suitable subject for *on dits* and loose talk."

"But—she is Lord Linton's wife! Surely she must know better than to talk of political events. Can't you impress on her that I'm a state secret or something?"

"I make no doubt it was Linton's hinting at just that which brought her around so quickly."

Riki sighed, then realized he was leading her down the stairs. "Where are we going?"

"My bookroom. It's the only place we're likely to get any peace until Clarissa and her brood leaves." He stood back for her to precede him down the corridor.

"Yes, I noticed how you disliked your nephew and

niece."

Bedford chuckled. He ushered her into a comfortable book-lined apartment. Two sofas were arranged at one end of the room, on either side of a blazing hearth. A table had been placed between them, and a rich rug stretched beneath. Riki crossed to the hearth and stood before it, looking down.

"What will you do if Warrick won't listen to you?" The question sounded gentle—deceptively so.

"He will." She allowed no doubts to sound in her voice.

"And then?"

She studied the flames for a moment. "Then, as you requested, I must get him out of your vicinity."

"Yes, you must."

She looked up, startled by how much savageness he packed into those three words. He stood just two steps behind her, his brow lowered, which gave him a ferocious expression. His eyes burned into hers.

"Bedford—?"

"Gil!" He snapped his name at her. "Oh, damn it!" He closed the space between them and dragged her into his arms.

His mouth came down over hers, urgent, a release of his frustration. For a long moment she clung to him, knowing she shouldn't, that it wasn't wise. Yet she wanted Gil with a desperation that went beyond reason.

His hands, so gentle for a man of his solidity and strength, caressed her throat, then trailed over her shoulders, making her long for them to explore the rest of her body. The pressure of his mouth became less intense, more seductive, driving any semblance of intelligent thought from her mind. She only *felt*, and the sensations that coursed through her were unsettling and erratic and wonderful.

Abruptly he released her, and took several unsteady steps away. He ran a hand through his already disordered locks.

"That was unpardonable."

"No, it wasn't." Her breath still came rapidly, and she ached for his arms to fold about her once more. "If you regret kissing me, that would be unpardonable."

A rueful smile touched his firm lips. He strode back to her and cupped her chin between both his hands. "Dear God, what is it that makes you so irresistible? Those adorable freckles?" He drew his finger along the side of her nose and along her cheek. "Or that you're forbidden fruit?"

She caught his hand and pressed it against her throat. "Not forbidden—only temporary. Just because it can't last forever doesn't mean we can't share *anything*."

He pulled his hand free as if her flesh burned him. "You're not—" With an effort, he controlled his voice. "You're a lady, not a courtesan," he finished stiffly.

"I'm also from a different time." She traced the line of his jaw, then tangled her fingers in the thick pepper and salt hair that just brushed the nape of his neck. "Women have learned it's all right to express what we feel."

He set her from him, gently but firmly. "I haven't."

She raised a skeptical eyebrow.

Dull color flooded his face. "Not with a lady," he snapped. "Damn it, Riki, we come from vastly different worlds! It may be all right for you—" He broke off, as if the concept were inconceivable to him.

"We must forget this happened," he asserted. "We have work to do—the work that brought you into my world in the first place."

Suddenly—annoyingly—he was his normal efficient self. He turned off his emotions as if they were one of the light switches he'd found so fascinating on her island. She tried to follow his example, but it wasn't easy.

"David," she stated. "Why don't we try to call on him? Even if we don't find him, we might learn where he is or when he's expected back."

Bedford nodded. "I'll go at once."

"We'll go."

He shook his head. "A lady cannot call at the residence of a single gentleman, even if they are cousins."

Her face fell. "What will you do? Bring him to me here?"

"No, there are too many people in the house. I'll set up a meeting place and make it sound so intriguing he won't be able to resist."

"Why not just tell him I'm here?"

"I don't think that's wise."

"You don't think he'll want to see me?" Even to herself, she sounded hurt.

He hesitated. "If he's as fanatical as you say, do you think he'll willingly give up his games-come-to-life?"

Bedford was right. David might well refuse to listen to reason. If that happened—if she couldn't convince him— Bedford might well call him out as he'd threatened to do. David wouldn't stand a chance.

Bedford departed, leaving her sitting in the bookroom, staring moodily into the fire. After half an hour of fruitless worry, she roused herself, feeling stifled in the warm chamber. She stood and shook out her skirts, only to stop as she heard a vaguely familiar voice outside the door.

"Don't fret, man, don't fret. I'll just wait for Bedford in here. Have you topped off the Madeira decanter?" The door opened and Sylvester Randall strolled in, leaving the distraught butler standing in the corridor.

He saw Riki and stopped dead. "Miss van Hamel?" His voice came out as a squeak. In a moment, he recovered. "How delightful, my dear." He came forward to take her hand, as if he had not just parted company with her the evening before, after their arrival in London.

"Mr. Randall." She allowed him to raise her fingers to his lips.

He released her and strolled to the table where two decanters and several glasses stood. He filled one of the crystal goblets for himself, and closed his eyes as he took a sip. He rolled the wine about his mouth, swallowed, and sighed in pure ecstasy.

"Heaven. Absolute heaven, my dear Miss van Hamel. No one could stock a cellar like my late and dearly lamented brother."

"If you are looking for Bedford, he has gone out."

"So I have been informed. I merely sought refuge from my niece, whom I already had the dubious pleasure of meeting this morning. Has Lady Linton been here long?"

Riki nodded and bit back a grin at Sylvester's shudder. "Do you not delight in your great-niece and -nephew?"

He fixed a disapproving eye on her. "I have no affinity for children. Doubtless I shall like them well enough when Lawrence learns to hold a dice box and Emily can sit a pony." He refilled his glass and lovingly swirled the contents.

Sensing her presence was *de trop*, and that she interfered with Sylvester's *tête a tête* with the Madeira, she made her excuses and slipped out of the room. What to do now? Gossip with Clarissa? She had a much better idea. Bedford had taught her the rudiments of piquet and she intended to improve and surprise him at the next opportunity.

She ran Hillary to earth in the music room, where he sat idly strumming his fingers along the pianoforte. "Are you busy?" she asked unnecessarily.

He made a face at her. "That depends. Has Clarissa left?"

She shook her head. "I need your assistance with something."

His whole face brightened. "No, really? Some errand you need run to Whitehall?"

"You are doomed to disappointment, I fear. I need a partner for piquet."

His face fell. "Is that all?"

"What do you mean, 'is that all?' It has become my goal to defeat your brother."

At that, Hillary laughed. "No one beats Bedford."

He was more than willing to exchange pastimes, however, and she shortly found herself listening to his rapid and frequently unintelligible explanation of scoring and strategy.

The door opened, and Bedford leaned negligently against the jamb, a slight smile touching his lips as his gaze rested on Hillary, who remained intent on his cards.

"She says you taught her to play," the young gentleman declared without looking up.

"Yes," Bedford admitted.

"She's like to beat you all to flinders in another couple of months." He tossed down the cards he held and shook his head. "Damn if I've ever met a female with such a grasp for cards!"

"Language, Hil," Bedford said mildly.

Riki, who had been studying his face for clues, finally gave in to her anxieties. "Did you see him, Bedford?"

The viscount nodded. "I did. And I kept my

183

hands off his throat."

"Whose?" Hillary looked from one to the other, hopeful. "Are you planning to darken someone's daylights, Gil?"

"What did you say to him?" Riki demanded.

"Very little. He has promised to meet my 'friend' in the Park tomorrow morning."

Riki let out the breath she held. "That's settled, then." The next moment, her smile of relief faded. "Isn't it?"

Bedford straightened slightly, his expression unreadable. "We shall have to wait and see."

Twelve

Riki, dressed in the forest green riding habit given to her by Felicity, perched precariously on her sidesaddle and shivered. It was freezing in Hyde Park. No wonder the fashionable world didn't venture to London until the late spring, if the ladies were expected to wander around in flimsy gowns with only the slightest protection from the elements. A late January morning was no time to venture out of doors.

Bedford reined in beside her. "How are you doing?"

"Fine." She made a face at him. "You'd never believe I was brought up with riding lessons, would you? I can't imagine anything farther from dressage than a sidesaddle."

Bedford shook his head. "What I can't imagine is a female riding astride." He looked down the long expanse of tanbark, where not so much as a single rider could be glimpsed, then looked for at least the fifth time at his watch.

"David never could get anywhere on time."Riki shifted in her saddle, trying to find a more comfortable position, and merely succeeded in setting her horse sidling.

A slight smile relieved the severity of Bedford's expression. "I just want this over with."

"You're not the only one," Riki murmured, and turned her attention back to the riding path before them.

Bedford started his horse moving, and Riki's went right along with him. They had gone no more than twenty yards when a tall chestnut came into view. The rider slowed to a walk, approaching with care as if watchful of trouble. As he neared, Riki recognized the tall, slender build of her cousin, his curling blonde hair so much like every other van Hamel except Riki.

David was alive. Elation surged through her. She hadn't really believed it until now. Her heart beat, rapid and strong, and unshed tears prickled her eyes. David was here, unharmed, not lost beneath the icy waves of the English Channel.

He came forward until his beloved features were clear, from his classically straight nose down to his squared chin. His gaze passed briefly over Bedford and he nodded, then he turned his attention to Riki. His eyes widened and his mouth dropped open.

"Riki?" Her name came out in a shocked gasp.

"Hallo, David. Surprised to see me?"

"Surprised? Good God, I—I'm stunned! Riki!" He swung off his mount, ran the last few steps toward her startled horse and grasped her about the waist. Easily he swung her free of the saddle, then around in a circle as he hugged her, laughing, clasping her slight body to him. Tears streamed unashamedly down his cheeks. "Riki! I can't believe it! It's really you! But how—"

He set her on her feet at last, controlling his ecstatic delight with a palpable effort. Still, one hand cupped her cheek and an expression of disbelief mingled with doting fondness lit his bright hazel eyes.

She sniffed and sought for a pocket her riding habit didn't possess. David located a handkerchief and handed it to her.

"*How?*" he repeated. "Dear God, Riki, I've never been gladder to see anyone! But how did you get here?"

"The same way you did." She mopped at her streaming eyes. If he weren't here, before her . . . She hugged him once more. "I thought you were dead. We all did."

He managed a shaky laugh. "I doubt that upset the others very much. If there were any way of letting *you* know I was all right, though, I would have, you know that. But *you!* Why—" He broke off, unable to find words. Somehow, he held her hands, gripping them tightly. "Did—did you go sailing, too?"

She nodded. "On purpose. Oh, David, what we've gone through! Bedford washed up on Falconer's Folly after being boatwrecked."

"On—in the future? Our time? So that's why the sailors thought him lost." David drew a deep breath and turned to regard his associate. "Why didn't you tell me yesterday?"

Bedford, still atop his horse, looked down on the other two, his expression unreadable. "I didn't want to take the surprise out of this meeting."

"Lord, it's a surprise, all right." The shock began to wear off, leaving David thinking more clearly. He returned his attention to Bedford. "You—you made the journey across time *twice?* It's possible to get back? I—I thought it was some fluke, a once-in-a-million-years happening!" He grabbed one of Bedford's reins and gazed up intently into the viscount's face. "Is there a—a key? Or some trick to it? Can you do it whenever you want?"

Bedford shook his head. "I have no idea."

The grim lines of Bedford's face finally penetrated Riki's euphoria, and she came back to earth with a resounding crash, She had been so very relieved to find David still alive, but now anger surged through her, directed at her cousin for causing such trouble, for the danger of the journey she made, for all of her pent-up fears and terrors.

"David, how could you!" She grabbed his arm and shook it. "How could you try to alter history?"

"Alter what?" He dragged his searching gaze from Bedford's rigid face. "What are you talking about? Oh, you mean just my being here. I didn't have a choice, did I? Lord, when I woke up on that beach, then found everyone dressed so strange—" His voice tightened and he broke off. "God, I was scared. I—I couldn't believe it, at first." A shaky laugh broke from him. "I thought all that gaming must have affected my mind, that I'd either gone insane or I was dreaming. But it didn't go away."

"So you decided to continue your wargaming *here!*" Riki accused.

A sheepish grin replaced his frown over his uneasy memories. "Well, can you blame me? Lord, I had the chance actually to take part in it all! As soon as I began to believe I was really here, that the Peninsular campaign was actually taking place *now*, I presented myself to the War Office and told Lord Bathurst enough about French strategy so he took me on as a junior advisor."

"To his expense! Oh, David, how could you betray him?"

"*Betray* him? You couldn't have wanted me to *help* the British, could you?" He stared at her, aghast.

"That might change history! Lord, I could have told them enough so they'd have given Boney a rousing trouncing last summer! But then the war would have been over and God knows what would be different in our time." There was no trace of blasphemy in his words.

"But—" Riki stared at him, bewildered. "Haven't you been feeding them misinformation to help the French? You always took Napoleon's side in your gaming. Isn't that what you've been doing here?"

"Lord, it was a temptation," he admitted. "Do you know, I honestly considered it? Wargaming for real? I would have given anything if I thought I could get to France and see Napoleon's field marshals in action. He's making such a serious muddle of his affairs."

"Why didn't you?" Bedford sounded merely polite, as if he weren't really interested in the answer.

"You've never heard me try to speak French, *that's* why I didn't. I can read it, all right, but not even living near Jersey for a couple of years could make me understand it when someone talks. You should hear Marie's—" He broke off abruptly.

"Would you have helped the French if you could?" This time, curiosity sounded in Bedford's voice. The cold fury Riki had glimpsed in his face only minutes before had faded into skepticism.

David hesitated, then shook his head, setting his carefully curled blond locks ruffling in the wind. The Regency-era hair style suited him, Riki thought.

"No, I wouldn't have dared give them any advantage. Oh, the temptation was there, you better believe it was." A wistfulness entered his hazel eyes, and he shook his head in regret. "I wouldn't have dared, though," he repeated. "If Boney routed the British in the Penininsula, he'd have been free to take his full forces into—" He broke off, casting a guilty glance at Bedford.

"Into Russia," Bedford supplied for him.

David stared in surprise at his superior.

"You're forgetting," Riki broke in, destroying the illusion of omniscience. "He's seen your gaming room on the island. And speaking of taking unfair advantages of the other side, I seem to remember you making detailed notes on everything you saw while you were in there."

"Every detail is accurate," David nodded, smug in spite of the rather unusual circumstances.

"I'm delighted to know it." Bedford's voice sounded tight. "And you are quite right, Miss van Hamel, I will not be able to pass on the information I learned in that manner."

On the whole, she decided it was for the best. Then the meaning of David's words of the last few minutes suddenly sank in. "He's not a traitor! Bedford, I *told* you David would never do such a terrible thing!"

"If you believed that, then why did you insist on coming back in time to talk to him?" he snapped.

She couldn't answer that, for in truth she *had* suspected David of trying to live out his fantasies. Or had there been another reason she'd wanted to accompany Bedford on that crazy, impossible journey? She looked up, met the brooding gaze from those gleaming, hawk-like eyes, and knew there had been.

"Whatever made you think I was fouling things up?" David demanded, affronted.

"Because one of the battle scenes had been—" Riki broke off and stared at Bedford. "One of the scenes *had* been changed, remember? To give a definite advantage to the French! We both were convinced."

Bedford nodded, and returned his glare to David. "But you claim you haven't been interfering."

David looked from one to the other, encountering only accusation. "Now look, Riki, you know me better than that. *I didn't try to change history.* Period. End of discussion!"

"But if you didn't, then who *has* been? David, there is no doubt about it. Something happened that changed the course of the battle at—what was it, Bedford?"

"Ciudad Rodrigo."

David nodded slowly, but frowned. "That was an eleven day siege, wasn't it? Lord, anything could have happened. If one person was killed at the wrong time, particularly an officer, utter chaos could have broken out."

"The French nearly won."

David nodded absently, intent on his thoughts. "I'd need to see all the dispatches and learn all the details before I could tell you what went wrong." He shot a half-humorous look at Bedford. "The reports aren't in, yet, needless to say."

"Needless," Bedford agreed. "But the point is, something did happen that changed the course of the battle."

"It wasn't me."

"What else could it have been?" Riki looked from one to the other as terrible thoughts jostled each other within her. "If David didn't do it, then someone else did. *Something* happened differently."

"Because I'm here." David said the words slowly, as if they were dragged out of him. "But that—that's impossible. I've been so careful! Damn it, Riki, I *know* the potential consequences! I've taken the greatest pains only to suggest or endorse those plans the British actually followed, and warn about the French moves that the British effectively blocked."

All three fell silent for a moment, considering.

"Could just the mere fact of David's presence be making a difference?" Riki asked at last. "Aren't there some laws of physics, or something, that say there can only be just so much matter in the universe? Have you—and now me—upset the balance?"

Bedford looked skeptical. "That might explain the frequency of the thunder storms, not the change in French strategy."

"It *might,*" David said slowly. "If atmospheric conditions were altered sufficiently. Say it rained for so long that the ground was soft enough for easy trench digging. Or maybe it was too wet and trenches had to abandoned?"

Bedford frowned. "That might be part of it, but I can't believe it explains it all. There were far-sweeping changes in the course of the battle. No, I think there is more to this."

He drew out his watch, glanced at it, then closed it with a snap. "I think it will be for the best if you go with me to Whitehall at once and resign your position, Warwick."

"But—" David broke off, his expression harried. "You don't believe me. Damn it, Bedford, I'm not misleading your War Office!"

"I didn't say I didn't believe you." The viscount's face remained devoid of expression. "I merely said it would be best, under the circumstances, if you were to resign. That way there can be no slip of the tongue."

"Please, David." Riki added in her plea, averting an argument. "We've got to return home as soon as possible, anyway."

"Return." An odd half-smile just touched his lips.

"God how I've wanted that sometimes. But how?"

Riki met Bedford's glowering gaze. "The very next electrical storm, we'll have to try. We can't stay here, you must see that."

David's face took on a mulish expression. "No, as a matter of fact, I don't."

Riki stared at him blankly. "But—"

"I'm not ready yet. Look, Riki, I've been *living* here for over two years. I have friends, a whole life, people I don't want to walk away from."

Riki knew exactly what he meant. Deliberately, she didn't look at Bedford. "All right, there's no sign of any thunder and lightning, anyway. I suppose we can stick around for a few more days."

"You'll like it here, Riki. I never cared much for doing the pretty back home, but it's different, now. It's more fun."

"Just another of your games." She didn't even bother to keep the dryness out of her voice. "You've been wanting to live in this period for as long as I can remember, so quit trying to kid me. But home we must and shall go, David, before we — any lasting damage here."

He nodded, though he didn't look convinced. He cast an uncertain glance up at Bedford, still atop his stamping horse. "What will I tell Bathurst?"

"That you've received a summons from home. From your family. Ri—Miss van Hamel tells me our countries are about to become embroiled in a rather nasty war. Let's not add to it by making him think it is your government calling you back."

"Why don't I set sail immediately then? And before you say 'you should,' let me tell you I have no intention of leaving London at present."

"Just say you're waiting for me, and I still have unfinished business," Riki declared.

"I will escort Miss van Hamel home, then meet

193

you in Whitehall." Bedford held his gaze, commanding obedience. "I imagine our business will occupy us most of the day. You may see your cousin at dinner this evening, if you will join us."

David cast Riki a rapid glance, and a dull flush crept under his tan. "I've got another engagement that I—I can't cry off from. Can I meet you somewhere later? The Dalmonts' card party, maybe?"

Bedford nodded. "Very well. But I will see you in my office within the hour. You may oblige me by assisting your cousin into the saddle."

Meekly, Riki submitted to David's surprisingly adept help. The suspicion crossed her mind that he had assisted many young ladies into saddles during the last two years. The dreadful thought that perhaps David had met a young female and formed a—what did they call them in this time, a lasting passion?—yes, a lasting passion, dawned on her and refused to be banished.

Her eyes drifted to Bedford, who spurred his horse ahead. Grasping David's hand, she bade him goodbye until evening, then hurried after her companion.

They rode in silence for some time, and at last she risked a peek at him. Deep lines marred his high brow and his eyes gleamed with a dark, piercing light. At a rough guess, she would say that viscount Bedford was not pleased.

"What's wrong?" she asked finally, when he showed no sign of speaking.

"Do you believe him?" he asked abruptly.

"About not helping the French? Yes, I do."

"You thought him capable of it when we were still in your own time."

"Yes, I did. He knows all the reasons why it would be disastrous to alter history, though. I didn't even need to point them out to him. He wouldn't do it."

"But someone is changing things. Remember those two renditions of the battle scene for Ciudad Rodrigo! They were so much alike. And you know very well there is only one person who could provide the necessary information to make them that way. Your cousin! At the moment I can't even be sure that getting him out of the War Office will be sufficient. If he's passing information direct to the French— Damn it, it's all nothing but one of his games to him," he exploded suddenly. "He has played the battles so often in mock recreation he is unable to see the suffering or horror of real war."

"Could he be passing information without being aware of it?"

Bedford gave a short laugh. "He'd have to be incredibly thick in the head not to realize what he was doing. Or whom he was telling."

"What if it's someone he knows well, someone he likes? No, I suppose he'd have to be pretty drunk to let something slip without realizing it. And that's something David doesn't do."

Bedford turned to gaze down at her. "He drinks like any other gentleman."

"I'll bet he doesn't have a hard head, though." She looked up, her excitement growing. "That must be it. Someone he trusts is a traitor."

"We know most of them. And anyone with whom Warwick socialized would be closely scrutinized. He is an outsider and a newcomer, remember. We are not completely gullible in the War Office."

"You've got a traitor," she repeated. "And it's not David."

"Who, then?"

"Someone who must be above suspicion."

"Are you back to your conspiracy theory? I believe you mentioned something about that before we left the Court."

She stared at him as new ideas whirled in her mind. "Your Uncle Sylvester, Sir Julian, and Lord Linton! Well, why not? Who could be more likely—and less subject to investigation—than three men closely connected to *you?*"

Thirteen

"To me!" Bedford exploded. His hands clenched and his tall roan danced nervously sideways. "Next you'll be saying *I'm* the traitor."

"No, I was just trying to get your attention and wipe that ridiculous condescending smile off your face."

He glared at her. "Condescending?"

"Yes, that look that means a poor female like me can't possibly know anything about such matters, so let's just humor her. I don't like it."

"Apparently." This time, he sounded almost amused. "All right, then, what do you suggest— bearing in mind the only sure way to stop the French from being assisted is to remove your cousin from my time and take him back where he belongs."

"Don't worry, we'll go," she snapped.

They returned to the house in stony silence. Riki swung down from her horse quickly, before he could help her, and handed her reins to the footman who came running down the front steps.

She strode into the house, drew off her gloves,

and barely prevented herself from flinging them onto the table. Down the side hall, the door to Bedford's bookroom opened and Sylvester stuck his head out. Seeing Riki, he waved with his Madeira glass, then disappeared once more inside.

In spite of her ill temper, she smiled. She liked Sylvester. She hoped he wouldn't prove to be involved with traitors in any way whatsoever. He did make that almost unprecedented call in Whitehall, though, and he showed up at the Court at almost the same moment as she and Bedford. He *could* have passed them in that carriage, and he also could have hit Hillary over the head.

Hit Hillary over the head. The words repeated themselves, demanding her attention, driving all thought of Sylvester from her mind. She could hardly wait to argue with Bedford again.

He did not return until late afternoon. When he strolled into the salon where she sat with Felicity's long-ignored embroidery, she flung it aside at once and rounded on him, triumph lighting her eyes.

"Why did someone hit Hillary at the Court? David wasn't even there! Whoever did it must not have wanted to be caught trying to overhear us."

A slow smile lit his eyes. "Whoever he was, he wouldn't have heard much, as I remember."

Warm color seeped into her cheeks. "You are hardly a gentleman to mention that," she informed him in what she hoped was a fair imitation of the so-very proper ladies of his time.

His frown returned. "Don't affect airs and graces. They don't become you."

She glared back. "And just what is that supposed to mean?"

"That I prefer you the way you are. Natural."

This offered a beguiling sidetrack, and firmly, though not without considerable regrets, she turned back to the main path. "What if someone thought we went into the rookery to speak in private. That's possible, isn't it?"

"Why would anyone be interested?"

"Because," she pointed out patiently, as if to a child, "we advertised the fact I'm supposedly an American agent."

"If you are implying my servants—"

"Of course not. But there were three people there who were not members of your staff and who might have more than a passing interest in what I might supposedly want to tell you."

"They wouldn't hit Hil over the head to do that."

"They might, if they had been startled, and desperately wanted to avoid being seen."

"This is ridiculous." He turned on his heel, but took no more than three steps before he halted, "Linton has little interest any more in affairs of state."

"I think you're wrong. He seemed very much concerned, to me."

"You mean my sister insists that he stay involved."

That seemed possible. "It was he who told your sister that you had gone on a mission," she pursued. "And she who told Sir Julian."

"And what have you to say about my uncle?"

That momentarily stumped her. "I don't know. I *like* him. I can't really imagine him involving himself in the war, not even for money, which he always seems to need."

"He obtains as much as he requires from me or my mother. We will rule out Sylvester, if you don't mind."

She let it pass. One hardly won assistance from a man when one accused his uncle of treason.

"And Sir Julian had barely arrived," he went on.

"On a very flimsy excuse. There is something about Sir Julian I don't trust. He could very well have been the one in that carriage following us in that very peculiar manner. You can't tell me *that* person was up to any good."

He didn't try. He merely watched her, an infuriating touch of amusement lighting his piercing eyes.

Her mouth tightened. "I suppose you next will point out that a mouse like your brother-in-law would never have the nerve to involve himself in anything nefarious."

"He wouldn't."

Riki glared at him. He was right, of course, Linton simply lacked the nerve. *Did* that leave Sir Julian? She would have to find out how well David knew him—and how freely they spoke to one another. Irritated with Bedford, and mad at herself for not being able to think up a scathing retort, she stalked off to change for dinner.

She entered the drawing room where they gathered before the meal almost an hour later, dressed in a lovely creation of pale green silk with a half apron of blonde lace. Bedford, who stood by the mantel, straightened on her entrance, then remained immobile, his gaze resting on her as if he were unable to tear it away.

A wave of satisfaction washed over her. After all, she had gone to some effort over her appearance—oh, all right, she'd dressed to please him. There, she'd admitted that fact to herself.

The meal passed pleasantly, as meals tended to in this household, and they lingered at the table. At last, Lady Prudence gave the signal for the ladies to rise, and they made their way back to the drawing room. Bedford and Hillary did not remain over their wine but accompanied them. The viscount barely had time to take up his position once more by the mantel before Newly entered to announce the carriage. They gathered their wraps and set forth for the card party.

As soon as they arrived at the Dalmonts', their little group drifted apart. Felicity joined several other young ladies, daughters of government officials whose positions kept them in London even during the unpleasant winter months. Lady Prue, Riki noted, already gathered about her a large and deferential court. That left Riki standing with Hillary and Bedford. She moved slightly away.

Clarissa sat on the far side of the room, playing silver loo with three others. Her husband, at a piquet table nearby, leaned over his cards, peering intently at his elderly opponent. Sylvester stood at Linton's shoulder, watching the play through his quizzing glass.

"And where are you going?" Bedford asked Hillary.

"Oh, just off with a few choice spirits." Hillary grinned at his eldest brother. Before Bedford could read him a lecture, Hillary hurried off.

Riki had little interest at the moment in Hillary's enterprising undertakings. Across the room, she saw David. He bent low, offering a wine glass to a young woman seated on a sofa before him. Lovely golden curls fluffed about the beauty's delicate face with its upturned nose and hollow cheeks as she laughed at whatever David said. Riki's heart sank.

She started toward them, slowly, with Bedford at her side. Resignedly, she noted the full, reddened lips and the brilliant blue eyes. Riki had seen her cousin in the throes of an infatuation before, and knew the symptoms all too well.

The woman looked up, saw them making their purposeful way toward her, and said something softly to David. He glanced across and smiled broadly. Excusing himself, he strode quickly over to take Riki's hands.

"There's someone I want you to meet." He pulled her back with him.

He was definitely head over heels this time, deep in trouble. Hiding her dismay, she accompanied him to greet the Vision.

"Riki, this is Mrs. Marie Marley. I want you to meet my cousin, Miss Erika van Hamel, Marie."

"Your cousin?" The slightest trace of a French accent just touched her words.

Riki stiffened, then realized why the name sounded so familiar. So this was Felicity's close friend. At least the woman wasn't likely to be a spy, but she posed another—and serious—threat to David.

How could he resist a widow whose marriage had been as unhappy as Felicity had hinted Marie's had been? She was so lovely, so fragile, just the sort of sad, wistful creature that brought out the knight errant in the stodgiest of men. And David was far from being stodgy. No wonder he was in no hurry to return to their own time.

Mrs. Marley smiled at Riki in unmistakable invitation. "Will you sit with me? I wish so much to know Mr. Warwick's cousin."

And Riki wouldn't mind learning a little more about *her,* either. She excused herself to the others and allowed Mrs. Marley to lead her aside to a quiet sofa.

"Have you known David long?" Riki asked.

A soft flush stole into the woman's cheeks. "No, not very long. We were introduced only a little over a month ago. Yet it seems as if I have known him all my life." Her eyes strayed to where David sat opposite Sylvester, playing cards.

Riki bit her lip. Unless Marie Marley was a consummate actress, there was real affection for David on her side. She was going to have her hands full. "Has he told you much about his home?"

Marie shook her lovely head and a wistful sigh escaped her. "No, he never talks of himself or his past, only his plans for the future. That is why I am so glad to meet someone who has known him since childhood. I would so much like to learn of his family."

Felicity joined them, and conversation turned to fashion. Fascinated, Riki listened to such obscure terms as "sontag sleeves," "Spanish puffs" and *"emarginate"* without the least hope of comprehension. Instead, she kept her eye on Marie while the other two ladies planned *toilettes* designed to take the *ton* by storm this coming season. Marie, she noted, kept her besotted eye on David.

Riki glanced over to where her cousin gathered up the cards and shuffled for another game with Sylvester. That worthy signaled a footman to pour them each some more wine, and David laughed at something he said. They appeared to be on very friendly terms.

Up rose her dreadful suspicions again. A friendly game of cards, a little too much wine, a joking argument about the war . . . It would be so easy for David to forget himself, to get caught up in his ruling passion, then retain none but the haziest recollections in the morning.

In the far corner, Lady Prudence rose in a sparkle of purple satin. One gesture of her lavender gloved arm sent her court scurrying, and Felicity rose at once.

"Mamma is sending out her minions in search of us. She must be ready to leave." She clasped Marie's hand. "We shall see you soon, I hope."

Somewhat to Riki's surprise, Sylvester joined them as the family gathered by the door. He strolled up with his arm linked through Bedford's, an expression of benign good will spreading across his wine-reddened countenance.

"A trifle above par," Felicity whispered to her.

"We must broach a bottle of that Madeira your father and I brought home with us from that trip to France, Bedford," the elderly gentleman declared as he happily—and quite uninvited—climbed into the already crowded carriage. He shook his head and sighed. "Before the war, that was." He fixed Bedford with a stern eye, as if he held his nephew personally responsible. "Damned war, making it so hard to get good wine. Had the devil of a time collecting my keg from the gentlemen. I'd give a great deal to see the war over, my boy, a great deal."

"How did you get your keg?" Riki asked, disliking her suspicions.

He gave her a sly wink. "Connections, m'dear.

Connections. I know a few people in the right places."

Like spies or agents or whatever they called them during this time? The thought left her chilled. She couldn't imagine smugglers being friendly—but then, she and Bedford had met up with a gang and escaped with their lives. Still, it would be interesting to know how well Sylvester and David knew each other. He might pass on information gleaned from her cousin in exchange for brandy, if he were indeed as broke as he implied.

The carriage pulled up before the house in Half Moon Street, and they all climbed out. Sylvester, still intent on his wine, accompanied them into the house. Bedford cast Riki a searching glance, then led off his uncle in search of whatever treasures the cellar might hold.

Riki started up the stairs with Felicity. "Mrs. Marley is very pretty," she commented.

"Beautiful," Felicity agreed with a sigh. "How I wish I were fashionably fair. She's as delicate as a rose, isn't she?"

And possibly as thorny, but Riki kept that reflection to herself. "She's a widow, you said?"

Felicity cast her a sideways glance. "You seemed well acquainted with Mr. Warwick," she said, not in the least changing the subject.

"For my sins, he's my cousin."

Felicity stopped dead and stared at her. "Your—I had no idea." A slight frown marred her normally smooth brow. "Are you particularly attached to one another?"

Riki caught on. "If you're matchmaking, you may forget it. We were raised as brother and sister and yes, I am fond of him, but no, we aren't *in*

205

love."

Felicity grinned. "Well, that's all right, then. I—I didn't want you to be hurt. I don't know Mr. Warwick all that well, but when I saw him with Marie tonight, I thought that at last she'd found someone who would make her happy."

"Hasn't she been?" Riki asked promptly, seizing her opening. "I believe you said something about that, once before."

Felicity nodded, her expression soulful.

They had reached Riki's room, so she obligingly invited in the other girl. "Tell me!" Riki sank down on her bed and patted the place beside her.

"She is the daughter of emigre parents, as you may have guessed," Felicity told her with all the hushed awe of one about to unfold a delightfully sordid tale to an appreciative audience. "They had absolutely nothing when they fled France. As soon as Marie was seventeen, her pappa forced her into marriage to cover his gaming debts. And with the most odious man! An officer, you must know, though how he managed not to be drummed out of his regiment I have no idea. She lost a baby because he beat her so badly. I vow, it was a relief when he was killed at Talavera just over two years ago."

Riki closed her eyes. An unhappy young woman would make the perfect tool for the French. She might well have encouraged David's infatuation in order to gain information about the War Office. And then she would have discovered what a gold mine he was about strategy and the campaigns . . .

"Do you know her *very* well?" Riki asked.

"I met her through Clarissa, who cultivated her because she speaks such exquisite French." Felicity made a face at her elder sister's snobbish ways. "She—"

"She?" Riki prompted as the girl broke off.

Felicity regarded her through narrowed eyes. "You seem quite interested in her."

Riki shrugged. "As you pointed out, my cousin is taken with her."

"It's more than that, isn't it?" Suddenly, Felicity's jaw dropped and her eyes opened wide. "You came here because you thought an American was aiding the French . . ."

"Don't be ridiculous!"

"It's Mr. Warwick, isn't it?" Felicity pursued, torn between ghoulish delight at guessing a traitor and sorrow for Mrs. Marley.

"No, pray, don't even suggest such a thing!" Riki made hushing gestures, but could see it was to no avail. "It isn't that at all! We're afraid someone is *using* him. You see, he's a—a specialist on military strategy. If a clever person got him relaxed and talking about his favorite hobby, there is no telling what they might learn."

"What makes you suspect it?" Felicity, no slow coach, went direct to the point.

"A change in the French strategy. A highly successful change, I might add."

Felicity considered a moment. "And you think the traitor might be Marie."

"It could be. She certainly seems a good prospect—of French parentage, possibly idealizing the France she remembered as a child? Her life certainly hasn't been happy here, from what you've said. Does she have any money?"

"Just her jointure, not much," Felicity said slowly. Then: "No! It's absurd! I *know* Marie. If she's an agent at all, it's far more likely she's working for the British, trying to entrap Mr. Warwick into revealing he has been sabotaging our cause. And I'll bet it was Bedford who set her onto it!"

Fourteen

"Bedford!" Riki stared at Felicity, her turn to be aghast. "No, he wouldn't—would he?"

"My brother is intensely loyal," Felicity nodded, not realizing the effect of her words on Riki. "If he had even the tiniest doubts about his assistant, you may be sure he would have him investigated."

Had he started an inquiry two years ago that even now continued its subtle way toward entrapment? No, it wouldn't have taken this long—would it? Unless . . . She stared at Felicity without seeing the girl. Unless he deliberately had surrounded David with trusted government employees. What better way to keep under control an unknown American with strategic military knowledge? Then, if his loyalty ever became suspect, it would be a simple thing to drop a word in the right ear and abruptly curtail any potentially traitorous activities.

And that word had been dropped, of that Riki was suddenly certain.

How dare Bedford! If they were to speak of traitors, he made a fine candidate! He wouldn't denounce David himself because of his promise to her, but he had done it in a sneaking, round-about fashion. Was that what he did in Whitehall the morning before, while she waited for him all unsuspecting in the carriage?

This was one matter she wasn't about to let wait a minute longer. With more determination than grace, she packed Felicity off to her own bedroom with the feeble excuse that she had a headache coming on. As soon as she saw the girl's door close behind her, Riki slipped out of her own chamber and marched back down the stairs.

She encountered Bedford in the hall, in a low-voiced conversation with Newly. The viscount looked up at her determined approach, and instantly dismissed the butler.

"What the—the *devil* do you mean by setting a spy onto David?" she whispered in furious tones.

He picked up his candle, took her arm and led her toward his bookroom without answering the charge. Once inside, he lit a sconce and placed his own taper with deliberation on the desk. "You will sit down quietly, then tell me what in heaven's name you're talking about," he said at last.

"As if you don't know." But she complied and waited until he closed the door firmly behind them. "You dropped a few hints in the War Office about David, didn't you?" she demanded.

He reached into his pocket, drew out a snuff box, but paused before opening it. "What ever gave you that idea?" His voice betrayed curiosity—and a touch of bewilderment.

She told him of her suspicions concerning Marie. "Do you deny she was introduced to him on your orders?" she finished.

"I do." He stuffed the unused box back into his pocket, took a few pacing steps, then stopped once more before the brocade sofa on which she sat.

"The first part of your accusation is correct—I did order a thorough investigation into his activities outside of Whitehall. I'd have been a fool not to, under the circumstances. But I have said and done nothing since I learned the truth about him. I only want him back in his own time, where he belongs."

Riki studied her hands in her lap, uncertain whether to trust his words or not. "What about Mrs. Marley? Is she a British agent?"

"Not a British one, no. There has never been any reason to suspect her of being a French agent, either. But it will now be looked into, just in case, I assure you."

She watched the closed expression of his face, but gained no clues. "You don't believe him."

"My dear Miss van Hamel—"

"Oh, stop patronizing me! You think he's guilty, don't you? Well, he isn't! You'd better find out who is before all your secrets are given away!" She stood, shook out her delicate skirts, and glared up at him.

A sudden smile touched his lips and the blazing light in his eyes faded to a tender glow. He rested his hands on her shoulders so this thumbs could stroke her throat. "I know you don't want to believe him guilty, Riki, but—"

"But nothing!" She shoved his hands away. "Are you forgetting the person who hit Hillary?"

"You seem to be. Mrs. Marley was not at the Court."

She glared at him.

"You are also assuming," he went on remorselessly, "that your supposed traitor possesses a great deal of knowledge about the French and British plans of battles not yet fought."

She almost stamped her foot, knowing in her heart she'd much rather kick him. "I mean, your traitor has probably been getting my cousin drunk

211

and at his ease, and gaining who knows how much information."

"Which brings us back to my point. Once your cousin is removed, so will be the source of the information."

She saw the force of that argument, but was not about to admit it. "That still leaves you with a traitor."

"Possibly," he said with maddening calm.

Her fists clenched. "How can you be so—so stupid and stubborn?"

A slight smile touched his lips. "It's an art."

He watched as she jerked away from him and marched out of the room. How could he be so stupid, indeed? It took every ounce of resolve not to drag the fiery little termagant into his arms and kiss her until she was breathless and yielding. Then—

He broke off that thought. He knew damn well what he'd like to do, then. *Too* damn well, in fact. He lay awake nights trying not to think about it, and it was beginning to drive him mad.

Where Miss Erika van Hamel was concerned, only two possibilities existed. Either he kept her beside him for the rest of his life, or he got rid of her as quickly as possible, keeping his distance until he banished her back to the future where she belonged before he lost the last vestiges of his self control.

He ran a frustrated hand through his hair. *Damn* Miss Erika van Hamel. Riki. He caught a tender thought creeping into his mind and squelched it. He had a great deal of thinking to do this night—and probably a day of intense activity on the morrow. He didn't need to lie awake, yearning for something—or rather, someone—he couldn't have. He snuffed the flame in the sconce with undue force, picked up his candle and made his way upstairs to where Pervis awaited him.

As he prepared for bed, he glowered at his reflection in the mirror. If David Warwick *were* guilty, he was more than willing to consign the man to the devil. He'd only have to engineer his passage through time, and then he'd be rid of him and that would be the end of the matter. If he were *not* guilty . . .

Almost, he didn't want to think about that possibility. What would it leave? Someone he knew—and trusted—betrayed their country. It was easier to believe Warwick and his ridiculous passion for "wargaming" was behind the change in the British fortunes in the Peninsula.

Either way, though, the person to whom Warwick passed the information—knowingly or not—had to be discovered and dealt with.

By morning, he found himself no closer to an answer. Barring David Warwick, and taking into consideration the attack on Hillary, he had three logical suspects. Four, if he were to take Riki's fears about Marie Marley seriously.

He climbed out of bed, too restless to lie still, and stared down into Half Moon Street below his window. His uncle, his brother-in-law, his best friend. Lord, what a choice! He couldn't visualize any of them in the role of traitor. Sylvester lacked perseverance at anything but the gaming table, Sir Julian cared for nothing but cutting a dash in society, and Linton was nothing but a mouse, and a sickly one at that.

He'd dismiss them all out of hand except for the one motive that could not be ignored. Money. Any one of them might have been induced to pass on information for a sufficient sum.

And now that he and Riki had come blundering

onto the scene with their talk of American agents, the guilty party would be alert for trouble and probably not approach Warwick in any but the most innocent manner. Frustration sent him off to the Park for a brisk early morning ride.

He returned well over an hour later to find Sylvester in possession of the front salon, basking under the undeniable pleasure of Riki's flattery. Damn the chit, why did she have to sit so close to him on that inviting sofa, listening so avidly to every word he spoke as if he were the most fascinating man she had ever met? The old reprobate positively preened himself!

Sylvester leaned closer to Riki, and Bedford's brow snapped down. He had always known his uncle to be a roue, but he had never thought him to be a shameless libertine! What was the chit about, allowing him to fondle her hand and stare blatantly at her shockingly low decolletage?

No, at least she had the sense to draw away and resettle her shawl. He resisted the impulse to do it for her, to make sure that not one inch of that creamy skin showed — or even that delightful freckle at the base of her throat. No one should look at her like that, except him.

Except him? He stifled that thought. No man of his time could possess her. His hand turned on the door knob as he started back out of the room.

Sylvester broke off at the slight noise, taken aback to discover his nephew standing only a few feet away. "What the devil are you doing here, Gil? I thought you'd be off to Whitehall by now."

"I have ample time," Bedford said shortly. "Does my being here interfere with your plans?" Abruptly changing his mind, he strolled over to the hearth where he leaned negligently, watching the couple on the sofa through narrowed eyes.

"Of course not, why should it? I have come to entertain your charming guest. It must be dreadfully dull for her, with so little company in town and not knowing anyone. Where were we, my dear?" Considerably put out, Sylvester turned back to Riki.

"You were about to tell me about the last time you were in Paris," she prodded.

"No, really." A flush crept into his cheeks. "Was I? Not the sort of story to be sullying a young lady's ears with. I thought you were going to tell me all about your adventures."

Riki cast a quick, meaningful glance over her shoulder at Bedford, then turned back to Sylvester with a silvery laugh. "I already told you all about how I was chosen for this work. Any more and I vow I'll bore you."

Bedford stiffened. Had his uncle been questioning her? Without compunction, he interrupted his uncle's assurances that he would hang upon her lips, no matter what she uttered. "Miss van Hamel, a word with you?"

"Certainly." She rose gracefully. "I won't be but a moment," she promised Sylvester, and crossed to the door that Bedford opened for her. He slammed it behind them.

"Yes?" She looked up at him with a semblance of innocence that made him long to shake her.

"Just what the—the *deuce*—do you think you're about? Getting to know your suspects?"

Infuriatingly, she laughed. "Let us say advancing our investigations, shall we?"

His jaw clenched. "You have no business mixing so freely with my family. If you will remember, I agreed to permit you to come back with me on the strict understanding you would avoid talking to people. Damn it, your mere presence poses a con-

215

tinual threat to the—the *integrity* of current events and the war effort! Why can't you just go to your room and remain there out of trouble?"

"How dull you would have me be! I am perfectly capable of guarding my tongue. You see how easily I have already picked up the phrases of your time."

He did indeed. She fitted in all too well for his peace of mind. "At any moment you might say something that could be proved a lie—or worse, might betray our position in the Peninsula."

She shook her head. "Only if the person to whom I speak is a traitor. Do you really enjoy suspecting your own uncle? This is the fastest way to find out."

"My uncle is not—" He broke off.

She regarded him with her lovely head cocked to one side. "Yes, as little as you like to admit it, it's a real possibility. He is shockingly expensive, you told me so yourself." She laid a hand on his arm, and her tone cajoled. "We do have a villain, you know. The best way to discover him is to learn what we can of each suspect and clear them one by one. So I have begun with your uncle. Besides," she flung over her shoulder at him with a disconcerting twinkle in her eye. "I like him."

He resisted the impulse to throttle her. Instead, he turned on his heel and stormed up the stairs. He had a long and undoubtedly unpleasant day ahead of him. If things didn't improve, he could always murder her tonight. That would make him feel better.

He was being ill-tempered and jealous and he knew it, and that knowledge didn't make a pleasant companion on the familiar drive to Whitehall. He should be glad Riki had been so completely accepted by his family. She was no fool; she knew what topics to avoid. What damage could she possibly do?

That thought haunted him throughout the long hours that dragged before him. She'd do nothing wrong, of course. She'd continue to behave in a delightful—and infuriating!—manner, becoming more a part of his family's life every day. As tempting a thought as that might be, she didn't belong here. She had her own family, her own life—and her own time.

He did not leave the War Office again until late afternoon. None of his coworkers were pleased over Warwick's resigning without warning, and he'd borne the brunt of it all day. A foul mood gripped him, but he determined not to let it show. He stormed in the front door of his house, stripping off his gloves as he went, only to be brought up short by Felicity.

"Gil, you've been an age!" She bounced down the last two stairs. "Have you forgotten we are pledged to attend the Allertons' musical *soiree* this evening? Mamma has been in a pelter, wondering if you would be in time to dine with us, before."

"I have not forgotten," he lied. Of all the unwelcome tidings. "Where is Miss van Hamel?" At the moment, he only wanted to get hold of Riki and find out what she had been about in his absence.

To his further annoyance, Felicity lowered her head demurely—to hide the mischievous twinkle in her eyes, he was certain.

"She has not yet returned."

"Returned? From where?" He pulled off his shallow curly beaver.

"Sir Julian has escorted her to the British Museum." She peeped up at him, her expression unreadable.

He shoved his hat back on his head, heedless of his appearance. Sweeping up his gloves, he shouted to the footman to order his curricle brought back

217

around.

"Are you going out?" Felicity fluttered long lashes at him, bearing a distinct resemblance to a kitchen cat who had gotten at a jug of cream.

"Out with it, minx. What are you up to?" he demanded.

She blinked innocent dark eyes at him, not fooling him for one moment. "What should I be about?"

Trying to make him jealous, he realized. Without another word, he turned on his heel and strode outside to wait.

So his little sister had selected Riki as her potential sister-in-law, had she? He stifled the intriguing response that sprang to life within him. Riki was not for him. Hadn't he just gone through that argument? And he couldn't care less if Sir Julian Taggart were interested in her, either. There wasn't a chance for either of them. She'd be gone all too soon.

And he was only going to the British Museum to protect her, he assured himself as his curricle returned and he took the ribbons once more. After all, Julian was one of their potential suspects! He maneuvered through the traffic, muttering to himself the whole time about how many people chose to remain in London in this dismal weather.

Nearly twenty minutes later, he pulled up before the beautiful old Seventeenth Century mansion that housed the museum and left his groom walking his pair while he went inside. A further half hour passed in frustrating and fruitless search through the crowded rooms, and he found himself wondering why he bothered. It was hopeless. He only had Felicity's word they had come at all. They might well have changed their minds, or even left by now to go elsewhere.

Still, he kept on, his mood growing fouler by the minute. He had decided to abandon his pointless attempt, and be damned to Riki, when he spotted them. The surge of relief he felt startled him.

Why shouldn't she have been safe? Good God, did part of him really suspect Julian? He wracked his conscience and realized that in truth, he did. There was that touch of sarcasm that had developed in his old friend, turning him from a youth bent on a lark to a hardened roue bent on enjoying himself at someone else's expense.

Was it that carriage that followed them from Brighton that loomed large in his mind, refusing to be dismissed? Or did he perhaps fear his friend intended to seduce Riki? If ever he met a female able to take care of herself, it was she. But what if she didn't mind being seduced?

"I do wish I might have seen it," Sir Julian laughed as Bedford strode up behind them, unseen. Julian appeared particularly—and irritatingly—resplendent this afternoon in a new coat of a brilliant blue superfine.

"He was the soul of heroism, I assure you," Riki said. "Had it not been for Bedford, I doubt I would be alive today."

Sir Julian drew her hand more possessively through his arm. "I still don't see why you were subjected to the rigors of a journey to Portugal. Not at all a pleasant undertaking for a delicately nurtured female."

"You forget, I'm an American. I already traveled all the way from New York. And the messages I carried were of considerable importance, I assure you."

"But could not a man have taken them, thus sparing you? Not, of course, that I am not delighted your mission brought you to our humble

219

shores."

Bedford resisted the urge to drag Riki free of that cloying hold and plant his old friend a facer.

Riki untangled herself neatly on her own, under the pretence of peering more closely into a display case. When she straightened up from her scrutiny of an Egyptian figurine, she fluttered her lovely lashes at Sir Julian with devastating effect. "I *wanted* to go. I can see you don't approve, but there it is. And since there was no reason why *I* must be the one to deliver the messages, I was forced to exert all my powers of persuasion. Fortunately, I have an uncle highly placed in government circles."

Sir Julian reclaimed her arm and led her on. "You sailed from New York, you said? I have never been there myself, but I have heard it is a pleasant enough town. Are you from there?"

"No." She stopped once more to examine a vase, and Bedford drew back behind a small knot of people to keep from being seen.

"I'm from a place so small I am sure you'd never have heard of it," Riki went on. "Are you interested in America?"

To that, Sir Julian was forced by politeness to answer in the affirmative. Bedford continued to follow them, listening with amused approval to Riki's improvised and undoubtedly fictional account of life in the former Colonies. Though Sir Julian listened with the appearance of fascination, Bedford knew him to be bored.

So why did his old friend question Riki so closely? Concern that they were being taken in by an adventuress? Not for one moment did he believe Sir Julian interested in the supposed political ramifications of her visit. But the messages she carried to Portugal — indeed, Bedford's own aborted journey there . . . Damn it, if Julian were attempting to aid the French for whatever reason, he might well behave in exactly this manner.

Riki drew back from the display case and saw Bedford. Her whole face lit up—and suddenly, his ill temper evaporated. Only a slight edge of distrust remained.

"What are you doing here?" Impulsively, she stepped forward, holding out her free hand.

Her other, he noted, remained firmly within Julian's arm. Bedford raised her fingers to his lips before releasing her, then turned to Julian.

Languidly, the dandy raised his glass, the better to survey the viscount. A taunting smile played about his lips. "Dear boy, has something put you out of temper?"

"A difficult day. My assistant has resigned, you see. Whatever brings you here? I hadn't thought antiquities to be one of your delights."

"No, I prefer much younger objects of beauty."

He smiled down at Riki in a manner that made Bedford's fists curl into punishing bunches of fives. With a concerted effort, he relaxed them.

"Miss van Hamel expressed an interest in the Museum, so what could I do but offer to escort her? Ah—and what brings you here?" He swung his quizzing glass by its riband, his sardonic gaze never leaving Bedford's face.

"Solicitude, my friend. I couldn't imagine your making the rounds without desiring company to alleviate your boredom." He offered his arm to Riki and the little minx took it promptly, fighting back a smile. Lord, he must be behaving like a jealous fool. Deliberately, he avoided her eye, and struggled with his growing irritation with Riki—and with himself.

He did not have a chance for private speech with her until after Sir Julian drove her back to the house and took his leave. Bedford consigned his curricle to the care of his groom and followed her up the front steps.

"Miss van Hamel?" He intercepted her in the entry hall, where Newly relieved her of her pelisse. "A word?"

"A whole one?" She smiled up at him. "We've become remarkably talkative, haven't we?"

He clenched his teeth. "I see it amuses you to turn everything into a jest."

"Yes, it does, rather. You should try it, yourself. It makes life so much more enjoyable."

He took her elbow and propelled her into the front salon, which stood empty. "Were you pursuing another suspect this afternoon?"

"I'd hardly call it pursuing. He called to take me driving in the park, but it was really much too cold. So I seized my opportunity."

"Does this mean you've cleared my uncle of all charges of treason?"

At that, she frowned. "I wish I could." A rueful smile just touched her lips. "Really, I don't believe I'm very good at being a spy. They both asked searching questions that could be interpreted as no more than a concern for you."

"For me?" That startled him.

"Yes, they both seem to regard me as a 'suspicious person.' Really, you can have no idea how lowering that is. I always considered myself respectable."

"Clearly this has given you a new insight into your character," he couldn't resist murmuring.

She made a face at him. "At least Felicity likes me."

"That's probably because she isn't on your suspect list. Did you arrive at any startling conclusions?" he asked abruptly.

222

She shook her head. "I'd say I wasted my day if I hadn't enjoyed myself so much."

"You mustn't let yourself fall prey to practiced rakes." He drew his snuff box from his pocket, opened it with an expert flick and helped himself to a pinch.

She regarded this activity with a reproving eye. "Felicity considers Sir Julian to be the most likely traitor."

He paused in the act of returning the enameled box to his pocket. "Does she? Why?"

"She doesn't like him. She calls him a simpering fop."

Bedford shook his head. "Purely affectations. But why did she tell you and not me?"

"Probably because she knew you'd simply defend your friend. If it escaped your notice, it was your first impulse right now."

Bedford bit back his retort. As much as he hated to admit it, she was right. "When do you intend to subject Linton to your questioning?"

"Subject?" She fluttered her long lashes in feigned innocence. "It was my impression Mr. Randall and Sir Julian enjoyed my company this day."

"If you have a try at Linton, you will have my sister Clarissa to deal with."

Riki laughed and shook her head, then sobered abruptly. "I promise I won't cause any trouble. But we must uncover our traitor."

"I think you've done quite enough. Leave it to me—and my department."

Riki bit her full lower lip. "Have you learned anything about Marie Marley?"

"I mentioned her name to the proper office this morning."

"Did you? I am very grateful. But I take it from your expression you drew a blank."

"If you mean nothing was known of her, I warned you that would be the case. But discreet inquiries are now being made."

She nodded. "That's all I ask."

She hesitated, and Bedford received the impression she was about to ask him something more. Instead, she turned abruptly away.

"I—I'd better change before dinner. We go to a musical *soirée* this night, do we not? It is very kind of you to permit me to attend."

His gaze rested on the back of her head, where her thick, smooth hair just brushed her delicate shoulders. There was another freckle, one he hadn't noticed before. He looked away. "You seem well able to guard your tongue."

She glanced back, and awarded him a shaky smile that didn't quite reach her eyes. "I won't commit the one offense I have come here to prevent."

"No, you won't." But he spoke the words so softly she couldn't have heard as she went out the door.

He stared after her a moment, then pulled himself together. Riki was not the only person who wished to do some investigating this night. He made his way to his chamber to dress for the coming event.

They took their time over dinner and arrived at the Allertons' townhouse a little after the appointed hour. Bedford watched Felicity drag Riki off to meet several of her friends, and knew no more than a momentary worry. He had other things to occupy his mind.

Sir Julian stood in a corner with a young matron of delicately fair complexion and delightfully fast reputation. The strategy that obviously occupied his mind had a great deal to do with conquest, but nothing to do with the military. *Damn* suspecting his old friend. That was Riki's fault. But the questions

224

remained.

Warwick, after exchanging warm greetings with Riki, settled a little way off with the dazzling Marie Marley at his side. That lady leaned back in her chair, her languid air only adding to her sultry allure. She might well coax secrets from the most ardent loyalist.

Several acquaintances hailed him, and Bedford joined the whist table they started. From there, he could keep an eye on most of the assembled company. Riki, he was pleased to note, moved to his mother's side, and listened with apparent delight to that lady's undoubtedly scurrilous monologue on the failings and foibles of everyone who caught her eye.

Clarissa strolled into the card room, resplendent in a gown of yellow silk that must have set Linton back a considerable sum. She hesitated as she scanned the room, spotted Bedford, and bore down on her brother.

"Bedford, how disagreeable of you to hide in here. I most particularly want you to talk to Linton. It is the most dreadful thing. He has actually spoken of retiring, again. This time I fear he means it!"

Bedford played his next card without looking up. "That might be the best thing for his health."

"Bedford! Oh, do finish that silly game and come with me." She waited in seething impatience until the last trick was taken, then grasped his arm.

With a pained expression, he removed her fingers from where she crushed the sleeve of his velvet coat, and stood. "Please, Clarissa, strive for a little decorum."

Thus admonished, she released him. "You will talk to Linton, will you not?"

"I will not." Still, he strolled with her to the other room. Why did Linton's possible retirement distress

Clarissa? Was there some reason for her wanting her husband to remain in the War Office? He broke off that thought. He was getting as bad as Riki, seeing potential traitors everywhere. He might as well suspect Clarissa as — as Sylvester, perhaps?

Linton spoke freely before his wife, though. Too damn freely. What if he spoke of military strategy? Would Clarissa pay attention? He cast a considering glance at her as she hung petulantly on his arm.

"Are you acquainted with Warwick?" he asked suddenly.

"Your assistant? Oh, no, he resigned, did he not? Linton told me. We don't know him very well, if you mean socially. Why?" She looked up, nothing but mild curiosity in her dark eyes.

Bedford shook his head. "Just wondering."

For across the room, David Warwick sprang to his feet to greet the stooped figure of Lord Linton as if he were a long lost friend.

Fifteen

Lord Linton? Riki watched from her seat at Lady Prudence's side as David greeted Bedford's brother-in-law with untrammeled delight. Somewhat embarrassed, Linton drew back.

With a visible effort, he recovered. "I understand you've resigned from the War Office." Linton shook his head. "Sad business that. You'll be missed."

"You'll miss our card games, you mean." David chuckled. "So will I, for that matter. You play a devilish fine game of piquet."

"As do you, much to my dismay upon many an occasion." Linton smiled in response and the indefinite sadness seemed to lift from his brow. "This was rather sudden, was it not? You had spoken no word of this to me."

David grinned. "You might say it hit me by storm. Miss van Hamel brought news from my family. I must return to America as soon as she is finished with her work here."

"I might—" Linton broke off as he saw his wife approaching. With a hurried excuse to David, he disappeared rapidly in the opposite direction. On the other side of the room, Sylvester caught him, and with elbows linked, the two gentlemen headed for the card room.

Bedford came to a halt, watching them with

227

frowning intensity. Clarissa stood rigid for a moment, then turned with an artificial laugh to greet a friend.

Riki shivered. All they needed now would be for Sir Julian to join them and the three stand in a corner whispering. With Marie Marley, of course.

Still, she would like to know what went through Bedford's mind at this moment. She excused herself to Lady Prue and took an impulsive step toward him, then turned away. She'd better wait until they returned to the house. They seemed to argue as much as discuss things these days, and a musical *soirée* was hardly the place to start a fight with a man.

Not far from her, Marie beckoned David and he returned with alacrity to his usual place at her side. Riki watched them closely, searching for something to convince her that the seeming affection on Marie's side was feigned. But her observations only left her with the sinking feeling that the attachment was very real indeed.

There could be no mistaking the strength of the infatuation on David's side. In that, of course, lay the most likely point of treason. How could he help but want her to share in his delights? If she played the devoted listener, David would ramble on *ad nauseam* and in all innocence about his hobby.

But to whom did *she* pass the information? She must have a contact. Riki chewed her lower lip, frustrated. Neither Linton nor Sylvester had done more than glance at Mrs. Marley, as they might at any lovely young woman.

What about Sir Julian? She hadn't seen him this evening, but that might mean he was in a drawing room she hadn't yet entered. She set off in search.

She found him at last, standing by the pianoforte, turning pages of a musical score for a particularly fetching young thing in a gown of gauze so fine as

228

to embarrass Riki. It seemed to please Sir Julian very well, though, for it was on this and not on the music that his eye rested. Riki sauntered up and leaned on the instrument, watching with what she hoped was an expression of rapt admiration.

"That was lovely," she sighed as the performance drew to a close. "I didn't realize you were a devotee of music, Sir Julian."

"I am a lover of everything beautiful." He awarded her the slightest bow. "Would you care to stroll about the rooms?" He took his leave of the musician and offered his arm to Riki.

"I wanted to thank you again for escorting me to the museum. I had a delightful afternoon." At least she would have, if she'd felt easier in his company.

His gaze rested on her, an unreadable expression in the depths of his hazel eyes. "You must permit me to be your guide on other expeditions about London. Would you care to see the Tower?"

"Very much. But I did not think a fashionable gentleman would care for such vulgar pastimes as sightseeing."

"Not vulgar, merely tedious," he corrected. "Unless the company makes the effort worthwhile."

She held her tongue and pretended to look down in pretty confusion at his compliment. It wasn't a *liking* for her company that prompted his invitation, though. He didn't seem to trust her any more than she trusted him. Obviously, he intended to discover as much as he could about her.

And that reminded her of her own purpose. She directed their steps into the other room where David and Marie still sat close together. As they passed through the doorway, Marie looked up and a flicker of recognition—or acknowledgment—crossed her face as her gaze rested on Sir Julian. Quickly, she looked back to David.

They knew each other, all right, Riki thought triumphantly, and didn't care to own up to it. Sir Julian must be her contact. That would settle everything so beautifully. She didn't like Sir Julian, and he was a far better villain than either Sylvester or Linton.

She would keep a close eye on him this evening and see if he tried to speak privately with the beautiful Mrs. Marley. That seductive air the woman cultivated would provide her with an excellent excuse for slipping off with a man for supposed dalliance. Then perhaps Bedford would listen to her about David's innocence. If her cousin were the traitor, he would have no need of the likes of Marie Marley to act as a go-between.

The musical portion of the evening did not prove enjoyable for Riki. Lady Prudence demanded her attendance, holding court with Riki displayed at her side like a prize, talking throughout the singing and playing in an overly loud voice. Though Riki tried to keep either Mrs. Marley or Sir Julian in sight at all times, craning her neck to catch glimpses of them drew unwanted attention to herself, and she was forced to subside.

At the beginning of the first interval, Felicity slipped off with a group of young friends and stood giggling in a corner until the resumption of the music forced her to return to her seat. Lord Linton, she noted with a touch of amusement, stood with a group of people loudly decried by Lady Prue as the most boring members of the government she had ever had the misfortune to see gathered together under one roof. Bedford divided his time between Sylvester and Sir Julian. Riki felt unaccountably irritated with him.

The evening dragged on, but at last the program drew to a close. They sent for their wraps, and Lady Prue paused just inside the drawing room doorway and looked back toward where David and

Mrs. Marley stood close together in earnest conversation. "Been sitting in his pocket all evening," she announced in tones calculated to draw the notice of everyone standing near. "Shouldn't be surprised if there were to be an interesting announcement in the near future."

The couple looked up and becoming color crept into Marie Marley's cheeks.

"You're embarrassing them, mother — as if you didn't know." Bedford strolled up behind them. "I believe the carriage has arrived." Firmly, he escorted them out.

Riki waited in seething impatience until the carriage at last pulled up before Bedford House. Bedford jumped to the street and let the step down, then assisted his mother and sister to climb out. Riki came last, and the firm pressure of her fingers as they gripped his carried their own message. He allowed his family to go on ahead.

"What did you wish to say?" he murmured as they followed the others up the stairs.

"Quite a bit, actually."

"My bookroom, then, I believe." He nodded to Newly, who admitted them to the house, then led the way down the hall.

As soon as the door closed behind them, Riki began. "There is a tie between Marie Marley and Sir Julian."

Something flashed in the depths of Bedford's piercing eyes, but he veiled his reaction almost at once. "Indeed?" was all he said.

"When she saw him, she looked instantly away, as if she were afraid of acknowledging him."

"More like she was afraid if she gave him the least encouragement he would join her."

Riki blinked. "What do you mean?"

"There are other reasons than espionage why a gentleman and a lady might be acquainted, my dear

231

innocent."

"You mean they—"

"I mean Sir Julian was quite interested in pursuing an acquaintance with her. She, I believe, was not."

"Oh." Riki considered a moment, then rallied. "That doesn't necessarily have to be true."

"I fear in this case, it does. I was myself an observer of his determined and unsuccessful courtship."

Riki studied her hands, feeling as if the ground had just caved in beneath her feet. "The best way to get to the bottom of all this is to find out the truth about Marie Marley!" she declared, refusing to give up.

Maddeningly, he shook his head. "We will leave that to the War Office, if you do not mind."

"But are they taking my suspicions of her seriously?"

He regarded her through half-closed eyes. "As seriously as any other case, I assure you."

She glared at him. "You didn't give this top priority, I take it. You're so convinced David is lying, you won't even bother to take precautions!"

He took a step toward her, hesitated, then rested his hands on her shoulders. "Her background and connections are being investigated. What more do you want me to do? Personally follow her around, night and day? What would you expect me to accomplish?"

"You might discover to whom she's passing the information. Or are you afraid it might prove to be someone you know—and like?"

It wasn't easy ignoring the warm, gentle pressure of his hands on her bare skin. *Damn* low-cut dresses. They left her all too vulnerable. She pulled away and strode purposefully to the hearth, where a small fire still crackled in the grate.

"We know where the information is coming *from*,"

he reminded her gently. "You could warn David of your suspicions, if you think that would help."

"It wouldn't. And not because he wouldn't care. He just wouldn't believe me. He's in love with her."

"Take him back where he belongs!" he snapped.

"I can't!" She spun about to face Bedford, her eyes pleading with him to understand—to help. "I can't force him to go. But if I could give him proof Marie has been betraying him, he'd *want* to leave."

"He'd leave fast enough if offered his choice between that or a firing squad."

"You wouldn't—you promised!" she cried, alarmed by the grim note in his voice. "You said you wouldn't denounce him as a traitor."

Bedford drew a deep, unsteady breath. "Unless I have to. Damn it, Riki, I'm not going to let him wreak havoc with our Peninsular Campaign—and with the future!"

Her heart sank. He meant it—and what was worse, she couldn't blame him. Nor would she have him change in the least. He was stubborn, proud, loyal to his country above all . . .

And that didn't change her problem any.

There was only one thing to do, and she knew it. She'd have to convince David of the danger he posed to everything they knew—and destroy his blind happiness and faith in his hopeless love.

It wouldn't be easy. If she went to him without proof, telling him her suspicions of Marie Marley, he'd think it nothing but a desperate ploy on her part to make him go home. No, she couldn't breathe a word of her fears until she could back up her accusations with incontrovertible facts.

How to go about getting them, though? She could always follow Marie herself until the woman met with a French agent. Would she know if that happened, though? Traitors had a bad habit of *not* walking around with labels on their backs saying "French spy."

She made her way up to her chamber, deep in unhappy plans. The best person to consult, she decided, would be Felicity. She was Marie's friend, she must know some of the woman's habits, certainly where she lived. The only problem would be how to get the information without alerting the girl to what she intended to do. Felicity was spirited enough to demand to help. She had better not ask her anything directly; she could not risk dragging Bedford's young sister into a potentially dangerous situation.

On the whole, it was easier than she anticipated. By dropping the merest hint over the breakfast table the following morning, Riki found herself carried off by Felicity to pay a morning visit to Marie Marley within the hour. Lady Prudence, fortunately, decided to remain at home, for she was herself in the expectation of receiving callers.

Marie Marley resided in a very small townhouse on Mount Street which, Felicity told Riki, had been purchased by her husband shortly before his death. The butler who opened the door to them was every bit as austere and proper as a good British butler should be. He bowed them into a front salon and withdrew to find his mistress.

The room was charming, Riki thought, tastefully decorated without any lavish wasting of money. Probably because Marie didn't have any. No evidence existed here of a lucrative business of selling military information. For the first time, Riki began to think she just might have been wrong.

Five minutes later, she found herself plagued with even more doubts. Marie swept into the room, exquisite in a fluttery gauze morning gown of a delicate shade of pink that set off her creamy complexion. No wonder she aroused David's protective instincts, Riki reflected. Who could ever believe such a delicate, lovely creature could be a dangerous spy?

"Will you not be seated?" She waved them toward a comfortable sofa nestled before the burning hearth and sank gracefully into a chair. "Ah, thank you, Addison," she added as the butler entered with a tray of lemonade and cakes. "Will you have a glass?" she asked her guests, already pouring.

Mrs. Marley turned her sweet smile on Riki. "Mr. Warwick is so very pleased that you have been able to come to England."

"I only wish I could go to France, as well." Riki managed a sigh. "You must know it has always been an ambition of mine to see Paris. It doesn't seem right, to have come this far and not be able to manage those last few miles."

Marie Marley shook her head. "It is indeed a pity. England is a beautiful country, *n'est ce pas*, but France! I lived in Paris when I was a little girl. I don't remember it well, but the stories my mother could tell! We had an estate near Chartres, and she spoke of it constantly as the most beautiful place on earth."

Riki tried to watch her closely without appearing to do so. "You must long to go back."

Marie agreed. "It is a great sadness that it is impossible."

"But the war will end, someday," Riki pursued.

Her hostess brightened. "It is my greatest hope, to be able to see Chartres and Paris once more."

Who wouldn't idealize her happy childhood, when her adult life had been spent in poverty and unhappiness? That provided an all-too-perfect motive — and one with which Riki almost found herself in sympathy.

But if she did pass on information, then Mrs. Marley was using David. That thought broke across her instinctive liking for the woman. Even if Marie had no idea of the real importance of the details of

235

strategy she gleaned, she still betrayed David's trust and that Riki could not forgive.

"Mr. Warwick, he is not very like you." Marie regarded Riki with interest.

"He looks exactly like all the other van Hamels — tall and fair. I'm the odd one out."

The conversation dwelt briefly on David, then Felicity neatly turned it to a ball at Woking House they would attend that evening, and whom they might expect to see other than just stuffy politicians. London before the season began, Riki gathered, was dull work for a lively young damsel.

By the time they took their leave, Riki's mind once more seethed with formulating plans. Marie Marley *must* be their traitor. But how to catch her out? She wouldn't meet with her confederates unless it was strictly necessary.

So that meant Riki had to feed her some information, deliberately though not too obviously, and see what — if anything — she did.

The rest of the day passed with Riki being fitted for a ball gown. Any number of minor alterations had to be made to the one Felicity eagerly bestowed on her, and then, when she at last thought she could relax for a moment, a hairstylist arrived to do something with her thick auburn locks.

And between all this, Felicity insisted she learn some of the basic movements of the dances that would be performed that night. That Riki didn't want to dance, but to take the opportunity to set a trap for a traitor, she couldn't explain.

When at last Felicity pronounced her ready to go down stairs that evening, Riki was amazed at the transformation in herself. No ruffles marred the purity of her appearance. The robe of celestial blue crepe opened up the front, revealing an unadorned undergown of dazzling white gauze. A delicate edging of lace peeped from the low scooped neckline.

Two silver rosebuds peeked out from among her thickly rolled curls, and a borrowed fan dangled by a blue riband from her gloved wrist. Austerity suited one as small as she, Riki decided. For once, though, she didn't feel in the least insignificant.

Holding her breath, she descended the grand staircase. Bedford stood in the hall below, resplendent in a coat of rich claret-colored velvet over a white brocade waistcoat, elegant in a quiet way that commanded admiration. Why must he so perfectly epitomize her every secret dream? It simply wasn't fair.

He looked up as she reached the last landing, and her heart gave a delightful double beat at the arrested gleam that lit his eyes. He came forward slowly, holding out his hand. She placed her own in his and descended to the hall.

Not one compliment passed his lips; there was no need. Breathless, she stood at his side, aware only of him, of the desire that pulsed between them. Only with the belated arrival of Hillary and Lady Prudence did she recover her composure and step hastily away.

The ballroom at Woking House, Berkeley Square, was already filled when they arrived. Riki looked about, curious, and fought back a sudden laugh. She knew these types; they were the same pompous blowhards and old geezers she had avoided when she was a child and her parents entertained some ambassador or other high muckety-muck.

She suppressed a chuckle. She hadn't thought in those silly terms in ages. Her mother had almost succeeded in "civilizing" her—before she broke away and took to camping and hiking instead of playing cards and dancing at the country club.

Their names were announced, and the others moved off in search of acquaintances. Riki remained near the door, scanning the crowd for her cousin.

Bedford stood protectively over her—glaring at the several young bucks who dared to venture near. He seemed pleased when she declined all invitations to dance.

David entered a few minutes later, escorting Marie Marley, and a tingle of nerves raced up Riki's spine. There was nothing dangerous about what she was going to do, she reminded herself. But she must be very clever if she didn't want to raise the woman's suspicions. If Riki did that, she might never be able to trap Marie.

"What's the matter?" Bedford murmured in her ear.

Riki jumped, then looked up and managed an innocent smile. "I just hope I don't behave too oddly."

His fingers closed briefly over hers. "You'll do very well."

She moved away from him. Bedford distracted her thoughts too much—and she was too willing to let him do it. Glancing back, she caught him watching her with a puzzled frown creasing his brow. She gave him a tremulous smile, then turned and made her way across the crowded floor to where David stood with Mrs. Marley.

She might as well just barge ahead. If she tried to do anything too smoothly, it would be obvious. This way, she'd get the conversation onto the war, blurt something out, and let David believe it was by accident.

As she neared, Mrs. Marley spotted her, waved, and said something to David. He turned and his face lit with pleasure.

"Riki!" he called, gesturing for her to join them. She did.

"How delightful to see you," Mrs. Marley said, the soft accent warming her voice.

No wonder David was ensnared. Her affection for him, Riki would swear, was real. But how could she betray the man she supposedly loved? What sort of treacherous heart beat behind that lovely facade?

"It's quite a crush, considering the season hasn't begun," David said with all the air of one who knew from vast experience.

"The war must be keeping a great number of people in London." Riki looked about. "I don't see many uniforms present. Is this strictly a political gathering, or are most of the officers still in the Peninsula?"

David laughed, though he sounded a touch uneasy. "We don't talk about military matters at balls." He obviously intended the edge in his voice to give her a hint.

Riki decided to be extremely obtuse this evening. "No one's listening to us. Besides, they all know better than I what's going on. Isn't that irritating, Mrs. Marley, to never quite understand what is happening?"

"It is, *du vrai*," she nodded in agreement. "*Men*," she added. "They do not think a woman has a mind."

"Now, that's a pack of moonshine," David objected, smiling.

"But it is true!" Mrs. Marley assured him. "It may be different in America, where one hears things are not at all as they are here, but in England, a lady must not discuss military strategy but only how handsome the officers appear in their regimentals."

Now, if ever there was an opening, here it was! Or was that a deliberate lead to David to tell her something?

"I agree." Riki stepped in quickly, seizing her chance. "Only consider. Here are the British troops, deep in their plans for an assault across the Tagus, and how many women in England know?"

David laughed. "Got that wrong, Riki. Lord, you

239

never could keep one battle straight from another. They're really planning on—" He broke off and managed a highly unconvincing cough. "Well, that's neither here nor there, is it?"

Riki frowned. "But David, I *know* Bedford said the Tagus. I *heard* him."

"Then you shouldn't be spreading it about, should you?" For perhaps the first time in his life, he snapped at her.

She blinked, startled by this vehemence.

He grabbed her elbow and led her off. "For God's sake, Riki," he hissed, "remember the—the privileged nature of your information!" He met and held her eye in a manner meant to both abash and warn her against further incautiousness.

Her heart swelled. If she'd needed anything to prove her cousin wasn't a traitor—and she hadn't—he'd just provided it. He had spoken with the strength of his convictions. She lowered her eyes, knowing she had to go on.

"Don't you ever get tempted to talk, just a little?" she asked. She looked up and met his gaze squarely.

"I—" He broke off, shaking his head. "God, I try not to. I suppose it would be easy for something to slip out, but—" He left the sentence unfinished.

"I know." Riki felt more relieved than she could have believed.

The music started and David hesitated. "Hadn't you better look around for your partner?"

Riki shook her head. "You two go ahead. I don't know the steps, remember?" She drifted back toward a seat against the wall where she could watch, well satisfied with her meddling so far.

She had reason to be even more satisfied barely two hours later. She had been sitting out the dance with Hillary, who was only too glad of the excuse not to stand up with any fubsy-faced daughters of the M.P.'s, as he darkly told her, obviously having one, and not many, in mind. When the guests began to go down for supper, Hillary rose with a sigh.

"Better go see what Felicity is up to," he said. "Bedford's taking you down, isn't he?"

Riki froze, barely hearing the last of his comment. She moved away without answering, her gaze focused on her cousin.

Near by, David hovered solicitously over Marie, who raised one hand to her brow as if with the headache. A crumpled piece of paper fell from her gloved hand and landed on a sofa at her side. Neither seemed to notice it. David coaxed her down onto the seat, then signaled a footman and sent the man on an errand.

Riki stared at them in mingled alarm and excitement. She hadn't really been prepared for such immediate results.

She hurried up to them, trying very hard not to look at the paper that barely protruded from between the cushions. "Is something the matter, Mrs. Marley? Can I help?"

"Yes." David didn't give Marie a chance to answer. "I don't suppose you've got a vinaigrette or anything like that on you, have you?"

"Lady Prudence will, undoubtedly. Shall I ask?"

"No, please." Mrs. Marley held up her hand, brushing Riki's arm with a feather-light touch. "Pray do not put yourself to any trouble. I shall go home and lie down. Nothing else works, I assure you."

"Migranes, I think," David murmured to Riki.

She nodded in spurious sympathy. Either that, or one heck of a good excuse to be left completely alone.

"Have you sent for the carriage?" Marie raised pain-filled eyes to David.

He grasped her hand and gave it a sustaining squeeze. "I have. Don't worry, I'll have you home as soon as possible."

Riki remained with them until the footman returned with the information that their carriage awaited outside. While David fussed over Mrs. Marley, locating her fan and shawl, Riki pretended to help. With a deft movement, she scooped up the crumpled slip and shoved it down the bodice of her gown. She trailed them into the hall, then watched as they descended the steps. Marie clung artistically to David's strong supportive figure.

Her heart beating rapidly with excitement, Riki unfolded the note. *"Meeting — two-thirty"* was all it said. For her, though, that was enough.

She crumpled it once more, and returned to the ballroom, which was almost empty now as the couples made their way down to the supper. She tucked the note back where she'd found it, though she had a strong suspicion Marie had received rather than written it, and now had discarded it. This was too chancey a way to pass a note.

Now, all she had to do was figure out how to get out of here herself and discover just what Mrs. Marley would do and whom she would meet — once that lady rid herself of David's company.

Sixteen

The obvious solution struck Riki at once. A feigned headache had worked admirably for Marie Marley; why shouldn't it do the same for her?

It should and it did. Half an hour later, Newly admitted Riki, with Felicity and Lady Prudence in solicitous attendance, into the house. Bedford and Hillary remained at the ball, under protest, but also under obligation to their promised partners.

"I do wish you would both go back," Riki repeated for perhaps the twentieth time as they escorted her up the stairs to her bedchamber.

"When you have been taken ill?" Felicity exclaimed, shocked. "Of course we will do no such thing."

"It is only a headache, after all. I will go to bed and probably to sleep at once. There is no need for you to miss the rest of the party. You cannot tell me you weren't enjoying yourselves. Please, do not make me feel guiltier than I do already."

Felicity hesitated. "Why do not you return, Mamma, and reassure Bedford? You know how

243

anxious he will become if at least one of us does not."

To that, Lady Prue agreed. As soon as she assured herself that all possible was being done for her guest, she took her departure. Felicity settled herself in a chair by the bedside, watching with a knowledgeable eye as Riki's abigail placed a cloth soaked in lavender water on her forehead and waved burning feathers before her.

"That is the awfulest smell!" Riki gasped. "Please, get it out of here. It's only making things worse."

The maid drew back, uncertain.

"Yes, do go." Felicity waved her to the door. "I shall stay with Miss van Hamel until she is more the thing."

"There is no need," Riki assured her.

Felicity regarded her with anxious eyes. "Are you quite certain?"

"Yes. I just want to lie here quietly."

Felicity nodded. "Then I will wish you good night. Do not hesitate to summon me should you have need." She let herself quietly out of the room.

A long sigh of relief escaped Riki. Now, she mustn't rush things, she still had well over an hour . . .

She waited fifteen minutes, until her nerves could take no more. What if Mrs. Marley left early? She might be about her business and Riki would miss her. Not daring to delay any longer, she rose, drawing off her nightdress and casting it aside in one swift movement.

She pulled on a dark green kerseymere gown, and by dint of some athletic contortions, managed to button it up the back. She fastened the matching pelisse up to her throat and pulled a dark shawl over her head. A quick survey in the mirror satisfied her; if she kept her face covered, she would disappear nicely in the shadows.

How, though, was she to get a hackney at this time of night? She hoped the few coins in her reticule would be sufficient. For that matter, how did she go about letting herself out of the house without raising the servants? Well, she could either sit here and worry and let her quarry escape, or find out by that good old fashioned method of trial and error.

She opened her door a crack, peered down the empty hall, then eased herself silently from her room, afraid to breathe for fear someone might hear and demand to know what she was about. At this time of night, the main stair would most likely be safer—and less used—than the servants' at the back of the house. She started for it.

Before she had taken ten steps, a door opened and Riki spun about, her heart stopping. Felicity waved to her, gesturing for her to join her in her chamber. Riki took a long, steadying breath and complied.

"Now, what is this all about?" Felicity demanded.

"I needed to go out for a few minutes."

Felicity pressed her full lips together, but her twinkling eyes betrayed her amusement. "I can see that, silly. Where are you going? If you don't answer, you know, I can make quite the greatest fuss."

"That I can believe. All right, I want to see what someone is doing tonight."

Felicity nodded in satisfaction. "I thought so." She removed her dressing gown to reveal a dark blue merino beneath. "You didn't look to me like someone with a headache. Who are we following?"

"*We* aren't following anyone. *I* am."

"You sound exactly like Bedford," Felicity giggled. Riki blinked. She had sounded *exactly* like him.

245

And what was worse, she knew how Felicity felt, not wanting to be left out. Firmly, before she let sympathy get the better of her, she shook her head. "It might be too dangerous. Bedford would never forgive me if I let anything happen to you."

"Then you can come along to keep an eye on *me*, because I intend to prove to you that Marie isn't a traitor and didn't leave the ball early just to meet with some spy."

"You knew what I was doing!" Riki stared at her in dismay.

Felicity returned the regard with surprise. "Well, of course I did. Are you coming or not? I can get us out of the house without being caught, which I'll wager you can't."

With the distinct feeling that the situation had been taken out of her control, Riki followed Felicity out into the hall and down the main stair.

The girl did not go to the front door as Riki expected. Instead, she slipped silently down the corridor to Bedford's bookroom. There, as Riki watched in dawning alarm, Felicity jimmied up the window, perched on the sill and swung her legs in their narrow-fitting skirt over the edge to the outside. She eased herself to the ground with all the expertise of one who had practiced this particular unseemly maneuver on more than one occasion.

Riki followed her example, found it more difficult than it looked, and landed on her knees at Felicity's side.

"Hush!" The girl fought back a giggle as she helped Riki to her feet. "Do you want old Newly to hear?"

Riki bit back her questions. Since silence was necessary, she had best keep her curiosity under control until they let themselves out through the gate into the mews. But once safely away from the house, she intended to demand a few answers from the girl.

Felicity didn't pause to give her the chance. Instead, she set off briskly toward Piccadilly. "Shall I pretend to be your abigail?" she asked brightly.

"How often have you done this?" Riki demanded, torn between exasperation and a reluctant appreciation of her companion's resourcefulness.

"Oh, lots of times, when we were children. You won't tell Bedford will you? No, of course you won't. He'd want to know how you found out, and that you couldn't tell him, could you?" She accompanied the remark with a look of wide-eyed innocence.

It didn't deceive Riki for a moment. "I'm beginning to sincerely pity your brother," was all she said.

Felicity just grinned. "Tell me everything."

Riki hesitated, then told her about the information she "let slip," the note, and Mrs. Marley's sudden illness.

The laughter faded from Felicity's eyes. "I don't believe it of her! You'll see for yourself how wrong you are." Her small hands clutched the edges of her cloak and she walked faster. "It's cold, isn't it?" she said presently.

It was likely to get colder, Riki reflected ruefully, glancing up at the icy clear sky. Stars glittered, bright and piercing, and a half moon bathed the almost deserted street in light, making walking easy. But it left Riki uneasy. Her skin crawled with an eerie sensation of being followed—or did she mean stalked?

A noise reached them, a rumbling rattle that rose in volume—and settled safely into the sound of hoofbeats on the cobbled stones. Riki let out a ragged breath of relief—which she cut off the next

247

second. Grabbing Felicity, she dragged her into the shadowed recesses beside some area steps, where they waited until two horses trotted past, drawing a covered carriage.

Felicity giggled again, nervous. "How dramatic of you."

"We're crazy," Riki breathed. "For heaven's sake, Felicity, can't we hail a cab or something?"

Felicity nodded. "We won't find a hackney until we reach Piccadilly, though."

Riki cast a quick glance up and down the street. Four young men — bucks, Felicity called them — laughing and conversing loudly, came out of a well-lighted house and set off none too steadily in the opposite direction. The ladies started forward again, following them at a safe distance.

Riki dragged her borrowed watch out of her borrowed reticule and peered at the face. One-fifty. That left them only forty minutes until two-thirty . . .

She quickened her pace, and Felicity almost ran to keep up. If Marie went out to keep the appointment, who knew how early she'd have to leave? What if they ruined everything by being too late? Once someone checked the veracity of her information, they'd quickly discover it was a lie. Would they guess it was a set-up?

The young men ahead of them paused in heated argument, and Riki fumed at the delay as she waited, once again hugging close to the iron railing surrounding area steps. Whatever the cause of the altercation, it blew over quickly, and both parties resumed their ambling stroll to the busier street that now lay only a few dozen yards ahead.

To Riki, it seemed an odd time of night for so many carriages to be out, but in the absence of television, she supposed people held more parties.

Card games, she had gathered, could go on until dawn.

Felicity stopped abruptly beneath a glowing gas light. "Wait here," she ordered, then stepped to the edge of the street and waved at a passing hackney.

The vehicle clattered by without so much as slowing. Felicity tried three more times before an empty carriage pulled up.

She turned back to Riki and winked. "If you please, m'lady?" She spoke loudly so the jarvey would be certain to hear. "Mount Street, and hurry. Her ladyship's frozen with the cold." She swept Riki into the vehicle.

" 'Her ladyship?' " Riki whispered as she seated herself.

Felicity grinned and shrugged. "Why not?"

Why not, indeed? The jarvey probably thought her some not-so-respectable matron on her way to keep an assignation with her lover, afraid to call out her husband's carriage on such an errand. It was probably more believable—and much more commonplace—than the truth.

Inside the hackney, it was not much warmer than outside. Riki huddled into her pelisse and looked out the window, wondering what they would encounter at their destination. An empty house? If Marie Marley really had retired to bed with the headache from which she had claimed to be suffering, they would never know. It could be a long, cold night ahead of them.

She glanced at Felicity, who sat shivering and trying to pretend she enjoyed every moment of their adventure. Bedford would be furious with her for involving his sister—if he ever found out. And with her luck, he undoubtedly would. Riki forced down the surge of panic that accompanied that thought, and bent her mind instead to figuring out how to make the inevitable interview with Bedford a little less traumatic.

All too soon, they were set down only a few houses from Mrs. Marley's. Felicity, in her assumed role of abigail, paid the man and followed Riki as she crossed the street to the covering shelter of a tree.

"Now what?" Felicity whispered.

Riki glanced at her and saw the girl's large eyes wide with excitement. "I haven't the faintest idea," Riki admitted, to Felicity's obvious dismay.

"We shall have to break in," the girl promptly decided.

"We shall do no such thing! What if we were caught?"

That sobered Felicity, but only for a moment. "We could say we were worried about her and called to find out how she goes on."

Riki threw her unwanted companion a withering glance. "We're going to find ourselves a semi-comfortable sheltered spot and wait. Surely someone will either come out or go into the house soon."

From Felicity's expression, it was obvious she thought this dull work. Still, she did as Riki bade and descended the first few iron area steps into the shadowed recess of a home across the street from Marie Marley's. The minutes ticked slowly by, and nothing happened. After half an hour, a carriage turned onto the street, but it drove by without so much as a pause.

"We should have brought a deck of cards." Felicity sank down onto the top stair with a sigh and arranged her skirts decorously about herself.

Riki drew out her watch once more. Only two forty-five. They'd been here in plenty of time—had she been wrong, and the note was about something else entirely? She refused to believe it. Yet she was glad she hadn't run with this plan to Bedford. He'd be in the advanced stages of "I told you so" by now.

Still, she determined to give it at least until four before she gave up and went home.

Felicity yawned and shifted to a more comfortable position. At least they weren't getting into trouble, Riki reflected, but at the moment that was poor consolation for the freezing night air when they might have been cozily asleep in their huge, down-shrouded beds. Felicity, though, she wagered, would not have missed this for the world, even if it proved to be naught but a wild goose chase.

And the wild goose, in this case, was probably sleeping peacefully in her own warm bed, her headache long faded away. Riki ground her teeth. As a spy, she was proving a pretty big wash out.

Felicity leaned against the iron railing beside her, her eyes closed. If it had been warmer out, Riki guessed her companion would have fallen asleep by now, despite sitting on the hard, cold step. She reached down to adjust Felicity's slipping shawl, but never got around to it.

Another carriage pulled onto the street and Felicity sat up straight. She sank back, though, as it drove past Mrs. Marley's house.

That did it. "Let's just—" Riki broke off.

The carriage stopped four houses beyond them, and a solitary cloaked figure climbed out, waved the driver on, and turned to silently retrace the way in their direction. A pale ruffle showed beneath the dark folds of cloth, and a glimmer of pale curls peeped out from beneath a hood.

"Bingo," murmured Riki, grinning.

"What?" Felicity glanced at her.

"That's Marie Marley, isn't it?"

"Shall we make sure?" Felicity rose, only slightly

251

stiff from her vigil, and would have hailed the figure if Riki hadn't stopped her. "Why not?" Felicity mouthed, eager for activity after sitting for so long in freezing boredom.

"We still have to discover whom she went to meet."

"You mean we aren't to accomplish *anything?*" Felicity demanded, her expression comic in her dismay.

"Oh, yes. We've proved to *my* satisfaction, at least, that Marie is our traitor."

"Have we?" Felicity sounded doubtful. "All we proved is that she went out tonight."

"Can you think of any reasonable explanation why she should, after that headache act she put on at the ball? Unless she wanted to meet someone other than David, of course."

The figure slipped up the steps opposite and was admitted at once by someone inside. The door closed so softly they couldn't hear it. A minute later, the wavering light of a candle showed briefly near a window, then faded.

Felicity bit her lip. "Was the—the false information you gave her *that* important?"

Riki nodded. "It was. I indicated a completely different line of attack for the spring campaign. Napoleon would need word of it at once in order to alter his own plans to counter it. They would have to act immediately, without waiting."

Felicity shook her head. "I still can't believe it. How—how *could* she?"

"She's had an unhappy life here in England. It wouldn't surprise me if she'd been raised on stories of how much better everything was back in France."

Felicity nodded slowly. "She—she was. Oh, how dreadful it all is!"

Riki closed her eyes, suddenly weary beyond reason. At least she now knew who made such treacherous use of David. But she shied from sorting out what to do next. She was so tired, she could hardly think straight. She yawned, unable to stop herself.

"Let's find a hackney," she said.

Riki rose at her usual hour in the morning, still tired and with a dull headache pulsing through her temples from lack of sleep. She yawned cavernously, donned the dress held for her by her abigail, and set about making herself as presentable as possible without makeup. At last, abandoning the effort as a hopeless case, she stumbled her way down stairs.

Felicity, she noted with a faint touch of amusement, was not present at the breakfast table. She couldn't blame her. Nor had the others, with the exception of Bedford, emerged from their chambers yet. His lordship, Newly informed her, had left for Whitehall an hour before.

That satisfied Riki. She wanted to conduct the up-coming and undoubtedly unpleasant interview with her cousin alone. She found paper and a quill pen in the bookroom, and after only three attempts, managed to compose a creditably neat note of summons that she gave to a footman to deliver for her.

This done, she returned to the breakfast parlor, poured herself tea, selected a sustaining breakfast, and settled down to wait. Outside the lace-curtained window, heavy clouds gathered, oppressive and threatening. How fitting, she reflected. Did they, perhaps, portend an electrical storm? With luck, she'd be in need of one.

David arrived just over an hour later, as Lady Prudence and Hillary were just finishing their breakfasts. Hillary raised a questioning eyebrow as Newly announced him, and Riki avoided his curious eye. With a murmured excuse, she hurried to the salon where her cousin awaited her.

He came forward, smiling, and took her hands in greeting. "Good morning, Riki. What's up?"

"Quite a bit." She pulled him down onto the sofa and sat beside him. "David, Marie Marley is a French spy."

"Marie—" He sprang to his feet. "Damn it, Riki, what the devil are you talking about?"

"You heard me. I believe Mrs. Marley is taking any information about the war you accidentally let slip, and reporting it to the French." She stood as he flung away from her, catching his hand to draw him back. "Listen, David. I told you about the battle scene that changed. If you weren't betraying the British, then someone else was, and someone before whom you spoke freely."

He shook his head. "I've never really talked about the war with Marie." A slow smile lit his eyes, momentarily shoving aside his anger. "We've had other things to discuss."

"You've talked about France, haven't you?" she pursued, determined to make him believe—to break his faith in the only girl she had ever known him to love. That hurt. She would give anything not to have to do this. . . .

David shook his head. "We haven't talked about the war." He met Riki's worried gaze with a steady regard. "For the first time in my life, I've found something of more interest than gaming."

Riki felt physically ill, as if she betrayed him. "David, you've got to—"

He placed both hands on her shoulders and

shook his head. "No, Riki. *We've never discussed the war.* Period. Now, tell me why you're so convinced. Jealous someone's finally replaced you as first in my heart?"

His tone sounded teasing, but she knew he was serious. She sank back down on the sofa. "I deliberately made something up last night and pretended to let it slip in front of her. Remember that bit about the British attack plan?"

"That nonsense?"

She nodded, hating this. "Soon afterwards, she claimed she had a headache and you took her home. I left the ball early, too, and went to her house and waited. At about three o'clock this morning, a carriage dropped her off half way up the street and she walked back to her house." She raised her bleak gaze to his face. "Tell me she was with you all that time, and you'll have no idea how glad I'll be."

David's jaw tightened. "She wasn't. But that's not an outrageously late time if she happened to go to another party. She might have felt better and been unable to sleep." But for the first time, his voice lacked conviction.

She laid an impulsive hand on his arm. "I'm sorry, David."

He shook her loose. "You haven't proved anything. Lord, Riki, I only *met* her just over a month ago. That isn't time for her to have sent any messages to the French troops in the Peninsula! She *can't* be responsible for anything." Without another word, he stalked from the room, slamming the door behind him.

Riki sagged against the pillowed back, her eyes closed. It was true, then, he'd only known her for just over a month? He was right. That wouldn't give the French enough time to alter their defense strategy—or would it? Could they change plans as late as a few days before the battle?

Suddenly, she no longer felt as sure of anything. Spying was a dirty, hateful job, *especially* when one spied on people one knew and liked! She gazed unhappily out the window, saw that the snow had begun falling, and returned to her chamber to try and rid herself of the headache that now throbbed against the back of her eyes.

She must have dozed off, for a light tapping on the door brought her awake. Her headache, she noted with relief, had all but vanished. She sat up gingerly and suffered only the slightest twinge.

Her abigail entered on her call and bobbed a quick curtsy. "His lordship's compliments, miss, and will you drive with him?"

She started guiltily. He couldn't have learned about her nocturnal expedition—could he? She wouldn't put anything past Bedford. David might very well have confronted him by now. Wearily, she allowed her maid to help her into a fresh gown and tidy her hair, then made her way down to where Bedford awaited her in the hall.

His expression, far from being angry, showed concern. "My mother said you weren't well."

"Only a headache. What I wouldn't give for an aspirin!" She descended the last steps and took the hand he held out to her. She looked down, wishing it weren't so difficult to breathe just because he touched her. Did David feel this way with Marie? If so, she could understand his refusal to believe anything terrible of her.

"I thought a drive in the fresh air might make you feel better." He led her outside to where his groom walked his curricle.

"Do we go to the park?" She shouldn't feel such pleasure in his company, not when it would be

256

taken from her in so short a time.

"No. We are going to pay a visit to my brother-in-law." He handed her up to the seat, then went around and took the reins from the groom. The man waited until Bedford put his horses forward, then swung easily up behind.

"I shall be delighted to see Lady Linton again." Riki regarded her hands demurely while she wondered what this might be about.

"Will you?" Bedford raised a disbelieving eyebrow. "Actually, we are going in response to a summons from my brother-in-law."

"A summons?" Her eyes flew to his face.

Bedford nodded. "It seems he has heard a rumor in the War Office and he is quite anxious to have it either confirmed or denied."

"It seems odd of him to send for us to come to his house," she said. "Why not his office?"

Bedford shook his head. "He's laid down with his rheumatism. He came in this morning, but left after only an hour. He has had clerks running back and forth between Whitehall and his home all morning."

A slight smile touched Riki's lips. "And now he has summoned you. Why me, though?" She kept her voice low, out of deference to the groom who could overhear almost every word they said.

Bedford slowed his pair as they neared the corner. "He didn't, actually. That was my idea. You will know better than I if he has heard any rumors he shouldn't. The faster we can track it to its source, the better."

Riki nodded but remained silent. It was David he really needed, not her. She only had the vaguest idea about the Peninsular Campaign; all she could state for certain was that Wellington won. But David, at this moment, was not likely to help her out with anything. She'd gone a long way toward alienating him this morning—and that was going to make it that much harder to get him to agree to go back to their own time.

They drew up before an elegant townhouse on Curzon Street and Bedford helped Riki down. The butler opened the door before they even reached the porch, bowed them inside, and took them directly to the library.

Lord Linton, appearing even more frail than Riki remembered, lay on a sofa before the blazing hearth, his slender figure covered with a shawl. He looked up at their entrance.

"Miss van Hamel?" Even his voice sounded weary. "An unexpected pleasure. Forgive me for not standing. Will you not be seated?" He turned to Bedford and gestured for him, also, to take a chair. "I—I expected you to come alone."

"I believe I explained Miss van Hamel's assignment to you. It will be best if we are open before her."

Riki promptly assumed an expression she hoped betokened both intelligence and discretion.

Lord Linton regarded her thoughtfully for a moment, then nodded. "As you will."

"Now, about this rumor?" Gently, Bedford prompted him.

"Yes." The elder man fell silent for a moment, his gaze once again returning to Riki. "I was sorry your cousin was forced to resign."

"He's quite sorry to leave, I assure you. Pressing family matters," she added brightly.

Linton closed his eyes and leaned back against the pillows that had been carefully placed to support him. "He knows so very much," he murmured. As if with a great effort, he focused on Bedford. "There seems to be much going on about which I have been left uninformed."

"Not to my knowledge," Bedford assured him.

Linton waved that aside. "So they all say. Then tell me, if you will, is there any truth behind this rumor of an assault across the Tagus?"

Seventeen

Riki started, then brought herself under control. That was *her* rumor, and the only people who had heard it were David and Marie Marley! Her heart lifted at this proof that Mrs. Marley really had passed on her information, then sank again the next moment. Marie *was* a traitor, even if not the one for whom they first looked, and David shortly would lose her to a firing squad.

"I've heard nothing of this." Bedford's calm voice broke across her thoughts.

"No hints at all?" Linton asked. His slight frame leaned forward as his worried gaze scanned Bedford's impassive features. "Nothing? Then who started the rumor?"

Bedford shook his head. "I have no idea. You may be at your ease, there is nothing of any moment occurring at this time of which you are not fully aware." He spoke gently, as if he understood—and fully sympathized with—his brother-in-law's desperation not to be excluded.

Riki sank back in her chair, her mind whirling. She'd only learned half of what Bedford needed to know; she still had Marie's contact to discover. "Where did you hear this rumor, Lord Linton?" she asked.

He looked at her as if he had forgotten her presence. "I really don't remember."

"But you only heard it recently," she pursued. "And it concerned you enough to summon Bedford."

The viscount's eyes narrowed as they rested on her, but he held his tongue.

Linton spread his hands in a deprecating gesture. "It must have been one of the clerks this morning, trying to impress the others with his supposed knowledge."

"Or was it before this morning?" Good heavens, what made her speak so directly?

A dull flush crept into his pale cheeks. "Of course not!"

Bedford's gaze swiveled from Riki to his brother-in-law. Never before had he seen the man so uneasy. A muscle twitched at the corner of Linton's thin mouth in nervous reaction. But to what? And what was Riki doing? He caught her eye.

She met it with a steady regard. "*I* started that rumor. Last night at the ball. And I only told two people—David Warwick and Marie Marley."

Linton blinked. "Then young Warwick must have told some of his friends at the War Office!"

Even to Bedford, that had the sound of clutching at straws.

Riki shook her head. "Actually, he laughed at me and said I must have gotten it wrong. He started to correct me, then caught himself. I don't think he told anyone. But Mrs. Marley went out again last night after she went home early from the ball."

Later, Bedford swore to himself, he would find out just what Riki had been about. At the moment, the stark fear on Linton's face was of more importance. "Did she come to tell you?" he asked, keeping his tone casual, without any trace of accusation, as if the unwelcome certainty had not dawned on him that moment.

"No!" Linton gasped the word. "No, why—why should she?"

"To confirm the rumor's truth, I should imagine. Did you tell Mrs. Marley you heard it from me, Riki?"

She nodded. "And David immediately denied it. So she would need to confirm it before passing it on to her—her contact."

Bedford threw her a look that promised retribution later for taking so reckless a course, but right now the results interested him far too much. He turned back to Linton, who sat erect in his chair. A gray cast had crept over his pale complexion and he held his hands clenched in his lap. That didn't prevent them from shaking.

"How long have you been providing her with information?" He kept his voice calm.

"I—" Linton shook his head.

"How did you get it from David, without his ever knowing?" Riki leaned forward.

Bedford gestured her back. "I believe the more pertinent question here is *why*. You're no traitor, Linton. How did they force you?"

Linton drew a ragged breath and let it out slowly. Leaning his head back against the cushions, he closed his eyes. When he spoke at last, it was the merest thread of a sound. "Blackmail."

Blackmail? Bedford regarded his brother-in-law in no little curiosity. As far as he knew, the man had led a boringly blameless existence, particularly since his health had begun to fail. "How—" he began, then broke off, not wanting to press.

Linton's eyes opened slowly, as if his lids were made of lead. "She—Mrs. Marley—contacted me. She had those letters." He turned his haggard gaze on Bedford. "Do you remember that brief peace, back in '01? Before your time, really, I suppose. But

262

there was a definite hope of ending the hostilities. I wrote several letters to highly placed French officials, promising to help smooth the way. I did it without authority—without the knowledge of my superiors, in fact. But the potential consequences were worth the possible risk of disapproval." His voice rose on a note of fierce determination, a belief in his convictions.

"There is nothing in that with which to blackmail you." In his brother-in-law's eyes, Bedford glimpsed the blighted ambition to be the great peacemaker of Europe. Almost, he could pity him.

"The letters, unfortunately, were sufficiently vague to serve the purpose of the French. They made one subtle alteration, that is undetectable. I saw them, you see. And anyone else privileged to read them would believe the author a traitor."

"What was that change?"

"They made the 'one' into a 'nine' in the date."

Bedford caught his breath. "And so your offers of aid to the French cause appear to have been made in 1809, when we were deeply engaged in war."

Linton nodded. He sagged back in the chair once more, spent.

"Why the devil didn't you tell me?"

"What could you have done? Who would have believed me? The disgrace, the—" He broke off. Traitors were shot. "Clarissa and little Lawrence—I couldn't bear it."

So he'd become a traitor in truth. Bedford bit back the acid comment that sprang to his lips. It wouldn't have occurred to Linton to fight back. He'd crumpled under pressure, and the strain ate steadily away at his already faltering health.

"Tell me the whole and I'll do what I can for you."

"I didn't give them much at first." Linton studied his clenched hands. "But they guessed I passed on useless information and—and they threatened me. They said they'd harm Clarissa if I lied to them again."

"Who threatened her?" Bedford demanded, his fists clenching at this cruel use of his sister.

"Letters. Always in letters, brought by Mrs. Marley. That—that made them seem all the more dangerous. Usually, she had no idea what her missives contained. She was only the courier." He wiped the damp palms of his hands together. "It was the—impersonalness—the coldness, that made them seem so deadly. I never doubted them at all."

"Did you keep any?"

Linton shook his head. "Always, she took them away again. They wanted me to write my information, but I refused. Then Warwick arrived in Whitehall."

Riki made a noise, but Bedford caught her eye and commanded her to silence. "Were they interested in him?"

Linton almost managed a smile. "Not at first. But later, yes. It seemed safe to pass on things he said, it sounded almost like the ravings of a lunatic, at times. By then, my health was going. I—I tried to ease myself out of Bathurst's daily affairs, but they kept demanding more."

"Did David talk freely to you?" Worry, almost agony, colored Riki's words.

"Only when he was in his cups. He doesn't have a hard head, you know—I'd say he probably wasn't used to drinking much. He couldn't even finish one bottle without rambling." Linton drew a shaky breath and continued. "It—it was easy enough to invite him over to my table at the club and start him playing piquet. Usually, he talked nonsense. But it sounded exactly like the sort of information the French would want, comments on their faulty strategy, where and how they should direct attacks. I don't think I believed in any of it for a moment. But the French have been doing so *well* of late."

Bedford nodded, his lips tightening in a grim line. "Go on."

Linton nodded. "They—they wanted to know my source of information. I told them, hoping they'd release me. And to an extent, they did. I was ordered to introduce him to Mrs. Marley, and since then—this past month—they've left me pretty much alone."

"David *was* being used!" Riki sounded elated. "I *told* you he didn't lie to us. He never knew!"

Bedford didn't answer. His thoughtful gaze rested on his brother-in-law. "Why did you hit Hillary over the head with that stick?"

The man shook his head. "God, how I hated that. I—I had to discover Miss van Hamel's business—they ordered me to find out what went on. Young Hil was seen to visit Whitehall when you weren't there, and they were convinced something was up. I had almost reached the rookery when he came along, shouting for you, and how could I explain my presence?"

"In short, you panicked."

Linton nodded, miserable.

"Do you know anything of a carriage that followed us from Brighton?" Riki asked.

Linton focused his eyes on her with difficulty. "No. Did one?" He shook his head, obviously not caring about it. "What—what are you going to do with me?"

"The first thing is to get you out of this." Bedford drew a deep breath. "I believe you are about to suffer a breakdown."

Linton looked quickly at him, panic in his pale blue eyes.

"Under your doctor's orders, you will withdraw

from public life, sell your townhouse and retire to your property in the Cotswolds where you will live retired."

"But—Clarissa . . ."

"My sister is not so heartless she would want you to continue jeopardizing your health. She may use Bedford House when she wishes to come to town, and you may be very sure that will delight her no end." He rose. "If I were you, I would begin at once. The sooner you are of no use to them, the sooner you will be free."

He took Riki's arm and almost dragged her out of the room, leaving Linton to accept the wisdom of his advice.

"So now we know," Riki breathed as they made their way down the front steps to the waiting curricle.

"We still must find Mrs. Marley's contact. And she was never even suspected until you brought her to my attention!" He made no attempt to keep the savageness out of his voice. He helped Riki in and they drove in silence back to Half Moon Street.

When they entered the front hall, though, he stopped her. "I believe you and I still have something to discuss."

Riki looked the picture of guilt. "Have we?"

"In my bookroom, if you please."

Without another word, she preceded him down the hall and into the chamber. He closed the door, then looked up to find her standing before the hearth, her posture rigidly straight. Only a touch of uneasiness showed in her lovely gray eyes.

"I'm waiting," he said.

Haltingly, she related her escapades of the night before. His first impulse, which was to shake her, he fought back. Such an action was far too likely to end in his kissing her. He wasn't about to give in to that.

Instead, he gritted his teeth and directed his frostiest glare at her. "Can you not keep from acting in the most reprehensible manner? Going out alone at that hour of the night! Your behavior has been shocking."

"And just what would you have done? You refused to believe me concerning David's innocence."

Probably, he'd have done much the same thing, he admitted—but only to himself. *Damn* the chit for coming into his world and wreaking havoc with his life! Abruptly, he turned on his heel and stalked from the room. He wasn't thinking reasonably, and he knew it. He encountered a footman in the hall, and sent him to the stables to order his horse brought around. Taking the steps two at a time, he went to change into riding dress.

The traffic on the London streets irritated him further, but at last he passed Regent's Park and approached Finchley Common. Once free, he urged his restive mount into a gallop. For a long, chill mile, he abandoned himself to the exhilarating exercise, then at last slowed, albeit regretfully. It was strange how the fresh air cleared his head; already, he could think more clearly. He brought his horse about and headed back toward town.

Before returning home, he stopped at Linton House in Curzon Street. A distraught butler opened the door, and a swarm of activity met his gaze. Everywhere, servants scurried about their unexpected jobs of packing everything that would be kept. A house agent, a furious Clarissa informed him when he at last found her, had already been summoned.

"Rather fast," Bedford commented, eyeing his sister narrowly.

"Oh, it is so vexatious of Linton to decide to remove from town just before the season is to begin, and without any warning!"

"But preferable to destroying your husband's health."

"But—" She broke off, startled. "Is he truly that ill, do you think?"

"Had you not noticed?"

She looked away, troubled. "I had thought—" She broke off, then rallied. "He—he will recover in the quiet of the country, will he not?" She raised large, worried eyes to her brother.

"I am sure he will." He took his leave, well satisfied with the results. Clarissa was not hard-hearted, merely too wrapped up in herself. Nursing an invalid husband back to health would do her a world of good.

When he at last returned to Half Moon Street, he found Riki pacing anxiously about his bookroom and his carefully recaptured control wavered. She looked so vulnerable. Again, he fought back the impulse to drag her into his arms and kiss that frown from her brow. She didn't belong in this time, she must return to her own, where she had her own future. Life without her, though, was going to be depressingly empty.

"What is it now?" he asked, doing his best to sound merely resigned to her latest folly.

She strode quickly up to him, her anxiety patent. In spite of his better instincts, he took her hands in a sustaining clasp.

"Now that we are certain about Mrs. Marley, we must warn David, stop him from inadvertently telling her or anyone else anything more."

"Yes, but first we must learn to whom she passes the information. And at the moment, I have not devised a satisfactory plan for how that might be achieved." Absently, he raised one of the small hands he still clasped to his lips, realized suddenly what he did, and released her abruptly. He turned away to the fire that blazed in the hearth.

"Can we not give her some more false rumors and see where she goes?"

Even her soft, husky voice did pleasantly distracting things to him. Firmly, he shook his head. "That wouldn't be subtle enough."

"Have we time for subtleties? We don't know what David told her about his resigning from the War Office. And now Linton is leaving abruptly. Aren't you afraid she'll realize he's told us about her and take fright?"

He looked at her over his shoulder. "She can only guess and worry at this stage. But if Linton remains in town, she'll be certain. He's no dissimulator." He rocked back on his heels, his eyes never leaving hers. "If you had told me what you were about last night, I could have placed an immediate watch on her and discovered where she went or who called upon her."

"Yes, I might have known this mess would all turn out to be my fault. You wouldn't have placed any reliance on one of my plans, and so you well know! You'd have told me to go home and go to bed and forget the whole thing."

Dull color warmed his face at the accuracy of her guess.

She awarded him her sweetest smile.

And there was more sweetness in that one smile than he could have believed. After a brief struggle, he said: "In the future, I'll thank you to keep me informed of your plans." Under the circumstances, he felt he had let her off with a mild rebuke.

Apparently, she did, too. Her eyes crinkled with suppressed laughter as she lowered her head in mock contrition. "Then I had best tell you now that

I am going to speak with David."

"I wonder what he'll do," he murmured.

"Come back to our own time with me, of course." Riki looked up, met his gaze, and looked away quickly. "You said yourself that couldn't happen soon enough to suit you."

"Did I?" He caught the wistful note in his voice and recoiled. Lord, he couldn't become a sentimental fool! There was too much at stake in this deadly game to allow blatant emotionalism to interfere.

He crossed to his desk and began to shuffle papers unnecessarily. "There's always the chance he'll try to get word to Mrs. Marley that she's been discovered."

"He—" Riki broke off her heated retort.

"He might very well. You have no idea what idiocies a man might commit when he's in love." And that was why he'd never succumb to that lamentable complaint himself. "I'll send a message to him to meet us in the park." He dashed off a quick note, then strode from the room, calling for Charles, the second footman.

Riki watched him go, her heart heavy. Her adventure was almost over. Once David learned the truth, that he had been tricked by the woman he loved, he'd be only too ready to return home.

And Bedford would be only too ready to see her leave. He liked her; he was even attracted to her. But he wasn't about to give in once more to that glorious wave of sensation that swept over them when he kissed her. That would only lead to heartbreak for them both.

She caught herself up on that thought. What absolute drivel she was thinking! Heartbreak, indeed! Her mind seemed to be trapped in melodrama mode, in some 1930s tear-jerker movie. But just because the words were so corny and trite, that didn't make them any the less true.

She trailed out of the room and found to her relief that Bedford, having entrusted his message to Charles, had gone to his club. That left her free until their meeting with David.

When the footman returned, however, she found the meeting had been put off. In a brief note, which David directed to Riki, not to Bedford, he pleaded a prior engagement for the afternoon but promised faithfully to look for them at the Blomquists' card party that evening.

With that, Riki had to be content. Bedford, upon returning and hearing the news, merely set his jaw, gave her a curt nod of acquiescence, and closeted himself in his bookroom until dinner time.

By nine o'clock, Riki found she could barely contain her nerves. Should she depart with David upon the instant? But that would mean she wouldn't see Bedford any more. Should they wait a few more days? But that only dragged out the inevitable parting — and gave David an opportunity to confront his lady love with the evidence of her treachery. No, they had better get David out of London at once. Perhaps they could journey to Falconer's Court and stay there until the weather turned favorable, which in this case meant stormy.

Carefully, Riki concentrated on not looking at Bedford during the short ride to the party. Opposite her in the carriage, Felicity kept up a lively chatter, but Riki paid her words little heed. She would miss them — all of them. Hillary, of course, was already set to depart on the morrow to return to Oxford. But she didn't want to say goodbye to any of them!

So this was what came of living alone on a tiny island for so long. She was starved for company.

271

When she got home, she would invite people for weekends — perhaps ask ornithologists and students over to observe the peregrines. She would surround herself with people, and then perhaps she wouldn't miss Bedford so terribly much.

The bouncing of the carriage as they pulled up before the Blomquists' house jarred her out of her depressed reverie. She still had a very unpleasant confrontation ahead of her. Squaring her shoulders, she marched forward to face it.

Her preparations were to no avail. After a quick search of the comfortably filled rooms, it became apparent that David was not present. With a sinking heart, she settled down at a card table, knowing there was nothing she could do but wait.

That quickly proved almost more than she could bear. David would not take this well; he would defend Mrs. Marley, probably refuse to believe the terrible things Riki must say against her. He would think she tried to trick him into leaving his love and returning to his own time. He would want to go back to the future as little as did she.

She caught sight of Bedford playing piquet with an elderly gentleman on the other side of the room. He showed incredible tact, she realized with a flood of gratitude. Instead of waiting like this, he probably should have gone directly to whichever office in Whitehall dealt with spies and told them the whole — except, of course, where David gained his knowledge of French and British strategy. David's very existence, the information he could be forced to give the French, was a danger to England. But Bedford, against his innate loyalty to his country, gave her the chance to save her cousin, to take him home.

The evening dragged on, and still David did not appear. Nor, Riki noted with growing uneasiness, did Marie Marley. Frustrated, she returned her attention to her game of piquet, playing with an intensity that soon brought a growing number of coins into a pile before her.

At last, Lady Prudence rose from her whist table and announced in tones that carried across the room that she wished to leave. With a sense of shock, Riki realized it was almost two o'clock in the morning. *Where was David?*

She glanced across at Bedford, whose eyes glittered in the candlelight. He must be burning with fury, with a sense of betrayal. She could only hope he didn't hunger for blood.

Quickly, she hurried to his side, just touching his arm. The look he directed at her left her cold and shaken.

"He didn't keep the appointment." He barely repressed his anger.

"He couldn't have known how urgent it was. Can we not go to his lodging?"

"I shall, certainly."

"I'm coming, too."

He didn't waste time arguing. He sent for his mother's carriage, begged her pardon, and informed her that there was someone he must see.

"Me, too," Riki added, urgently.

Lady Prudence regarded them both from her queenly height and inclined her head. "You will have a care for Miss van Hamel, Bedford. See that she gets home safely."

"That is my intention." He waited with barely disguised impatience while they took their leave of their hostess, then he ushered his family from the house and out to the carriage that had just pulled up to the door. He handed in his mother and sister, then waved the driver on.

"What about us?" Riki breathed easier now that

he hadn't insisted she accompany them.

"We are going to have a talk with your d—with your cousin."

He started briskly down the street and Riki almost ran to keep up with his long-legged stride. He didn't slow for her, and she was relieved when at the corner they spotted a hackney standing by the curb. Bedford gave her cousin's address, they settled inside, and Riki caught her breath. They rode in silence until the carriage pulled up before the lodging house in Albemarle Street.

"Wait here." Bedford jumped down and strode across the street.

Riki peered out the window. The large, dark building appeared in no way remarkable. She tired of staring at it almost at once. But before she had time to become bored, Bedford strode back out, alone.

"Half Moon Street." He gave the jarvey the direction of Bedford House, pulled open the door and climbed in.

"Where is he?" Riki caught his arm in agitation. "What did you do . . . ?"

"Nothing!" He spat out the word, then continued in a savage undervoice. "Your beloved cousin, my dear, has flown."

Eighteen

"What—?" Riki stared at Bedford, startled.

"Left. Vanished. His room's been stripped, and the fellow running the lodging says Mr. Warwick will not be returning."

"But—that's impossible! He knew we—" She broke off, shaking her head, fearing the worst. "He wouldn't leave like that, not without telling me." Even to herself, her voice sounded forlorn.

"Well, he has. Confound it! I never should have waited. I should have turned this entire matter over to our people as soon as I got to London!"

"You didn't because of me."

He turned dark, brooding eyes on her. "Yes, because I promised you. I've never let a woman cloud my judgment before."

And he never would again, his tone said clearly. Riki closed her eyes, feeling ill. "Where has he gone?"

"Do you really need to ask? To France, of course."

"No!" She grasped his arm, shaking it in her intensity. "You heard him, he'd never try to alter history! He would never go willingly . . ." Her voice trailed off on that last word.

"If he were abducted, his room wouldn't have been emptied of his possessions. No, he left of his own accord."

"Then he couldn't have gone to France!"

He grasped her hand and eased her grip on his coat sleeve. "I'm sorry, Riki. What else am I to think? He got my message today, he knew it was urgent, and the man who runs his lodgings says he paid his account and left, alone, with all his baggage."

Riki shook her head, trying to block out the knowledge that her cousin had betrayed her—and Bedford, England, even their own future. It was too much to take in.

With a palpable effort, Bedford resisted the temptation to draw her against himself, to offer comfort for the pain rampant in her strained face. Instead, he hunched his shoulder and glared out the window. Damn David Warwick. Damn himself, for not denouncing the traitor when he had the chance. And damn Riki van Hamel, while he was at it. He let his infatuation with this impossible female cloud his normally excellent judgment. Abruptly, he let down the window and shouted to the jarvey to take them to Mount Street.

Riki huddled in her corner. "I can't believe it," she murmured.

"And just see the result!" No, that wasn't fair. It was his own fault, for not acting on impulse—and good sense. They still had one chance, though a very slim one, he admitted. A watch had been placed on Marie Marley, only that morning. If she left her house, she would be followed. And if she carried any baggage, she would be arrested. Since he had heard nothing, perhaps Warwick had not gone that far.

The carriage jolted to a stop, he jumped down, strode across the street and vigorously applied the knocker. He was forced to repeat his rapping several times before a sleepy and highly affronted retainer opened the door to him.

"I must see Mrs. Marley at once," Bedford declared.

"I am sorry, sir, she is not at home."

"When do you expect her back?"

"I couldn't say, sir." He began to close the door.

Bedford stood his ground. "If you do not take me to her at once, you will be placed under arrest for treason."

"Treason?" The man's face paled and his hand dropped to his side.

But though the elderly man was quite willing to talk, he had little to say that Bedford found of use. Madam had simply vanished. No, he could not state with any certainty when she had left. After her nuncheon, of course, but she had not been there for dinner. No, according to her maid, she had taken nothing with her. She left only one letter, to be delivered on the morrow, and a note for himself, directing him to close up the house.

"To whom was the letter addressed?"

"A Miss van Hamel, sir."

"Give it to me."

As soon as the man returned with the sealed sheet, Bedford tore it open. At a glance, he recognized Warwick's fist.

Sorry I couldn't stay to say goodbye," he read. "*We're in a bit of a hurry. For obvious reasons, we have to get out of here today. There's a little business I have to settle in Spain.*" A scrawled "D" was the only signature.

Bedford swore long and fluently, drawing an admiring glance from the retainer.

"Will that be all, sir?" he asked.

"Yes. No. Don't go." He turned and waved both arms over his head. A minute passed, then a dark shape detached itself from a doorway just up the street and hurried over.

"Did you see anyone either come or go?" Bedford demanded as the young man joined him.

"No, m'lord. Only servants."

Servants. Warwick probably came to see her, disguised, and she must have left the same way. With that blonde hair shoved under a mob cap and an ill-fitting maid's gown, the watcher would have paid her little heed. Bedford left the man with orders to begin a thorough search of the house for anything that might help, and returned to the carriage where Riki waited. Without comment, he handed her the letter.

She read it quickly, then lowered it to her lap. "No."

"Yes! He's admitted it!"

"No!" She shook her head. "It *can't* be true. He—he must be going to help the British."

"My God, how naive can you be? He'd have come to me, if that were his intention."

Riki closed her eyes and drew a long, quavering breath. "I'm sorry, Bedford."

He let that pass. "Exactly how much good can he do Napoleon?"

"A lot, I'm afraid." Her voice sounded muffled, as if she didn't want to answer, but felt compelled. "You saw his gaming room. He knows Wellington's battle plans for the entire campaign in intimate detail. He's fought and re-fought every battle with his gaming friends. The—the result will be disastrous."

"There is only one hope." He sounded grim and

278

he knew it, but at this point he didn't care. Sparing Riki's feelings was the least of his worries. "I must find him at the earliest possible moment."

"*We* must find him," Riki avowed. "You're not going after him alone. This is my fault."

He looked down at her, his expression carefully veiled. "And what do you think you could do that I cannot?"

"He is my cousin. My money provided him with the leisure to indulge his fascination with war games. It's my responsibility to prevent him from causing further damage."

"And what makes you think I'll let him?"

Her eyes opened wider as his intent became clear to her. "You—no, you can't kill him! You promised me!"

"What else am I to do? Rely on him to agree to be a good lad and behave in the future?" He freed himself and took her by the shoulders, shaking her gently. "Damn it, Riki, he's proved we can't trust him. God alone knows what damage he'll have done before I can stop him. Once I catch up to him, I can't permit him another chance to aid the French. I gave him one, already." Bitterness hung heavily in his words.

"Because of me." Her huge, lovely gray eyes brimmed with moisture. "Gil, I . . ." A single tear, followed closely by another, slipped down her cheek.

He brushed them away with one finger, then stopped the next with his lips. That did it. His arms crept about her and he held her tightly, crushing her petite form against his chest, kissing her with all the passion he'd been trying for so long to deny. His mouth brushed her cheek, then her eyes, tasting the salty tears before he reclaimed her mouth once more. Sensation blended with primitive need, and his control hovered on the brink.

With an almost superhuman effort, he dragged himself back, thrusting her from him while he could still think. Had he no resistance when it came to this woman? Desire, more intense than any he'd ever before experienced, warred within him against the anger he *ought* to feel with her for influencing his better judgment. To possess her would be worth any price—except the betrayal of his country.

That brought him part way back to earth. She wasn't of his world. They didn't belong together. He forced himself to repeat that, over and over. He couldn't have her for more than just a little while longer. And that knowledge haunted him.

"Gil—"

He silenced her by pressing his fingers to her lips. "No, Riki."

"You *must* let me. Please, if we can find him, we'll go back to our own time at once, and then you'll be rid of—us." Her voice trailed off on the last word.

Lord, he'd like to keep her at his side every moment of the precious time they had together. The temptation was almost irresistible. "No," he repeated, before she could change his mind. "I won't expose you to the risks of searching for your cousin behind enemy lines."

She drew a deep, unsteady breath. "Damn it, Gil, this is no time for misplaced chivalry! I won't be left out. I'm not the kind of shrinking, fragile damsel you're used to. I was brought up very differently, to make my own decisions and accept their consequences!"

"No."

"Give me one good reason. And I mean a *good* one!" She looked up at him, challenging.

Bedford gave up. "Because I can't think straight when you're near." And somehow, he had her back in his arms where he wanted her—and where he knew she could never stay.

Two questions still bothered Bedford, but he was not about to mention them in front of that enterprising young lady. One, the identity of Marie Marley's contact, he might never know—unless he one day caught up with her. He'd choke it out of her, then, if he had to. The other problem might have a much simpler answer, and he intended to see to it at once.

Only one person, in his mind, seemed likely to have followed their carriage from Brighton. Therefore, as soon as he had seen Riki safely off on a visit with Felicity and his mother the following morning, Bedford strolled around the corner to Clarges Street, where Sir Julian Taggart kept rooms while in London. He knocked sharply on the door, and several minutes passed before Julian's valet answered.

The ever correct gentleman's gentleman regarded Bedford in haughty amazement. "Sir Julian is still abed, m'lord." His tone, if not his words, implied that anyone who had been so long acquainted with his master must surely be aware of the solecism of calling upon him before noon.

Bedford waved his objections aside. "I need to talk to him, Grooby."

"But my lord . . ."

Bedford set the affronted valet aside and took the stairs two at a time. He knocked on the inner door, then made his unceremonious way into his old friend's bedchamber without waiting for an answer.

Sir Julian, wrapped in an elegant dressing gown, sat in a wing-back chair by the window and sipped tea as he read the morning paper. He eyed his visitor with pained reproach. "Really, my dear Bedford," he protested. "So early?"

Bedford impatiently waved Julian's protest aside. "I intend to have a few answers from you. Now."

Sir Julian set down the paper and spread his hand in an inviting gesture. "Far be it from me to interfere in your plans, dear boy. You may have as many answers of me as you wish."

"What did you think would happen to me on the road from Brighton to the Court?"

A slow smile spread across Julian's face. "Was I that clumsy? I take it you lost me on purpose, then. I wondered at the time."

"I did. And you didn't answer my question."

Julian examined his immaculate manicure. "I didn't trust Miss van Hamel. Your story, you know, didn't sound completely true to me. It seemed quite possible *she* was responsible for your aborted trip, and had planted herself on you with the intention of working her way into your household. That would make her either a spy or an adventuress." He tilted his head. "Which would you have considered the more dangerous?"

In spite of himself, Bedford smiled. "She is neither, as a matter of fact."

"You relieve my mind. I do not believe I could have supported the sight of you in the toils of an adventuress."

"Neither could I."

"Tea, dear boy?" Julian waved the pot toward him, hospitably.

And that, he reflected as he left shortly, was that. Dear old Julian, a well-intentioned—if somewhat clumsy—meddler. Riki would undoubtedly take Julian in even greater dislike once she knew his opinion of her, but at least one mystery had been explained to his satisfaction.

The rest of that day and the better part of the next, Bedford spent at the War Office in Whitehall. The conferences were endless, the results not positive. Finding one traitor who had deserted to the French seemed a formidable and unnecessary task to the so-called "experts" on the war effort. Any other traitor, and Bedford would have agreed. But David Warwick represented a special case, a potential disaster not to be comprehended by any of the British officials.

Nor did Bedford feel capable of explanations. Instead, and knowing he sounded as if he were out for petty vengeance against his treacherous assistant, he remained unswervable from his purpose. Lord Bathurst at last gave grudging permission to what he referred to as a "damn-fool waste of Bedford's valuable time" and washed his hands of the business.

That left Bedford free to plan his venture, which he did with meticulous care and every bit of help and advice he could scrounge in the busy department. It seemed most likely that Warwick had done precisely as he said, and was even now on his way to Spain where he could be at the sight of the battles, giving his advice to the generals. Therefore, the sooner Bedford left for the Peninsula, the better it would be.

A supply ship would leave Newhaven in two days, which left him little time to make his personal preparations; he would have to depart for the port early the following morning. The worst, he realized quickly, was not knowing how long this venture would take. The letter he carried from Bathurst would give him the cooperation of every commanding officer in the Peninsula, but his would be a difficult and desperate search, with no guarantee of success — or even of his survival.

With that dark thought in his mind, he spent an intense morning with his man of affairs, ordering the disposition of his unentailed properties and assuring that all would run smoothly until his return, however long that might be. That left one last task, taking leave of his family. They were to spend a quiet evening at home for once, and that suited him very well.

Bedford dressed for dinner quickly and hurried down first, refusing to take any special pains with his appearance on this, his last night at home. Why should he care what memory Riki had of him? Probably by the time he returned, having dealt with her cousin, he would have recovered from his ridiculous infatuation and be only too glad to pack her off to her own time. Perhaps he should have arranged to send her home immediately. But that, he realized, he couldn't bring himself to do.

When the door to the Blue Salon where he waited opened, he looked up eagerly. But the exquisite gentleman who paused just over the threshold for dramatic effect bore little resemblance to Riki's dainty self.

"Good evening, Uncle Sylvester." He tried to keep the resignation out of his voice. "To what do we owe the honor?"

"I found myself forced to cry off from a little party this evening."

"Gaming, I assume. Are your pockets wholly to let — as usual?"

Sylvester crossed to the fire to warm his coattails. "Really, Nevvy, to hear you talk, one would think I'm perpetually under the hatches."

"You are," replied his dutiful nephew, but with no malice in his tone. "Have you informed Newly you will be joining us?"

"Certainly." Sylvester straightened his slight frame.

284

"What's this I hear about you leaving for the Peninsula? Think you'll make it, this time?"

Bedford's eyes narrowed. "Where did you pick up that bit of information?"

Sylvester made an expansive gesture. "Happened to drop in on Linton this afternoon. He had some fellow from the War Office there, picking up papers. Linton says he's resigned his post. The whole household was in an uproar with their packing and preparing to leave London." Sylvester fixed an accusing eye on his nephew.

Bedford nodded. "His health, you know. I believe this will be for the best."

Sylvester's gaze narrowed, but before he could demand any more information, the door opened again and Lady Prudence, Felicity, and Riki entered. Lady Prudence came to a halt in a rustle of purple silk.

"You here, Sylvester?" She raised her lorgnette and regarded her brother-in-law with quelling intensity.

"As you see, my dear Lady Prue. Felicity, you look lovely, as always. And Miss van Hamel, a never-ending delight." He swept an elegant bow in their direction. "I have come to bid Bedford farewell."

To Bedford's surprise, his mother merely nodded. "Very proper."

He cast a speculative glance at Riki, who made a show of seating herself on the edge of a gilt-trimmed sofa. "I see my journey is no secret."

"Did you expect it to be?" In a cloud of pink gauze, Felicity settled on a blue brocade chair. "Really, Bedford, you'd think you were the only person capable of finding out anything."

"And whom do I have to thank for informing everyone of my movements?" His wrathful gaze came to rest on Riki once more.

"It was only reasonable you'd be resuming that journey you were taking when your boat sank," Felicity declared. "And from your activities over the last few days, it was obvious it would be soon."

"So it was." Bedford fixed a penetrating eye on his sister, but decided she only spoke the truth. Actually, he'd forgotten that message he'd attempted to carry to Wellington. It seemed ages ago, as if it occurred in some dream — or to someone else. He hadn't known Riki, then.

Dinner passed with less confusion than was usual in his family, perhaps because Hillary had departed for Oxford and was no longer present to enliven the meal with his practical jokes. Afterwards, he allowed his uncle only one glass of brandy before steering him to the drawing room where the ladies waited. He saw the others settled at a whist table, then made his excuses because of the early hour of his departure and said his goodbyes.

When he came to Riki, he hesitated. The success of his mission meant she would leave him to return to her own time. It was for the best, he reminded himself savagely. Abruptly, he turned away, but she rose and went to him.

"I'll do my best." He spoke before she could. To his surprise, she merely nodded.

"Have a pleasant voyage this time." She gripped his hands for a moment, then returned to the card table and took her place.

Feeling considerably deflated, he made his way upstairs to where Pervis, his valet, already packed his trunks. He should be pleased to find Riki so docile instead of continuing her arguments to accompany him, but perhaps she realized how difficult and dangerous this undertaking would be. The fact that she didn't seem to mind being parted from him, though, hurt. Irritated, he paced about his chamber, hindering Pervis as he carefully folded and smoothed the numerous garments he deemed necessary to sustain his master among the officers in Lisbon.

The urgency of his mission proved an overpowering weight on his broad shoulders, robbing him of sleep as he tried to see his way to its successful completion. Yet as he departed before dawn the following morning to drive his curricle the considerable distance from London to Newhaven, it was Riki's indifference that haunted him. Had it all been pretence on her part to bend him to her will? Had she abandoned that ploy once she realized he intended, if necessary, to kill the traitorous Warwick? She hadn't even made one last plea for her cousin's sake. She must have known it was pointless.

By the time he reached the port shortly before two o'clock that afternoon, he was in a foul mood. He left his curricle and baggage in the charge of his groom and made his way along the teeming wharf, careful to avoid contact with the fishmongers.

Screeching gulls swooped low over the boats that rocked gently at anchor. He located the *Sea Witch* with little trouble, merely following the steady parade of soldiers carrying crates and baggage on board. Women and children gathered near the gangplank, bidding their menfolk farewell.

Bedford strode on board, unchallenged, and was directed to the hatch where he found the captain overseeing the securing of the cargo. He presented his papers, and in a very little time he was escorted by a boy to a small cramped cabin that would be his quarters for the duration of the voyage. He tossed the boy a coin, and was promised his luggage would be aboard in a trice.

He stood at the porthole, gazing out over the harbor, until the smell of pitch, barely noticeable at first, grew on him. He might be in the way on deck, but at least the fresh salt air would be clean and a welcome change from these closed quarters.

He strode up the companionway, dodging the hurrying sailors, and found a place in the bow where he could watch the bustling activity without obstructing it. The day promised to be clear with a strong breeze, perfect for setting sail. Wavelets slapped at the hull, but not a single white-cap showed its stormy head. He stretched, easing his stiff muscles.

He had made it to the ship with a bare half hour to spare. Already, the gangplank was being drawn back. The captain's voice boomed forth over the cries of the sea birds, and the lines that had secured the great ship to the dock were cast off.

A creaking protest of heavy chains sounded as five strong sailors dragged up the anchor. Canvas snapped in the wind as more men raised the sails, and the deck rose beneath Bedford's feet as the *Sea Witch* slipped free of her berth and turned her bow toward open water.

They moved slowly at first, until they passed the last line of moored boats. Then the sails were hauled fully into position, the wind caught them, and the heady salt spray lashed against Bedford's face as the ship picked up speed. His spirits surged, filling him with that familiar energy and joy of being on the sea.

Behind him, the dock would be growing distant, half-hidden by the lines of bobbing boats. But he looked forward, on toward his journey. Behind him. . . .

Behind him, voices raised in angry shouts.

"What's this about?" The captain's voice reached

him, rising on an incredulous note. "A spy? Why were you stowing away, lad?"

Bedford spun about. Two sailors stood before the captain, clutching between them a youth garbed in ill-fitting clothes. A short, slender youth with bright auburn hair hanging to his shoulders.

The captain drew his pistol, and Bedford, fury filling him, strode quickly to intervene. Shoving one sailor aside, he grabbed the youth's shoulder.

"Damn it, Riki, what the devil do you think you're doing?" he exploded.

Nineteen

Riki, despite her bravado, trembled in Bedford's clasp. The sailors, even the captain with his threatening gun that had terrified her a moment before, now seemed unimportant.

"We found 'im below in the 'old, sir." The sailor who still gripped her responded. "Stowin' away, 'e was."

"Do you know the fellow, Lord Bedford?" The captain, still holding the pistol, came a step closer and peered at Riki's face.

Bedford drew a deep, ragged breath. "This, captain, is Miss Erika van Hamel. She has been assisting our government, but it was the decision in Whitehall that it would be too dangerous for her to continue her assignment. You will note the rebellious spirit so common among the American colonists in her behavior."

"American, is she?" That seemed to explain everything to the captain. He tucked the gun away. "What are we to do with her, my lord?"

Bedford cast a quick glance back the way they came. "It's too late to turn about," he said, not without considerable regret.

"You might try taking me with you." Riki, annoyed at being left out of the discussion, shook off her remaining captor and faced Bedford squarely. "This is my affair—even more so than yours. I told you days ago I wouldn't be left out."

"Your damned precious cousin—"

"He deserves to be heard before you shoot him out of hand."

Bedford grabbed her arm. "Excuse us, captain. I'll find something to do with her. She need not be your concern."

He dragged her back toward the bow of the ship where they could continue their rousing fight without an audience. The men would be busy for some time still, coping with the sails as they advanced into the uneven currents of the Channel.

"Now, you will tell me where you got those clothes and how you got here—though I don't suppose I really need to ask. Hillary's?"

Riki nodded, refusing to look chastened. "He left quite a few things in his room. There was no trouble finding something that fit well enough. Nor would he grudge them to me."

"That goes without saying. And how did you follow me?"

"I didn't. I left first—last night, in fact. I'd won some money at cards, and your sister loaned me more, but between us we could only manage enough to hire two horses with the carriage instead of the four you'd have. Felicity said you'd probably overtake me unless I left hours ahead of you."

"I suppose she even told you which ship I'd be on?" He spoke through clenched teeth.

Riki shook her head. "No, your Uncle Sylvester discovered that for me. He was only too delighted to be of service."

"I can imagine." Bedford glared at her and ran an agitated hand through his already wind-blown hair, changing the pattern of salt and pepper in a fascinating manner. "You'll have to come with us," he said at last.

"Thank you."

"To Lisbon, but no farther!" he asserted, exasperated. "I will leave you with some poor officer's family there."

"No, you couldn't be that cruel to them." She met his fulminating glare with a bland smile. "Only think how distressed they'd be when I vanished."

"You—" Alarm flickered momentarily across his face.

"No, not back to the future. I fully intend to follow you. You realize, of course, it would be much simpler if you just took me with you. I don't speak a word of Portuguese and my Spanish and French never got beyond high school. You'd probably have to turn back to rescue me from some ridiculous scrape or other before we'd gone ten miles." She peeked up through her long lashes with a look calculated to disrupt his thinking.

He remained visibly unmoved. "You're a damned nuisance," was all he said.

She stuck her tongue out at him.

"Quit playing off your tricks on me, my girl." A grim note crept into his voice, and the lines about his mouth set in determination. "I'm not taking you into danger."

"Why should you worry about me? Your sole purpose seems to be to murder my cousin. After all, neither of us belongs here. If I get killed as well, what does it matter?"

His hands clenched. "It matters too damned much, and you know it does." He barely breathed the words.

The intensity of his gaze held her spellbound. The movement of the deck swayed her toward him, and she didn't resist. He reached out and caught her, steadying, and his strong hand remained on her arm, his fingers caressing her borrowed coat sleeve.

"Gil?"

The throaty whisper sent a shiver through him. He drew her closer and she closed her eyes as his head descended toward hers.

Abruptly, he released her. "Damn you," he muttered, with considerable heat.

"That seems to be one of your favorite occupations of late." It was a struggle, but she recovered her equilibrium. No easy task on the unsteady deck of a ship, she told herself by way of excuse.

"You bring out the best in me, I suppose." He gazed down at her, and his expression softened. "Be reasonable for once, Riki. It's too dangerous for you to venture into Spain."

"No more dangerous for me than for you. No, listen, Gil." She laid a hand on his arm and his own came up to cover it. "I *am* fond of David, but I don't think I'm letting that cloud my judgment. Give me one last chance to save him. Please, Gil. I just can't believe he'd intentionally try to change history. He *knows* the potential consequences. Marie Marley must have tricked him in some way. Let me talk to him. If you're right. . . ."

His fingers tightened over hers. "I must make certain he can't aid the French."

She nodded, then mastered her voice. "If he really is tampering with history, and if he refuses to stop and return to the future with me, I understand he must be — stopped."

"Killed, if there is no other way." Bedford said the words deliberately, making her accept them.

"Killed," she repeated, though it went dreadfully

293

against her very nature to agree.

"All right, then. I'll take you with me. And may heaven preserve me from strong-willed females who thrust themselves into men's business." But the last was said with a touch of his more usual good humor.

Riki let it pass. He didn't really want to spare David. Bedford considered her cousin a traitor—and possibly with good cause. For her sake, though, he had made that promise. And he would abide by it. With that she had to be satisfied.

The weather, which had been so stormy of late, turned fair and tranquil, as if out of sudden perverseness. The ship lay becalmed on the seas with barely a breeze to move it slowly forward. The skies remained clear, without so much as a cloud to offer the promise of more favorable sailing conditions. The days crept by, slipping inexorably into weeks.

Only the slightest touch of *mal de mer* troubled Riki at first, but she quickly emerged from the cabin Bedford had turned over for her use. They spent their time strolling about the deck for exercise, or playing piquet at night until Riki's skill almost equaled Bedford's. Always, the urgency of their mission hung over them, and they both chafed at the wasted hours.

Then at last they reached the Portuguese coast and rounded the tip of land that led to the mouth of the Tagus. Riki leaned eagerly over the side, staring into the darkness of night as they sailed silently along the river and into the wide estuary and the Mar de Palha beyond.

We'll sleep on board tonight." Bedford joined her against the rail as the sailors ran to toss lines over the side to men waiting on the lighted docks.

"And tomorrow?"

"I will consult with military headquarters and arrange our transportation to wherever the army is currently advancing. And then we will find you something a little more suitable to wear."

That brought a slight smile to her worried lips. "You don't like your brother's taste in clothing?"

"Minx," he murmured. "It's bad enough on him. On you, it's outrageous. As well you know."

She cast him a sideways glance. "You don't like them on me?" she pursued, deliberately provoking him further.

"Far too much. You're an unconscionable baggage."

"I've rather gathered you're of that opinion. And now I suppose you'll lug me across Portugal and Spain like some extra saddlebags."

"Not quite." The smile sounded in his voice.

She looked up, but the torches and lanterns that illuminated the sailors scrambling over the deck and wharf didn't penetrate to the dark fastness of his eyes.

"It will be a hard ride, I warn you," he went on.

"I'll be glad of the exercise after being cooped up for so long. Can't I keep these clothes so I can ride astride? I can't imagine anything worse than fighting with a sidesaddle for long stretches."

"No!"

She glanced up at him, startled by his vehemence.

"You have been stared at quite enough by the sailors. I won't have you walking around like that among an army on the march. You'd be taken for a common camp follower."

"Not a common one, surely," she responded promptly, though his words stung.

He pushed away from the rail and stood erect, towering over her. "You are the most shocking hoyden with whom it has ever been my misfortune to come into contact."

"You've mentioned that before," she pointed out in a spirit of pure helpfulness. "Look, we'll compromise. If I can find a seamstress and something resembling a riding habit, I can have a split skirt made."

"A what?" Suspicion sounded rife in his voice.

"A full skirt, only divided, like very loose pants— I mean breeches. When I'm on the ground it will look every bit as prim and proper as you could wish. But I'll be able to ride astride."

With that, he agreed, though he obviously held some reservations. Satisfied, Riki bade him goodnight and made her way to her tiny cabin where she lay awake, wondering about the adventure to come.

She must have drifted off to sleep at last, for she awakened to a soft tapping at her door. Dragging herself back from the depths of a hazy dream, she yawned, then struggled to a sitting position. Light streamed in through her porthole, announcing that the morning was already advanced. Another cavernous yawn prevented her from calling out in response.

"Riki?" Bedford's muffled voice reached her.

"Just a moment," she called back. She swung out of her bunk, steadied herself on the gently rocking floor, and reached for her clothes.

"Pack everything and come up on deck."

She heard his booted footsteps retreating down the narrow companionway. Picking up one of Bedford's valises, she began to toss in the few articles of clothing she had borrowed from him. Not for the first time did she regret not bringing anything with her when she stowed away.

Today she would rectify that problem. Lisbon was no backward town, but a bustling city inhabited by any number of British officers' families as well as well-to-do Portuguese nobility. There would be shops—provided Bedford would once again loan her some money.

This, she quickly discovered, he was more than willing to do. His only regret, which he expressed freely and with a certain amount of heat, was that she had to set forth in that scandalous costume. With amazing tact, she refrained from pointing out that Hillary hadn't thought it scandalous, and instead promised to purchase a simple gown at her very first stop and pack away Hillary's garments at once. To this Bedford agreed, and after handing her a sizable purse, he took his departure to visit Admiral Berkeley at his headquarters.

A tentative question of the ship's captain set her in the right direction for the shopping district. This, she discovered, was already bustling with business. Not speaking one word of Portuguese proved a considerable drawback for a young lady garbed in men's clothing, but she managed to purchase a plain round gown of figured muslin that didn't fit that badly. Wearing this and the pair of slippers she purchased at a cobbler's next door, she set forth with the assurance that the proprietess of the next establishment she entered would not be shocked by her appearance. Only by her request for a split skirt.

But she found a seamstress not only able to understand her gestures, but also willing to make the necessary alterations to a riding habit that hung on display in her shop. Recklessly, since Bedford was footing the bill, she purchased an already made-up light woolen gown and pelisse as well.

She would still need a hat to suit Bedford's notions of propriety. While the seamstress went to work, Riki visited a haberdasher's to purchase undergarments, a toothbrush, a shawl, and several other items of necessity.

297

Bedford, she found when she returned to the *Sea Witch*, had not wasted the morning either. She found him on deck, deep in conversation with a slender middle-aged gentleman in scarlet regimentals. Bedford cast a glance over her demure muslin gown, the warm shawl and the chip straw bonnet and nodded approval, then introduced her to Captain Belmont, who would be embarking with a supply train to Spain the following morning.

He was delighted to include them on this expedition, the captain informed Bedford, obviously not meaning a word of it. Women, his glance said clearly, should stay at home where they belonged. Riki contented herself with smiling sweetly at him, then thanked him coolly for his help and stalked off to stow her new possessions in the saddle packs provided by the captain.

The following morning dawned crisp and clear, with a promise of warmth by mid-day. Spring came early to the Peninsula, Riki thought, then the next moment it dawned on her it was no such thing. Somehow, between the parties in London and the never-ending voyage to Portugal, March had slipped away, becoming April without her realizing it.

Garbed in her new habit and Hillary's boots, she rode easily astride her mount, though she shivered in the early morning chill. Soon they left Lisbon behind. The company with which they traveled moved slowly, but the well-tended roads allowed them to cover more ground than she otherwise would have thought possible with supply wagons in their train.

Long before the commander finally called a halt at dusk, she had given way to exhaustion. Only with a concerted effort did she remain erect in her saddle. Every muscle ached, and the approach of nightfall brought a harsh nip to the air.

Beside her, Bedford swung off his mount, then

came around and grasped her waist, more than half lifting her to the ground. "Tired?" he murmured.

She made a rueful face. "It's been a few years since I've really ridden much—and never all day like this. I think I've discovered a few new muscles."

His fingers brushed an errant auburn tendril from her cheek. "Rest while you can. It will be another long day tomorrow."

"But my horse—"

"I'll take care of him." He pulled the reins over the bay gelding's head and led both her mount and his own a short distance away where the soldiers were engaged in unsaddling and rubbing down their animals.

Around her, men busily set up their make-shift camp. Riki took a tentative step, found her legs supported her, and hobbled stiffly off to find the captain in charge. A tent had been provided for her use, she discovered, and when an eager young lieutenant offered to oversee its erection, she made no protest.

She felt as if she had barely had time to eat dinner and fall asleep when Bedford was calling her again to get up. In the dim early morning light, she could barely make out the indistinct figures of soldiers leading their freshly saddled horses or breaking camp. The pungent odor of smoke from the breakfast fires that still burned filled her lungs. She stretched, discovered a couple of new muscles that had decided to jump on the bandwagon of complaint, and dragged on her riding habit. By the time she emerged, two soldiers were waiting to take down her shelter, and Bedford had secured breakfast for them both.

"Useful man," she declared. "I can't believe how hungry I am."

He grinned. "Unaccustomed exercise," he explained over a slab of bread and cheese.

She took a plate from him and settled at his side on a rock. "How much farther?"

At the weariness of her tone, his expression gentled. "We've come about a third of the way, the captain says. Badajoz is just over the border. We should reach it a little before nightfall the day after tomorrow."

She asked: "Do you think we'll find him there?"

"I wish I knew." He took a long drink of his steaming black coffee. "He had several days' start on us, and we lost I don't know how much time becalmed on the voyage. But we don't know how he traveled, if he went to Paris first, *anything!*" He dashed the dregs of the powerful brew into the dirt at his side. "It's most likely they'll want him where they're expecting a battle. Damnation! I wish I could be sure."

Riki touched his cheek, then quickly withdrew her hand. "We'll find him as soon as we get to Badajoz, you'll see."

He directed an almost humorous glance at her. "It's a city under siege, in case you'd forgotten. How do you intend to locate him? Ride into the town square and ask the French where they are keeping an American traitor to the British cause?"

She pretended to consider for a moment. "Well, I could, I suppose, but my French is rather poor, as I may have mentioned. Perhaps we'll have to be more subtle."

That brought an honest smile to his lips. "Let's worry about it after we've seen what we're up against. Mayhap the battle will already be over. I can't remember the exact date written on Warwick's displays, can you?"

"April the Sixth."

"That's—" He broke off. "Today is the Fourth,

300

isn't it?"

"I'm afraid so."

They finished eating in silence. As she stood and brushed off her skirts, the commander gave the order to prepare to mount, and Riki and Bedford hurried to where he had left their horses saddled and waiting.

The problem of finding David occupied her mind for most of that day and the next, at least whenever she could spare her thoughts from her aching muscles. If the first day had been agony, the next two were torture. After three days of being cramped in a saddle, she'd almost welcome a turn or two on a rack.

But just as she was about to abandon hope of ever again using her legs, an outrider who had ventured ahead returned with the news that Elvas, where the British had established their headquarters for this third siege of the city, was just ahead. Badajoz, the captain assured them, lay a bare ten miles farther.

Riki nodded, her nerves racing. "When do we go?"

Bedford shook his head. "That will depend on a great deal." A slight smile at her eagerness just touched his lips.

When he emerged from the British headquarters a little over an hour later, though, his expression was grim. Riki, who had waited near the horses, hurried across to meet him.

"What is the news?"

"You were right about the date. The assault is on for tonight."

Riki's throat suddenly felt dry. "Then—"

"I'm leaving at once. I *must* know if Warwick is there."

"And just what do you intend to do? Climb the

walls or fortifications or whatever they have, right along with the army?" she demanded.

He looked down at her, his expression somber. "If I have to."

Riki swallowed, fighting back a wave of fear. "Then I'm going with you."

Twenty

"You will do no such thing!" Bedford rounded on Riki, his expression explosive.

"Of course I will. You think you can slip in there and kill my cousin without my knowing. I won't stand for it!"

"So you'll risk your life for a traitor."

"We've been through this before." She spoke through clenched teeth, not permitting her frustration—or fear—to show. "Gil, you don't even know if you can do anything. Let me ride up with you. We'll stay behind the action, wait and see what happens. You can tell whoever is in charge that it is imperative you see any prisoners. Then, if the town is taken, we can enter safely and search for David."

A wry smile barely touched his lips. "You have a very simplified notion of how war works, my dear. Very well, if you think you can stand the sight of that much carnage, you may come with me to the British camp. But under no circumstances will you enter Badajoz!"

"Then promise me you won't kill David if you find him. Promise!"

He took her hands, his expression grim. "I swear to you, if I find him alive, I'll bring him to you."

Riki met his unwavering regard and could only wonder at the emotions that raged behind his

303

sparkling eyes. He had been in battle himself, taking active part, not just a mere onlooker. Was it the horrors he remembered now, or that thrilling surge of adrenalin that overcame caution and made an ordinary man charge bravely toward death? And Bedford was no ordinary man.

She dropped her gaze, feeling as if she trespassed into the privacy of his soul. She wanted to share it, but it must be at his offering. "Bring him to me," she agreed.

They left their baggage at Elvas and rode in silence with a lieutenant, who carried messages to Sir Thomas Picton, who was in charge of the assault. Sir Thomas had made his camp with the Third Division on the far side of Badajoz, and dusk already obscured the landscape as they worked their way around the south, toward the Albuera road. Nothing, though, not even the approaching darkness, could hide the scarred and ravaged landscape that bore its mute testimony to the heavy bombardment from the French defense. Even a river had been dammed so that it formed a vast, impassable lake.

Riki shivered in sudden foreboding. The distant sporadic gunfire provided the perfect musical score for the setting.

The city looked exactly like an ancient fortress, formidable—impregnable—standing on a slight hill in the midst of flat land. Toward the eastern end, a craggy castle rose high on a towering rock, a symbol of defiance to those mere mortals who dared to breach its walls.

In its great shadow lay the British camp, and Riki caught her breath. Trenches slashed across the fields; heavy artillery pointed at the walls. A second city seemed to spread out before her, consisting of a hodgepodge of tents, wagons, and horses. Everywhere, men swarmed, moving solemnly about their deadly business. Riki raised her eyes to the barren grey walls above and wondered if even that great stronghold could long endure this mustering on-slaught.

According to history, it didn't. This was the night of April Sixth, the night the British at last scaled the walls. But would all that be changed? Were the French fortifications all that much stronger, because they had been warned of the British strategy? Was David even now within those walls, telling the com-manders where the British would strike first, and how best to repel their attack?

If the French were forewarned, how much dead-lier would be this assault! The British plan was to move up under cover of darkness and scale the walls where they couldn't be seen. What if the French didn't *need* to see them?

Tension tied her stomach in knots. Could one man — one she had loved as a brother since child-hood — destroy history with a simple warning spoken at the wrong moment?

The young lieutenant who served as their guide took them directly to Sir Thomas's tent. Riki, who had once again donned Hillary's clothing for safety's sake, remained with the horses while Bedford went inside to present his authorization and explain his request. He emerged shortly, and from the rigidity of his stance, she feared their request had been de-nied.

"Gil?" She swung down from the saddle and hur-ried over to clasp his hands. "What happened?"

He shook his head and managed a slight smile. "Nothing. All is well. You are to wait here until I come for you. You'll be safe in Sir Thomas's tent."

"And what of you?" Her foreboding grew.

With one finger, he gently stroked her cheek. "I want to see the preparations."

305

"Can't I—"

"No." He cut off her request. "I want you here, away from it all." He drew her a step closer and stroked her hair back from her face. "You would see much that would distress you terribly. You also will remain here because the French continue to shoot, as you may hear, at irregular intervals. I can't risk your being hurt."

Suddenly, it became extremely difficult to breathe. "Why?" she whispered.

He dropped a light kiss on the top of her curls. "Then who would there be to argue with me?" He released her abruptly and gave her a slight shove. "Inside with you. I'll come back and report if anything is about to happen."

She glared at his back as he disappeared into the darkness, moving carefully among the clustered tents and numerous campfires.

Waiting throughout the early hours of the night quickly proved unbearable. Between the pervading aura of excitement and the constant activity, Riki couldn't bring herself to sit still. She paced about the narrow confines of the tent, peeking out regularly in the hopes of catching a glimpse of Bedford's sturdy figure.

Suddenly, a distant explosion, followed by rapid gunfire, shattered the night and she ran outside. She could see nothing, she was too far away. Impulsively, she started forward, desperate to know what occurred.

Before she had taken twenty steps, she saw Bedford and broke into a run. "What is happening?" she cried, anxiety quavering in her voice.

He put an arm about her shoulders and led her inexorably back to the tent. "The assault has begun. Somehow, the French either saw the preparations or they were forewarned."

Riki stopped dead and looked up at him. "David?"

"I don't know. But I intend to find out." Every line of his rugged face bespoke his grim determination, the cold, murderous hatred in his heart for his ex-assistant who betrayed the trust Bedford placed in him.

A falcon swooping to his kill, Riki thought. A cold hard lump of fear formed in her breast.

"Stay here," she begged.

He looked back the way he had come, where innumerable flashes of gunpowder now illuminated the dark facade of the castle.

"There's nothing you can do to help. They *will* take the town tonight." She put more assurance into those words than she felt.

They stood where they were, watching from that considerable distance, waiting because they could do nothing else. His strong hand gripped hers painfully, his tension never lessening. Did he relive battles from the dark recesses of his memories? He had been wounded, he had known the searing pain of a bullet. Her thankfulness that he did not take part in this engagement left her weak.

Then the firing slowed, the cannonading became less constant. Bedford stiffened, and started walking with Riki hurrying at his side.

The camp was not empty. Groans and occasional cries reached them from the wounded who had been carried to their tents. Women—wives, camp followers—busied themselves heating water over the fires, tearing linen into strips for more bandages than had been prepared. Everywhere, the putrid smells of blood, smoke, and untold miseries reeked.

Bedford's hand tightened on Riki's and they strode on, drawn by the necessity to know what occurred. Then through the darkness came a trio of

307

soldiers, two staggering as they supported their limp comrade between them.

Bedford hailed them. "What's the news?"

"We've breached the wall, sir," the nearest gasped. "Won't be long, now," he added as they passed.

"Then we do take the town!" Riki breathed, and realized with a sense of shock that she'd identified completely with the British. She had only been here for less than three months. How could David, who had lived among these people for over two years, turn against them?

Bedford's stride lengthened and she had to run to keep up. The next soldier they encountered confirmed the report, adding the bastions on the western end of the town were now overrun by the British.

A shout rose in the distance, rippling back through the camp as weary voices joined in triumph. The castle had been taken.

Bedford halted, his expression torn. "You're going back to the tent," he finally said.

"And you?"

He drew an unsteady breath. "I'm going up as far as I can. As soon as it's permitted, I'll enter the town and see what I can learn of Warwick."

"The fighting hasn't stopped," she pointed out unnecessarily, as rifle shots could still be heard, though neither as frequent nor as loud. "It's in the streets of the city, now."

His hand cupped the back of her head as he stooped to kiss her quickly. "I'll be careful. Go, now." He watched as she turned and walked slowly back the way they had come.

Ten steps later, she stopped and looked over her shoulder. Already, Bedford was vanishing from sight. That was something she had no intention of permitting him to do. She slipped stealthily after him. Fortunately, it didn't occur to him that she would disobey his order; he focused his attention entirely upon the last remnants of the battle that would not be easily abandoned, and paid her no heed.

As the first creepings of dawn lightened the sky, silence reigned at last. Wellington, Riki heard from a passing soldier, had entered the town, and the last French forces had thrown down their weapons, though the gates remained blocked. Riki huddled amid the gathering soldiers, waiting for decisions to be made. When at last the British broke up into patrols to enter the city, Sir Thomas Picton permitted Bedford, in the company of a battle-weary lieutenant, to begin his search.

Fighting back her fears, Riki mounted the assault ladder in the wake of the others. Lord, how she hated heights! She closed her eyes, clinging to the wooden rungs in much the same manner as she had clung to the rocky cliff face not all that long ago. At least now there was no accompanying thunder storm to add to her horrors.

Step by precarious step, she climbed up, then at last scrambled over the breached wall after Bedford's escort. She slipped to the rear of his small entourage, keeping far enough back so he wouldn't notice her, yet close enough to the party for safety's sake.

Badajoz did not appear to be a place for anyone not in a British uniform. Riki shivered and moved a step nearer the others. The streets appeared to be deserted except for scarlet coats, or an occasional French soldier being forced against a wall. The small party with Bedford moved quickly, driven by an urgency that left Riki taut with nerves.

So far, the British soldiers were held under strict control. But once the French troops were rounded up and marched out under guard, the British would be turned loose to sack the town and release the blood-lust built up throughout the long dark hours of the siege. Riki narrowed the distance between herself and Bedford once again.

"Can anyone escape?" Bedford's voice reached her.

"Not easily, m'lord," the lieutenant answered.

"But it is possible?"

"For a few men, yes. They'd only have to steal uniforms, and no one would question them. A good many Spaniards may slip out before it's fully light. They won't want to remain and be thought French collaborators."

They followed the walls, and the carnage of bodies that met her horrified gaze left Riki ill. She averted her eyes, but the stench was overpowering. She had never thought her stomach particularly weak, but she now fully sympathized with Bedford's declaration that this would be no sight for her. For the first time, she could understand Bedford's deadly fury with her cousin. But there had been too much death already this night.

Rifle shots and shouts broke out ahead, where several French soldiers sought to fight their way to possible escape. Bedford and his guard rushed forward and Riki followed.

Bedford stopped short and Riki almost collided with him. As she drew back, she caught his sharp intake of breath. The next moment, she, too, saw David.

Two French officers gripped his arms. One raised his rifle and fired at their party, and a British private standing beside Bedford fell. The two officers with David dodged down a side street, little more than an alleyway, and Bedford dragged a pistol from his coat pocket and took aim. Riki grabbed his arm.

"Don't!" she screamed.

He ignored her. The pistol flashed and the sound exploded in her ears. An answering shot came from the alley and Bedford threw himself against Riki, knocking her to safety beside a stonewall, then collapsed on top of her as his three guards dashed in pursuit.

Riki struggled free of Bedford's weight, and rolled his solid body slightly so that she could rise to her knees. "Gil?"

He didn't move. She caught hold of him and stared in horror as the pale morning light showed blood oozing between her fingers and spreading rapidly over the side of his coat.

Twenty-one

"Gil!" The cry tore from Riki. She reached for his face and her hand came away covered in blood from where his forehead had struck the stone wall. She looked about, frantic.

More shots sounded from down that alleyway where their guards had disappeared. This was no place to be. If they were mistaken for residents of Badajoz, perhaps French sympathizers . . .

It was too dreadful to consider. They'd be shot, or worse. She grasped Bedford's shoulders and struggled to drag him toward the sheltered recess of a doorway, but she couldn't budge him more than an inch or two. Her attempts started his wound bleeding dreadfully.

"Gil!" She shouted his name, mostly a plea for him to regain consciousness. Only once before could she remember feeling so completely helpless. But then it had been her falcon, not her beloved Bedford, whose life had been at stake.

Tears slipped unheeded down her cheeks as the full realization of her love for this strong, capable man flooded through her. Why couldn't she help him as he had many times come to her aid? Why couldn't she be stronger?

Six soldiers, under the command of a sergeant, marched briskly toward them. Riki half-stood in relief, but before she could speak, the men saw her. Raising his bayonet, the sergeant advanced, a deadly gleam in his eye that caused Riki to fall back and clutch Bedford's inert form protectively in her arms.

"Don't!" she managed, and knew it was a feeble attempt. The man kept coming, the blood-streaked point of his weapon looming ever closer, and she screamed: "He's been wounded, we need help!"

That brought the sergeant to a halt, and his men behind him. "Who are you?" he demanded, suspicious.

"This is Viscount Bedford. He's been shot, and I can't move him. He needs a doctor." She cradled Bedford's head in her lap.

The sergeant considered a moment, obviously disappointed at being denied his prey, then nodded. "Right, then. Heave to, lads." He gestured for two of his men to pick up the unconscious viscount.

"He's bleeding terribly!" Riki looked about, then on inspiration dragged free Bedford's neckcloth and folded it into a pad, which she pressed against his side. She tore off her own but found it too short to go about the viscount's rib cage. "Give me yours," she ordered a private who stood by, and the man, after a brief glance at his sergeant, complied with a crumpled looking handkerchief that appeared as if it hadn't seen a washtub in months.

It added the necessary length, though, and as the men lifted Bedford, she was able to secure the bandage about him. The sergeant resumed his patrol with four soldiers, leaving the other two for Riki to command. Keeping close to their sides, she let them lead the way out of Badajoz by the easiest route, through a gate that had been partially cleared. Bedford looked so dreadfully pale, as if his life's blood drained inexorably away . . . .

She dashed tears from her eyes to clear her blurred vision and stumbled along with the men over the uneven road. She no longer saw the maimed bodies lying where they had fallen, nor smelled the sulfurous stench

313

of powder mingled with the untold horrors of death. Only Bedford mattered, that he wouldn't have been hit if he hadn't thrust her to safety, that she loved him so desperately she would *make* him live, for her own life would be an unbearable emptiness without him.

Soldiers streamed past in an unending line, casting glazed, incurious glances at them. Solemn processions such as this were all too common. Ahead of them, beside them, even following behind, she could see other fallen gallants being carried by their comrades from the battle site back to camp. Some would receive medical attention, others were beyond help. Riki could only pray Bedford was not of the latter's number.

There seemed almost as much activity in the trenches beyond the walls as there had been during the fighting. Sorting the wounded from the dead, she supposed. She clasped Bedford's dangling hand and found it distressingly cold.

"Where is his tent?" the private carrying Bedford's shoulders asked.

"We were using Sir Thomas Picton's. I — I don't remember where. . . ." She broke off and looked about helplessly, rather hoping there might be a sign saying "headquarters."

The lack of one didn't bother her helpers. The name of their commander worked like magic on the two men. "This way, sir," the private addressed Riki, and they worked their way through the bustling camp.

Sir Thomas's tent was in use, but his batman directed the soldiers to carry Bedford to one next door. Its owner, she gathered, had been an early fatality.

Ducking inside the canvas flap, Riki took rapid stock. She strode at once to the cot and stripped the dirty bedding from it. No more than a fleeting regret did she spare for not having time to make it up fresh. Bedford, in his present state, wouldn't care.

The men laid him down, and Riki slid the pillow beneath his head and tightened his bandage to stop any new onslaught of bleeding caused by moving him. She covered him with the blanket, then turned to thank her assistants. They were already gone.

Satisfied Bedford was as comfortable as possible for the moment, she hurried to Sir Thomas's tent to ask where she could find a doctor. The man assured her he would send someone as soon as possible, and Riki returned to Bedford's bedside, wishing there was something — anything! — she could do.

She passed an anxious morning, trying to staunch the flow of blood and praying one minute that he might revive, then contradictorily the next minute that he would remain lost in blissful unconsciousness and not be aware of the pain.

Not even the magical name of Sir Thomas Picton was able to secure the services of a doctor. So many soldiers had been injured, no one had time to spare for a mere civilian who did not need an arm or a leg ruthlessly hacked off. She was on her own.

Riki remained at Bedford's side, changing the pads and keeping them tight until at last the blood slowed to a sluggish flow, then stopped almost completely. His forehead burned to the touch. Riki went to the entrance of the tent and waylaid the first person she could stop, a strange little man of uncouth accents but clean appearance whom she suspected to be a dead officer's personal groom.

This individual, who gave his name as Menchen, seemed glad to be pressed into service. He brought her water, and together they sponged down the viscount's fiery skin.

That drew a low groan from Bedford, and his eyelids slowly raised. "Riki?" he murmured, her name barely intelligible.

She gripped his hand tightly. "Don't talk."

"Safe," he muttered, and she knew he spoke about her, not himself.

She raised his hand to her lips and kissed it fervently.

315

A slight cough brought her attention to Menchen, who held out a cup to her. While he supported the viscount, Riki held the water to his lips. Bedford managed a sip before his eyes closed once more and he slept.

Toward the early afternoon, Menchen slipped out of the tent. Probably in search of food, Riki thought, surprised to discover she was hungry. But she wasn't about to leave Bedford's side. When Menchen returned, though, he not only brought bread and cheese with him, but also a doctor. Riki almost fell upon the man's neck in gratitude.

The doctor, obviously exhausted himself, helped Menchen to remove Bedford's coat. He then unfastened Riki's make-shift bandage and tore the fine linen cloth of his shirt from the wound. He gave it a cursory exam, then produced a satchel of instruments.

"If he wakes up, give him a shot of this," the doctor declared, handing Riki a bottle of brandy.

She stared at it, horrified.

"Hold him down," he ordered Menchen.

The man complied with a determination that startled Riki, but a moment later she saw the need. Even in his weakened condition, Bedford was a strong man. She was forced to aid Menchen before the doctor finished extracting the bullet, and Bedford's sharp exclamation and the trembling of his tensed muscles beneath her gripping hands brought a beading sweat to her own brow. What it did to Bedford, she didn't want to think.

"Give him the brandy," the doctor directed.

Riki did, with shaking hands, filling the cup and encouraging Bedford to swallow enough to deaden any pain. By the time he'd drained the cup, the doctor had dusted the wound with a heavy coating of basilicum powder and strapped him up with a new bandage. Menchen eased their patient back onto the pillows.

"Nothing vital's been touched," the doctor remarked as he stuffed his instruments away without washing them.

Riki bit back her shocked protest. They didn't know about bacteria and germs yet, she reminded herself. She cast an anxious glance at Bedford. More patients died of infection than wounds, as she remembered. Dear God, what she wouldn't give for a good shot of penicillin, or even some sulfa powder. If it would do any good, she'd gladly boil water to sterilize something, but the damage had already been done.

Bedford's ragged breath reclaimed her attention from wistful longing to the immediate necessities, and she went to smooth the bed and make him more comfortable, if possible. She supposed the hangover he would suffer from the brandy would be the least of his problems. Right now, his skin felt so hot and dry it alarmed her, and she sent Menchen for more water.

The doctor returned in the early evening, looking even more exhausted than before. He checked the wound, said all was as well as could be expected, then produced a small cup and a knife from his bag.

"What is that?" Riki asked, alarmed.

"I'm going to cup him." He began removing Bedford's shirt.

"Cup him? You mean *bleed* him? No!"

The doctor eased the shirt off the broad shoulders and down Bedford's arms. "Best thing for him." His forced joviality betrayed his weariness.

"No." Riki simply placed herself between the man and his intended victim. "He's lost too much blood already, and the brandy has put him in a high fever."

"He needs cupping." The man tried to put Riki aside, but she held her ground.

"No. It—it's a new medical theory that has been put into practice in America," she improvised. "They have proved cupping *isn't* as good as has been thought."

"America, is it?" The doctor's derisive snort showed what he thought of ex-colonials. "Let me—"

"I'm sure you have other patients who need you. Let him be for this night. If he is worse by morning, you

317

may cup him then." She could only pray he'd be better.

This compromise proved acceptable to the doctor, but he still took his leave of her with much the air of one shaking the dust from his sandals. With a shuddering sigh, Riki returned to her chair beside the bed.

Bedford passed a restless night, tossing on the cot, mumbling in a delirium produced from the cumulative effects of fever, pain, and brandy. Riki alternated between mopping his brow with cooling damp cloths, and holding him tight, trying to still his thrashings. When he at last became calmer, she began a steady, soothing monologue until he drifted back into an easier sleep. She fell silent and finally nodded off herself, his hand cradled between her own in her lap.

She awoke stiff to an eerie light she finally identified as dawn. Menchen was no longer in the tent, having returned to his own quarters. The hand she still held felt no more than warm.

That brought her more fully awake. Bedford's breathing came steadily and deeper. She touched his forehead and found it no longer burned. Succumbing to temptation, she ran a finger along his rough, stubbly cheek.

She had work to do. Going outside, she encountered her neighbor's batman already astir, with a fire started and water almost at a boil in a kettle. She begged a cupful, then returned to her patient. Drawing back the blanket, she gazed at the bare chest covered in dark curling hair, and knew the impulse to bury her face in that tickling mass and breath the scent that would be so uniquely Bedford. That, she promised herself fervently, she could — and would — do later, when he was awake and well enough to share the experience.

She turned her attention to unfastening the bandage while disturbing him as little as possible. The bullet had caught him as he swung sideways with her, and it had torn a long gash through the skin before lodging itself against a lower rib. He was lucky; it might so eas-

318

ily have struck some vital organ.

The wound, when she exposed it, looked horrible to her. Steeling her nerve, she probed the edges with a cloth dipped in the still steaming water.

He stirred and opened his eyes. "Wha — Riki?"

"It's all right, Gil. The wound looks clean." Tenderly, she brushed the lank pepper and salt hair off his forehead and dropped a kiss there instead. "Let me change the bandage."

He fell silent, obviously exhausted by the effort of speech. When a fresh pad was in place and tied to her satisfaction, she drew the blanket back over him.

"What happened?" His eyes remained closed, but he reached out to her.

She took his hand and sank into her chair. "You were shot, in the ribs. The doctor has removed the bullet and I refused to let him bleed you."

He began a shaky laugh, but broke it off. "Good girl." He said nothing for a long while, but just as she thought he had gone back to sleep, he spoke again. "Warwick?"

"I don't know." She kissed his fingers, simply because they were there. "If you're all right for a moment, I'll see about getting you something to eat."

He made no protest, which she considered to be a good sign. She emerged once more from the tent, to the welcome sight of Menchen coming toward her with a small earthenware bowl in his hands. His sharp-featured face cracked into an oddly uneven smile.

" 'Ow's 'is lordship this mornin'?"

"Much better, he's awake. Is that food? Menchen, you're a treasure."

"Yes, miss." He grinned lopsidedly at her from beneath his shock of graying brown hair. "Gruel."

She laughed, and knew it was relief and exhaustion. "He'll hate us both for that. I don't know how to thank you."

The little man looked embarrassed. "I'll be back

319

later, if you need me."

"Oh, yes, please. His lordship will want the services of a man, I'm certain."

Menchen nodded in commiseration and hurried about his morning business. He was back before Riki had managed to spoon more than a dozen mouthfuls of what Bedford termed "that foul concoction" into her patient. With him, Menchen brought a wooden box and a tray laden with cheese, bread, and coffee.

Riki didn't bother to ask where he had found such welcome fare. She retreated outside to have a few mouthfuls herself, and felt considerably better for it.

The doctor, upon his arrival, grudgingly admitted Bedford was no worse for his not being bled. The wound progressed as well as might be expected, he agreed, and he took his leave to visit patients less recalcitrant about receiving his prescribed treatments.

Riki returned once more outside while Menchen tended to the viscount, and when she at last re-entered the tent, Bedford looked considerably more human. The wooden box lay open still, revealing its contents to be shaving tackle and brushes. Bedford's chin had indeed been scraped, albeit not quite expertly, and his hair, though still lank from fever, had been combed into some semblance of its usual order.

Bedford greeted Riki with a feeble but definite: "Menchen has joined our service."

"I'm glad to hear it. He's been wonderful."

The little man flushed with pleasure and busied himself with putting things away.

Riki returned to her seat beside the bed. "Are you more comfortable?"

He nodded, though weakly. "Need to know what happened to Warwick."

Riki glanced at the former groom and decided he'd do. Giving him the name of the lieutenant who had served as their escort/guard the morning before, she sent Menchen to discover what he could.

Once more, the man proved his worth. He returned an hour later with the information that both Warwick and one of the French officers had simply disappeared, and must have gotten out of the city. No trace of either had been discovered anywhere, and though the soldiers who had plundered the city would not have looked for him, there were enough officers who had inspected the prisoners who had been alerted to the importance of this one traitor. If he had been among them, he would already have been found.

Bedford received the news with an impassive countenance. Riki eyed his seeming calm with grave misgivings.

"You can't go after David," she informed him.

"I have to!" But the weakness of his voice told a different tale.

Riki looked him over and decided it was time for a little gentle subterfuge. "If you'll try to sleep for a bit, Menchen will ride to Elvas and retrieve our baggage. I'll speak to Sir Thomas myself about sending out search parties for David."

Bedford nodded, and she guessed he had only half taken in what she said. She left him to rest, and Menchen departed on his errand.

The information she received satisfied her very well. Small scout parties would be sent out immediately, Sir Thomas promised, though he didn't hold out much hope for results. Neither did Riki, but at the moment she didn't mind. After repeating several times that it was imperative to capture David Warwick alive, if at all possible, she returned to the tent to try for a few hours of sleep herself.

This she managed with surprising success. When she awakened at last, Menchen had not only returned with their luggage, but had managed once more to procure a meal for them. Blessing the happy occurrence that brought the little man to them, Riki fed Bedford a chicken broth with soaked bread, then settled down to her own meal.

Bedford lapsed back into sleep, and Riki took the opportunity of changing out of Hillary's much crumpled clothes and into one of her dresses purchased in Lisbon. She could also use a bath. She glanced at Bedford, whose steady breathing assured her he would not readily rouse. She then secured the tent for such privacy as could be arranged and stripped off her soiled garments.

A quick sponge-off in tepid water was the best she could manage, but it felt like heaven. She dried herself briskly on a towel, then donned her few undergarments and chemise. From her valise, she pulled the light woolen gown, shook it out, then glanced at Bedford.

He was watching her. Warm color suffused her cheeks. "You — you're awake," she stammered.

He nodded slowly, his steady gaze not leaving her. "A gentleman should leave at this juncture." His tone held no trace of apology, but more than a little longing.

She laid the dress over the top of the case and went to him, taking the hands he held out to her. Emotion welled within her, so powerful she could no longer deny it.

"I love you, Gil," she whispered. No embarrassment accompanied the words, only a vast relief filled her that he was alive to hear them.

His breath caught in his throat and he pulled her down, grasping the back of her neck to bring her mouth against his. It was a gentle kiss at best, and he released her all too soon, his hand dropping weakly back to the bed.

"What a — a damnable thing to say to a man in my condition."

She laughed, albeit shakily, and sank onto the chair at his side. "I'm sorry if it doesn't suit your convenience, my lord."

"It suits me perfectly." A rueful, boyish smile touched his lips. "I just wish I could do something about it. It feels so mawkish to just lie here like some great, useless lump while I tell you the earth stood still when I first saw you." He drew another breath, resting from the effort of the words. "You're the part of me I've been searching for all my life."

"It doesn't sound mawkish to me in the least." Riki kissed his brow, then his lips, which were still dry from the fever.

The flame that lit his dark eyes belied his weakness. For several blissful moments, she forgot everything except the feel of his roughened hands on the bare skin of her shoulders.

She kissed the hollow at the base of his throat where the dark curls began, and a groan broke from him, though not of pain. His lips sought hers, and her hands roamed across that broad, hairy chest, reveling in the firmness of muscle. Then her wandering fingers encountered his bandage, and his murmurings stopped abruptly as his entire body tensed.

She released him at once, anguish filling her. "I only cause you pain," she whispered. "Just look at the suffering you've gone through because of me!"

"Riki —"

She cut him off, tears filling her eyes. "If David and I hadn't invaded your world . . . If we'd never come, you wouldn't have been in such danger!" And she'd never have experienced this hopeless, devastating love. "I don't belong here," she cried in agony, knowing it to be the truth. Half blinded, she pulled away and dragged on her dress.

Twenty-two

By the time Riki had mastered her trembling hands enough to fasten her gown, she had herself somewhat under control. She might not be able to stay with Bedford forever, but she had a little time left, at least, and she intended to make the most of it. She turned back to the bed and saw that his eyes were closed, but an expression of such unhappiness lingered on his face that she knew he couldn't be asleep.

She knelt beside him and took his hand tightly in her own. "Gil?"

He turned his head on the pillow to gaze into her eyes. "I love you, Riki. How can I lose you?"

It was his weakness, the trauma of his injury, that caused him to speak so freely, she knew, but that didn't matter. Hearing those words filled her with a deep happiness she would carry with her forever. "We'll build a few memories, as soon as you're stronger, I promise," she whispered.

"Will there be time?"

"We'll make the time."

"I've never longed for fair weather more." He managed a weak smile.

That brought the topic back from its emotional peak, and Riki settled herself for a discussion. "It may take us some little while to find David, you

324

know. Did he see us, do you think?"

"I couldn't tell." His voice still sounded exhausted. "I don't think so."

"Then he won't try to hide. That should make it easier. We've got to find him as soon as possible, for the sake of the British war effort. When—and how—I take him back to our time we can discuss after that. Now, I'm certain he'll remain on the Peninsula, where all his wargaming interest has been centered."

'Where else might he go?" Bedford roused himself.

"Russia—but I don't think it's likely."

Bedford considered. "No," he said at last. "There weren't any signs in his gaming room that he'd studied that campaign enough to be of any use."

"He hasn't. We can safely count on Napoleon being defeated there—and on David remaining here to assist the field marshals."

"The next major battle—" Bedford broke off. "Not until late July, is it?"

Riki nodded, recalling the labels on the glass domes with an effort.

"At Salamanca," Bedford continued. "That gives us a little over three months in which to find Warwick."

"There will probably be minor skirmishes in a variety of places." Riki chewed her lip, thoughtful. "I imagine the French will keep him as near the center of the action as possible."

"Then that is where we will head—provided Sir Thomas's scouts don't pick up any trace of him." He drew a deep breath, resting from the effort of talking. "I believe we will do best to be in the thick of things, ourselves, and if there's any whisper of trouble elsewhere, to get there as quickly as we can."

"I don't like it, Gil." She tightened her hold on his hand "I never wanted you put in such danger."

He managed a creditable grin. "I wouldn't have it

any other way."

Not one more word of the limited time they could share passed between them. They would make the most of what they had, Riki vowed, and spent every possible moment at his side.

By the following day, he got out of bed for a little while and ate a regular meal. After that, his strength returned rapidly though his wound progressed at a slower rate. About them, the army remained restless, not yet moving on. The severely wounded were evacuated back to Elvas, the dead were buried, and search parties were sent forth by Wellington to harry the retreating French troops who had escaped before Badajoz fell.

Bedford returned to their tent after one of his information-gathering strolls one evening with the news that they would depart at dawn, riding with one of these parties as escort.

Riki, bending over a stew pot that hung in the fire, set down her wooden spoon and regarded him with considerable alarm. "You're not well enough, yet."

He eased himself down beside her. "What is this? Rabbit? Menchen is a resourceful devil, isn't he?"

"Yes, he is, and quit changing the subject." She laid her hand on his shoulder. "Are you sure it's safe for you to ride?"

He covered her fingers with his, pressing them none too gently. "I can't sit around here waiting while your cousin tells Marshal Marmont how to carry the day at Salamanca. We must follow as quickly as possible."

"But which way? To Marmont's headquarters in Valladolid?"

Bedford shook his head, his eyes gleaming. "The marshal was reported in Sabugal on the Eighth, five days ago."

"And you were wounded only seven days ago."

But she made no further protest. Marmont's current location was their logical goal, and Bedford was not one to lie abed. If anything, the sheer frustration of inactivity would be more harmful to him than riding. "Shall I have Menchen pack for you?"

Bedford nodded absently, his mind already on the difficulties of the journey ahead.

Riki couldn't be satisfied, though. Throughout the remainder of the evening, she kept a close eye on him. He betrayed no outward signs of pain, but he moved with care and tiny lines remained etched on his face.

He left the tent while she prepared for bed. When he re-entered, she was ready for him.

"I want a look at your side."

He met her gaze steadily. "It's healing well enough."

"I'll be the judge of that, if you don't mind. Take off your coat."

"A gentleman might be pardoned for thinking that a provocative command."

"If you're hoping to embarrass me, you can forget it." She strode up to him and eased the smooth woolen cloth off his shoulders. He slid his arms from the sleeves, and she draped it over the foot of the cot.

He removed his neckcloth, hesitated, then pulled off his fine lawn shirt with only a wince and cast it aside over his coat. He faced her, a challenge lighting his dark, brooding eyes. 'Well, doctor?"

She dragged her gaze from the black hairs that liberally covered his broad chest and stomach. Damn the man! There wasn't a thing wrong with his muscle structure. Quite to the contrary, in fact.

She unfastened the bandage with undue force and exposed the wound that slashed across his lower ribs. By the light of the lantern that hung from one of the tent supports, she examined it, gently touch-

327

ing the edges. It looked better than she'd expected—a long way from being completely healed, but neither did it seem in immediate danger of tearing open again. He'd bear a ragged scar later.

"Verdict?"

She turned away and busied herself finding new lint with which to cover it. If she kept looking at him, she'd forget his weakened state and the ordeal that faced them on the morrow. The possibility of what might happen—of what they mustn't share this night—flooded through her mind, and her hands trembled as she knotted the new bandage about him.

She hadn't even kissed him—not the way she longed to, at least—for so very long. . . . Unable to stop herself, she trailed her fingers up his side, knowing she wanted so much more. Once they left this camp, how many opportunities would they have?

"Riki?"

The huskiness of his voice broke the last of her control. Her arms slid around his back to hold him tight, and she buried her face in the dark tangle of hairs that covered his chest. Deeply, she breathed in the scent of the coarse soap that mingled with the mustiness that was so uniquely him. Her lips moved, kissing him as she had longed to, and his body tensed.

He gripped her shoulders and held her away from him, his expression tortured. "Don't, Riki. I want you too much already."

"Your side—?" Alarmed, she glanced at the bandage.

"No, that's well enough. For your sake. If I kiss you now, I won't be able to stop."

A slow smile of relief and anticipation played about her lips. "Who's asking you to?" She caressed the backs of his hands with her fingers.

He groaned. "Riki, you can't know—"

"Oh, can't I?" She slid her hands up his bare chest and over his shoulders, feeling the tautness of those lean muscles. She wanted him, with a yearning that went beyond the merely physical.

"You're in my care!" The protest sounded weak. "A gentleman can not take advantage of a lady—"

"Who's taking advantage of whom?" Her lips found his throat.

"I—"

She silenced any further objections by dragging his head down until she could reach his mouth with her own. His resistance crumpled, and he swept her into a crushing embrace that made conscious thought extraneous. Her shift went the way of his shirt and coat, and it was not long before they sought the comforts of the cot.

They departed in the early morning light, with Riki astride her bay gelding, huddling in her pelisse in the dawn chill. Bedford, at her side, sat stiff and erect in his saddle, only the slightest bulge against his side betraying the bandage that Riki had tied as thick and tight as possible. She wasn't really worried, though; he had proved to her last night just how strong and fit he really was.

The remembered glow of love washed over her, leaving her warm and tingling. It didn't seem possible any man could have been so perfect, so exactly anticipating her every desire, so gently yet thoroughly fulfilling her every need. That she had done the same for him before they had at last fallen asleep, arms and legs still entangled, had been obvious.

He glanced at her, and the grimness of his expression faded beneath the smoldering passion that lit his eyes. Last night was one neither of them would ever forget. She wondered, not the least bit irrelevantly, what sort of camp they would make that evening.

Their party started forward, and Menchen, who had waited with them, dropped back to the rear with their baggage. Riki dragged her thoughts back to the task at hand. David was undoubtedly on his way to Marshal Marmont; and now, so were they.

The thirty mounted soldiers with whom they rode traveled swiftly—too swiftly, as far as Riki was concerned. Bedford remained silent, only the tenseness of his jaw and the pallor of his skin beneath its weathered tan betraying his pain. She should have left him alone last night to rest—yet she couldn't be sorry. She kept her horse close to his, casting anxious glances in his direction, though she knew he would scorn any suggestion that they stop to rest.

Over the next couple of days, very few words passed between them. There wasn't the need. Bedford seemed content to have her at his side, as if her mere presence sustained him. At night she slept near him, but never close enough. She had to content herself with the clasp of his hand and a memory that kept her awake and yearning for a repetition.

In the early afternoon of the third day, the commander of the troops reined to an abrupt halt. Riki shielded her eyes and gazed ahead along the road. A cloud of dust formed in the distance and the indistinct form of a horseman began to take shape; the outriders were returning with their reports.

"Stragglers, sir!" the first cried as he came within hailing distance. "A mile ahead, in a village!"

"Right, then." The commander signaled the neat double line of cavalry behind him, and they proceeded forward at a brisk distance-covering trot that would leave the horses rested enough for a charge, if that proved necessary.

Around them, the pines grew more thickly and the forest closed in. Riki peered through the trees but could see little except the dense mat of underbrush. Everything felt so still, so silent . . .

Stragglers. She shivered. They might well be riding into a skirmish. Unless . . .

She glanced at Bedford's grim face. "Do you think David . . . ?" She let her voice trail off.

He shook his head. "He has a week's start on us."

"But we've covered a great deal of ground, and you said yourself this is the most likely direction for him to take."

He threw her a smile of such warmth that her heart seemed to turn over. "My little optimist," he murmured.

They soon glimpsed the "village," which proved to be a euphemistic name for a collection of crude dwellings and dilapidated buildings. It lay a short distance up a cart track, which cut off from the main road at a sharp angle. Overhanging trees all but obscured their view.

Riki eyed it uneasily. What would French troops be doing here? The scouts must have panicked after spotting a few injured soldiers, who had been left behind by their fleeing comrades. If only David might be there . . .

A shot rang out from the trees on their left. More answered from the right, almost drowning out the commander's shouted orders to reform. Rifles and pistols seemed to be firing from everywhere.

Riki's horse reared. Dozens of mounted French troops charged out through the sheltering pines and undergrowth. Her gelding spun about, and Riki found herself facing more of the attacking French cavalry who had circled around to their rear.

She grabbed her reins and dragged her panicked mount's head about, digging in her heels to reinforce her order. Bedford, she saw, was on the ground, shooting, using his trembling horse as a shield. Menchen came up on his side, and in moments produced shot and powder to reload for the viscount.

The forest, which had proved such excellent cover for the French, now hampered their attack, limiting their movements. In minutes, the British had them on the run. Bedford swung onto his horse's back and spurred it forward, joining the patrol on their frantic pursuit of their enemy into the village. Feeling somewhat like unnecessary baggage being dragged along, Riki followed, loathe to let Bedford out of her sight.

They galloped headlong onto the narrow main street, and a fresh volley of shots greeted them. A British soldier fell almost at her side, and Riki reined her gelding to a stop and swung out of her saddle. The wounded man needed attention, to be gotten out from under the horses' feet. Menchen, she saw at a glance, remained with Bedford.

Her mind relieved on that account, she concentrated on the fallen soldier. With a few short tugs, she succeeded in loosening his neckcloth, which she formed into a pad to stop the flow of blood from his arm. The man, still conscious, took it from her and staggered to his feet, freeing her to go on.

She did, slowly, looking about her with a determination that barely overcame her nausea at the bloody carnage that met her gaze. Many of the wounded, she knew instinctively, were beyond her help. But there were others . . .

She wasn't alone. With a wave of relief, she recognized the patrol's "doctor," a lieutenant who had assisted with the wounded at the last battle. He looked up from where he knelt beside a fallen soldier and gestured to her. She hurried to his side, only too glad to obey the orders of someone knowledgeable.

332

The shots continued as the French tried to repel the British intruders, and the sulfurous odor of powder filled the air. Riki crouched low, following the lieutenant, helping him to drag injured men to the comparative safety of doorways. Doggedly, she kept at her work, too tired to think, knowing only she couldn't do enough good and that she couldn't stop.

A single shot rang out nearby, startling her. It must have been silent for several moments, she realized, and she hadn't even noticed. Another shot answered the last, then stillness engulfed the village. Riderless horses, gathered together like the gregarious animals they were, stamped restlessly at the far end of the narrow street. One by one, the French threw down their guns to their weary British captors.

Where was Bedford? Riki looked about, frantic for a sight of him. It wasn't his broad, sturdy figure that caught her eye, though, but a taller, more lightly built man. His fair hair caught the westering sun as he limped, half-supported by a fair-haired girl, into a tavern.

David, with Marie Marley. Riki hesitated, knowing she should follow them, yet desperate to find Bedford.

"Riki!" His well-beloved steady steps came up behind her.

With a half-moan, half-sob, she spun about and threw herself into his arms, hugging as much of him as she could manage; his sharp intake of breath made her release him at once. "Your wound—I'm sorry, Gil. Are you all right?"

He nodded, though a long gash across his cheek seeped fresh blood.

She would deal with that later. "He's in there." She took his arm and started for the tavern.

"Who? You mean—?"

She no longer dragged him. He marched ahead,

his longer stride easily outdistancing her. She ran to overtake him.

They weren't even hiding. David lay sprawled in a chair, his injured leg raised onto a table. Marie bent over it, cutting back the buckskin of his riding breeches to reveal a nasty, searing tear in the flesh just above his left knee.

Bedford stopped only feet away from them, his freshly reloaded pistol in his hand. David looked up, met that deadly gaze, and the blood drained from his face.

"I ought to kill you." Bedford's voice was almost unrecognizable, a cold thread of deadly steel.

David thrust his chin out, and a spark of indignation lit his eyes. For a moment, it almost replaced the unbearable pain reflected in his face. "That's hardly the way to greet the hero of Badajoz."

"Hero?" Bedford's lip curled. "I suppose the French couldn't make enough of you after your assistance."

"Non!" Marie Marley straightened up, placing herself between Bedford and David. "Until the arrival of your patrol, we were their prisoners."

Bedford thrust her aside. "You don't really expect me to believe such humbug, do you? Give me one reason why I shouldn't shoot you here and now."

"You promised me!" Riki cried, but he paid her no heed.

"I told you what I was about in my note. You got it, Riki, didn't you?" David directed a pain-filled glance at her.

"I did." She bit her lip. "All you said was that you had unfinished business here in Spain."

A slight, ironic smile just touched his lips. *"Et tu,* Riki? I was trying to set matters to rights."

"I am sure the French were very grateful."

"Damn it, Bedford!" David broke off as a shudder ran through him. "Because of what I let slip, the

French got off easier at Ciudad Rodrigo than they should have. That meant there were more troops available to defend Badajoz. I had to repair that damage—equalize things—or we—the British—would have lost a battle we should have won."

"And precisely how do you claim to have done this?"

David drew an unsteady breath. "We blew up a gate and created complete chaos."

Bedford straightened. "Are you trying to pretend you *didn't* help the French?"

David's gaze rested on his wounded leg, on the ragged, torn skin and the blood that soaked his clothes. "Obviously you don't believe it, but I didn't."

"If it were your intention to help the British, you could have done that from outside the walls."

David shook his head. "You didn't spend enough time in my gaming room, Bedford. The siege was conducted well. It was the French defense that had to be altered. And for that, I had to be inside."

"So you asked a French spy to help you?"

"Methinks I detect a note of skepticism," David murmured with a faint attempt at humor. "Yes, I did. Only someone already helping the French could have induced them to let me enter the city walls."

"I see. Mrs. Marley, I presume, was only too glad to switch loyalties?"

"I owed it to David." Her soft accent made a caress of his name. "After using him—" She broke off, and large, misty tears filled her lovely blue eyes. "And after seeing what Felicity thought of me—"

"Felicity?" Bedford broke in. "What the devil has my sister to do with this?"

"She came to me, the morning after I tried to confirm a rumor with Lord Linton, and begged me to tell her I was not a traitor." Mrs. Marley shook her head. "I had never thought of it like that, never seen myself through her eyes."

"Felicity," Bedford repeated. "*She* warned you."

"Not on purpose!" Mrs. Marley held out her hand toward him, then drew it back. "You must not blame her. She could not believe me capable of— such treachery. She only wanted me to deny it."

Recovering somewhat, he shifted his hold on the pistol, still not lowering it. "So you and Warwick concocted this scheme to redeem yourselves?"

David's lips twitched. "There, my dear Bedford, you have it in a nutshell. Riki and your sister already knew about Marie, and we guessed Linton would shortly be telling you the whole, so Marie had to get out of England. And I wanted to make up for the unintentional damage I'd done."

"You *trusted* Mrs. Marley?" Bedford demanded, his eyes narrowed, still not believing. "After the way she'd been tricking you, turning you into a traitor?"

David's eyes flashed. "I'm an American, not British, I'll thank you to remember. And that was only at first. She didn't try to 'use' me after we came to know one another." His gaze transferred to Marie, and his expression softened. "What she did was her job."

"A mission I came to hate once I met you." She raised his hand and gently pressed his fingers to her lips. "It was to betray my own heart."

"Why didn't you stop?"

Riki cast Bedford a nervous glance. Marie had been not so much a traitor to England as a patriot to France. Bedford, though, was not about to see it in that light.

"I had no choice." Marie still clung to David, but she raised huge, miserable eyes to Bedford. "They would not let me."

"You could have come to us, confessed and named the traitors."

"Ah! You do not understand, *du vrai!* How could

I do anything so foolish? I am French, an *emigrée*. I would have been shot."

To that, Bedford did not seem to have an answer. He returned to the basic facts. "You are a spy, you used my assistant for your treachery."

"*Non!* Not any longer."

"You left England when you knew you had been exposed, and you went directly to where you could do the French the most good."

"I told you why we came." David straightened his shoulders as if squaring off to fight with his former superior. "I gave the French no aid, though they asked."

Bedford allowed his lip to curl in a sneer. "I saw you at Badajoz, in the company of an officer."

"I was under arrest! Dammit, we'd just been caught blowing up—" He broke off under the coldness of the viscount's expression, and his lip twitched derisively. "I suppose I should be glad that damned colonel hustled me away. What did you intend to do, shoot me?"

"Yes."

David closed his eyes for a moment. "Contrary to what you think, I spent my time figuring out how to do the right amount of damage to the French, not in helping them. The approach of the British assault troops was seen without my intervention."

"Are you trying to tell me you weren't even tempted to aid them?" Bedford didn't relax his rigid stance.

David shook his head slowly. "My God, it was—" He broke off, searching for the right word. "It was *unreal*. I *knew* I could help them win, that I could change history! Imagine that, Bedford. To know the future of the entire world lies in your hands. I could have made Napoleon emperor of all Europe—and England—by the end of next year. But I didn't." His gaze met and held the viscount's.

337

'Why not?" Bedford didn't sound the least bit impressed, merely skeptical.

David gave a half-laugh, and the visions of grandeur he painted the moment before faded into oblivion. "God, it sickened me." He raised a suddenly haggard face to Riki. "To re-enact the battles . . ." He shook his head. "It wasn't real, any of my miniature world. It was just a game. Recording casualties and counting the wounded—they were nothing but metal figures. They didn't matter, they'd just be reused in the next battle we staged. And they didn't bleed or have their faces torn open or their arms and legs blown off."

He lowered his face into his hands. "That gate—it was awful. The French soldiers—I actually *killed* them. A whole unit! I—" He broke off, too choked up to speak. He looked at Riki with eyes that had seen too many unspeakable horrors.

Riki took his free hand, knowing there was nothing she could say to ease his misery.

Bedford regarded the trio with an icy glare. "Spare me the Cheltenham tragedy, Warwick."

David paid him no heed. "God, Riki, it's enough to make you sick."

"I know. I entered Badajoz."

He looked up quickly, his eyes flashing in anger at Bedford. "How could you let her? Damn it, that's no sight for her."

"He didn't know," Riki broke in. "I followed him— to make certain he didn't haul off and shoot you."

David smiled weakly. "That was decent of you, Riki, considering what you thought I was doing."

"Had your fill of real war?" Bedford's sneer sounded more pronounced.

David met that angry glare and didn't look away. "We both have." He glanced at Marie and she nodded, her eyes wide with remembered horrors. "We traveled with the so-called 'ambulances.' Reading—

338

even studying in detail—about the Peninsular campaign couldn't have prepared me for the reality. To have taken part in it, even in mock re-creation, now makes me sick."

"It is true," Marie whispered. "Never have I done more than pass information from the so very elegant drawing rooms of London. It was a game, as David says. But now—I want no more part in aiding such savagery to continue."

David's fingers closed protectively over hers.

"What now?" Riki asked, holding her breath.

David met her searching gaze steadily. "I want to go home, back to my own time. With Marie."

Bedford stared at him, speechless.

"I can't leave her," David said simply.

Riki glanced at the other young woman and recognized the adoration in her expression as she gazed at David. "Gil?" She laid her hand on his arm.

"No!" The word exploded from him. "You can take your precious cousin, he doesn't belong here. But Marie Marley is guilty of spying and she's not going to escape."

"Would it be so dreadful?" She clutched his arm, shaking it slightly in her urgency. "Let Marie go with David—she will only be shot by the British if she remains."

"Damn it, Riki!" Bedford shifted his grip on his pistol again in order to pull her hands from his upper arm. He held them tightly. "I shouldn't be letting Warwick go. Do you think I'm not having to struggle with my conscience?"

"I didn't betray the British." David spoke softly, the pain of his wound strong in his voice.

"But Marie Marley did!" Bedford glared the others down, then addressed himself to Riki. "I will not permit you to turn me into a traitor, as well!"

David rose shakily to his feet, thrusting Marie behind him. "I won't leave without her."

"Then you may consider yourself under arrest."

David squared his stance, wincing as he moved his wounded leg. "You'll have to take us, then." Threatening, he raised his fists. "Or do you intend to shoot an unarmed man?"

Bedford's mouth tightened. He set the pistol aside and began to unfasten the buttons of his coat.

"Gil!" Riki grabbed his arm but he shook her off. "For heaven's sake, Gil, he's been wounded! And so have you."

"Stay out of this," He thrust her aside and she staggered back.

"Run," David hissed the order to Marie, then took an unsteady step forward, placing himself strategically between her and Bedford.

"I cannot leave you." The fear-filled cry came from Marie's heart. She backed away a step, but made no move to escape.

Bedford cast his coat across a chair and raised his own fists, wincing at the strain to his barely-healed rib muscles. David tensed.

The door to the tavern burst open before he could launch his attack. Half a dozen British soldiers barged in, their rifles in their hands, with the captain who led the patrol at their head.

The officer stopped dead five paces into the room and took in the tableau with one glance. "You've captured them, m'lord! Well done." He jerked his head to his men. "These are the spies. Take them outside and shoot them."

Twenty-three

"No!" Riki screamed. "Gil—?" She turned to him, horrified.

Bedford took an unsteady breath. "No," he confirmed. "Take them into custody, but I don't want them harmed. Yet," he added, holding David's gaze. "They are to return to England for trial."

"Gil—!" Riki broke off under the fury of the gaze he directed at her. In silence, she watched her cousin and Marie Marley shackled.

Bedford remained where he stood, his rapid, shallow breathing betraying his rigid control. David cast them one last, unreadable look before he and Marie were marched out between the soldiers.

"How could you?" Riki cried as soon as the heavy door closed behind the dismal little procession. Shock and fury overcame her. "How could you? You betrayed me, you gave them David!"

Bedford caught her hands, gripping them until she flinched from the pain. "Be quiet! Damn it, Riki, I had no choice."

"But David isn't a traitor!"

"We only have his word for what he did. What did you expect him to say when he'd been caught?"

"But what if he's telling the truth? You can't be so certain,

Gil. The only thing we *do* know he's guilty of is talking too freely over his wine with a superior in the War Office."

Bedford drew a long, steadying breath. "There is no doubt about Marie Marley. I'll help Warwick because I promised you, but not that French—" He broke off whatever choice descriptive term he had intended to use. Dropping Riki's hands, he straightened. "I already told you, I will not permit you to turn me into a traitor as well by releasing her." He swung about and strode from the room, his booted footsteps echoing on the floorboards like a death knell.

He was right, Riki realized, her heart sinking even lower. Even if Marie Marley *had* assisted David to make amends, that didn't erase the years she had spent serving as a spy. By begging Bedford to forget that, Riki asked him to behave in a manner less than honorable by his standards. She averted her eyes from his stiff, retreating figure. They truly were of different worlds.

She started after him, her steps dragging. At least he wouldn't make David stand trial for treason. He wouldn't dare, not with all that her cousin could blurt out. She probably ought to be thankful witch burning was no longer a craze.

Outside in the now quiet street, the British soldiers rounded up the French prisoners. David, limping badly, fell into line with them, Marie at his side.

Riki stomped off to where her gelding stood with the other horses in the charge of the grooms who rode with the unit. Grasping her reins, Riki led the animal toward the prisoners. The first of the guards stepped forward, stopping her.

"One of the prisoners is wounded and can't walk," Riki snapped at him. Her furious glare defied the man to stop her.

"Against orders, miss." He stood his ground, his gun raised diagonally across his chest.

He made no move to point it at her, but she sensed

the threat. "Viscount Bedford!" She shouted his name in clipped, determined accents.

Bedford, who stood with the captain and a lieutenant, deep in conversation, turned a wary eye on her.

"This prisoner is unfit to walk. Have you not the common decency to permit him to ride?"

He strode over, his dark brows lowered over his hawk-like eyes. "These two are not to be kept with the others. They are to ride with me."

"And your escort," the captain nodded. "They're too dangerous for us to run any risk of their escape."

"As you say," Bedford nodded.

Riki glared at him, furious, but kept her lips together. At least David would ride.

She glanced back to where two soldiers assisted David to mount a horse. Disillusionment mingled with the pain on his normally animated countenance, and her heart cried for him. Poor David, he had been such an eager, naive little boy over his favorite pastime. He'd been granted his dearest wish, to see the Peninsular campaign in reality, and he'd never again be able to think of it with innocent pleasure. Now he saw his hobby as a thin veil covering the real horrors of war. Her spirits sinking even lower, she rode in silence as they began the long journey back.

In the three days it took them to reach Lisbon, Riki spoke not one word to Bedford. He rode at a distance from her, both his rigid posture and grim features defying her to approach. She made no attempt. What they had shared, she realized, was over.

The city, somewhat to her vague amazement, remained unchanged. They had been gone only a little more than two weeks; it felt like an eternity.

Bedford left his party under the care of the lieutenant and went immediately to make arrangements with Admiral Berkeley. Preparations for their departure began at once, and took depressingly little time. The morning following their arrival in the city, they boarded a British supply ship returning to England with the wounded.

Bedford's expression remained rigid, unbending, and steadfastly he avoided Riki. Did his promise to her mean nothing any more? She watched his distant figure as he conversed with the captain. Had he become so determined to administer punishment that he closed his mind, willingly sacrificing David along with Mrs. Marley? Or did he actually want to destroy his assistant who had caused him so much trouble — who had been the cause of bringing Riki into his world? That last thought hurt unbearably.

The voyage stretched out, long and lonely, as Riki sought some way to soften his mood, to make him see reason. She could think of nothing.

Nor was she permitted to speak with David or Marie, who remained secured in their separate prison cells deep in the hull, smothered in darkness and the vile smells of pitch and tar. Menchen, allowed more freedom than she, brought her word that they did as well as could be expected. Their jailer, though, he warned, did not permit his giving them anything from her.

She entrusted a message of hope for her cousin to the ex-groom and turned away, only to see Bedford striding in her direction. As he neared, he looked up and saw her. Deliberately, he headed a different way.

Her temper flared. Probably he was ashamed to face her! He betrayed her. She repeated that thought over and over, and found it more painful every time. She loved him, yet he wouldn't spare David.

And Bedford loved her, too — didn't he? He had said so once — when barely out of the throes of a fever. And he had proved it, so very eloquently, that one night they shared together. Now, though, the memory must be a constant source of embarrassment. Gilbert Randall, viscount Bedford, was not one to wear his heart upon his sleeve.

Good heavens, she was even beginning to *think* in the

terms of his time. She leaned against the rail and stared bleakly out to sea. Whether Bedford loved her or not would make no difference to his decisions. He was a man of honor, and as such, he would never let his infatuation with a woman interfere with his duty. For once, she could not count on his aid.

That gave her something new about which to be depressed, and she proceeded to indulge to her heart's bitter content. The sooner she returned to her own time, she decided, the better it would be. And instead of brooding over the irritating, frustrating behavior of men in general, she had best concentrate on rescuing David.

By the morning of the seventh day out, the already rough seas churned and darkened with an approaching storm. Waves slammed against the hull, and the sailors ran to their posts, securing the sails against the wind that set Riki staggering as she stood in the bow. Salt spray stung her face, whipping wet, clinging tendrils of auburn hair into her eyes, blinding her as she stumbled toward the sheltering causeway.

Sailors bustled past, some offering a steadying hand, others too intent on their errands to do more than sidestep to avoid plowing through her. The deck lifted and dropped with a relentless thoroughness that left her stomach somewhere riding the crest of the last wave.

She pulled her cloak closer about herself as she stood in the doorway, reluctant to go below where the smells would be her undoing. Determinedly, she refused to think of her cousin and his fair but treacherous love locked in the bowels of the ship. She felt ill enough here on deck where the icy wind and spray kept her senses from dissolving in nausea.

She and boats weren't getting along lately. The voyage out to Portugal hadn't been bad, merely endless, of course, but the one before that, when she and Bedford set forth in her ketch. . . .

She shivered, but not with the cold, as the pitching of

the deck brought forth vivid memories of that lashing, thundering storm . . . that storm that had brought her back through time. There was only one way to save David, she had known that from the start. She had to take him forward nearly two hundred years. And for that, she needed an electrical storm!

She left her shelter in one surging motion, running to the starboard side where she clung to the rail to keep from being flung overboard by the erratic lurches of the heaving deck. Her intent gaze scanned the charcoaled skies, willing an elusive flash of lightning to break the darkness. None came, but she did not give up hope.

Her mind whirling, searching for ideas, she scanned the ship. Could a vessel of this size make the nearly impossible voyage across time? As far as she knew, the boats involved had all been small, holding no more than five people. Somehow, she must get David transferred to some small ketch or yacht before they reached England.

The storm continued for four days, during which Riki clung to the rail, searching the savage sea for some small craft suitable to her purpose. None came into view, though, and for the first time in her life, Riki watched the passing of a storm with heart-felt dismay. Once again, calm water stretched as far as she could see, unbroken except by an occasional whitecap.

She paced the deck that rocked gently, and tried to think up a way to approach Bedford, to whom she had been barely civil of late. She found him in the stern, quite at his ease among the sailors, laughing at some joke that set deep color to the men's faces as Riki approached.

Bedford turned to discover the cause of the disturbance, and his brow creased over suddenly narrowed eyes. The sailors took their hasty leave.

"Am I interrupting something?" She offered a hesitant smile, unsure of her reception. His eyes roamed over her face—missing nothing, she supposed ruefully.

His pleasure faded beneath cynicism. "What is it you wish me to do for you?"

Ouch. She fought back a wince at his words. "Must I want something?" She moved closer, one hand barely touching his sleeve.

She did want something, of course, but his nearness played havoc with her senses, creating unbidden visions of herself clasped tightly in his arms, of his firm mouth seeking hers or brushing feathery kisses along her throat, drawing moans of yearning from deep within her. She opened eyes she hadn't realized she'd closed and found him gazing at her, his expression unreadable.

With one finger, he raised her chin so he could look down into her face. His dark eyes burned like coals, smoldering with a desire that set answering sparks flickering deep within her.

"Gil—" Her whisper faded, carried away on the salty breeze. It was impossible to speak, with his thumb caressing her throat. Hunger gnawed through her, a starvation only he could assuage. She clutched his arms, drawing herself nearer, pressing her slight body against him.

His finger trailed across her freckled cheek, then down her neck, setting a riot of sensation through her. A soft sigh escaped her lips as she raised them to meet his. Warm breath fanned her cheek, then her mouth, as his lips hovered so close she could taste the salt spray on them.

"It won't work," he murmured, though his hand drew her ever closer.

"Why not? You know it will." Her lids, heavy with desire, veiled her eyes. The late afternoon stubble of his chin prickled against her cheek.

A soft chuckle shook his sturdy frame. "You won't seduce me into freeing your cousin and Mrs. Marley, you know."

She pulled free, her skin burning, then chilled as the

blood drained away. "I wouldn't! I—"

He clasped her hands, bringing them unresisting to receive his kiss. "Don't think you're not tempting me, but I'll not be turned traitor."

She pulled free, furious. "I wouldn't stoop to seduce—"

That falcon-like gleam lit his eyes and he swooped like a striking tiercel, his mouth covering hers, stopping her angry words. She struggled a moment, then abandoned a fight for which she had no heart. *This* was what she wanted, to be lost in his mesmerizing spell, to sink into the whirlpool of sensation he created.

As abruptly as he claimed her, he set her aside. Her eyes fluttered open, startled, and for a moment she saw clearly the effort it took for him to control himself. A purely feminine elation surged through her, akin to smugness, that she could so stir him.

"I didn't come to seduce you," she said.

"It just seemed a good idea?" He managed a wry smile that was touching in its vulnerability.

"Yes. A very good idea. It still does. I can't think of a better one, in fact."

He drew a deep, steadying breath. "I'll remember that. What did you want, then?"

She blinked, then refocused on her plan. "To talk. To ask you something." He waited, one eyebrow lifted in inquiry, so she pressed on. "Do you still believe David to be a traitor?"

"I don't know." He answered in all honesty. "I'll accept that he didn't consciously betray me—my department."

"But?" she prodded as he fell silent.

"He went to Spain in the company of a spy, and we saw him in the company of French officers at Badajoz."

"You heard his explanation."

Bedford nodded. "I did. And it *might* be true."

She touched his arm, then succumbed to the temptation to caress it. "It would be a pretty rash act, to enter a besieged city he knew would fall shortly to the attackers. Unless he intended to intervene to save himself."

"Mrs. Marley still hasn't given me the name of the man to whom she passed the information. Does that sound like a woman who would deliberately betray her own people, after she'd been spying for them?"

Riki hesitated, then nodded. "People do crazy things when they're in love."

"Do they?" The look in his troubled eyes could only be described as skeptical.

Riki's heart sank. *Yes,* she wanted to scream at him. *She* would do something every bit as foolish—to be near him. Hadn't she followed him into Badajoz through a breach in the wall while the fighting continued? It hadn't been for her cousin's sake, no matter what she told herself. She had gone to be near Bedford, and, as he himself would say, the devil take the consequences.

"What did you want?" He interrupted her thoughts, bringing her back to the point at hand.

With an effort, she dragged her gaze from his face. "To take him back to the future, where he belongs. Like we agreed at the beginning."

"And?"

She swallowed hard, then persevered. "I think our chances will be much better on a smaller ship. Before we reach the Channel, will you request that we and the—the prisoners be transferred to some smaller vessel we'll undoubtedly encounter? You can say you want to take them by the most direct route to London."

His lips twitched. "No."

"Gil!" She shook the arm she still clutched.

"Riki!" His tone mocked her desperation. "No, only consider. The chances of a lightning storm breaking in the next few days are non-existent. We've just had a regular downpour."

"You mean I won't be *able* to take him—home?"

"Not at the moment." His serious tone reinforced his words. "And whatever happens, I will not permit Marie Marley to escape."

She glared at him, but knew it did no good. She stalked off, depressed and afraid for David and Marie. Pace the deck as she did, though, wracking her mind, trying to hit on another plan, nothing came to her.

When she again applied to Bedford for help, sympathy shone in his eyes, but his only advice was an unhelpful: "Wait."

She bit back her angry retort, knowing a rousing fight would not help her cause. Before she could speak incautious words, she left him. Even as she did so, though, she knew she was unable to be furious with this infuriating man she loved.

At last, England lay ahead. Riki stood in the bow through the long afternoon, watching the land mass grow steadily larger and clearer as the wind drove the ship relentlessly toward home port. And David's destruction, she reminded herself.

Afternoon faded into the haze of evening when the vessel at last neared the wharf at Newhaven and the sailors ran to secure the lines. Disheartened, Riki retreated to her cabin until the activity slowed.

A sharp rap on her door brought her out of her reverie. In answer to her call to enter, Bedford strode in.

"I have made arrangements for you to spend the night at an inn near the docks."

She glared at him. "What of David and Mrs. Marley?"

"They'll remain here. Under guard."

"And you want me off the ship? Why? Are you afraid I'll overcome their guard and make off with them?"

He shook his head, but he didn't smile. "I'll be riding for London with Menchen at once. I'd rather you were safely on land."

She barely heard his words. Her own had planted an obvious, if extremely foolhardy, solution in her mind, and the longer it remained there, the more certain she was this could be her only possible course of action. She nodded slowly.

"It will feel good, not to have the deck swaying beneath my feet every moment." And Bedford would think her safely out of the way and never suspect her intentions. She managed a sad smile for his benefit. "Give me a few minutes to repack my things."

Half an hour later, she watched from her low-pitched bedchamber at the front of the inn as Bedford and Menchen mounted their hired hacks. Bedford waved to her, then urged the animal forward out of the lighted yard into the dark streets. She drew a deep breath to steady her shaky nerves and turned back into the room.

For this expedition, she needed Hillary's clothes again. She didn't hurry, though; there was plenty of time. Midnight or later would be the best hour to set forth. She rang for the meal Bedford had ordered her to eat in her room, and settled down comfortably on her bed to plan her attack.

She must have dozed off, for she awoke to the last chimes of the clock as it announced twelve o'clock. Bedford must almost be in London by now, she reflected, then shoved that thought aside. It was as well he wouldn't be around to stop her.

Quickly she changed, then slipped into the narrow passage lit only by a single, smoking lantern, her feet still unsteady from her long days aboard ship. She made her way through the maze of corridors, at last finding the back stairs. After reaching the ground floor without incident, she let herself out through the kitchens, where only one minion dozed fitfully in a huge rocking chair beside the great hearth.

She found herself in a crooked, unlighted alley-like street, where houses and shops crowded against each other. With determination filling her — primarily to keep her nerves at bay — she set forth to locate the ship. The night was overcast, with that eerie, still warmth that so often presaged a thunderstorm. An old, familiar fear welled within her, but her surging hope took firmer root, supplanting it. If only . . .

In spite of her growing excitement, she slowed her pace to keep from tripping over every uneven cobble stone. Tonight might be their only chance in weeks — if they were ever able to try, at all. If she failed to rescue David, she couldn't bear to think of the consequences. And how was she to distinguish the right ship from amongst all the others in this darkness?

To her relief, it wasn't hard. The sleek vessel bobbed peacefully in its berth, oil lamps illuminating the gang plank that lay in place. A deep sigh of relief escaped her. She hadn't even begun to consider the multitude of problems that most assuredly would face her. At least she'd be able to get aboard.

At the foot of the plank, though, her nerve almost deserted her. It would be easier if she didn't tremble so. She had no choice; it was now or never. Once the prisoners were brought from the boat onto British soil, they would never be turned loose.

She squared her shoulders, decided stealth was better than a direct attack, and slipped out of the shadows and up the wooden planks, crouching low. About half way up, it struck her that it might be immensely practical if she were to carry some large blunt instrument with which to knock out any guard who challenged her presence. She glanced back to the wharf, saw nothing movable, and mentally shrugged. This way, if she were caught, she might be able to talk her way out of it. A weapon would clearly betray her intentions.

She stepped onto the deck and ducked down, and her hand encountered a loose wooden object. A belaying pin! She hefted it, testing its weight; it made a perfect club. So much for her logical reasoning of a minute before. A good stout stick gave her confidence.

Her spirits lifting at this bit of luck, she crept slowly forward, keeping as much in the protective darkness of the ship's side as she could manage. At last, though, she had to run for the companionway, and felt every moment of her exposure as if it were an eternity. Still, no shouts were raised from the deck to shatter the stillness of the night.

So far, so good. She reached the doorway, found it ajar, and ducked inside. Having opted for the Portuguese slippers rather than Hillary's hobnailed boots, she descended without a sound into the darkness of the cabin deck.

At the end of the long hallway, another oil lamp shone, and she started toward it. Rather than feel safer, this total lack of guards made her even more nervous. She crept silently, holding her breath, her teeth clenching her lip until they drew a fine drop of blood.

She reached the next flight of steps that led down to the crew's deck. Her heart beat so loudly, surely someone must hear — if there were anyone about. Doggedly, she kept on. She reached the next level in safety.

Again, another lamp hung at the far end, lighting the way into the cargo hold where the prisoners were confined. Dizziness swept over her. *You're crazy*, the thought kept repeating through her mind. *You'll get caught*. But by forcing one foot to follow the other, she proceeded inexorably though unsteadily forward.

She stood at the head of the last flight, peering down into the darkness. Why hadn't a guard come forward, yet? Was there only one, watching David and Marie? That was possible; no one in England knew of their presence on this vessel. No one would be expecting a rescue attempt. And it was also possible the guard, bored and tired, had fallen asleep.

Heartened by this hope, she descended, step by cautious step, until at last she reached the hold. Still no one. She braced herself, inched forward, and a rough hand clamped firmly over her mouth from behind.

Twenty-four

"Quiet!" A deep voice hissed in her ear. "What the devil are you doing here, Riki?"

She swallowed the scream that welled in her throat, and the hand eased on her mouth. Her breath escaped in a ragged gasp. "Gil?"

"What do you think you're doing?" he repeated, the savageness of his voice not the least bit dimmed by his words being whispered.

Reaction swept over her, leaving her too weak to answer. She lowered the belaying pin she had started to raise. Then a sudden—and hateful—idea occurred to her. "You're the guard!" she accused. She pulled free, torn apart in an agony at his betrayal.

"No." He took the wooden weapon from her limp grasp before she dropped it, and tucked it into the waistband of his breeches. He glanced over his shoulder, and the action emphasized the tension in his voice. "But he'll be upon us if you make any noise."

"*Us?*" Her lip curled. "Don't you intend to hand me over along with David?"

"That would be rather pointless, when I've gone to a great deal of trouble to set him free," he hissed back, exasperated.

She eyed him uncertainly. "*Have* you?"

"Damn it, Riki, a gentleman doesn't go back on his promise. I said you could take him back to the future, and so you shall."

She looked about. "Where's Menchen?" she demanded, still suspicious.

"I made up a story about expecting trouble and sent him ahead to London. I don't think he believed a word of it, but this way he won't be involved if we're caught. Now stay here." He extinguished the lantern and shouldered past her, starting through the maze of crates for the far end of the ship where another light dimly shone.

Riki caught his arm and pulled him back. "You can't!" she whispered.

"Would you care to tell me why not?"

She tried to see his face, but only an occasional gleam from the distant, swaying lamp touched his piercing eyes. "Because for *you* to set him free would be a traitorous action! It wouldn't be, for me."

"No, just a damned dangerous one." He pulled away once more. "All you want is a chance to free Mrs. Marley, as well."

Again, Riki caught him. "I can't let you do it." Her fingers caressed the smooth material of his coat. "I can't let it come to this, Gil. Even if you're not caught—" She shook her head. "This is exactly what you've tried to avoid! I can't let you become a traitor because of your promise to me." She reached her hand out to him, just touching his cheek, and felt his jaw tighten.

"I became a damned traitor the moment I returned to my time and didn't instantly warn Bathurst of the danger Warwick—my own assistant!—presented." He gripped her upper arms, hurting her. "All I want is for you to take your cousin and both of you get the hell out of my life." He released her abruptly and slipped away in the darkness, not a single sound betraying his presence.

Get the hell out of my life. Riki stared after him, seeing only the dim shapes of crates, only the slightest impression of movement. She had done it, forced on him the choice between honor to his given word and duty to his country. It was a no-win situation. Either way, just by making the decision, he destroyed the honor he sought to uphold. For that, he would hate her, and she couldn't blame him.

Unable to remain behind with her miserable thoughts, she crept forward until she could see the single guard, propped in a chair, a gun lying limp in his lap. Across from her, she caught a glimpse of Bedford's rigid form as he seemed to hesitate, probably calculating various risks and chances.

Riki bit her lip. She couldn't let Bedford make the first move . . . Then inspiration hit. It was time, she decided, for the oldest trick in the book. And she could only hope the guard had never heard of it.

If only Bedford hadn't taken her weapon. But he had, and that meant she had to improvise. She stooped, careful not to make a noise by brushing against anything, and groped cautiously around on the floor until her fingers encountered a small chunk of wood, apparently left behind when the sailors secured the crates.

Perfect. She weighed it in her hand, made a guess at the best direction, and hurled it as hard as she could. It struck another crate some twenty feet away with a satisfying smack.

The guard jerked, gripped the gun, and his head came up in a pivoting roll as his suddenly alert eyes searched the shadows for the source of the noise. Slowly, he came to his feet, raising his pistol as he came, and started away from the dark cells that had secured who knew how many prisoners-of-war in their time. Bedford inched his way from his hiding place, and before the man took more than five stealthy steps, Bedford brought the butt of his own pistol down on the back of the guard's head. The man crumpled to the wooden deck.

"Very neat." Riki joined him.

Bedford knelt, felt for the man's pulse, and nodded. "Let's get on with it." He subjected the guard to a rapid search, found the key ring that hung from a chain, unfastened it, and rose.

"Gil—" Riki tried to take them from him. "Leave it to me. Please. I can't ask this of you."

"I'm deep in it already."

"Riki?" David's voice called softly. "If this is a rescue mission, I'm sure glad to see you. Is that Bedford with you?"

"It is," the viscount snapped.

"So you finally decided to believe me, did you?"

Bedford's jaw clenched. "You don't belong in this time. You must go back to your own."

David's lips twitched in a rueful smile. "And you hope I drown in the process? Don't worry, I probably shall. But I never thought I'd be so glad to try."

Bedford shoved a key into the lock, but it didn't work. He repeated the process three more times to no avail, with Riki hanging on his arm, casting uneasy glances over her shoulder, afraid that at any moment they would be discovered. The fifth key, at last, produced a protesting creak as the rusty inner workings responded. The door to the iron cage swung open.

David bounded out. "Lord, it feels good to be free of that place! I was afraid I might only come out feet first, the way he kept looking at us." He gestured toward the inert form of the guard.

He turned with no more ado to the other cell. By the dim light, they could just make out a sleeping form curled beneath a blanket on the rough bunk. "Marie, my love," David called softly. "Here, Bedford, unlock this, will you?"

Bedford knelt beside the still-unconscious guard again and refastened the ring of heavy keys where they belonged. "No."

David swung about. "What do you mean?"

"I mean she's staying. I'm committing one treasonous act already, releasing you before a trial. But you've got to get back to your own time before you do any more damage to mine. She's a different case. She belongs here, and I'm going to see to it she pays for her treachery."

"You'd take it out on her, make her the scapegoat!" David's hands clenched.

Bedford glanced up from his work. "She's no innocent caught in a trap, Warwick. She knew what she was doing — she used you, if you'll wipe that besotted look off your face and try to remember."

"Please, Gil." Riki laid her hand on his shoulder. "What difference can it make if she goes with us? If she's to be shot, anyway, her disappearance won't affect history. She'd be as good as dead, as far as this time is concerned. She'll simply vanish. And she may die, we all may drown, as we try to go home."

Slowly he turned his head, and his cold, furious expression made a stranger of him. She fell back a pace.

"Leave me some scraps of my honor, madam."

That look, unbearable, frigid contempt, sliced through her. No trace remained of the earlier love that had burned so brightly in his eyes. She had killed it.

So why must his unyielding sense of honor and duty make him that much dearer to her, that much more worthy of her own love? His withdrawal — no, it was more than that — his utter rejection of her, proved unbearable. Pain welled up, robbing her of coherent thought.

Bedford started to rise, only to crumple on top of the guard. He didn't move.

"Gil!" Riki stifled a scream and sank beside him, feeling for the pulse in his neck that beat faint but steady. Frantic, she cast a glance behind her to David.

Her cousin, his face unnaturally pale, held Bedford's pistol by the barrel. "He—he'll be all right, Riki."

"How could you?" She hugged Bedford, unheeded tears starting to her eyes. "David, he was helping us!"

"He was leaving Marie! Damn it, Riki, I'm not going to let them murder her. She means more to me than my own life."

He shoved Bedford's sturdy body aside and found the keys that were once more attached to the guard's chain, and jerked them free. "I didn't want to do that, but I had to, Riki. I *had* to. Marie," he called, soft but urgent.

She was sitting on the bed, her tousled blonde curls falling about her pale face. She clutched the top of the rough navy blanket about her as she watched, wide-eyed. "David?"

He rammed the first key into the lock, attempted to turn it, then tried another. "We're getting out of here." At last he found the right key and thrust the squeaking door open.

In a moment, Marie was on her feet and in his arms, holding on to him as if she had thought never again to find that haven. When she at last turned her face from his, she saw Riki kneeling on the floor beside Bedford. "What have you done?" she whispered, her lovely eyes widening with horror.

"Bedford knocked out the guard to free me. I had to hit him to save you. Riki, I'm sorry. I had no choice, you must see that. Would *you* have me leave her?"

Riki shook her head. "No." She cradled Bedford's unconscious body in her arms, holding him tight.

"Come on." David grabbed her hand and dragged her to her feet.

She released Bedford slowly, reluctantly. "What—"

"We've got to lock them up before they awaken. What are the odds of their recovering and raising an alarm before we're safe?"

Marie went instantly to Bedford and grasped his shoulders. "I need help."

"No!" Riki pulled her away. "David, he *saved* you!"

"And now I'm going to save him. Do you want *him* accused of treason for helping us? This way, no one can blame him. He can say he suspected you of trying to free us, so he came back to the ship, but I was already free and overpowered him. This way, his precious honor remains intact."

He pushed her aside, and she made no protest as he and Marie dragged him into the first of the iron cages. The guard went into the other.

Riki went inside, then knelt beside the bunk where Bedford lay and clutched his limp hand. It was all for the best, she told herself. David was right. It would have come out anyway, somehow, that Bedford hadn't ridden to London with Menchen that night after all. This way, he'd be cleared of all blame.

She arranged him more comfortably on the narrow bed, which was no easy task; he was not a light man. Then she bent to kiss him, one last time.

"Come on, Riki!" David looked anxiously over his shoulder. "We're wasting time."

Time, that horrid dimension that must always separate her from her beloved Bedford. She brushed his lips once more with her own, then allowed David to fasten the cell behind her.

Believe me, Gil, this is for the best. She willed him to hear her thoughts, to understand why this had to be. She couldn't stay with him, she belonged in the future, not here where her heart yearned to remain. She was a nobody in his world, not someone of whom he could be proud. If she stayed, she wouldn't continue to bear the glamour of being an American spy. She'd be only Riki . . .

And how much damage might she do, all unintentionally, by knowing things a person of this era had no right to know? No, Marie might be able to go to a future that was not yet determined, but Riki could not remain in a past that had already been decided.

She turned, blindly, and hurried after the other two, who wasted no time now that they were free. None of them spoke again until they had gone several hundred yards along the dock, leaving the ship far behind.

"What now?" David said at last when they stopped for breath.

Riki shook her head, too depressed to really care what David said or did at the moment, her thoughts still with Bedford. "I don't know."

"What do you mean 'you don't know?' " The strain of the last few weeks—or possibly years—sounded in his voice. "Damn it, Riki, didn't you have a plan for once you got me out of there?"

"Not really. I—"

"Oh, my God, you never were one to prepare for anything properly, were you?"

"That's not fair, David. It was always you who—"

"This is no time to argue!" Marie broke across their childish flareup. "You have rescued us and for this we are grateful. We shall now merely hide ourselves."

"For how long?" David glanced at the overcast sky and excitement replaced his tension. "Look, you can't see any stars showing. Has there been any lightning, Riki?"

With a massive effort, Riki rallied. They wouldn't know, of course. They'd been in that horrid dark hold, where Bedford lay now . . .

"No, only rain." She shook off the last remnants of her lethargy. "The weather has the *feel* of thunder and lightning, now, though. Don't you think so?"

David stood still for a moment, his eyes closed. "Yes, it does. Almost . . ." He looked about, eager. "Let's find a small boat and head out into the Channel."

Find. He meant steal, of course. Under the circumstances, there was no other way, she supposed. But she hated doing it.

"It looks like it may break at any moment." Excited, Marie scanned the thickly clouded sky.

"This is our chance! Let's not miss it." David cast a quick glance up and down the wharf. "There are some small crafts over there. Let's go."

"We—we may need some supplies." Vividly, Riki remembered the unpredictability of a raging storm. It might take no more than moments for them to encounter the lightning, or it might take all day—or even a week.

David frowned. "Think you can find some? We can't waste much time."

Riki nodded. The kitchen at the inn where she stayed should provide ample food—even if they didn't know. That, at least, she could pay for—with the coins Bedford had left with her. She hurried off on her errand, leaving the other two to "procure" transportation and fasten an iron chain to the top of the mast.

Re-entering the inn wasn't difficult. Nor was locating enough food to last them for a day or two. She packed this up quickly in a basket that stood on a shelf, all the while casting anxious glances over her shoulder to where the scullion slept peacefully in the chair.

By the time she returned to the dock almost an hour later, her nerves were tied in knots. Marie was waiting for her, and grasped the basket Riki carried. She hustled Riki along the long, dark wharf to the end, where David had already partly raised the sails of a small ketch, preparing for casting off. Riki jumped to the deck, then turned to help Marie.

"Free the lines, will you, Riki?" David, busy with the sails, didn't even glance at her.

With the practiced ease of years, Riki clambered

back out, unfastened the lines and cast them to the bottom of the boat. Marie gripped the wooden edge of the wharf to hold them close until Riki was once more safely aboard. Together, they pushed free, and David dragged the mainsail into place.

The breeze caught it and the cold spray hit Riki full in the face as they slipped into the dark harbor. At first, they remained close to the shadowy outlines of ships riding silently in their berths. Bedford lay a prisoner in one of these, and by their hands.

Riki closed her eyes, fighting back her tears. He would never forgive her for what she had done to him. Was this why he would retreat, leaving the pleasures of London behind to build Falconer's Folly on that tiny, almost inaccessible island? And would his "dearest lady" of the journal be his memory of her, or would he find another woman, one who would wipe clean his feelings of betrayal and dishonor?

That thought proved almost unbearable. With a last, whispered "goodbye," she turned resolutely away and stared ahead, into the darkness of the Channel.

Riki had no idea how long they sailed. She huddled in her cocoon of unhappiness, the vision of Bedford's fury her constant and uncomfortable companion. At last, the icyness of the unrelenting spray coming off the churning sea penetrated her misery. It froze her, stinging, but it wasn't as salty as she expected. She glanced up into the cloudy sky and realized this was more than a drizzling mist.

"Rain!" Marie cried, as the realization struck her at the same moment. She hugged David, who sat close at her side, his arm about her. "The storm's beginning!"

He grinned, excited, at Riki. "We'll make it!"

Riki nodded, her heart aching. They had to make it. She couldn't stay here, even if Bedford still wanted her—which he didn't.

She scrambled to her feet and lurched forward, gripping the low railing to keep from being pitched overboard as the craft tossed on the choppy waves. Huge drops pelted down on her, faster and faster, washing away the sheen of salt thrown up by the prow.

Ahead of them, a thin silvery streak appeared briefly in the sky, only to vanish the next moment. Her eyes narrowed as she studied the spot. "Did you see that?" she called over her shoulder.

"What?" David leaned forward. "Is there something out there?"

"I thought I saw—"

The next streak of lightning obliterated the need for her explanation.

"We did it!" David cried. "Marie! We'll make it!"

Riki gripped the rail, trembling. Lightning, all right. And she still hated it.

The storm inched closer. The next fiery slash through the clouds would be accompanied by that rumbling roar of thunder that always left her ill. *Damn* old—and unquenchable—fears. And there it came. Riki huddled down in the boat, cursing herself, cursing the storm that she both needed and dreaded.

It wasn't close, yet; she counted nearly ten seconds between the flash and that not-distant-enough sound. That meant more than a mile—almost two, really—yet to go.

Clinging to the rail, Riki stared fixedly into the sky, waiting for the next vivid flash of electricity to slice through the night. Blackness surrounded them for several minutes, then two jagged streaks lit the charcoal clouds, one right after the other. The savage drumming followed three seconds later.

They'd make it. Riki repeated that, over and over. They'd make it, and as soon as they did, she'd move far away from her island, to somewhere where she'd never again have to hear that dreaded sound. Somewhere that wouldn't constantly remind her of Bedford, and the love she'd managed to turn to hate.

The clouds split with streaking light just to their right, and thunder exploded about them. Riki cringed, then forced herself to look up. The first fury of the rumble barely faded when a second flash brought a renewed onslaught against her ears. Closer . . .

The boat swerved as David tacked to compensate for the driving wind and current. Steadily, they headed deeper and deeper into the heart of the storm. The thunder rumbled, unending, the flashes became constant jagged streaks of unharnessed electricity.

Riki's teeth clenched on her lip, controlling her fear by the merest thread. Then directly above them, the brilliant light flashed, and the entire boat glowed with bluish light.

Marie's scream echoed in her ears, becoming part of the rumbling thunder that reverberated through Riki. The eerie light danced up her arms from her hands, which gripped the rail. They had been hit!

With a crackling hiss, flames shot up from the mast, licking at the sail, dancing along the yardarm.

"We're going to burn!" David yelled, stark terror in his voice.

Twenty-five

"Fire!" Marie cried, adding her voice once more to that of the storm. "David!"

Fire? It couldn't be! Riki stared at the flaming canvas in disbelief.

Then reaction took over. Clinging tightly to the side, Riki eased her way back along it until she found the basket of food. Heaving the contents unceremoniously toward the cabin door, she turned to face the unanticipated danger.

She leaned over the edge, scooped up water, and heaved it toward the burning sail. The next moment, David was beside her, using a wooden bucket he must have found below. The beating rain helped, and soon only smoldering remnants of cloth remained.

Riki dropped her basket, staring mutely up at the tattered wreck. "Did—did we go forward through time?"

David stared at Riki, both his pallor and the unsteadiness of his voice betraying his shock. "It wasn't like this before."

Riki looked about, bewildered. The storm still raged, and lightning flashed off to their right. She barely flinched as the thunder rumbled across the sky. "Nothing has changed," she breathed. "Last time—I can't remember what happened. I lost consciousness, I think."

"Me, too." David looked at her helplessly.

"David?" Marie's quavering voice interrupted them. "Where are we?"

He turned and gathered her into his arms. "I don't know."

We'd better find out." Riki looked back at the sail. "Do you think we can get anywhere using the mizzen, if we try to rig it onto the mainmast?"

They tried it, and it worked with a considerable bit of finagling. The smaller triangle of canvas had not been designed for the larger frame, but with extra line, it stretched. David fastened off the last knot, and Riki grabbed the tiller and steered them into the wind. Their sail caught and filled, driving them forward.

"Which way?" she called.

David shrugged. "If we could see the stars, we might be able to make a guess. That way?" He gestured to the port side, where France might conceivably lie unless they had been driven drastically off course.

Steadily, they inched away from the heart of the storm until the rumbles of thunder retreated in the distance. Rain continued to beat heavily down, adding to the puddle in the hull caused by the swamping waves. David and Marie turned their attention to bailing.

Riki shivered in her drenched clothes, but steadfastly ignored her discomfort. Straining her eyes, she stared ahead, trying, by the occasional flashes of lightning, to catch a glimpse of land. It was easier to see, but only endless waves and thick clouds remained. A soft glow lit the horizon. Dawn, she realized with amazement.

The storm continued throughout the morning, with the occasional rumbles and flashes fading farther into the distance. Still, they sailed on, seeking the land they couldn't find. Riki, hunching over the tiller, steered as straight a course as she could toward what she hoped would be southeast. She had no idea how wide the Channel ought to be at this point, how much longer they'd have to endure the cold and wet. But at least she could do something about the gnawing hunger that assailed her.

"David, did our food get ruined?"

"Food?" He turned from the bow where he peered into the charcoal clouds.

Marie rose from where she'd been curled against him on the bench and hurried to the cabin. She emerged a moment later with the loaf of bread, chunk of ham and knife Riki obtained. She took it to David, and he cut their meager supplies into slabs to create something that could approximate sandwiches. He swallowed his in six bites, then brought one to Riki. She released the tiller into his charge and tried to enjoy her meal.

An hour passed and nothing changed. Fretful, unsure in which era they now existed, Riki paced forward. Where was Gil, now? Still lying in that dreadful cell aboard the boat? Or had he lived out his life long ago with his dearest lady at his side, assuaging the pain that for Riki would remain raw?

She blinked back the moisture from her eyes, knowing it was neither rain nor salt spray, and returned to relieve David at the tiller. At least steering the ketch through the rough swells gave her something to do. She settled once more in the stern, staring ahead. There seemed to be a pale outline in the distance, one that grew steadily, one that lay too low to be clouds. She oriented on it and followed as straight a course as she could.

Land!" she cried, as soon as she was sure.

"Where?" David lurched forward against the boat's

tossing and peered through the unnatural darkness of the storm. "Land!" he breathed in confirmation.

Minute by minute, the solid mass grew clearer. Another hour passed, and the hazy outline of a fishing village began to take shape. No boats ventured forth in the remnants of the electrical storm, but Riki could make out shapes moving about on the docks. She couldn't quite determine what they wore. She tacked against the wind, bringing their ketch nearer the harbor entrance, but staying well out in the safe, open Channel.

"What do you think?" Riki called to her cousin. David stood in intent silence, studying the details of the small anchored crafts as they neared the sheltered cove with its rickety wooden docks. The vessels looked old—not just from constant use and lack of care, but in design as well. Not one modern sail boat or motor boat could be glimpsed.

"Can you bring us closer?" He sounded dubious. None of them had any desire for contact with people until they knew where—or when—they were.

Riki complied, barely entering the wide harbor mouth. A figure kneeling beside a pile of nets rose slowly, staring at them, and her heart sank. She shoved the tiller hard, bringing them about, and threw the boom until the sail caught the wind.

"We're still in the past," David exclaimed. "Damn it! Why didn't it work?" He swung around to face Riki, as if accusing her of creating this disaster. "We should be *home!*"

Riki shook her head. As much as she might wish to doubt the evidence of her own eyes, it was irrefutable. Unless they had just wandered into an antique boat show, where the participants all dressed the part, they were still in the past.

"What are we to do, now?" Marie looked from one to the other, beseeching.

"Get out of here before anyone decides to chase us. If we're captured by the French. . ." Riki bit back that thought. Marie was French—an agent. A spy. It would be so easy for her to turn them over to her side, and be welcomed as a heroine.

David stared blankly at the clearing blue of the early morning sky. "I was so sure we could get back to our own time! What went wrong?"

"What will become of us? We cannot return to England." Marie shifted her gaze, turning so she could regard the ramshackle fishing village that vanished behind them. There was longing—and a certain amount of speculation—in that glance.

"I cannot let you go to France!" Riki glared them down, refusing to show any fear. They could take control of the boat easily, go wherever they chose, and she knew it.

"Our only choice is to keep trying. We *must* get back to the future."

"What do you want us to do, sit in the middle of the Channel until the next electrical storm brews up?" David sounded frantic—as frantic as Riki. "That could be months—and there's absolutely no guarantee we'd make it next time, either!"

She shook her head. "I owe Gil that much, not to turn you two loose in this time, where your knowledge could do damage. You said yourself you wanted nothing more to do with the war. What do you think the French would force you to do, if they caught you again?"

David's hand closed over Marie's, and the bleak look they exchanged sent a quavering sigh of relief through Riki. They were done with war, both of them, just as they had said.

"America—?" David suggested, but without much conviction.

"You're forgetting the War of 1812. You'd only be

370

pitchforked into another conflict."

"Canada?" Marie regarded them hopefully. "I have cousins in Quebec who would welcome us."

Riki shook her head. "I *promised* Gil I wouldn't leave David in this time. That goes for you, too. Nothing will make me break that promise."

"Except circumstances beyond our control," David pointed out.

"Not even that. Damn it, David, I promised I'd take you back to our own time, and that's what I'm going to do!"

David drew an unsteady breath. "Well, we'd better follow the storm, then."

Riki's fingers clenched white on the tiller as they headed once more into open water. They *had* to make it home.

There was nothing for her here. Without Gil, life would be unbearably empty. At least at home, in her own time, she might be able to throw herself heart and soul into her worthy causes to keep from thinking about him every moment.

"Perhaps next time it will work," she said softly, mostly to herself.

"What was different?" David demanded. "Think, Riki. What did you do differently?"

She shook her head. "It *should* have worked."

"What is the key to traveling through time?" David sank down before her, his weight on the balls of his feet. Marie hovered at his elbow, anxious.

"I assumed it would be easy." Riki gazed ahead, unseeing, lost in thought. "You and I have each done it once before and Gil managed it twice. The chain is on the mast, there is an electrical storm, we've even been hit by lightning."

"There's *got* to be something else!"

Riki closed her eyes, racking her brain. Memories flooded back, fear-filled, terrifying — and vivid. The rumbling thunder, the waves that crashed over the sides of the boat, swamping them, dragging them down . . . into a whirlpool!

She grabbed one of David's hands. "We were pulled into a whirlpool, and I lost consciousness as we went under water. *That's* the missing element!"

David nodded, his eyes blazing with his own remembered horrors. "The whirlpool," he breathed. "Lord, I remember it. But how do we find it?"

"It is somewhere near my island, where few ships ever stray amid the rocks."

"Why didn't we know about it before?" David objected. "I spent a lot of time exploring in the boats."

"Maybe it only appears during a violent storm. Rather like having a Bermuda Triangle in our own back yard." And as she spoke the words, she knew it wasn't a joke. "That was why it seemed so easy for you, then Gil and me, to go back through time. The whirlpool was practically on our doorstep. The real miracle was Gil, coming from England, being swept into it to come forward."

A deep rumble in the distance caught her attention. Riki gripped the tiller in new determination. "Let's go. We've got to get there before the storm vanishes completely."

David nodded, excitement filling his face. He strode to the prow and gripped the forward mast as they hazarded a guess on the direction of Jersey.

"To shift through time, all the elements must be present," she shouted over the remnants of the storm. "We *must* reach the whirlpool while there is still a chance of being hit by lightning."

The ill-fitting sail caught the whipping wind and Riki found her hands full as it strained against its unorthodox fastenings. If they lost it . . . She held the tiller with all her strength, steering toward the crackling lightning that was their goal. They would find Jersey, all right. She only hoped the storm wouldn't be driven on before them, just beyond their reach.

Morning faded to noon, and the black clouds gathered more thickly above them. Rain pelted down with renewed fury, making it impossible to see more than a few feet to any side. The wind buffeted the small craft, tearing at the canvas until it flapped free of its fastenings.

Forward motion halted, and the raging waves pummeled their hull. Marie clung to the cabin, pale and ill. David struggled to re-attach the sail to the metal chain, but the pitching of the boat made maneuvering unsafe. Riki gripped the tiller, knowing it no longer did any good, but unwilling to abandon her last illusion of control.

David collapsed at last on the bench beside Riki, exhausted. "I can't get it."

"I'll try." Before he could stop her, Riki stood unsteadily, lurched against the cabin wall, and grabbed the whipping canvas. It had torn loose, ripping the material so the line could no longer be threaded through. Nor was there enough spare canvas to tie it into place, as the sail was already too small for this mast. If she only had a knife, she might be able to make a new hole.

A knife. She stumbled into the cabin, half fell down the few stairs, and landed in the middle of the remnants of waterlogged food. She steadied herself, and sought the knife she had shoved in the basket. Holding it carefully, she clambered back on deck and went to work.

It took the combined strength and determination of Riki and David to hoist the sail once more into place. The wind snatched at it, threatening to destroy their efforts, but at last they fastened it tight. Riki once more grabbed the tiller, and wondered where, in the vast expanse of Channel, they'd been driven by the wildly tossing waves. Amazingly, they had not sunk.

The storm's fury increased and the rumbling of thunder reached her once more. She hadn't heard it for some time, she realized. She braced herself and steered toward a distant flash of lightning.

The next jagged streak flashed closer and the accompanying timpani roll of thunder sounded only moments later. She shivered, her old fear rising through her exhaustion. She gripped the tiller for support.

Never before had steering been so hard. Again, they neared the center of the electrical storm, but they had absolutely no idea where they were. They had to find the right place before their metal chain drew another bolt of lightning—one that might well finish them if the whirlpool were too far away to be reached in time.

If only they could hold out until they neared the rocky outcroppings that surrounded Falconer's Folly, where that swirling vortex must be concealed . . . If only their mast were struck at the moment it drew them in . . . If only this time they might return to their own time and not drown!

If they succeeded she would never see Gil again. Torn between her longing for him and the knowledge she pursued the only possible course, she headed the ketch directly into the high winds.

Only the intensifying of the darkness about them revealed the coming of night. She shivered, drenched with spraying waves and the rain that washed the caking salt from her face.

"Riki!" David's excited shout reached her over the tumult of sea and storm. "There!"

She peered into the growing blackness. Ahead, but still in the distance, lay the jagged outlines of

374

tiny islands. Her heart filled her throat, choking her, pounding so hard she could barely breathe.

Lightning flashed with an accompanying thunderous roar, right on top of them. Marie's high-pitched scream sounded over the protesting groan of the mast as the wind drove them toward the rocky outcroppings that could rip their hull to shreds. About them, foam-capped waves reared high, crashing against their shuddering hull.

The wild pitching of the ship threw Riki to the swamped deck. Toward the bow, Marie clung to David while he gripped the rail, struggling to keep from being swept overboard.

And nowhere could she see the whirling vortex of water. Riki struggled back to the tiller, panic rising within her. They couldn't last much longer. If they didn't locate the right place, they would be torn apart, dragged beneath the freezing waves, vanish from the face of the earth.

Another jagged flash lighted the sky, and thunder reverberated overhead, rising in intensity until it rumbled within her and found an answering voice in her scream. Hands trembling, she pushed the rain from her eyes, and saw the dim outline of another small boat.

She stared in disbelief. No, she hadn't been mistaken. Dear God, had they been followed from France? No sane person would venture forth in this storm, though. Nor was this a ghost ship, floating at the mercy of the waves. The sail bowed out with wind as it came steadily, purposefully closer.

A brief streak illuminated the single occupant. Riki's heart stopped, then beat faster, her reaction for once having nothing to do with the thunder.

"Gil," she breathed. "Gil!" The wind swept his name from her throat.

She saw him wave, and thought he shouted, also.

There was no hope of hearing. Riki waved back. He was here, she could make out the outline of his beloved face—and he was in as much danger as they.

"Riki!" This time, she heard him—and the fear for her rampant in his voice.

She blinked back sudden tears. He risked his life, setting out in such a storm, to find her. "Gil!" she cried, her heart tearing.

"—Don't care . . . Warwick . . . Marley!" Only a few of his words reached them, thin but distinct. "—Can't lose you, Riki! I—"

A shimmer of lightning and clap of thunder ravaged the rest of what he said. Riki shook her head, trying not to cry, knowing only that she loved Gil more than life itself—and she had to leave him.

"I must go back where I belong," she shouted.

"Why? Are you—" The wind carried off the rest of his words, then the last reached her. "—Afraid? Don't . . . nerve . . . just to be yourself—with me?"

She wasn't afraid anymore! The shock of the realization jolted through her, but her surging elation evaporated at once. It didn't matter. She *couldn't* stay.

"Riki—!" He broke off as a wave rose high and crashed over the side of his boat.

Horrified, Riki saw it suck back, away from the small vessel. The deck was bare. Then she breathed again as Bedford struggled up from where he had been thrown. He grabbed up a bucket and began to bail.

Another wave slammed across the low prow, swamping the hull. Bedford struggled forward, still heaving bucket-full after bucket-full of water overboard as he went. But even faster than he could empty it, the waves brought back more.

Suddenly, the wind caught his slack sail and the vessel teetered. He gripped the cabin as for a long moment, it heeled dangerously. Then the sail seemed to dive toward the seething swells. The hull sank low, a black mass dragged ever downward.

"Gil!" Riki screamed again, shouting his name over and over.

But there came no answer from the capsized boat.

The next moment, their own ketch began to spin, slowly at first, then faster and faster. Water swirled about them, luminescent, sparkling. Riki looked about in horror as they were drawn inexorably into a spiraling funnel that opened up about them.

A blinding light flashed directly above, and a shimmering, eerie flame danced down the mast, outlining the vessel in iridescent electric blue. The mast had been struck!

For one, life-long second, her world spun wildly. Bedford struggled in the water, beyond her reach, beyond her ability to help. Her own boat spun crazily, sucked downward toward the heart of the whirlpool. David and Marie clung to each other and the mast. And just beyond them, Riki glimpsed the dim outline of her short-wave radio antennae on the island of Falconer's Folly.

She couldn't leave Gil. In that split-second, before time converged and she was drawn into the future, she dove overboard.

Cold blackness engulfed her. She couldn't breathe, then her head broke water and she gasped, only to be drawn down by the outer rim of the whirlpool. She flailed, frantic, fighting for air.

Something solid grasped her and she broke the surface. Somehow, miraculously, it was Bedford's voice that shouted in her ear. She turned in his arms, clinging to him, crying and laughing. The sea no longer dragged at her.

Steadying herself, she pulled away and struck out for the nearest solid mass. Bedford's long, even strokes kept him at her side.

It was farther than she'd thought. As they neared the island, she could see no place to approach without being dashed against the craggy boulders. Bedford pulled ahead, fighting the current and waves that lashed against the jagged outcroppings, leading the way. She followed, and with relief sighted a less dangerous stretch of shore that sloped toward the crashing waves.

Bedford caught her hand, drawing her toward it, toward safety. Gasping for breath, she pulled herself onto the rocks, then remained where she lay, too drained to move. Bedford stood slowly and reached down to help her.

Her fingers closed about his hand, and she felt his warmth and strength. They were together, the impossible had come true . . . She rose to be enfolded in his strong arms, and for several very long minutes, nothing else mattered.

"Where—or when—are we?" she gasped at last.

"Look." Bedford's voice held a shaky laugh.

She did. Rain beat steadily down on an island that would have seemed more familiar had the rookery already been built. She shook her head in disbelief. Over there, only minutes before, she had seen her short-wave radio antennae. Now there was nothing.

Except the cliff-like boulder that towered over them. Riki looked up its uneven surface and her breath caught in her throat. Several falcons perched in the uneven crannies, where her own bird Guinivere had sheltered with her broken wing . . .

"We—we climbed that," she whispered. Had it only been months ago, or ages in the future?

The roughness of his unshaved chin brushed against her forehead as he nodded. "To rescue that falcon of yours. And you were so afraid of the storm." An unsteady laugh shook through him.

He moved his hands to her shoulders and held her slightly away. "You were in the whirlpool. How did you come back to me? You should have been dragged into the future."

"How—" She broke off until she could command her voice. "How could I leave you? I jumped overboard."

"My God," he breathed, with no trace of irreverence. "You might have drowned." He pulled her against himself, holding her shivering body as tightly as he could.

"You came after me," she offered as her only explanation.

"But—can you stay?" Fear of losing her brought a husky, alluring note to his voice.

Riki made no attempt to stifle her response. Her lips brushed his throat and her pounding blood warmed her. "I *must!* Somehow . . ."

"Do you think Marie Marley has taken your place in the future?"

Riki hesitated, then nodded. "Perhaps that would reestablish the balance David broke when he went back. I wonder . . ." She wiped the rain from her eyes, then wrapped her arm about him once more.

"I never did learn the name of the person to whom she passed the information." He merely sounded rueful, not angry.

Riki couldn't help but smile. "Leave her some scraps of her honor, sir," she murmured in a fair imitation of Bedford's tone. "It's probably someone your department is already keeping an eye on, anyway."

Bedford's chin rubbed against her forehead. "At least she and Warwick are where they can't do any more damage."

Riki nodded against his coat. "They—Oh, dear!"

"What?"

"I left the island to Mr. Fipps!"

A deep, appreciative chuckle shook Bedford's shoulders. "Did you? I wonder what they'll do?"

"Vindictive," she murmured. "They'll be all right. In my original will, I left a few things to David. They'll have to start over somewhere, but it'll be good for them."

"And what will be good for us?" He looked about. "Know of any shelter?"

She managed a shaky smile. "Feel like building a rookery?"

A deep chuckle escaped him and his lips brushed hers. "My dearest lady." He spoke the words, which appeared so often in the journal he had yet to write, as if testing them for the first time. "My dearest, dearest lady."

She stiffened, and her eyes widened as she stared at him. "Gil! I *do* stay," she breathed, conviction filling her for the first time. She held him tight, burying her face in his drenched coat, her shoulders trembling with emotion as tears slipped unheeded down her cheeks.

"Riki?" Concerned, he tilted her chin so he could see her face.

"I *do* stay—I belong here! Don't you see, Gil? I was *already* in that journal you kept." In her growing excitement, she gripped his arms. "David's presence only affected history from this date onward, in the future—because the changes he caused had no far-reaching consequences. Mine must! I'm a part of history as it was actually recorded. That means I must have a life here, that I'm not just a chance visitor."

"My dearest lady," he repeated. He drew her even closer, and his hands wandered, leaving her in no doubts as to his sentiments.

"My lord!" She drew back, fighting the sudden

laughter that welled within her. "Is that any way for the very proper Viscount Bedford to behave?"

He regarded her with mock hauteur. "I was merely considering one way in which your presence in this time will affect the next generation. It *is* the duty of my viscountess to produce an heir to the title, you know."

"Your—" Her breath caught in her throat.

"As soon as I can procure a Special License."

The prospect intrigued her, but she couldn't resist murmuring. "To marry in such unseemly haste. What will your family and friends say?"

"That you'll keep me from growing old and stuffy." He chuckled, a deep, enticing sound she adored. It broke off abruptly. "Will you miss your own people?"

"A little—but we were never really close." Her brow puckered. "Besides, it's not as if they've died—they're all still to come. And we'll have our own family, soon."

"You won't regret this?"

She ran her finger along the dripping lapel of his coat. "Well, I *will* miss my blow dryer. And my microwave oven, of course."

He grinned. "So will I, for that matter. Lord, what a lot of work we have ahead of us."

"Not that much." She hugged his arm, knowing what joy their lives would hold. "We only have to lay the foundation for preserving the endangered peregrines."

"And, as you mentioned, build our rookery."

"At the moment, I'd settle for a boat. All that fine talk about a Special License! You know perfectly well we're stranded on a rocky island without food, shelter, or any means to get off."

"Not quite. Look over there."

She did, and saw the smashed hull of his yawl,

which had washed up on the rocky shore about a hundred yards away. With a cry of delight, she started toward it. "We can repair it and get back!"

"Oh, no you don't!" He caught her about the waist and hauled her unprotesting back into his arms. "I'm not about to risk letting you go sailing again in weather like this. Menchen can rescue us tomorrow. He didn't go to London as I ordered, devil that he is, so I told him to look for me around these islands as soon as it was safe. Knowing him, that will be in the morning, whether or not the storm has ended."

Riki brushed her hand across his stubbly chin. "That leaves us alone for a very long, cold night. Do you think we'll be able to keep ourselves warm?"

A slow smile lit his eyes. "Oh, I think we'll manage."

Under the watchful eyes of the falcons, Riki took his hand, and they made their way to the shelter of the battered boat, where they managed quite well indeed.

Epilogue

David Warwick gazed at the serenely beautiful face in the portrait. A smile as familiar to him as his own parted the woman's full lips, though soft white curls replaced the auburn he had known. At age seventy-eight, Erica Randall, Viscountess Bedford, had still been lovely.

His attention moved on to the erect, still-sturdy figure of the man who stood at her side. Gil's eyes, even in that painted rendition, sparkled with an inner contentment. A falcon perched on his gauntleted wrist. David shook his head. He only hoped *he* looked as good when he reached his eighties.

Marie Marley tugged at her calf-length skirt as if she wished she might make it longer. Unsuccessful, she abandoned the attempt and turned to the housekeeper, who escorted them on this tour of Falconer's Court. "You said they had five children?"

"That's right, miss. Two sons and three daughters. This is a delightful portrait, isn't it? Not at all stiff, like so many of the Victorian era. One might almost fancy one knew them."

"They must have been very happy," Marie murmured.

383

The housekeeper nodded. "Theirs was a love match—or so I've heard tell."

David, his gaze once more on Riki's face, nodded. "It was. It must have been," he corrected hastily. "Just look at them."

Marie's hand tightened on his. "They were living the life they wanted—together."

They continued their tour, then thanked their guide and stepped outside into the fading light of the late afternoon. David slipped his arm about Marie's shoulders and drew her toward the white BMW they had left parked on the drive. He opened the door.

Marie hesitated. "What now, David? Where do we go?"

He turned and for a long, silent minute stared back at the stone facade of the old house. "Home," he said at last. "To California—and my family. They believed my amnesia story and they can't wait to meet you."

"And after that?"

"We'll stay there." He straightened, and his chin rose a fraction with his new-found determination. His arm tightened about Marie, and a smile of anticipation lit his eyes. "Riki left me one of the family businesses. This time, I'm going to make a success of it."